Two
Swordmasters

To My Mother
The source of my life
And the stories

Special thanks to
Jennifer Au Shimizu
Lesly Coelho
Rosemarie Bagdasarian

Two
Swordmasters

Chiang Shiao-ho   Lee Mo-bai

江小鶴 李慕白

Shiao-shen Yu 于孝慎

To order additional copies of this book, contact:
Xlibris
1-888-795-4274
www.Xlibris.com
Orders@Xlibris.com
776845

CONTENTS

CHIANG SHIAO-HO (江小鶴) AND A WILLOW TREE

Prologue 1

Chiang Shiao-ho (江小鶴) and a willow tree................................3

1...3

2...9

3...23

4...34

5.. 46

6...69

7...84

8...102

9...108

10...121

11...129

12...150

13...161

14...172

Epilogue..179

LEE MO-BAI (李慕白) AND A LIVING WIDOW

1...183

2...197

3...212

4...226

5...239

6...254

7...271

8...282

9...295

10...309

11...323

12...337

Epilogue...357

Chiang Shiao-ho (江小鶴) and a willow tree

Prologue

It was a cold night, the only sound was the village dogs' barking. Chiang ran to the south and hoped that he could cross the mountain to N. Szechwan and then Beijing. Twice he fell on the rocky path. Once he almost fell into the rushing creek. One moment he felt hopeless and preferred death, in another he felt like turning back and fight them to the death. However, he kept going. With his muddy, bloody, body and sword, anyone could have mistaken him for a bandit. So he dropped his sword and kept struggling ahead on his blistered feet until he was exhausted. Sitting on a rock to rest and with excruciating pain, he took off his battered cloth shoes, squeezed the blisters and bandaged his feet with strips of his torn shirt.

'*What terrible crime have I committed that makes me an inexcusable criminal? Do I really deserve to be chased like a sheep by a pack of wolves? The law of the ruling Chin Dynasty has no 'death penalty' for adultery. Will I live through this? Will I see my wife and sons again?*"

Chiang Shiao-ho (江小鶴) and a willow tree

1

Chiang hid in the hills and lived on wild berries for three days. An old hunter he met shared some coarse food with him and told him the shortest mountain path to North Szechwan. Earlier he had taken a chance by going home to get some silver and gulping down some cold rice. He had asked his wife for forgiveness, and told her that he would be going to Beijing. His two sons--twelve-year-old Shiao-ho and the baby -- were sleeping as he caressed them with his cold fingers. His tears dropped on their checks. He wondered whether he would stay alive to see them again; he wondered whether he had crippled the sadistic Bo Zhi-lin. He hoped that Master Bo and his son won't kill his family. '*Oh, what have I done? I should have considered the terrible consequence of my illicit, adulterous act, and...*" Suddenly he heard horses' hooves and then saw his pursuers. Two ferocious-looking men in their late-thirties rode ahead of old Bo. He knew that they must be the Lung Brothers, Master Bo's most capable students. '*Master Bo had sent for them to kill me*'. He desperately climbed up the rock, slipped and fell on his back. One of them whipped him.

Nearly blind with fear and anger, he shouted, "You are all murderers...." He was killed before he could finish his accusation, before Master Bo could shout, "Wait! Don't kill him..."

The furious old Bo gazed at the dead body with regret. He ordered, "It's done; keep quiet about it."

In the evening, Master Bo went to Chiang's house and threw the silver that had been found on Chiang's body over the fence. The baby cried, and the remorseful Master Bo felt sad and very old.

Chiang Shiao-ho did not pay too much attention to his father's absence at first. He was used to his father traveling to some big city to work for days or half a month and coming back with nice toys for him and pretty clothes for his mom. But somehow, he knew his father's absence was different this time. His mother sobbed softly while she nursed his baby brother. He missed his father.

Shiao-ho asked his mother, "Mom, when will Daddy come home?"

His mother, trying to suppress her tears, said rather harshly, "He went to Beijing and he won't be back for at least a year or two. I told you already."

"But why are you crying so much? It cannot be true!" Without knowing why, tears rolled down his dirty cheeks. *'It's bad. Mom will not tell me, so I will ask Uncle Ma. He should know.'* Uncle Ma married his mom's cousin and was also a student of Master Bo. His father told him that Master Bo's two sons and students were all sworn brothers. Each of his students keep his own surname and has the word "Zhi", meaning ambitious, as part of his first name.

The next morning, Shiao-ho went to the training field and watched Master Bo teach. He proudly recalled that his Daddy moved quicker than most of Master Bo's students. At break, he ran to Uncle Ma, held onto one of his legs, and asked, "Uncle Ma, where did my daddy go? Mom won't tell me the truth. She just cries."

"Get out! You dirty, little bastard! How dare you come here!" Bo Zhi-lin, Master Bo's second son yelled and then slapped Shiao-ho as if he were chasing away a dog.

Chiang Shiao-ho punched him in the stomach and Bo Zhi-lin bent over in pain, "You dare attack me! I'll kill you!" However he held his saber in check. He knew that his father and others were watching. Meanwhile, Shiao-ho jumped high and would have punched Bo Zhi-lin again if Uncle Ma had not held him back. Uncle Ma had a hard time restraining the boy.

"Stop! Shiao-ho!" Master Bo called thunderously, his face glowed deep red and his long beard bristled. He looked murderous, but Shiao-ho was not going to show any fear. Instead, he pushed his chest forward,

"I'm here to ask Uncle Ma about my father. Grandpa Bo, your son attacked me first."

Master Bo laughed, "Shiao-ho, brave boy! Your father has not been here lately. I miss him, too. Go! Go home and ask your mother."

"I'm not going. Mom will only cry; she won't tell me. I've come to ask Uncle Ma. Unless you, all of you, tell me the truth, I will stay won't let you practice in peace."

Master Bo smiled, "Don't be naughty! Here are a few coppers. Go and buy yourself some candy and be a good boy."

Shiao-ho knocked the old man's hand forcefully and the coins scattered. "I don't want your money. Tell me where my father is and I'll leave."

Uncle Ma held Shiao-ho and said, "My good nephew, don't bother us. I'll take you home and I will tell you." Uncle Ma sensed that Shiao-ho's life was in danger. He added, "Let's keep quiet. The officials are investigating Chiang's whereabouts already. We don't want the neighbors reporting us again." Master Bo understood readily. Uncle Ma dragged the belligerent boy away.

"The boy is a bad lot, just like his father," Bo Zhi-lin stated. "Why should we not beat him and kill him now?"

Master Bo whipped his son in the face and said angrily, "You're my son and you are not like me at all. You are a shame"

"Grandpa! Please don't be angry!" May-lin, his ten-year-old sole granddaughter ran to him. Master Bo caressed the girl's long, black shiny ponytail with trembling hands.' *Neither of my two sons will be very good at martial arts. If I die, my skills will be lost, and there will be nobody to protect my family against my enemies' revenge. I'd better teach this little girl all my skills in my remaining years.*' He asked Uncle Ma, a blacksmith, to forge a small, lightweight saber for May-lin.

In the next few days, Shiao-ho led his group of mischievous village boys to harass Bo's students, especially Bo Zhi-lin. Bo Zhi-lin dared not go out of the gate any more. One day a student showed up with a bleeding forehead, and another one came with a torn shirt. They claimed that Shiao-ho's gang had cornered them. Master Bo said furiously, "Terrible!" and Uncle Ma was afraid for Shiao-ho's life.

One day at dusk, Master Bo passed Chiang's place and walked toward the wheat field. He looked back and saw cooking smoke rising from every house and some boys heading homeward with the animals.

It was getting dark. With his long graying beard waving in the breeze, old Bo looked this way and that way, and stood like a hungry tiger awaiting his prey. Soon he saw Shiao-ho, holding a club, coming fast. Master Bo stopped the boy on the narrow pathway winding through the tall wheat field.

"Grandpa Bo, you dare fight me!" Shiao-ho swaggered to hide his fear but his voice trembled. "Out of my way!" With a low laugh, Master Bo unsheathed his sharp dagger and aimed it at the boy. His eyes blazed while the thought ran through him, *'If I kill you now, I won't have to worry about you killing me later'*. Somehow Old Bo missed; he was too slow or the boy instinctively jumped back fast; he could not kill the boy. Immediately, the cunning Old Bo put the dagger flatly on his palm as if he wanted to show the boy his dagger. Shiao-ho did not realize that his life had been in danger and, because he wanted to have a real sword, he exclaimed, "A real dagger!"

"Shiao-ho, be a good boy and I will give you a dagger." Master Bo said.

"Grandpa Bo, I promise that I will be good. Can I really have it now?" Shiao-ho's genuine joy and innocence softened the old man's heart. Master Bo handed it to the boy. "Do not harass my students. They are your uncles. You HEAR?"

"Thank you! Thank you! I promise that I will be good." Shiao-ho examined the dagger fondly.

Master Bo watched the boy for a while, torn between his fears of what the boy might do to him ten or twenty years later, and his love of an innocent and courageous boy. He contemplated the opportunity, wanting to grab back the dagger and kill the boy. But he stopped himself. *'I'm over sixty. I don't want to be cruel anymore. It's bad enough that I had his father killed'*. He ruffled the boy's hair and said, "Shiao-ho, it's getting late. You'd better go home. Your Daddy has gone to Beijing. He will be away for a while."

"Grandpa Bo, I won't be a bother anymore. I don't think you're cruel,"

The next morning, no students came to Bo's training field with any unpleasant encounters with Shiao-ho. Master Bo taught them with high spirits and he began to teach May-lin seriously.

At the end of the session, Master Bo called Ma, "Take these ten ounces of silver to Chiang's wife. Chiang Zhi-shen was my student for three years. He broke my rules and I forced him away. I don't think he will be back soon. I am sorry for his wife and children and I'll try to help them."

On his way to deliver the silver to Shiao-ho's mother, Uncle Ma thought. *'Why? Master Bo had the husband killed and now he wants to help the widow and orphans. Lately Shiao-ho has been making a lot of trouble and Master Bo seems to tolerate him. What's going on? It's strange. Maybe Master Bo really does have regrets.'*

Shiao-ho called to him excitedly, "Uncle Ma, see my shiny dagger, it's real and very, very sharp!" He brandished the seven-inch dagger happily.

"Be careful! Where did you get it? Don't cut yourself."

"Grandpa Bo gave me this dagger. Last night, he waited for me in the wheat field. He showed me how shiny it was first, and then gave it to me. He didn't want me to bother the uncles any more. He is not a cruel old man."

"He waited for you and gave you the dagger! Let me have a look at it!" Ma Zhi-min felt a chill all over. He took the dagger, rushed inside and told Shiao-ho's mother, "Cousin, you and the boys must move to my home in town right now. Old Bo could not give your son a dagger out of kindness. He...Never mind, just pack some clothes and I can come back for the rest." He tried very hard to keep the fear out of his voice.

"Uncle Ma, give me back my priceless dagger. Please!"

Ma handed the dagger back to Shiao-ho and said, "Keep it and learn how to use it well. In the future you can use it to...."

Shiao-ho's mother sensed danger, "You think we must move, Cousin Ma?"

"You must move. Hurry up and pack. I'm going to borrow Brother Lu's mule for you to ride. I am taking you and the boys to my home in town."

Her teeth chattered and she agreed, "Yes, yes, I'll pack quickly."

"Shiao-ho, help your mom pack. Tell you what, I'll teach you how to fight, and how to forge a dagger and a saber in my shop. If you learn the blacksmith trade, you can forge many swords and you can earn a living." Ma said.

Shiao-ho jumped up and yelled, "Good! Let's move to town. I want to learn how to fight. I want to fight better than you, daddy and even Grandpa Bo."

Ma went to Lu's place to get the mule and told Lu his strong suspicion, "Master Bo wanted to kill Shiao-ho last night. He changed his mind at the last moment."

Lu agreed, "If Master Bo wants to *'weed the roots'*, he must kill Shiao-ho now to assure he doesn't take revenge in the future."

Ma said, "Old Bo is cruel and ruthless. Brother Lu, you better go to Master Bo's place to do some work for him. I am related to the Chiangs and I do not want to get you in trouble. I better go."

Ma moved the Chiangs to live with him in town. He dared not tell his wife or Chiang's wife the depth of his fear. He sold Chiang's house. It did not bring too much. Chiang Zhi-shen had borrowed heavily against the house.

He behaved with extra care around Master Bo and Bo Zhi-lin. One day, Master Bo told him, "You are good to take care of the Chiangs. Here is some silver. Take it. I'll help you."

A month later, some villagers reported that they saw Chiang's remains lying in the creek up in the mountains. Chiang's wife knew for sure that her husband was dead. She remarried soon afterwards. Ma told her, "I'm not merely a relative. I'm Chiang Zhi-shen's sworn brother. Cousin, I'd like to keep Shiao-ho with me. I would like to see Chiang's name and bloodline continue through Shiao-ho. You can take the baby with you; your new husband probably will adopt him."

2

Uncle Ma taught Chiang Shiao-ho martial arts and blacksmith skills for two years. Shiao-ho grew tall and strong. His father's tragic death and his mother's remarriage had made him bad-tempered. He learned to drink and fought frequently with the town roughnecks. Uncle Ma understood him and treated him with kindness but his wife did not. She resented that the growing Shiao-ho ate too much. She was also jealous of the boy's good looks and the attention that her husband paid to the boy. So she wanted Shiao-ho to leave. The boy was not happy about staying either.

One day, Ma dragged himself home through the deep snow after his daily practice at Master Bo's. His wife complained, "Look at you! You have been practicing martial arts every day for seven years now. Are you skilled enough to be an armed escort and get rich? We would be better off if you had enough time to manage your shop."

Ma sighed, "You don't understand. I dare not stop going to Bo's. I have learned enough to be a second-rate guard. But, I have seen enough of the cruelty, and I honestly do not want to be a guard anymore. I must go there every day lest Master Bo get angry. If he is mad at me for any slight disobedience, we'll be in real danger. See what happened to the Chiangs!"

"Ah! Chiang Shiao-ho is just another mouth to feed. He's lazy. Why can't he go live with his mother? We hardly have enough food to feed our own children," Ma's wife grumbled.

"Be patient, woman, you hear! It's I who kept him with us when your cousin remarried. I just cannot throw a homeless boy out now. Shiao-ho is smart and strong; he forged some very nice pieces and he sure earned his keep. Anyway, Shiao-ho will be sixteen years old in two years. Then he can go out and make a living for himself. Listen, I don't want to hear any more talk of this."

"Uncle Ma, hurry! Your Shiao-ho hit Donkey Sam hard. Shiao-ho may kill him." a neighborhood youth shouted. Ma said on his way out, "Never mind. Donkey Sam deserves a good beating." He resented that the greedy Donkey Sam had arranged the adulterous meetings between Jade Flower and Shiao-ho's father.

Later, in Ma's cluttered shop, Shiao-ho knelt and said to Ma, "Uncle Ma, please tell me the truth. Who killed my father?"

"Sit, Shiao-ho. Your father violated certain rules set by Master Bo for his students. He verbally insulted the Bos and wounded Bo Zhi-lin and Chen. Later he was afraid he would get caught and left town. We heard that bandits killed him."

Shiao-ho sobbed, "It's not true. Donkey Sam called me names and said my father was a braggart and a coward. He also said that the Lung brothers helped Master Bo hunt my father down and killed him. Besides, he said that it was you, Uncle Ma, who fetched the Lung brothers from Zie-Yin City for Master Bo. He ordered them to hunt down my father. You must know the whole truth."

"Shiao-ho, I've tried to cover it up for two years, and even your mother does not know the whole truth," Uncle Ma told Shiao-ho the details.

"Shiao-ho, we really cannot blame Master Bo entirely. Your dad was to blame, too. Your father and the rest of us all knew that old Bo is uncompromising when it comes to the 'death penalty' for anyone who commits adultery. It's said that Master Bo killed his wife and her lover. He was jailed for life but he escaped. It's no wonder that he hates anyone who commits adultery. Whenever he accepts a new student, he makes it very clear that anyone who defies this rule will be killed. Your father knew that; he deliberately violated the rules and insulted Master Bo. He was conceited about his skills, and he thought Master Bo, old and slow, could not control him. Master Bo almost died of a stroke, and that's why he ordered me to fetch his accomplished students back home to enforce his rules. I dared not refuse to go, and besides, he could have sent someone else. I knew then that your father had no chance fighting against them." "Uncle Ma, I'm grateful that you've taken care of me. Now I hate no one else but the old Bo, not only because he killed my father but also this." He showed Ma the dagger and continued, "Master Bo gave me this dagger two years ago. I remember that night very well.

It was dark and there was nobody around in the wheat field. In the beginning, he looked terribly vicious. I was afraid that he would beat me, but I didn't understand why he changed his mind and gave me the knife instead. I've been thinking about it again and again. Now I believe that Master Bo wanted to murder me."

"Lower your voice, Shiao-ho. That's why I insisted on moving you and your mother here the moment you told me about this dagger. I knew then that your family was in danger. I also taught you the martial arts for your own protection." Ma continued, "For two years, Master Bo has known that you're living with me and he has showed true concern once in a while. He often gave me some silver for your keep. I think that he truly regrets what had happened. I advise you to be forgiving. You'll have no chance of surviving if you want to go after him. Not only will you be killed, my family will be in danger too. Think about it."

Shiao-ho gazed ahead for a long time. Then he kowtowed thrice. He thanked Uncle Ma for keeping his mother, his brother and him alive.

"Come and eat!" Ma's wife called.

Ma patted Shiao-ho on the shoulder affectionately and said, "Let's go in and eat. Don't dwell upon this any longer. Try to preserve your life, behave well, become a successful person and carry on your father's bloodline. That will be a better way of being a good son than dying a senseless death."

During the meal, Ma's wife complained about Shiao-ho's shortcomings again. Shiao-ho kept quiet and did not quarrel with her as he usually would.

It was still early when they finished eating, and the snowstorm worsened. Ma frowned, "It looks bad, and I still have to go to Master Bo's tomorrow." When he noticed Shiao-ho's melancholy, his heart went out to the poor boy.

"Shiao-ho, here are a few coppers. Buy yourself a drink. It's no use to brood over the past. We cannot do anything about it."

About six inches of snow had fallen and it was still snowing. The only tavern in town still remained open with a few noisy drinkers. Shiao-ho bought a drink and then wandered around town. His hand touched the sharp blade of the dagger in his pocket. Master Bo had intended to use it to kill him two years ago.

He decided that he would go to Bo's village to challenge Master Bo. *'I know I am only a boy, but I am strong and fast while he is old and slow.*

Maybe I can win.' Pulling his worn padded jacket tighter around him, he thought, *'Anyway, if I kill him, with luck, and escape successfully, I will go far, far away and never come back. If I'm killed, folks around here will know that I've tried to avenge my father's murder and it'll be an honorable death. I just cannot stay here and depend on Uncle Ma any longer.'* He walked fast against the cold and snow, and was bursting with bitter hatred when he passed by his old home. He knew the gate of Master Bo's must be closed at night, so he walked around and found a lower part of the earthen wall and jumped up. He could not reach the top at first. He jumped again, barely made it, and then he fell awkwardly inside the yard.

"Thief? Who dares come here?" Master Bo yelled.

"I come to kill you...." Shiao-ho charged at Master Bo with his dagger.

"You dare!" Master Bo raised one foot and kicked Shiao-ho in the stomach. "How dare you come to kill me! Boy, you would have been dead already if I didn't pity you. Ah! You are Shiao-ho!"

Shiao-ho managed to hold his dagger tightly, tried to get up and charge again. May-lin came, holding her saber, and shouted, "My uncle is away. I can protect my Grandpa!"

"Don't kill him!" Old Bo stopped his granddaughter and took the dagger away from Shiao-ho with bare hands. Shiao-ho charged ruthlessly at Master Bo again. The old man kicked the boy harder this time.

Shiao-ho cried, "I have to kill you. You killed my father!" Then he jumped up, like a trapped young tiger, and charged again. Master Bo grabbed Shiao-ho's two hands. He wanted to kill Shiao-ho at once, so he loosened one hand to pick up the dagger. Shiao-ho struggled and freed one of his hands. He reached up and grabbed the old man's long beard.

"Donkey Sam told me that you murdered my father. I have to kill you even if I die!"

Master Bo clubbed Shiao-ho on the head with the back of the dagger. Shiao-ho passed out. Master Bo held the dagger, but somehow he did not have the heart to kill the boy. Instead, he pulled Shiao-ho up.

"Shiao-ho, I did not kill your daddy. I should have killed Donkey Sam, he was the instigator, and he was the one to blame."

Shiao-ho was dizzy and he protested weakly, "Don't deny it. Everyone says that you are the killer."

May-lin hit Shiao-ho hard on his back. Shiao-ho sobbed.

Master Bo's two daughters-in-law rushed out to see what the commotion was about. Master Bo told them, "Nothing's wrong! Go back to bed!" He examined the dagger, gave it back to the boy and said, "I gave you this dagger two years ago; I cannot believe that you want to use it to kill me now. It's too bad that you're so young and you really don't know how to fight. You have to learn how to fight for a few more years." Shiao-ho lowered his head in defeat.

Master Bo then ruffled Shiao-ho's hair kindly and said, "Good boy! You're the bravest boy I have ever met. Although you came to kill me tonight, I don't hate you. But I must tell you that I did not kill your father. On that day, I did not intend to kill your father, but ...." He stopped before he said the name, "I don't want to tell you this person's name. This person is very good at martial arts and you're definitely not his match. If you challenge him, he will kill you for sure. He is not softhearted."

Shiao-ho was convinced and he thought, '*The Lung brothers are the killers and I shouldn't have come here. I'd better leave.*' He stamped his feet and said apologetically, "Sorry! I should not have come here and I won't bother you anymore. I am going."

"May-lin, open the gate!" Master Bo ordered. He thought, "*He is better than his father. He's brave, handsome, without his father's overbearing arrogance and obviously knows 'right from wrong'. Maybe I can...*'

May-lin called, "You! Stop right there!"

"What? Grandpa Bo let me go and now you want to fight me? Let's fight."

"My grandpa does not have the heart to hurt you. Everyday my grandpa burns incense and prays to Buddha. He could have killed anyone without a second thought before. He spares your life tonight, but I won't let you go free." She chopped at Shiao-ho fiercely.

Shiao-ho backed a few steps and shouted, "Stop! I'm not going to fight a girl. A good man never fights against a woman." But May-lin came after Shiao-ho with her Kung Lung saber. Shiao-ho had no choice but to fence with her.

Master Bo watched. Shiao-ho managed to jump aside after ten passes. He said, "I don't want to hurt a girl! Do you dare fight me with fists? I don't want to wound you with my sharp dagger."

"Sure! Who's afraid?" Throwing her saber on the snowy ground, they started a fistfight. Shiao-ho was stronger and taller but the girl was more skilled. Many times the girl's fist hit his body, but Shiao-ho felt nothing at all. He observed that the girl applied the same styles that Uncle Ma had taught him, and he started to fight with growing confidence. A few minutes later, Shiao-ho hit the girl and she fell.

"Stop! You two young heroes! It's a good fight!" Master Bo called.

"Grandpa, he beat me," May-lin cried.

"Hush! He is taller, but you are more skilled. May-lin, it's a fair fight!"

"Shiao-ho, did Uncle Ma teach you what I have taught him? You fight with the Kung Lung styles." Remembering the importance of not getting Uncle Ma involved, Shiao-ho replied, "My father taught me two years ago."

"It's a pity that your father died early. He had only been my student for three years, but he learned better than the others. He could have been an expert by now. Your father was an accomplished scholar and he was not happy. He was torn between learning martial arts and passing the civil examination to become a magistrate, even a governor. Shiao-ho, it's late. The town gates must be closed for the night already. Stay here and go home tomorrow."

"Thanks. I will stay one night only," He added, "Tomorrow I'm going somewhere faraway. Uncle Ma does not know that I came here. He will be very mad at me. I cannot go back to his house."

"Where are you going?"

"I must find a good teacher and learn the martial arts well so I can avenge my father's death."

"You are a child and a very naive one, too. Without a good recommendation, no one will readily accept you as a student. Besides, Master Lee, Master Hsu, and I are the leading masters of martial arts in this area. Why not stay right here; I'll teach you. Think about it." Master Bo and the children had a snack together.

Everyone was asleep; Master Bo was awake and thought, '*for forty years I have wandered around China. I never hesitated nor was afraid to fight; I killed quite a few. Why do I let a mere fourteen-year-old boy threaten me? I really do not know what to do about him. If I spare his life now, he surely will be a threat later. It is better that I kill him now. But, I am very fond of him, he is so brave. I can't bear the thought of killing him.*' Master Bo stood outside the window of the room where Shiao-ho slept and listened. All he could hear was the sleeping boy's soft breathing. '*I worry too much. He is only a boy. I'll talk to him tomorrow and try to keep him here with me. I must keep him from going* away *to find a good teacher. With his physique, his talent and a good teacher, Shiao-ho can be a real threat later. I'll teach him some skills and make him work for me. A couple of years from now, he will forget about revenge and will be just like a grandson to me.'*

The next morning, when Master Bo was drinking a cup of tea, Shiao-ho told him, "Grandpa Bo, thank you very much! I'm going now."

"Where?"

"Last night I was wrong to come here to kill you. I'm sorry that I offended you. Now I'm going to find a famous teacher and beg him to teach me. In two or three years, I'll be back to kill my father's murderers."

Master Bo felt a sudden chill again. He smiled, "You are too young to go away all by yourself. It's better that you stay with me. You do odd jobs for me and I'll teach you all my skills. I'll point your enemy out for you and help you." He added emphatically, "You must know that you are only a boy and you have no silver. You'll starve to death. Besides, the bandits may kill you. Don't say that I did not warn you!"

He knew that he really had nowhere to go. Shiao-ho said, "I'll stay with you. But I don't want to be your student, and you'll have no control over me. I'm free to do anything and I can leave any time." Master Bo sneered, "I would not accept you as my student even if you begged!" He took a sturdy steel poker and shaped it into a circle effortlessly with his hands. Holding it against his knee once, he broke the poker into two pieces.

"Did you see that, Shiao-ho? You can avenge your father's death successfully only if you can do this, too. Otherwise, you'll just get yourself killed." he added gently, "Good boy, go out and shovel the snow now. We'll have breakfast soon."

Shiao-ho realized then that Master Bo indeed was highly skilled and had indeed spared his life last night. He thought, *'I will learn well. Besides, where can I go? I have no place to go. I'll stay here for a while. I may find out more about my father's death'.*

Uncle Ma came and saw him, "Here you are, Shiao-ho. We were so worried. Why are you here? Ma whispered, "You cannot stay here..." Master Bo and May-lin came out together.

Master Bo asked his students, "Do you remember this boy? He's Chiang Zhi-shen's son, Chiang Shiao-ho. He was told that I killed his father." Master Bo looked fiercely at every student, particularly Lu and Ma.

Ma said, "Teacher, Shiao-ho has stayed with me and helped me in my shop for two years. I never tell him lies. Last night he ran away and I'm surprised to see him here."

"Ma Zhi-min, I did not say that you told him any lies." Master Bo continued, "I want you, all of you, to hear this. I swear in the names of all the gods and ghosts that I did not kill his father and I have a clear conscience. I'm very fond of Shiao-ho even though he tried to kill me last night. I'll keep him here with me and I'll teach him. He is not one of you. He's not a student. I will treat him as my adopted grandson. *Ha! Ha!*" Master Bo closed his announcement with a hearty laugh. Everyone joined the laugh as if on cue. They congratulated Master Bo in unison. Ma also laughed and said the proper words of congratulation, but he was frightened.

The students soon started their daily training. May-lin learned in earnest. Shiao-ho stood aside and watched, he wasn't told to join the practice. He carefully observed the forms and techniques of the other students and realized that everyone was far superior to him. It was impossible for him to avenge his father's death now.

Shiao-ho watched the others practice and was often ordered by them to do chores. Master Bo treated the others very severely, but he was extremely kind to Shiao-ho. Sometimes he ruffled the boy's hair fondly. Master Bo also did not object that Shiao-ho and May-lin played together, even though the girl's mother did not think that it was proper. When it was nice outside, Master Bo would take the children out for a walk in the evening after he lit incense and prayed before Buddha.

Ma came to practice and did his share of chores every day. He looked at Shiao-ho often, and was constantly waiting for a chance to have a private talk with the boy.

Bo Zhi-lin came home from Xian, and he dared not show his objection to his father's decision to adopt Shiao-ho as a grandson. He complained to his wife, "My father is surely not right in his mind. Instead of '*Weeding the Roots*' and killing Shiao-ho now as an assurance against the young boy's revenge in the future, Dad adopts him and keeps him here. That boy is a young wolf; he will be a killer soon."

"It's really not your business. Your father wants to keep him. How can you object to his wish? Besides, Shiao-ho is only a boy. Your father gets his father killed and now you want the boy dead, too. If the officials won't stop you, the gods and the ghosts will surely punish you later."

Bo Zhi-lin slapped his wife hard and said, "If everyone had a soft heart like you, nothing can be done." Bo Zhi-lin wanted to hit his pregnant wife again, but he restrained himself and walked out. He saw that Shiao-ho was feeding the horses and he mercilessly took out his anger on the poor boy.

"You! Good for nothing! You give the horses too much feed. You want to stuff them to death?" He kicked the boy hard. Shiao-ho jumped up to strike back but Uncle Lu held him back.

It was spring and it got warmer. The newly sprouted leaves and grass, the rushing creeks, made the country fresh and alive. Shiao-ho was far from being happy. Every day Bo Zhi-lin would found ways to torture him. Chen was also mean to Shiao-ho. Now, with the novelty wearing off, Master Bo treated him with cool indifference, and he did not teach Shiao-ho martial arts as he had promised.

One day when Uncle Ma and Shiao-ho were cleaning the weapon-stands together, Ma whispered, "You can't stay here. It is a plot to keep you here and use you as a servant? Master Bo won't kill you as long as you're useful. But his son will not tolerate your existence. Do you know that the Lung brothers will be here for the Spring Memorial Festival? They, may be one of them, killed your father. If they know that you're Chiang Zhi-shen's first born, they will kill you. You better leave. You can hide at my place for a few days. Somehow I'll borrow some silver for you to go to Szechwan, you'll be safe there. Lung brothers are afraid of Master Hsu." Shiao-ho did not follow Ma's advice. He seemed to have a scheme of his own, and he sharpened his dagger whenever he was out of the other's sight. In the afternoons when the students have left and the Bos were inside taking a nap, Shiao-ho took a horse out and rode secretly. Even though the horse repeatedly threw him off in the beginning, with perseverance, Shiao-ho rode very well.

One afternoon while he was riding, Shiao-ho heard May-lin and other little girls singing. His face suddenly lit up.

"Nice singing!" Shiao-ho clapped his hands.

May-lin said, "Shiao-ho, you're riding again! If my uncle see you, he'll beat you up again. Go! Go! He isn't taking a nap now. Grandpa has sent him out on an errand, and he may be back any minute. Go back quickly."

Shiao-ho laughed, "I want to hear you sing."

Another girl said, "Forget it. We're not singing for you."

Shiao-ho got off the horse, opened his arms wide and laughed, "No! I won't let you pass if you don't sing."

May-lin replied, "There's no way we'll sing for you," then she added softly, "Shiao-ho! You better listen to me and go back quickly. Why do you want to irritate my uncle? You know he will beat you up." She laughed suddenly, "Girls! Let's run! See whether he can catch us." The girls all giggled and ran. Shiao-ho started to chase them.

"Shiao-ho! Stop right there!" Bo Zhi-lin galloped up and yelled. The girls and Shiao-ho stood still. Bo Zhi-lin yelled at Shiao-ho, "Thief! Lazy Bones! You're riding again!" He hit Shiao-ho hard on the head and Shiao-ho saw stars. He wanted to challenge Bo Zhi-lin, but he realized that he, a boy and empty-handed, could not win. He sat down at the roadside and pulled at the grass and stared blindly at the ground. May-lin sat down beside him.

"Shiao-ho, are you all right?"

Shiao-ho did not answer and she touched his shoulder, "Are you crying, Shiao-ho?" He wasn't crying before, but he started to cry now. His tears dripped onto the earth and May-lin started to sob too.

After a while, May-lin said, "You better get away from here. Sooner or later they will kill you." She wiped her tears with the back of her hands.

"I know. Uncle Ma and Uncle Lu told me to leave too. But I...have unfinished business here, and I don't want to leave yet."

"What business? Are you worried that you don't have silver?"

"It's true that I don't have silver, but..." Shiao-ho hesitated and then continued, "Silver is not the issue. I want to...." He grabbed her hand and said seriously, "You mustn't tell anyone that I want to leave. If they know, they will kill me for sure." Her face turned white and she promised, "I won't tell."

May-lin practiced with the others in the morning and flew kites with her girl friends in the afternoon. Her father sent her a beautiful kite shaped like a butterfly. She liked it very much and she was very happy.

Shiao-ho's life became pure misery. Bo Zhi-lin ordered him to feed the pigs. At night, Shiao-ho was ordered to sleep in a little hut beside the pigpen. In a few days, Shiao-ho smelled and looked like a pig. However, after finding out that the Lung brothers would be here soon, he seemed to be in good spirits.

Ma and Lu were anxious for Shiao-ho to run away. Uncle Ma secretly gave Shiao-ho two ounces of silver and Uncle Lu gave him some, too. One day Uncle Lu gave Shiao-ho a few articles of clothing that were too small for his own son. Shiao-ho accepted the silver and clothes but refused to leave. He carried the dagger with him day and night and it seemed that he was waiting for something to happen.

One afternoon, Shiao-ho herded the pigs along the creek. He let the pigs drink and feed nearby. He sat and daydreamed.

"Shiao-ho! Come and help!" May-lin ran to him and said urgently, "My kite is caught on the tall willow tree. I can't reach it, please come and get it down for me."

Not knowing why, Shiao-ho was always glad to see and to talk to May-lin. He only knew that whenever he saw her, he could temporarily forget his problems. It seemed to him that May-lin had the power of comforting him. Sometimes he wondered if she was the only reason he stayed.

Shiao-ho shook his head and said, "No. It's not mine, and I don't care."

"Please, please. It's my favorite kite. I beg of you." She stomped her feet, pushed her lips out and she was ready to cry.

"After I am gone, who will get the kite down for you?"

"After you leave, it will be too hot to fly the kite. You won't go away forever, will you? I will wait and fly the kite again when you are back." Shiao-ho sighed. '*Will I and can I come back? I may be dead.*' There was a huge willow tree beside the creek, and the kite was caught on the tallest branch. May-lin wanted Shiao-ho to go up the tree and get her kite down, so she looked up at the tall boy and begged, "Please, please get the kite down for me."

Shiao-ho thought, "*If I can escape safely, when will I be back? By then I'll be a big man and she a grown woman. Maybe she'll be married before I'm back. If we meet again, she probably won't recognize me. How could she ever remember that I once had retrieved her kite from this willow tree?*"

"No, I can't get up this tree."

May-lin grabbed his arm and begged, "I know you can do it. You can climb any tree." Shiao-ho said nothing for a while, and then he suddenly laughed, "Good. I'll get it if you will promise me one thing."

"Anything you want."

"If I call you 'my wife', will you answer me and call me 'my husband'?"

May-lin blushed but she wanted the kite really bad; she bit her lower lips and nodded. She secretly did not mind calling Shiao-ho husband.

Shiao-ho climbed to the top branch quickly and freed the kite. On the ground, May-lin looked up with open hands and called, "Throw it down to me!" Shiao-ho did not throw the kite down, instead he held the kite in one hand and descended from the tree sure-footed, and he jumped to the ground from about ten feet high.

Holding the kite high in his hand, Shiao-ho also blushed and said, "I'm going to call you my wife now." His face turned red and he called softly, "May-lin, my little wife!"

May-lin's face crimsoned. Looking around and making certain that there was no one about, she hesitated and murmured, "Yes, my husband." She took the kite and ran away.

The exhilarated Shiao-ho picked up the bamboo stick and started herding the pigs back. *'Great! I have a wife. Later, maybe ten years from now, I will be a skilled martial arts master, or even a first grade guard with a lot of silver. One day I'll dress up nicely, ride a good horse back here and marry her.'*

Two sweaty horses stood in Bo's stable. Shiao-ho heard someone call one of the riders Brother Lung; he knew that the moment came and the waiting was over. He was terrified and excited.

Shiao-ho closed the gates of the pigpens, he intended to join the others with his head high showing that he was not afraid. But he had a second thought, and he lowered his head and dropped his shoulders instead. He was not going to be conspicuous before he could take measure of his enemies first.

When Shiao-ho walked into the big room where everyone was, Bo Zhi-lin grabbed him by the shoulder. Shiao-ho tensed up and thought that they were going to kill him. He prepared to draw his dagger out and fight them to the death. Uncle Lu walked up and put his hand on Shiao-ho's shoulder and said, "Shiao-ho, go and give the horses a good rub down!"

Bo Zhi-lin sneered, "Brother Lung. Do you know this dirty rascal? He is Chiang Zhi-shen's first born. Remember how handsome his father was? Look at him; he is nothing but a dirty pig." The Lung brothers laughed. Bo Zhi-lin continued, "My father thought Shiao-ho a smart and brave boy earlier, but now he agrees with me that Shiao-ho is nothing but a coward and a simpleton." Uncle Lu pushed Shiao-ho out of the room lest Shiao-ho would fight. But Shiao-ho said not a word. Uncle Lu did not like Shiao-ho's submissive attitude at all. *'Why did Shiao-ho take the insult? He must be up to something. I better stick around tonight.'* Master Bo sometimes asked Lu to stay overnight, so it seemed quite natural that Lu would stay

The pigsty stood between the house and the stable. Shiao-ho deliberately left the exit unlocked and he pretended that he was busy feeding the horses and cleaning the stable. He had to wait. He paced around and the sun seemed to set extremely slow. Uncle Ma came into the stable and said, "How come you are still here? Don't you know the danger? You are fourteen years old now and you can work anywhere to stay alive. You know that the Lung brothers will be here at least seven or eight days. Sooner or later the Bos will tell them that you tried to kill Master Bo, and the Lung brothers will not let you live. Go! Go now. They are drinking." Shiao-ho said nothing.

May-lin came and handed Shiao-ho a small package of steamed dumplings with meat filling, "They are delicious. I'll try to steal more for you." Shiao-ho hid the food. They were as warm as his tears.

Lu went to the kitchen to help out and noticed that May-lin seemed to be very nervous. Her mother greeted Lu, "I am glad that you will stay overnight. I will pack some of the dumplings for you to take home tomorrow." She liked the steadfast Lu Zhi-chun and she hoped that later May-lin and Lu's second son would get married. Lu thanked her and then carried a plate of fruit to the dining area.

On his way to the kitchen for his usual leftover, Shiao-ho met the drunken Master Bo. The old man, with his extra bright eyes, looked at Shiao-ho fiercely.

His look sent a chill down Shiao-ho's spine. *'Did he see through my plot?'*

After he ate, Shiao-ho talked softly to the horse he used to ride when he saddled her. He then carefully packed his silver and the hot dumplings in a piece of cloth tied tightly across his back. He could hear his own heavy heartbeats and the Lung brothers talking coarsely, almost sounded like quarrelling. One of them shouted, "Damned that Hsu Min! He surely fights well with the sword. It's lucky that there were two of us." Now Shiao-ho knew for sure that Master Hsu must be superior to the Lung brothers and he hoped that he could be Hsu's student.

He quietly took the horse out and rode fast toward the foothills. There he tied the horse to a big tree and walked back to the stable and waited. When he heard the village night watchman sound the gong three times, he walked out of the stable, holding his dagger, stood in the dark and waited. He could hear the Lung brothers' loud snoring but the old Master Bo still coughed once in a while. It seemed to Shiao-ho that the old man had seen through his plot and deliberately coughed aloud to warn him. As the fourth night call sounded, Shiao-ho knew that he could not wait any longer. It would be dawn soon.

His heart pounding, Shiao-ho dashed to Lungs' sleeping room but could not push the door open. Holding the dagger between his teeth, Shiao-ho pushed the door with all his strength. As the door gave in, he fell into the room, but he quickly regained his footing and knifed someone, and dashed out of the room. Lu was lurking around the corner. He pretended to grab Shiao-ho but he actually gave Shiao-ho a powerful kick, sending the boy rolling down the foothill fast. Everyone was out. Lu shouted, "The stable! He steals a horse."

Shiao-ho rode breathlessly toward the mountains, the same escape route his father used two years earlier. Hearing riders coming after him, Shiao-ho hit the horse with his fist again and again to urge it to run faster. A little while later, he heard no horses and he thought he was safe. He started to relax a bit when he suddenly heard Uncle Lu, "I saw him running to the west!" Shiao-ho trembled.

The sounds of all other riders but one became faint. Shiao-ho wondered who was shadowing him. Uncle Lu whispered, "It's me. Shiao-ho! To the east and then south. You just follow the creek and the narrow pass and you will be out of the mountains. You will be safe in the north part of Szechwan Province. Take care." He handed Shiao-ho a package of dumplings.

3

Shiao-ho rode southward and now was in North Szechwan. He watered the horse at the creek and let the horse graze. He had a drink of water and washed the blood off his dagger and his arms. *'A lot of blood! I must have stabbed someone's abdomen! I might have killed one of my father's murderers, or at least I wounded him good. Didn't they find my father's body at the bottom of this creek?'* He was not sure, but he knelt and kowtowed trice. "Daddy, I may have killed one of the murderers. If not, someday I'll be back to kill whoever murdered you so you can rest in peace." He didn't want to mention that his stepfather was mean and abusive. He thought about his mother, his baby brother, May-lin, Uncle Ma, Uncle Lu and wondered when and how he would see them again. He was hungry and swallowed the dumplings and tears.

The carriages parked outside a restaurant each had an identical small white triangular flag with red trim and words on. Shiao-ho could not understand the words but he knew that they were not the ones of Master Bo's Kung Lung companies. The Kung Lung's flag was yellow with black trimmings and black words. He had seen Kung Lung's caravan passed by Uncle Ma's blacksmith booth. His father once explained the folks call Master Bo 'Bo Kung Lung'. Master Bo's superb martial arts skills as mighty high as the 'Kung Lung (dinosaur) mountain range. *'one day I will defeat the Kung Lung School. But, how about May-Lin, Isn't she a member of the Kung Lung school?'* He mounted the stairs as an adult.

"Hi! Boy! Are you looking for someone?" a waiter asked.

"I will have a drink and a meal. Serve me wine first! and see to it that my horse is fed." Shiao-ho pushed his chest out.

"Yes, Sir! You really want a drink? Not water?" The waiter laughed,

"You think I'm too young? Tell you what! You see I have silver here," he put his sliver and the dagger on the table with a bang, "Serve me wine and a meal quickly, and feed my horse too."

"Yes, sir!" the waiter chuckled. Other guests laughed, too.

He gulped down the food and noticed that every other guest dressed neatly. He looked at his torn jacket stained with pig poop, his dirty bare feet. *'Where can I get some silver to buy some decent clothes? I only have enough to eat for a few days.'* His dagger lying on the tabletop reminded him of Master Bo's savage expression before he was given this very dagger. *'He was going to kill me then'.* Shiao-ho renewed his oath of revenge. He tensed up when he heard heavy steps coming upstairs, and he was ready to run when he saw Uncle Lu and Chen. Uncle Lu said, "Shiao-ho, I'm taking you back." Lu's eyes glared, signaling danger and compelling the boy to run. Shiao-ho darted between the tables when Chen tried to grab him. "Let's see which one of you dares to..." Shiao-ho shouted. Lung Zhi-chi came upstairs; Shiao-ho pushed the paper-paneled window open and jumped just as Lung Zhi-chi's heavy saber cracked the window frame. He landed on the back of a horse and cut the horse loose, held on for dear life when the horse bolted and ran through the frightened pedestrians. He imagined that Lung Zhi-chi was in pursuit and gaining on him, Shiao-ho hit the horse rapidly. When he lost control, he jumped sideways off the running horse.

"Boy, Are you all right? You were smart to jump off the horse, and lucky to be alive. Is this your dagger?"

"Thank you, Sir. It's mine."

"This is a spirited horse. It is not easy to ride." Another man led the runaway horse back to Shiao-ho. It was Lung Zhi-chi's big black horse, not the white one Shiao-ho had. He knew now that he had not killed Lung Zhi-chi. *'Had I killed or only pierced someone else? perhaps I killed his brother.'* Besides an expensive looking saddle, there was nothing else on the horse's back. He had lost his scanty silver in the restaurant. *'No silver! How am I going to eat?'* A wedding procession passed by with a troupe of musicians accompanying a red curtained palanquin. The bearers and the musicians all looked at Shiao-ho and his torn clothes with contempt. Shiao-ho thought angrily, *'Do you think that I'm too poor to marry a pretty girl? Never mind, I have May-lin. She is waiting for me, and I'm going to have a grand wedding. You wait and see!'* Immediately he recalled another sad scenario. An old palanquin stopped at Uncle

Ma's to carry his sobbing mother and his baby brother away to her new husband Ton's place, and left him a bona fide orphan. Ton was a miser and he was also abusive. Once, Shiao-ho's mother made him some new clothes. When Ton found out about it, he came to Uncle Ma's place and demanded them back. Shiao-ho wanted to fight him but Uncle Ma held him back and said, "At least your mother and brother have a roof over them and food to eat. Not many men would marry a penniless widow with a child."

His tears mingled with the blood dripping from his nose. He passed a few village eateries, but he had no silver to stop and eat. *'I'm going to die of hunger in a few days and that is that.'* He remembered the stories about the vagabonds who stole or earned a living with performances of boxing or swordsmanship on the roadside. *'Of course I won't steal! But I can put on a show of boxing tomorrow at the market. Now I wish that I did not eat all the dumplings. But I was so hungry then.'*

He was afraid that he might be mistaken for a highwayman if he kept riding through the night so he stopped at an abandoned temple. *'Poor horse, be patient. I know you're hungry, me too. Tomorrow, I'll buy you some feed if I can.'* He tied the whining horse to a big tree, lied down on the cracked floor beside a shattered statue of Buddha and slept. The horse's loud neighing woke Shiao-ho. He heard the sound of horse's hooves fading in the distance, *'Thief! Someone stole my horse.'* In the dark, he tripped and fell face down on a broken piece of brick. Somehow he got up and started to chase the horse thief on foot through the fog. He ran a while and heard the horse no more when he suddenly saw a person sprawled on the roadside. He was so scared and he ran for his life. He stopped to catch his breath and realized that no one was chasing him. *'poor guy. He maybe dead'.* The horse had thrown the thief and ran away, only the saddle left on the roadside. Chiang Shiao-ho walked away from the body at first, but he had an idea and he turned back to the body and searched. Sure enough, he found a small fortune in the dead man's pocket. He also picked up the saddle.

"Best saddle for sale. Very Cheap! Best...." at the market he shouted, Two soldiers seized and manacled Shiao-ho. "Why? I did nothing wrong! How dare you arrest me?" Shiao-ho kicked the soldiers to get free. "Buster, you kicked me." One soldier slapped Shiao-ho hard and the older one said gently, "Boy, come with us to the court, we won't jail you if you're innocent." But the headstrong Shiao-ho, like a trapped young tiger, kicked and shouted all the way when they dragged him to the magistrate's office. The older soldier tried to calm him down, "Little brother, we're just doing our job. Someone reported that you are selling stolen goods. Please keep quiet and wait for the trial. Magistrate Fan is nice and just, he won't punish a young boy too harshly." But the indignant Shiao-ho continued to struggle and shout, until he nearly lost his voice.

"Are you soldiers or robbers? Give me back my dagger and my silver!" Shiao-ho protested when they searched him and took away his dagger and a small amount of silver. "Little one, we'll give you back everything if you're innocent. Don't worry! Howling will do you no good." They locked Shiao-ho in a small dark room, paying no attention to the boy's cursing and begging until Shiao-ho was finally reduced to hopeless sobbing. In the afternoon, four officers took him to court and pushed Shiao-ho to kneel in front of the seated old Magistrate.

"Little one, what's your name?" With a Southern accent, the Magistrate asked gently,

"Chiang Shiao-ho. I'm innocent and you better order them to give me back my stuff. Do you hear?"

"Ha! You're nasty. Why did you kill a man and steal his saddle and silver? The truth! Before I order you clubbed!"

"Honorable Sir, I'm innocent. Last night a thief stole my horse and...."

"Stole your horse? How could you own a horse? I see you won't tell the truth without a beating. Club him twenty times!"

"Pardon me and please have pity on me. I'm a runaway orphan. Master Bo killed my father and then...." Shiao-ho broke down.

"Hold him now and make inquiries! If he is telling the truth, I'll deal with that Master Bo," Magistrate Fan ordered.

They threw Shiao-ho into a cell with twenty-some other prisoners. They locked his feet, but took the chain from his neck and untied his hands. The cell had one pail in the corner for the night soils, and the smell was unbearably repulsive. Shiao-ho threw up and then sat against the cold, damp wall and sobbed. One of his jail mates came to comfort him. During the night, Shiao-ho found that the shackles on his feet were for an adult and they were loose on him. He secretly freed his feet, and then put them back on and slept with the hope that he could escape in the morning. It was customary for the newest prisoners to empty the latrine bucket in the morning. With one hand carrying the odious pail, Shiao-ho was trying to loosen the cuffs on his feet, he slipped and fell. The night soils spilled all over the guard, who cursed and kicked Shiao-ho. Shiao-ho rolled away, freed his feet and then ran. Twice he fell, but he picked himself up and ran even faster out of the courtyard and out of town. There were sound of horse's hooves behind him; he thought that the soldiers were chasing him and ran even faster until he fainted. His last memory was of being lifted up by powerful arms. A man held him on a running horse, and the stranger was not a soldier.

"You're a brave young rascal and cunning too. You acted like you have learned some martial arts. Who's your teacher?"

"Uncle Ma Zhi-min taught...." suddenly Shiao-ho was thrown off the horse. He regained his footing quickly and threw a rock at the stranger, who had doubled back. "Why? You've saved me and now you want to kill me? It doesn't make sense! Come down! Be a man and fight." Shiao-ho shouted. The stranger dismounted and laughed, "Oh, young brother, I really admire your guts. But I became angry as soon as I heard that your teacher's name has the word 'Zhi'. There is not a good man among Master Bo's Kung Lung gang," he continued, "is Ma not a student of that mean old Bo?"

"Yes. My father was Master Bo's student too. Master Bo and the Lung brothers killed my father. Uncle Ma helped me escape. Who are you and why did you save me?"

"I heard about the murder. you are Chiang Zhi-shen's boy, now the Bos want to catch you, alive or dead. I'm Wu Da, nicknamed Black Leopard. I have many friends. We rob the rich and help the poor. I witnessed your escape. I admire your bravery and cunning, and that's why I saved you."

"I won't be ungrateful. Someday I'll repay your kindness. Can you lend me some silver? I'm starved, and I need clothes and a weapon. The soldiers took my dagger and a bit of silver."

They stopped to eat. The used clothes they bought were too big and too long. Shiao-ho rolled up the sleeves and pant legs, tied the waist with straps torn from his old jacket. He also padded the shoes and tied them to his feet.

"You sure are resourceful, aren't you?" Black Leopard took him up the hill to the leader, a monk.

"Boy, Black Leopard said that you're brave and good at martial arts. We can use your help to do things that are difficult for us adults to do. But remember that we don't steal from or rob the poor or the old. Moreover, we never insult or hurt a woman," the monk told Chiang Shiao-ho. He did not want to be a bandit. *'Real heroes are not robbers. Master Hsu is a real hero and he won't teach me if I'm a bandit.'* He would leave this group as soon as possible.

The soldiers must have pities him for being so young, his wound from the twenty strikes were slight. Two days later, the rowdy group left to rob a convoy. Shiao-ho stayed behind. The monks said, "I'd like to see your wound completely healed. Next time we will take you with us." Shiao-ho escaped the next day. He did not hesitate to help himself to a package of gold nuggets and silver. *'this is the loot anyway'* He also took a saber. He escaped from the back slope. There was no path and he got lost and fell. He lost one shoe but he kept running on bleeding feet until it was dark and found an inn. He asked the innkeeper, "Where can I find Master Hsu?"

"Master Hsu has a huge estate in Min-An County. It's about two hundred miles to the south from here. You can get there by boat quicker than by land."

'I don't know how to swim. I'd better go by land.' Shiao-ho decided. He replaced his torn and unfit clothes and bought a horse, travelled uneventfully south to Min-An Town.

"How many students does Master Hsu have?" Shiao-ho asked around.

"None. Master Hsu does not accept any students. It's said that he set an impossible test for the admission. He wants to hand his skills down to his sons. One is a bit older than you. Master Hsu is very conceited. He does indeed have great skills and he's number one around here." The long-winded clerk told him. Obviously, Master Hsu was well-known. *'Now, what should I do next? I need to find a good teacher to teach me.'*

Szechwan province is one of the wealthy provinces in China and Shiao-ho found the folks there were all well-dressed and well-mannered. He started to learn to be polite. The hotel clerk advised him to talk to some profession security guards.

Shiao-ho visited the biggest security company. He met two very friendly professional guards and he told them his grievance. Nan, the older guard said, "Old Bo and his gang, especially the notorious Lung Brother were indeed have a bad name here. No need to worry. The Lung Brothers dared not come here anymore. Master Hsu punished them often. When the Lung Brothers knew that Master Hsu and his son were away last month, they sneaked into Master Hsu's plantation and killed two servants. They bragged that they had killed two of Master Hsu's best students."

Lee, the other guard said, "Master Hsu is conceited. He does indeed have great skills. He and old Master Lee are famous around here. But I'm not sure if he's Master Bo's match," he rambled on. "I do think you better seek the great Master Du '*Szechwan Dragon*' to teach you. Even if you can only learn twenty percent of his skill, I promise you that you'll meet no equals."

"Who is he? Where can I find him?" Shiao-ho asked eagerly. Nan laughed,

"He is only kidding. Master Du, the one called 'Szechwan Dragon' was very famous twenty years ago. But, nobody knew why he'd suddenly gone from this area, he might be dead. Nobody was his match even when he did not use '*Tien Hsueh*' technique. He only applied this most effective killing skill when he wanted to defeat two to three hundred bandits quickly."

"What is '*Tien Hsueh*'?"

"'*Tien*' means point at and '*Hsueh*' means nerve cavity. It is one of the elite secret techniques of the militant Tao priests on the Wu-Ton Mountain. It was used so rarely that not many people know about it. According to what I have heard, one who knows how to use it can kill or cripple a man, or make the man mute instantly simply by pointing his two fingers at one of the blood flowing pressure points, or a nerve cavity. Legend has it that only two masters in Szechwan Province knew how to do it. One is Szechwan Dragon Master Du in the north and another named 'Dragon Knight' Master Gi in the west. Both of them were very famous twenty-some years ago, and both of them retired suddenly."

"Are they still alive?" the awed Shiao-ho asked.

"There is no information about Szechwan Dragon Du. Someone said his grandchildren are still in Szechwan. A few years ago, a traveler from Xian said that both Dragon Knight Gi and his son had passed away. His daughter-in-law and a grandson live in poverty." He then added, "Master Gi was first a student of the *Sho-Lin* school, of the warrior monks, but later he learned some more improved techniques, including '*Tien Hsueh*' and *Tai-Chi* swordsmanship from the *Wu-Ton* school."

"What is *Sho-Lin*? What is *Wu-Ton*? Are they the names of mountain range like Kung Lung?" Shiao-ho asked.

"*Sho-Lin* is the name of a great Buddha temple. All the monks there knew how to fight well and the martial arts techniques they have developed was called '*Sho-Lin*' school. They emphasized physical strength. I heard that Master Bo's teacher was a master of the '*Sho-Lin*' school. They were usually big powerful men. '*Wu-Ton*' is the name of a mountain. *Tao* priests had their temples everywhere on the mountain. *Tao* priests developed the '*Wu-Ton*' school, emphasized the breathing and concentration methods called '*chi-kung*' (energy), and they improved the '*Tien Hsueh*' technique. A sick and weak person can become a deadly fighter too. *Wu-Ton* masters preferred a lightweight, sharp two-edged sword. I believe Master Hsu is of the *Wu-Ton* school. I hope I did not bore you with my long-winded explanation."

Shiao-ho stood up and bowed. "Thank you so much. I hope you will teach me more. My father died and I know nothing."

He asked again, "Does Master Hsu know the '*Tien Hsueh*' technique?"

"I don't think so. As I said earlier, Master Hsu is conceited. If he knows it, he won't hide it." Lee replied.

Shiao-ho felt hopeless. '*If all the great masters are dead, and Master Hsu may not be Grandpa Bo' match. It will be almost impossible for me to avenge my father's death. Still, I better beg Master Hsu to teach me.*'

"Why did both famous 'Dragons' retire the same time? Did they kill each other?" Shiao-ho asked again.

"No, they retired, or you can say that they withdrew themselves from the arena of the martial arts world. Master Gi, 'Dragon Knight', died a few years ago. One of the theories I heard was that another more skilled master defeated them and forbade them to bully anyone with their skills. They both were conceited with their superior skills until they met the best."

"Who is this supreme master?"

"No one knows. They said he is a short southerner, came from somewhere around Nanjing. That is all I know, Shiao-ho."

"Thank you both. I will tell Master Hsu my misfortune and hope that he will be sympathetic and be my teacher. Thank you both take time to talk to me." Shiao-ho bowed to both of them.

One day someone told Shiao-ho that Master Hsu was back. Shiao-ho saddled his horse and rode toward Master Hsu's villa. He led, not rode, his horse slowly and carefully passing through the crowded streets. Three horsemen rode from the north, the first rider was a well-dressed, scholarly looking man about forty and his two followers seemed to be servants. 'He must be Master Hsu....' Shiao-ho thought, 'It will be bad manners to trail them now. I'd better visit him tomorrow.'

Shiao-ho went to Master Hsu's villa and requested an audience. When Master Hsu came out, Shiao-ho kowtowed and asked to be a student.

Master Hsu refused, "I don't want to have any students. Stand up, Boy."

Shiao-ho kowtowed again and begged, "Please teach me the best martial arts. I must avenge my father's death. The Lung brothers killed my father.

I wounded one of them. Lung Zhi-chi almost killed me. Please..."

"Boy, I don't believe you. There's no way you could have wounded one of the Lung brothers. Get out of here."

Shiao-ho cried, "I stabbed him when he was asleep. The Lung brothers killed my father. Master Bo almost killed me...." His words of grief and suffering, gnashed out between sobs. Master Hsu was touched; he pulled the boy up, sat him on a bench and ordered a servant to bring him a cup of tea.

Master Hsu said, "You truly want to be my student?"

"I swear. If I'm not honest, may the thunder strike me?"

"Lung Brothers are my enemies, too. Chiang Shiao-ho, to be my student, you've got to be able to measure up to three requirements."

"I'll agree to a hundred!"

"I'm serious. First, you've got to have some martial art straining."

"I do. Uncle Ma taught me the basics and I can jump up on the roof from the ground, too."

"Good. Second, you must be able to endure hardship."

"Yes I can. I am a homeless orphan, and I was hungry for days. Aunt Ma never let me have enough to eat...." He shed tears again.

"All right then. Third and the last! You have to have strength! Can you lift up heavy weight?"

"Indeed I can! I helped Uncle Ma forge steel. I've strong arms."

"I want proof! Come with me, I'll show you."

Master Hsu led Shiao-ho to the three six-foot-long steel rods in a corner of the yard. Pointing to the smallest one, with the diameter of about an inch, he said, "Four years ago, Steel Rod Monk came here with this and demanded a donation of a thousand ounces of silver if I failed to lift this rod up and hold it over my head. I did and he left without the silver."

"Three years ago, Steel Rod Monk came back with this," Master Hsu pointed at the mid-sized steel rod with a diameter of about three inches and demanded two thousand ounces of silver if I couldn't lift it. I lifted the rod up and he left empty-handed again." Hsu stood beside the biggest rod and continued, "Last year, Steel Rod Monk dragged this huge solid steel rod here and demanded four thousand ounces of silver. I tried twice and failed to lift it, so I had to give him the silver. I had to borrow the silver. He left with the silver and a smirk on his face." Shiao-ho looked in awe at the rusty rod with a bowl-like diameter, half buried in the ground.

Master Hsu continued, "I swear that if anyone can lift the heaviest rod, I'll call him Teacher. I'll also call anyone my Brother if he can lift the mid-sized rod. To be my student, one will have to lift the smallest one, at least waist high. It's been almost a year now, and no one has been able to lift the small rod. Shiao-ho! You're brave and you have the determination to learn. I promise that I'll teach you all my skills without reservation the day you can lift it up to your waist, but not one day sooner. Agreed? Take it or leave it."

The smallest rod and the medium rod were there side-by-side. The slender, medium height Master Hsu, lifted the mid-sized rod, moved it and placed it besides the heaviest one. He said to the amazed Shiao-ho, "This is better. Not in your way."

Shiao-ho bent down, gripped the small one and tried to lift it. Giving all he had, he lifted it halfway to his knees and dropped it and almost toppled over it. Gritting his teeth, Shiao-ho tried again and did even worse. Master Hsu said gently, "You can come here to practice every day. When you can do it, I'll teach you. Keep trying." Shiao-ho tried and failed again. He was hungry and tired. *'Of course I can't do it today. I'm starving and I'm tired. Tomorrow I can do it.'*

Early next morning, Shiao-ho went back and tried again. He managed to lift it a little higher. Master Hsu encouraged Chiang Shiao-ho, "You can't build the Great Wall in one day! Come and practice every day, and soon you'll call me Teacher."

Shiao-ho tried again and again until he was too tired to walk. Every morning, he would go to Master Hsu's place to practice. Moved by his determination, Hsu and his oldest son treated him with kindness and the servants showed Shiao-ho sincere respect. One day, Shiao-ho almost lifted the rod waist high, but he dropped it when he saw stars dancing. He felt lightheaded and had a sweet taste of blood in his mouth. He looked pale. A concerned servant asked, "Would you like some refreshments?"

"No. Thank you very much. My stomach hurts, but I'll be back tomorrow."

When Shiao-ho did not show up at his villa to practice for the next two days. Master Hsu, he now was fond of the boy, sent a servant to see the boy. Shiao-ho was very sick. Master Hsu moved Shiao-ho to his villa and called a doctor to treat him. He said, "Shiao-ho, Don't worry. I'll look after you."

During his convalesce, Hsu Jan, Master Hsu's eighteen-year-old son, came to visit Shiao-ho once a while. Between sobs and teeth gritting, Shiao-ho told him: how did Master Bo exploited him as a servant, and let his son abused him, how did old Bo try to kill him one evening shortly after his father being killed, and ... Shiao-ho also told Hsu Jan about May-lin, the kindness help he got from Uncle Ma and Uncle Lu... His sad story was touching and also a necessary relief for him.

One day Master Hsu asked, "Shiao-ho, now you're well. Are you truly anxious to avenge your father's death?

"Yes! Yes!"

"Good. I am anxious to punish the Lung Brothers. We're leaving today! We'll go to Zie-Yin City first to punish the Lung brothers, and then we'll go to Chengba, Master Bo's lair. You'll have your revenge; I will challenge them and even the score. If we win and come back safely, I'll teach you."

"Thank you. How many of us will be going?" Shiao-ho kowtowed.

"Only you and me, and my sword, I'll make Master Bo admits his defeat, lest I kill all his students."

Hsu Jan said, "Daddy, take me with you."

"No. You stay home! I need you here to protect the family."

"But... there are many students and Lu Zhi-chun and the Lung brothers are very skilled. How can you fight all of them alone?"

Master Hsu said angrily, "I said that I, myself, am enough to stamp out the Kung Lung gangs. Say no more!"

4

Master Hsu wore a dark blue silk button up shirt and a pair of matching drawstring ankle length pants, and a wide yellow silk sash tied around his waist. He seemed relaxed on his white horse. His three-foot long sword was tied along the horse's flank. Shiao-ho rode behind him. Master Hsu taught him to roll up his silver in a wide strip of cloth and then tied it crisscross over his shoulders, how to have his saber tugged in the fold on his back. "Shiao-ho, this way you'll have your hands free and you won't lose your silver when you have to run. Don't put anything valuable in the saddlebag. You're a boy and your enemy might take your horse." Shiao-ho almost cried because of Master Hsu's fatherly words.

Shiao-ho though himself a good rider but now he sweated and had a hard time keeping up. No matter how hard he tried to quicken his mount, Master Hsu's white horse was always a few paces ahead. When they stopped to eat at noon, Shiao-ho wanted to have a drink but he didn't because his Teacher did not drink. Shiao-ho had never known anyone else, besides his granduncle, a magistrate, who talked and moved with such calm and authoritative manners the way Master Hsu did. He met his granduncle when his father took him to visit. Somehow he knew that Master Hsu was superior to his granduncle. Master Hsu was both a super martial arts master and a scholar. Shiao-ho admired Master Hsu very much and he tried to emulate him. *I'm so lucky to be his student and I hope he will teach me how to read and write, too.*

They came to a foothill with fewer pedestrians. At the entrance of the mountain path, Master Hsu stopped and handed Shiao-ho a small silver bell. "Shiao-ho, tie it to the neck of your horse." Master Hsu also had one. Their two bells jingled pleasantly together, echoing along the deserted mountain path.

Shiao-ho saw a group of rough looking men, probably bandits, waiting for them; he tensed up and prepared to fight. But, none of the bandits had any weapons, instead, one of them held a tray of refreshments.

The man said, "Greetings, Master Hsu. Please have some refreshments. You're most welcome to rest at our fort!"

"No, thanks!" said Master Hsu rode on without stopping. The highwaymen stood back respectfully for them to pass. When they crossed the mountain, Master Hsu told Shiao-ho to take off the bell and said, "You'll put it on again when we have to cross another hill." Shiao-ho understood then that the bells were Master Hsu's signal for the bandits to know that he was passing. Riding behind Master Hsu, Shiao-ho looked at his god-like teacher with awe and admiration.

One evening, Master Hsu led him to a villa. Mr. Yuan welcomed them.

Master Hsu said, "Chiang Shiao-ho is my student. Master Bo had his father killed. We're on our way to Chengba to confront him." Shiao-ho was so happy that Master Hsu acknowledged that he is his student.

"We've heard about the killing, and I don't think we should judge Master Bo too harshly. Shiao-ho's father was to be blamed, too. Shiao-ho, your father was conceited and he provoked Master Bo's anger."

"Both Uncle Ma and Uncle Lu agreed with what you've said. They explained everything to me. But, Master Bo tried to kill me, too." Shiao-ho told them about the incident with the dagger. Master Hsu said, "Someone has to restrain this high-handed Master Bo. This time I want to settle the score once and for all. If I win, I'll forbid them to set foot in North Szechwan. If they win, I'll stay out of their way, never to enter their territory again."

"We'll accompany you. Master Bo has more than thirty students, you will be outnumbered."

"No, thanks. Besides the Lung brothers, the rest of them are mediocre. Numbers do not mean too much. Judging by the Lung brothers' skills, I may not be able to defeat Master Bo. That's why I don't want you to get involved." Master Hsu said. Shiao-ho thought, *If Master Hsu loses the fight, I'll be in real trouble. Can I come out of this alive?*

Yuan's ten-year-old son came out to greet the visitors. When Master Hsu asked about the boy's martial art training, Uncle Yuan replied, "I started teaching him last year. He is skinny and weak and he needs to learn more than boxing and sword fencing. In a year or so, I'm sending him to Master Kac to learn the '*Tien Hsueh*' (Attack vital points) technique." Shiao-ho thought, '*If Master Hsu loses the fight and I come out alive, I have to seek Master Kac to learn this marvelous 'Tien Hsueh'*'

The next morning, they crossed another mountain and were in the Kung Lung School's turf. Shiao-ho thought, '*we're close to my hometown now. I hope I can see my mother, my little brother, Uncle Ma, and Uncle Lu. Definitely I will see May-lin soon. But what should I do? Will she talk to me if she knows that I'm coming with Master Hsu to wage war on her Grandpa?*'

Master Hsu did not take the bell off. He told Shiao-ho that he wanted everyone to know that he had come to this area. Outside Zie-Yin City, they met a convoy escorted by a Kung Lung Security Company. Instead of following the customary courtesy of travel, Master Hsu deliberately led Shiao-ho riding through the convoy. All the carriages stopped in confusion and the guards looked angrily at them.

"It's very rude to ride through a convoy like that, but the Kung Lung guards recognize me and they dare not protest," Master Hsu said. Somehow, Shiao-ho did not think that was the right thing to do. Later they met Uncle Yuan and nine armed robust servants. Uncle Yuan said that they came to applaud Master Hsu, but Shiao-ho knew they were coming to assist Master Hsu.

"Teacher, have you traveled in this area before?" Shiao-ho asked. Master Hsu seemed to be familiar with the area.

"I had been here twice; seven years ago and three years ago," Master Hsu explained. "Behind his back, some of Master Bo's students, especially the Lung brothers, are downright wicked. Years ago, Kung Lung guards had a booming business in North Szechwan. They were conceited and behaved unscrupulously, and I chased them out of Szechwan again and again. I don't think that Master Bo knows his students' vice and he must resent me. He is old now; otherwise, he would have challenged me already."

Master Hsu told Shiao-ho at the hotel, "It's only ten miles to Zie-Yin City. Keep your saber handy and be alert tonight. They know that we are here and who knows what they might do during the night." Fear and excitement kept Shiao-ho awake. He thought he heard someone on the roof, or try to break in through the window many times throughout the night.

He was jumpy the next morning. Master Hsu said kindly, "Shiao-ho, don't be afraid. The Lung brothers are nothing to be afraid of. But Master Bo is something else. He is old, but I dare not think it'll be easy to beat him."

They came to the Lung brothers' security company. Master Hsu rode through the gate. Lung Zhi-tin, whom Shiao-ho stabbed, was lounging on a cot with his stomach bandaged.

He shouted, "Ahe! Shiao-ho. You get Master Hsu here to help you!" He could not stand up. Shiao-ho wanted to stab him. "Stop! Shiao-ho, you're not going to beat an injured man!" Master Hsu called. Three armed men, Chen among them, came out.

"You, Rebel." Chen slashed at Shiao-ho and the other two fenced with Master Hsu. With his long, narrow, two-edged sword, Master Hsu disabled one quickly. Chiang Shiao-ho had a hard time defending himself against the experienced Chen. Master Hsu came to his rescue and pierced Chen's shoulder.

"Hsu Min! Damn you. Come and fight me!" with a ferocious shout, Lung Zhi-chi joined the melee. Together with Kao, they held Master Hsu off for a short while and then Kao was injured. Lung Zhi-chi dashed out of the guard station with Master Hsu and Shiao-ho in hot pursuit. Yuan and his men conveniently blocked Lung Zhi-chi's escape. Shiao-ho was so happy that his father's killer did not have a chance to escape now. To his dismay, Uncle Lu jumped down from a galloping horse, and immediately locked in a fight with Master Hsu. Lung Zhi-chi fled.

"Teacher, please stop! Uncle Lu is a good person." Shiao-ho shouted. Lu Zhi-chun successfully blocked Hsu's thrust with his heavy saber and pleaded, "Master Hsu, please stop. Let's talk over our differences."

"You know why I came. Lately your Kung Lung gang has behaved rowdily in North Szechwan. I'm here to teach all of you a lesson."

"Let's solve our differences peacefully. Besides, Shiao-ho's father was insolent and deserved to be punished," Lu Zhi-chun said.

"I have my own reasons to come here! The Lung brothers killed two of my servants. Then they bragged, saying they killed two of my best students. I don't have any students. I came here to even the score."

He called, "Shiao-ho! Let's go to Bo's village to catch the coward Lung Zhi-chi."

Uncle Yuan told Shiao-ho, "Someone said that Master Bo killed your father. Not the Lung brothers." Shiao-ho sobbed.

"Shiao-ho, don't cry. They cannot get away now," Master Hsu said.

Master Bo and his students waited for them at Bo's front gate. Maylin, dressed in pretty pink silk, stood under a tree and waved her small saber at Shiao-ho furiously.

The stout Master Bo walked forward alone, "Master Hsu, Welcome! Your fame is far-reaching. Have you come here to help the renegade Shiao-ho avenge his father's killer? It is I who killed Chiang Zhi-shen. Please kill me alone if you can. Leave my students out of it."

"I'm here also on my own account."

"I don't believe that I have offended you, Master Hsu."

"Not you yourself. But you're blind to your students' atrocities in North Szechwan."

"Which one? I have always kept my students' behavior in check. Shiao-ho's father committed adultery and I had him killed. Now if you name the students who have offended you, I'll punish them myself and order them to give you a proper apology."

"The Lung brothers killed two servants of mine while I was away. I came here to demand justice. Lung Zhi-tin is indisposed. But I'll take Lung Zhi-chi back to be hanged for murder."

"My students are my sons. I'll kill and punish them myself. But no one, not even Szechwan Dragon Du or Dragon Knight Gi, will be allowed to hurt my students. You better leave Master Hsu!"

Master Hsu advanced a few steps, but stopped when Master Bo said, "Wait! Hear me out first. Master Hsu, I know your skills are superior to my students. But I'm confident that I can beat you. If we could go back twenty years, I would never have allowed you to wound my students."

"Master Bo, let's talk no more! Let's fight!"

"Let me finish, Master Hsu! I'm old now and my two sons are not good fighters. After I die, my sons and my students will not be able to defend themselves against my enemies. That's why I did not kill Shiao-ho."

"It's simple. Let me have Lung Zhi-chi, and I'll leave the others alone."

"You heard me wrong. I'm not afraid of you. I'll protect my students regardless of what will happen."

Master Bo brandished his saber once. Master Hsu blocked it and he was surprised at Bo's strength. Stepping back, Master Bo continued, "Let's have a friendly duel and don't draw blood if it is possible. If you win, I'll kill myself and you can kill my students at will. But, first tell me what you'll do if I win."

Master Hsu bowed low and said formally, "I'll never come to this area and your students will have a free run in North Szechwan. Agreed?"

"Agreed."

Two weapons clashed and the fight began. Master Hsu thrust thrice in quick succession and Master Bo successfully blocked them just as fast. They moved very fast, sometimes their weapons clashed together, but they separated swiftly too. Shiao-ho and the others could not follow the fight fast enough to distinguish who's winning. Everyone watched with their mouths wide open and held their breath. Suddenly Master Hsu jumped out of the circle and Master Bo, pale and gulping for air, stopped too. Then, to everyone's surprise, Master Hsu ran to his horse and galloped away without saying a word.

Startled and confused, Shiao-ho stood there dumbfounded. Uncle Yuan called, "Shiao-ho. On the horse and let's go." He pushed Shiao-ho onto the horse and led them away. They followed Master Hsu and quickly rode southward along the curving mountain path; the same one where Shiao-ho's father was killed and Shiao-ho had escaped. Finally Master Hsu stopped when they reached North Szechwan.

"Why? Teacher, did you not want to hurt an old man?" Shiao-ho asked.

"Don't call me Teacher any more. I'm not good enough to teach you. Come closer!" Master Hsu raised his right arm and Shiao-ho could see the blood trickle through a cut and the blood stains on the pant and boots.

"Master Bo wanted to protect his sons and students from revenge. He deliberately slashed me enough to hurt but not to kill. If he had not held back, I would have lost my right arm." Master Hsu continued with a sigh, "Even in his old age, he is better and stronger than I am. If he were young, more agile and stronger, I would not have had a chance to hold him off more than ten passes." Shiao-ho's face was white as snow.

"Shiao-ho. I'll keep away from Master Bo's territory as long as I live. Even if I teach you all my skills, you wouldn't have a chance of beating the Kung Lung gang. Lu Zhi-chun is almost my match already. Ah! To get your revenge, you have to learn more superior skills."

"But, Teacher, where can I find a better teacher than you. Please teach me." Shiao-ho knelt and begged.

"Go to Kaifeng and seek Master Kac, to learn the 'Tien Hsueh' technique. When I visited him seven years ago, we had a friendly meet. He pointed his fingers at my leg once; my leg went numb and immobile immediately. Of course he cured me right away. If not, I might be a cripple by now. You go to him and tell him that I sent you and he will accept you. You know I have to keep my word to leave the Kung Lung gang alone. Otherwise, I would have let my son take you there. Take care and good luck."

Uncle Yuan said, "Shiao-ho, you're too young to travel to Kaifeng alone. Come home with me. I'll take you and my son to Master Kac's next year. It's very dangerous for you now. Every Kung Lung member will hunt you down and kill you."

"No, thanks. I can't wait that long. I'll be careful. Thank you."

Shiao-ho stood there watching them ride away and he felt very alone. *'I'm still close to home; I better go see my mother, my young brother and Uncle Ma. Who knows if I will be alive and back again? I know I have to cross Tu-Nan Mountain and Dart Hu Li's bandits might kill me. Hu Li's throwing darts are deadly accurate. He wounded May-lin's father before. Oh! May-lin! Please don't hate me. I did what I have to do.'*

He waited until dark, tied the horse to a tree, and went to his mother's place. Ton, his mother's husband would not let him in. "Go away! Your mother is my wife now, and I won't allow you to upset her. Every Kung Lung fighter is trying to catch you and kill you. I won't put my family in danger on your account."

He walked back to his horse when a shadow came out from behind a tree. Shiao-ho raised his saber.

"Shiao-ho. it's me," Uncle Ma said hurriedly. "Here is a bit of food and silver. Lung Zhi-chi is in town looking for you. You better run. Let me show you another route out of town and hope they won't ambush you. Don't stop for anything until you're safely far away."

"Uncle Ma. You're my true father." Shiao-ho kowtowed.

The next morning, he stopped at a small eatery close to the north entrance of the Tu-Nan Mountain pass. He shared the only table with an old scholar who was reading. Shiao-ho thought, '*I wish I could read and write. It's too bad my father died before he could teach me more. Uncle Ma is practically illiterate. If I could be Master Hsu's student, he may teach me. No one will teach me now. Ah! Master Kac may teach me if I am lucky enough to stay alive and reach him.*' He tried to not let his tears come.

With a Southern accent, the old scholar asked him, "Young boy, where are your folks? You can't be traveling alone on this dangerous mountain route?"

"I have a horse and I know how to fight. Anyway, I have no family now. I'm not afraid of the bandits! If they dare rob me, I'll kill them." Shiao-ho forced himself to laugh aloud lest the stranger saw his tears, but his voice cracked, giving him away.

"Where are you going?"

"I'm going to Kaifeng."

"It's quite far. Do you have a relative there?"

"No one. I'm going to seek the famous martial arts Master Kac and beg him to teach me, so I can come back to avenge my father's death. Master Bo killed my father...." Shiao-ho broke down and sobbed as he told the old man about his sufferings. And then he said, "Grandpa, you're a learned man. You probably do not understand all of this fighting and killing stuff." Shiao-ho felt better after the talk.

"How old is this Master Bo?" the scholar asked.

"Oh! He is old. My father was his student and I call him Grandpa Bo. He...killed my father because my father disobeyed him." Shiao-ho did not want to mention the name 'Kung Lung' school. He was afraid that the owner of the eatery might know some of the Kung Lung guards. '*I better not say anything more. Uncle Lu once told me that I should not tell strangers things.*'

They ate in silence. Shiao-ho thought, '*At least I have silver to buy food this time.*' He still had the silver and gold nuggets he took from the bandits. He touched the pouch that he tied across his shoulders for assurance.

Shiao-ho said, "Grandpa, we can ride in turn to cross the mountain."

"You go ahead. I'm not in a hurry. Take care," The old scholar picked up his book.

The owner told Shiao-ho, "Boy, you better wait here for a convoy and then go with them. It's not safe for a lone traveler, and you are so young." Shiao-ho figured that the only security company passing through here would be the Kung Lung guards. They were more dangerous to him than the bandits.

He replied, "Thank you. I don't think they will rob me, I have nothing."

The mountain path gradually became steep and narrow, and Shiao-ho had a hard time reaching the first peak. When he stopped to rest, he saw another lone traveler standing under a tree on the next peak. He pushed ahead to have a better look and found that the person was the same old scholar whom he had met at the eatery. When Shiao-ho bade him goodbye, he was still eating and reading.

He called, "Grandpa, is that you?" Catching his breath, "Oh! Grandpa, you must know how to fly. How did you get ahead of me on foot? I have a horse and I started before you did."

"I know a short cut," the old scholar smiled.

"No wonder. Am I on the right path?"

"Yes. After this peak, you'll have to pass two more before you'll be on a level road. There you will find a few houses. You can ask them for some water. You go ahead."

"Thanks." Shiao-ho let the horse gallop downhill. He looked back and saw the old scholar still standing there on the peak. *'He probably is composing a poem.'* He remembered that his father had said that scholars like to write poems about scenery.

It was too steep to ride uphill, Shiao-ho had to lead his horse, and the going was hard and slow. When he stopped to catch his breath, he suddenly saw that the old scholar was on his way down the next peak ahead. A chill went through him and the hairs on his arms stood up, *'Oh! He must be a ghost, or a mountain god. He is not human. What am I going to do? Hide? Where?'* He was scared, but he kept going and hoped that he would be out of the eerie mountain. Soon he was on the level road and he felt better.

He heard the faint sound of shouting and weapons clashing ahead, and he quickly pulled his horse behind a rock and hid. Finally he ventured out when it was quiet again. With his saber ready, Shiao-ho proceeded cautiously around a bend. What did he see almost scare him off his horse. About twenty men lay on the road. Their broken weapons scattered around. Shiao-ho thought they were all dead until one of them called, "Help! Young brother, go to the main camp and ask for help. We can't move...Ah! Who are you? You are not one of our men." None of them could move and some of them moaned in pain.

"I'm a traveler. Are you all wounded? How come you're not bleeding?"

The man said, "Please be kind enough to go to our main camp to get us help."

"Who hurt you? There are so many of you."

"We're Hu Li's men. A white-bearded scholar disabled us with 'Tien Hsueh' technique. When we ganged up on him, he did not seem to move but none of our weapons could touch him. He then pointed two fingers at us...."

Shiao-ho rode away fast, hoping that he could catch the old scholar. He knew that the old man must be a supreme master who had protected him. '*Who knows? He might be Master Kac. Doesn't Master Kac know 'Tien Hsueh'? Ah! He must have deliberately showed me his skills back at the peaks. I was too stupid to understand the hint. I should have realized that only a skilled master would dare travel alone. Wasn't he concerned that I was alone? I should have kowtowed to him right there and beg him to teach me. Now where can I find him? Master Hsu is a scholar, too. Why did I think that he is an old scholar who knows nothing about martial arts? And why did he ask me how old Master Bo is? Does he know Master Bo? But he was nice to me.*'

It was dark and Shiao-ho was tired and hungry when he rode out of the mountain pass. He wanted to find a place to eat first. But when he saw a convoy parked in front of the only inn, he turned back toward the mountain quickly. He did not want to take the chance of meeting any Kung Lung guards here. A man, probably a guard, saw him and called, "You! Don't turn back to the mountain; the bandits will surely come out at night."

Shiao-ho pretended that he did not hear him and kept going, but another guard stopped him and said, "If you want to die, it's your business. But I won't let you go, lest the bandits follow you here and rob us. Who knows if you're not a spy? Come with me to see my boss. We Kung Lung guards are not easily fooled."

"Let go of my horse! I'll...." Shiao-ho whipped at the guard, wanting to escape desperately now.

A familiar voice, "What's going on? A thief? Chiang Shiao-ho! How dare you...." It was Bo Zhi-lin. Bo Zhi-lin did not know about Master Hsu's duel with his father yet. He was travelling with a Kung lung Company on their way back to Xian.

Shiao-ho attacked Bo Zhi-lin ruthlessly. He knew that he had no chance of escaping and he decided to fight to his death. At least he could wound or kill Bo Zhi-lin, who had tortured him so much. Bo Zhi-lin ran, "Brother Feng, help!"

A strong hand snatched Shiao-ho's saber away and then a kick sent him rolling away like an egg. Bo Zhi-lin and the others attacked Shiao-ho with sabers and clubs. Shiao-ho fought back ferociously until he could not move any more.

Feng ordered, "Don't kill him. Tie him up and send him back to Master Bo."

Bo Zhi-lin echoed elatedly, "Tie him up...." He kicked Shiao-ho again, and suddenly his back became numb. He tumbled down.

"Brother Bo, what's the matter?" the others asked.

"Don't push me! What? It's an old man."

An old scholar, out of nowhere, pushed them away and stood protectively beside Shiao-ho.

Feng asked, "You old man. What do you think you're doing? Go away! You hear? I'm not going to hurt an old man."

"I'm the boy's teacher. No one is allowed to harm him!" a crisp reply with a Southerner's accent.

Feng waved his saber menacingly, "Get out of my way right now! I'll..." and then, "Ache! Let go of my saber!"

No one could recall what had happened exactly. The old man held Feng's heavy saber with two fingers, but the stout Feng could not pry it loose no matter how hard he tried. Next, the old man seized the saber, threw it on the ground and broke it into pieces with one foot.

There was silence. Everyone was too scared to move or talk when the old man lifted Shiao-ho up, carried the tall boy on the shoulder and walked toward Shiao-ho's horse. Shiao-ho smiled through pain and tears. He had a super teacher now, his hardship was over and everything would be all right.

"Wait. Please wait! Honorable uncle! Please tell us your name," the seasoned Feng Zhi-pan finally found his voice, "so we can tell our Teacher. We're Master Bo Kung Lung's students."

"No need to know my name. Just ask Bo Gen-fee to tell you whom he'd met thirty years ago at Tonby Mountain. He will know." The old scholar lifted Shiao-ho onto the horse's back and led the horse away.

"Ah! He knows Master Bo's real name! Who is he?" Feng Zhi-pan and all the Kung Lung guards whispered amongst themselves. They went to Bo's village with the now crippled Bo-Zhi-lin and the pieces of the broken saber.

Master Bo turned pale and almost fainted when he heard. "The old man said, "your should know whom you'd met thirty years ago at...."

"I sure deserved severe punishment for being cruel." Master Bo sighed, "Now all the gods and ghosts want to punish you, my sons and students, for my wickedness. How can I forget that scholar? Thirty years ago, I met him and received the only defeat and humiliation I have ever known. I was young and strong. I think he was a few years younger than me. But fighting him was like an egg fighting against a rock." He did not want to tell them that he was pulling a pair of gold earrings off a young woman's ears at that time. He continued, "Shiao-ho is brave and strong. If this scholar teaches him, Shiao-ho will be a super master soon. None of you will be alive when Shiao-ho comes back for revenge." He said again, "It's my entire fault. I should not have killed his father in the first place. I should not have let Shiao-ho live just because I'm old and have become soft and indecisive."

Ma Zhi-min said, "Teacher, please don't worry. I'll talk Shiao-ho out of it when he comes back."

May-lin said angrily, "Grandpa, I'll learn all your skills and I will beat Chiang Shiao-ho. Oh! I hate him!"

Lung Zhi-chi said, "Teacher, please don't worry. When the renegade comes back, we'll ask all of our friends to come to our aid. Beside, starting today, we'll practice more to improve our skills. We're so many, and he is alone. We'll win!"

Master Bo thought a long time and said with determination, "Your skills are not very good because I did not teacher you all my skills. I have been holding back and not teach you some of my secret techniques. From now on I'll teach you all my skills. Then every one of you will be as good as I am. I don't believe that thirty-some Bo Kung Lungs cannot beat one lone Chiang Shiao-ho.

5

Time flew by like one of Dart Hu Li's throwing darts. Ten years had passed since the old scholar took Shiao-ho away. Master Bo's beard had not a single black hair left at the age of seventy-six, and some of his students had grandchildren already. There had been many changes in the circle of guards and the field of martial arts. There was no news of Chiang Shiao-ho and his incredible teacher.

Master Bo would ask these questions whenever one of his students returned home or a friend came to visit him. Deep down in his heart, Master Bo knew that all his students put together couldn't stop Shiao-ho's revenge. He knew that Shiao-ho's teacher, the scholar, was truly superb. Some nights, when sleep evaded him, Master Bo shuddered with fear, recalling his complete defeat at the hand of that short scholar nearly forty years ago. Even at his best, Master Bo was as useless as an egg fighting against a rock in his confrontation with Shiao-ho's teacher.

"Any news of Chiang Shiao-ho? Are there any new outstanding young martial arts masters in your area?" Master Bo would ask these questions whenever any of his students returned home or any friend came to visit him. Deep down in his heart, Master Bo knew that all his students put together couldn't stop Shiao-ho's revenge. He knew that Shiao-ho's teacher, the scholar, was truly superb. Some nights when sleep evaded him, Master Bo would shudder with fear when he recalled his complete defeat at the hand of that short scholar nearly forty years ago. Even at his best, Master Bo was as useless as an egg fighting against a rock in his confrontation with Shiao-ho's teacher.

His oldest son, May-lin's father, taught many students, and his security station in Han-Chun City attracted good business. His second son, Bo Zhi-lin, had never fully recovered from the strange old scholar's execution of '*Tien Hsueh*' on the back. He was rendered a hunchback, and could walk slowly again only after many years of doctoring.

May-lin's mother had passed away years ago. Now, at twenty-two, May-lin was an average looking girl, and her bound feet were not small enough to be considered admirable. She was Master Bo's only grandchild, and he spoiled her. Master Bo had taught her all his secret fighting techniques, so she was now superior to Lu and the Lung brothers. Master Bo boasted often. "Master Hsu would not be able to last more than ten passes now in a duel with my May-lin." However, he never mentioned whether May-lin could beat Chiang Shiao-ho. He often wondered, '*How advanced are Shiao-ho's skills now? Could my granddaughter at least defend herself if they were to meet and fight?*'

He smiled whenever May-lin said, "I hope that damned Chiang Shiao-ho comes soon. The sooner he comes, the sooner I can beat him." Master Bo would think, '*It won't be that easy.*' and he would suddenly feel chilled all over.

Most girls would be married at the age of fifteen or sixteen, lest they become old maids. Because of her rather large feet and her mannish behavior, the ordinary country folks did not want May-lin to marry their sons, but many first-rate guards and martial arts masters came to Master Bo to ask for May-lin's hand for their sons. Master Bo refused them all. Sometimes he would say, "My granddaughter does not want to get married yet.

Indeed, May-lin said again and again that she was not ready to be married. She seemed to be carefree, but she never forgot Chiang Shiao-ho and their secret pledge under the willow tree. Whenever she recalled that Shiao-ho had called her "my little wife" and she had answered "my husband," she blushed. She knew Shiao-ho well; his determination, his resourcefulness, his inscrutable endurance, and most of all, his wisdom to hold back his anger whenever he knew that any action of his would cause his imminent death. Many times, she had witnessed Shiao-ho submissively receive her uncle's severe beatings. Once, after her uncle kicked Shiao-ho rapidly, she helped the wobbly boy up and tried to stop the blood flowing from his head. "It's bad," she had said. "Why did you not strike back? Maybe he will think twice before he kicks you again." Shiao-ho moaned, "I should not give him any excuse to kill me. Uncle Ma told me to endure everything and try to stay alive."

She knew in her heart that her Grandpa's fear of Shiao-ho was real, even though she boasted often that she could beat Shiao-ho. Even if Shiao-ho had just a mediocre teacher or no teacher at all, she knew that Shiao-ho would be difficult to fight if he ever came back. Now with his great teacher, Shiao-ho would be superb. With his strong physical condition and natural agility, Shiao-ho was a born fighter.

She wanted to be prepared and kept busy every day with martial arts practice. She rarely missed training sessions. At night while everyone was sleeping, she would drill herself, jumping up and down from the roof and hopping from roof to roof. Every afternoon she rode, quite often to that huge willow tree. There, under the branches, she often daydreamed about Shiao-ho. But she also hated Shiao-ho. She hated him for being a constant threat to her old grandpa. She hated him for the impossible love between them, for causing her simultaneous longing for and fear of his return. Sometimes she chopped the huge tree trunk to relieve her frustration. The old tree suffered so many cuts that it began to die slowly.

She was secretly dreading Shiao-ho's impending revenge. Her grandfather's dishonorable plot to use Shiao-ho as a servant and her uncle's relentless abuse would definitely guaranteed Shiao-ho's hatred for them. She often thought, '*If I'd been treated so badly, I would not be forgiving either.*' She recalled how every time they had some delicacies to eat, she had to steal for Shiao-ho, who got only leftovers.

May-lin despised her uncle Bo Zhi-lin. Her uncle even abused his own wife. Her aunt told her, "May-lin, your uncle is less than a bully. He's afraid of the strong, and he abuses anyone who is weaker than he is. He is so afraid of Chiang Shiao-ho. Sometimes he screams and then begs for Shiao-ho's forgiveness in his sleep. It's my misfortune to be his wife. I pity him."

She loved her grandpa very much and she was close to him. One day while they were having lunch, Master Bo looked at her and asked hesitantly, "May-lin, do you want to go out to see the world?"

"Where would I go?"

"Anywhere you want to go. You can travel through the mountain ranges to see the rushing rivers. You can see the real world that you would not have a chance to see if you stay home. You can also meet some martial arts masters and fighters from different schools."

"Sure, let's go. Grandpa, you have not traveled so long."

"No. I can't. I cannot leave home."

"Oh well! You can't or you won't? I don't want to be apart from you. So I'll not go."

"May-lin, you should not think that your skills are sufficient. They're far from excellent. You can't learn any special techniques if you stay home. I'd like for you to go to your father security station at Han-Chun City first, then Xian, and Kaifeng. At Kaifeng, you'll seek Master Kac to teach you '*Tien Hsueh*'.

"I don't want to learn '*Tien Hsueh*'. A true fighter would fight honestly with fists or weapons. I wouldn't call it an honorable victory if one wins with sly tricks."

"You have to learn this super skill. You have to know how to use '*Tien Hsueh*' to beat someone who might use it. Otherwise, you can be killed instantly or slowly be reduced to a cripple like your uncle. Chiang Shiao-ho's teacher made your uncle a cripple with '*Tien Hsueh*'. Shiao-ho must have learned it now. I want you to go out for two reasons. First, you may hear something about Chiang Shiao-ho...."

"If I go out, I'll find out something about that renegade for sure. If I meet him, I'll kill him right away."

"If he is not hostile to us, or if his skills are mediocre, we won't kill him. Secondly, I think you should get married soon. Not one young man around here can match your skills. You'll have to go out to find someone suitable. I hear that there are some exceptionally skilled young warriors out there. One surely must be good enough for you to marry. I want you to promise me that you'll find a decent looking young man who has skills superior to mine. As soon as you find one, promise me that you'll come back and let me make the proper arrangement. Although we are not of the gentry's class, we prefer propriety."

May-lin blushed when Master Bo stressed again, "Promise me that you'll only take a note of his name and background first. I have to give him a test, and I want to make sure that he is skillful and honorable before you marry him. I want you to behave properly and maintain our good family name."

May-lin was too shy to sound her opinion, but she did not protest either. She thought, '*If I leave home, I can start to look for Shiao-ho. If he still truly loves me, I will talk him out of the revenge business and have him marry me. We will be a happy family. If I stay home, I won't have a chance to talk to him alone when he comes back. Both of them, Grandpa and Shiao-ho, are strong willed men. They would start the fight for life and death right away, before I could say anything. I wish that I had the courage to tell Grandpa that I love Shiao-ho, but he is so strongly against this kind of man and woman thing. He will be so angry if he knows and he may kill me too.'*

Master Bo thought, *'It's said that one should not keep a marriageable girl too long at home. It's so true. My May-lin is thinking about marriage now.'*

They checked the calendar and consulted a fortuneteller to choose a lucky date for May-lin's departure. She left with the fifty-year-old one-eyed Uncle Yu on a bright day in April. Master Bo had Yu's left eye cut out because he had flirted with a woman while watching a roadside show. Yu knew very well of Master Bo's eccentricity, and he was not thrilled at all to escort a spoiled May-lin.

After they crossed the Bah Mountain, Uncle Yu told May-lin, "My good niece. We're away from home now and we have a long way to go. I know that you have no trouble fighting anyone and you will win, but I would advise caution and modesty. We'll be polite to everyone we meet. We don't want to show our weapons. We'll try to avoid a quarrel or a fight. We'll...."

May-lin was impatient. "You don't have to tell me again. Grandpa has already told me many times."

"Master Bo has a lot of experience and he wants us to have a safe journey. We have to be...."

May-lin said angrily, "Uncle Yu, will you stop lecturing me? Otherwise, I'll go by myself."

"My good niece. I just want us to be safe. That's all."

Her father did not like the idea of a young woman taking such a long trip. It was his father's idea; he could not send his daughter back home. He wanted to send some of his students to go with her, but he knew his willful and proud daughter would reject more company. He was worried that May-lin and Yu must pass the Tu-Nan Mountain, where Dart Hu Li wounded him ten years ago. He warned Yu, "Brother Yu, don't tell May-lin that Dart Hu Li and his gangs occupy the Tu-Nan Mountain lest she would provoke a fight. My father has spoiled her and she is too proud of her skills for her own good."

Fortunately, May-lin and Yu crossed the mountain with many other travelers, and no bandits showed up. Next they stopped at Uncle Lu's new Kung Lung security station. Uncle Lu did not like May-lin's itinerary either. He said, "It's dangerous to travel to the east, May-lin. It's all right for you to go to Xian; Uncle Feng is there. His house is big and his daughter-in-law is about your age. She will be good company for you. After Xian, you better go back home. There are a few young fighters out in the east. The most famous one is Gi Kon-jii, the grandson of the legendary Dragon Knight. This young man is about twenty and has great fighting skills. Even the famous Master Kac of Kaifeng was defeated when they had a friendly match. I heard that young Gi is on his way to the west. He said openly that he wants to have a duel with Master Lee and Master Hsu in Szechwan. He may even want to challenge Master Bo. If he meets you and finds out that you're Bo Kung Lung's granddaughter, he will surely want to fight you. You may win or you may lose. Either way, Master Bo, at his age, would be forced to come out of his retirement.

Yu said anxiously, "Szechwan Dragon and Dragon Knight were the two greatest masters thirty years ago. Master Bo told us again and again that we should not be conceited with our Kung Lung skills. We can beat a lot of fighters from other schools. Master Bo has told us repeatedly that any one student of these two famous Dragons will be able to defeat a hundred of us easily. May-lin, we better go home after Xian."

Lu said again, "There is something else I think that Master Bo should know. Customers from the east said that a young man with supreme swordsmanship is traveling northwest from the South. Someone speculated that he might be Chiang Shiao-ho. I assume that Shiao-ho must be a very skilled master now and will soon be on his way here to take his revenge on us."

Her eyes, so much like her Grandpa's, flashed anger. "Uncles, please don't worry. I'm going east to challenge that boastful grandson of Dragon Knight. As for the rebellious Chiang Shiao-ho, I'm going to find him and kill him." May-lin raised her voice considerably. Her angry countenance and her brusque gestures made her look like a typical roughneck, not a docile girl at all. Lu noticed Yu's look of disapproval and he signaled Yu to say nothing more. Later he told Yu, "It's no use to warn her any more. She is spoiled and she'll not listen to any advice.

May-lin quietly saddled her horse at midnight, and galloped along the well-used road to Xian. When she stopped for lunch, she drew curious attention for being a lone female rider carrying a weapon. She was told that there were only two more stops before Xian when she checked in at an inn for the night.

"Young lady, are you traveling to Xian all by yourself?" The inn attendant asked her. He noticed her two maiden-styled thick braids tied with red ribbons and knew that she was not married. May-lin only nodded.

She contemplated whether she should go to see Uncle Feng in Xian or not. She decided that she's not going to Uncle Feng's security station. *I'd better go to Xian and find an inn to stay by myself. I'll do some sightseeing there and then go to the east. Further to the east, there won't be any Kung Lung security stations and no one will try to advise me to go back home. I don't believe that young man Gi's skills are superior to mine. Chiang Shiao-ho's skills might be better. Maybe I will meet him there. I wonder whether we will recognize each other. Both of us are grownups now. He was tall and now he must be even taller.'* Her eyes were moist. She also wondered if Shiao-ho's teacher found him a pretty wife already. *'If he is married, I don't want to see him, and I won't kill him, even if I could.'* She heard that the southern girls are petite and pretty with delicate features. May-lin touched her rather large nose and looked down at her not so small feet and sighed.

She came to a wide river with more than ten huge ferryboats crossing to and fro. "Excuse me. I want to go to Xian. Do I have to cross this river?" May-lin asked someone standing beside a horse.

"Yes. There is a boat ready to go now. You better hurry." The man sounded familiar. May-lin recognized Uncle Lieu who had left Chengba two years ago. Now he was a guard at Uncle Feng's security station at Xian. She tried to turn around but it was too late.

Lieu was surprised to see her. "May-lin, who brought you here?"

She replied, "Uncle Lieu. It's my grandpa's idea to let me come out to see the world. He ordered Uncle Yu to accompany me. At Han-Chun City, my father agreed with Grandpa's idea. But Uncle Lu insisted that I should go home soon. I don't want to go home, so I left Uncle Yu there. Grandpa suggested that I go to Kaifeng and Szechwan later."

Lieu was worried about May-lin's safety too. He watched her grow up to be an arrogant, conceited and willful young woman. So he did not argue with her but said agreeably instead, "Your Uncle Lu is just like your Grandpa. The older and the more skillful he is, the more cautious he becomes. With your excellent skills, you'll meet no equals anywhere. Let's go to Uncle Feng's first. I will ask Feng's permission to let me go with you. I want to see the world too." May-lin said, "If I go to see Uncle Feng, will he stop me and send me home?"

Lieu laughed, "Who dares stop you? It's your Grandpa's idea and who dares not to obey. Uncle Lu is just too cautious."

The ferryboat docked. The crowd on board fought their way off and more fought to get on. The experienced Lieu had no problem getting them and their two horses on board. The flat boat was large enough to carry three carriages, five horses and more than ten persons. A crew of five stood on the deck and sculled the slow going boat.

"Uncle Lieu, Is it true that someone had met Chiang Shiao-ho?"

Instead of answering her, Lieu waved his hands slightly and tried to warn her not to talk about anything important in public. She did not understand the signal and said again, more or less to herself, "I'd like to challenge that famous grandson of the Dragon Knight, after I beat Shiao-ho."

"My good niece, don't you enjoy the scenery and the boat ride? Do you see the flock of geese flying by?" Lieu tried to say something unimportant to make sure that May-lin wouldn't say more. He noticed that everyone on the ferry looking at her.

After the crossing, Lieu sighed, "My good niece, do you know anything about being cautious on the road? Who knows if that young man Gi wasn't on board with us?" Lieu looked around to make sure no one was following them.

May-lin sneered, "So what! I hope that we would meet him. I will fight him right here. I left home to look for opponents to fight! You're as timid as Uncle Lu!"

Lieu tried to persuade her, "May-lin, be patient. It is better that we find out the opponent's strength first and weigh our chances of winning before we fight. Also we should enlist our friends' aid before the fight. Indeed you have great fighting skills, but you're a woman."

"Uncle Lieu, if you don't stop talking nonsense, I will not go to Uncle Feng's with you. I will go to the east to fight that young man Gi and Chiang Shiao-ho alone."

Lieu said, "Chiang Shiao-ho is indeed our enemy. We could never forgive him for leading Master Hsu to fight us. We have nothing against young Gi. If he does not provoke a fight with us first, we should leave him alone."

May-lin sneered and said nothing. She looked around with wandering eyes. There were even some women on the street shopping. And there were tall, dark-complexioned men who wore white or black long robes with a lot of cloth wrapped around their heads. She even saw one tall man with yellow hair and skin as white as a dead fish's belly.

Lieu commented, "Xian is a big city; it had been the capital for many dynasties in the past and it had many magnificent temples and palaces. There are many foreigners from other countries to the very west of us. They sure dress weird."

Feng Junior welcomed them warmly. He took May-lin to the inner court to meet his mother and his wife. When Uncle Feng came in later, May-lin stood up and said, "Uncle Feng! Greetings! You've grown a beard!"

Feng Zhi-pan smiled, "I'm an old man now, and you have grown tall. Master Bo and your father both agreed upon your journey to the east. We won't hold you back. Please stay with us for several days, while I find someone familiar with the route to go with you."

"I don't need an escort. I've enough silver and I've my Kung Lung saber to protect me."

Feng smiled, "Bravo! I heard that you want to challenge young Gi and Chiang Shiao-ho. I have no information of Chiang Shiao-ho's whereabouts. That young man Gi is at Kaifeng. I've sent him an invitation. He will be here soon."

"Good! I'll wait. If I can beat him here, he will not dare go to Chengba to challenge Grandpa. Afterwards, I'll go to the East to look for Chiang Shiao-ho. I hate him and I'll kill him." She started to cry. Feng and his wife thought the girl was homesick, and they did their best to make her feel at home.

Lu Zhi-chun had arrived ahead of May-lin and hid in another room. He complained that Master Bo was at fault to let a young woman venture out alone. He told Feng, "I'm not worried about Chiang Shiao-ho at this moment since he might be dead. The pressing problem is Gi Kon-jii. He is Dragon Knight's grandson and we are definitely not his match. I followed May-lin all the way here, and thank goodness there was no trouble on the road. Should we send someone to fetch her father? He can order his daughter home."

Feng Zhi-pan said, "I don't think so, May-lin is very stubborn. I lied to her that I had invited young Gi to come so she would stay here and wait. My son and my daughter-in-law can take her around to do some sightseeing. She can visit many temples and hopefully she will not want to go to the east soon."

"It's better to get her father here. She has a bad temper, and who knows what trouble she will get if she stays. You know that she is not afraid of anyone of us."

Feng laughed, "I don't think she is afraid of her father either. She is trouble all right. I hope my docile and smart daughter-in-law can keep her interested in something domestic and keep her in."

Lu said, "She won't stay in."

Actually May-lin did stay in. She enjoyed the woman's company a lot. Her mother died when she was only fifteen. The only woman at home, besides a couple of old female servants, was her Aunt who was older and was always sick. Now May-lin enjoyed learning how to sew and how to cook. She daydreamed, *'If I can talk Shiao-ho out of revenge, then we will get married. I want to be a good wife.'* Her face hot.

Every day she would ask Uncle Feng, "When will that fellow Gi Kon-jii be here?"

"Soon"

On the ninth day, Feng Junior invited May-lin to visit the famous pagoda sixteen miles south of Xian. He said, "Sister Bo, I'm taking my wife to the temple to burn incense and ask the deities there for blessings. Please come with us. We can visit the famous pagoda there. It was built during the Tong Dynasty almost a thousand years ago. The bones of the first monk who went to India to bring back Buddhism are kept there. It's a place you must visit in Xian."

May-lin put on her favorite pink outfit. She insisted on riding her chestnut mare even though Feng Junior hired carriages for her, his wife and a maid.

The seven-story tall pagoda stood at the center of a magnificent temple and had windows on each of its six sides. May-lin walked around everywhere. She looked up and saw that there were people looking down from the windows above. "Brother Feng, can we go up to the top floor of the pagoda?"

"Sure! There are circular stairs winding all the way to the top level." He looked down at May-lin's feet first and continued, "Only you and I will go up. Your sister-in-law's feet are too small."

May-lin was a bit annoyed and walked fast. There were paintings, poems on the walls and other displays on every level. May-lin looked at them briefly as she climbed quickly. She could not read anyway. One Buddha statue sat in the center of the small area on the top level. A young scholar was writing a verse on the wall. Feng Junior did not know enough words to read the poem, but he recognized the signature: Lee Feng-jii from Beijing.

May-lin noticed that the handsome young scholar's posture indicated good martial art training. The scholar finished the verse and picked up a sword with iron handle and iron scabbard from a corner. He started to walk down. *'Ah! He must be a sword master, and a pretty good one too,'* May-lin thought, *'Look at his sword. Didn't Grandpa once warn me to beware of someone who carries a heavy sword like his? He said whoever carries a plain looking heavy sword must be very good at swordsmanship. I wonder how good he is.'*

She started to walk down, following the young scholar. Feng Junior called her, "Wait for me! What's the hurry?"

"Brother Feng, that young scholar knows martial arts very well. Did you see his sword? I want to know who he is."

He replied, "I don't think so. These bookworms always like to pretend that they are good at both the literary and the martial arts. To show off, they write verses everywhere and carry a sword. See his signature? Lee Feng-jii, I never heard of him. He is not famous." On their way back to town, they saw the scholar riding ahead. May-lin was convinced that the young scholar must be one of the upstarts who were here to challenge the Kung Lung School. She was determined to follow him.

Feng Junior was somehow jealous of the attention May-lin paid to the young scholar, He said aloud, deliberately, "He simply wants to scare others with his sword!" When there was no response, Feng junior shouted in his usual bullying manners. "Hey, you! Stop! Who are you? What are you doing here?" When there was no reply, Feng Junior repeated it.

Lee Feng-jii turned around and shouted back, "None of your business."

"I want to know." Lee ignored him and kept on going. Feng Junior quickened his pace, so the two horses almost touched each other. Reaching out his right hand, the stout Feng Junior intended to push the slender scholar off the horse. Feng Junior was the one being pushed off his horse. Feng Junior unsheathed his Kung Lung saber and charged at Lee. Lee simply pierced Feng and rode away. May-lin managed to get the injured Feng Junior back home.

Uncle Feng said, "We have to find him and fight him even if he has superior skills. He wounded my son. We have to fight him to even the score. We can't live with the shame. We must fight him to restore our reputation. Otherwise, who will ever buy our protection again?"

Uncle Lu said, "Let us be patient and think of a perfect way to handle this. It's true he wounded my nephew, but the wound was only a surface wound. Lee Feng-jii could have cut off my nephew's arm, but he did not. We all know that only a superior fighter could hold back from inflicting serious injury and death. Master Bo told us to beware of two types of martial arts fighters we meet: monks or Tao priests and scholars. These two types would most likely have some special skills. The martial arts they have learned, the internal training that emphasized on *Chi-kong* (energy) are different from the external school we have learned from, and it is not easy to defend ourselves against them."

They found out where Lee was staying. Uncle Feng ignored Uncle Lu's advice, led twenty-some armed guards to the inn where Lee Feng-jii stayed. Lu Zhi-chun disapproved this course of action and stayed behind. He wondered, '*how can Feng Zhi-pan, Miu, and Pan be so gullible? They wanted to win by sheer numbers. The Lung brothers and these earlier students of Master Bo's are all bullies.*'

Feng warned everyone, "We will have a better chance of winning if we can surprise him. Lee was reading. Feng broke into the room through the paper window panels, chopped at Lee and shouted, "You wounded my son today. My name is Feng Zhi-pan."

Lee Feng-jii blocked Feng's saber, jumped out of the room and fought the Kung Lung group. He shouted, "Your son is rude, he provoked the fight. Ah! Twenty to one! Shame on you!" In a short while, six members of the Kung Lung gang were down with wounds. From the roof, Lee shouted down, "I don't want to wound more of you." May-lin jumped upon the roof and fought him. Lee Feng-jii. blocked her attack and force her down. He left at ease.

Among the six Kung Lung casualties, five with minor wounds were servants and assistants, the one dead was Uncle Miu, who had tried to slash Lee on the back. Miu and Feng had worked together for more than twenty years. Feng was sad at the loss and ashamed of the complete defeat.

Pan Zhi-sam said, "Let's see what he has written. We might get a clue." He thumbed through Lee's poems, and he yelled, "Ah! Lee Feng-jii is Szechwan Dragon Du's student." Feng said, "What? Didn't Szechwan Dragon pass away a long time ago? How could he teach a student in Beijing?"

May-lin and the others all asked, "Who is this Szechwan Dragon?"

"Szechwan Dragon Du and Dragon Knight Gi were two superb masters thirty years ago. They were equally formidable and were known as the Two Dragons of Szechwan." Uncle Feng explained.

The news of those twenty Kung Lung members suffered a terrible defeat in the hand of one lone young scholar spread all over Xian. Feng preserved Miu's casket in a vault at a nearby temple so that all of Master Bo's students and friends could have time to come to the funeral later.

Uncle Lu arranged a duel with Lee Feng-jii.

He said, "Mr. Lee, you've injured my nephew. You also killed one of my sworn brothers. We will have a duel tomorrow morning to settle the score."

Lee said, "The whole gang again! I do not want to wound more of you."

Uncle Lu said, "Just you and me."

A crowd gathered around an empty field besides the Ba Bridge next morning to see the duel. Uncle Lu declared that the he himself alone would duel with Lee Feng-jii, but Uncle Pan and the whole Kung Lung members, more than 30, ganged up on the lone Lee Feng-jii even before the duel. Lee Feng-jii wounded a few of them quickly and forced the rest of them to quit. Soon there were only Uncle Lu and May lin, who had insisted, fighting Lee Feng-jii jointly. Both of them could not gain an inch. About ten passes later, Lee Feng-jii was just about to pierce May-lin's shoulder, another short young man with a sword, rushed in and blocked Lee's thrust. Two young men and two swords locked in a swift duel. Lee Feng-jii started to show signs of defeat, and he ran with new comer chasing him. The newcomer hit Lee's shoulder with the flat of his sword slightly and called a halt. Lee rode away, his face red. The new winner stopped May-lin who wanted to chase after Lee. "Miss, let him go. He knows he is beat. So many of you fought one lone man. You're in the wrong. He is tired and he is alone."

Lu Zhi-chun agreed, "It was supposed to be a duel between Lee Feng-jii and me. We should not have ganged up on one man. we have lost shamefully."

Uncle Feng thanked the young man and asked his name. The young man answered rather proudly, "I'm Gi Kon-jii. I'm Dragon Knight Gi's grandson."

"Master Gi, please come to our security station and let us thank you properly over drinks."

"Thanks. I'll be in town for three months. I'm sure we'll meet again." Gi stole a glance at May-lin. Lu Zhi-chun noticed it and frowned.

"Where will you be staying, Mr. Gi"

"At my uncle's shop temporarily"

On their way back to the station, May-lin said angrily, "Lee Fong-jii fought us a long time and he was tired. I am going to find Lee Feng-jii and fight him alone. I also want to challenge that arrogant Gi Kon-jii." She did not want to admit, even to herself, that Uncle Lu had to help her to fight Lee, and that Lee almost wounded her." However, she cried when she was back in the woman's court. All the attendants and servants were subdued and quiet at Feng's security station.

Feng sighed, "What a shame! Our Kung Lung School's thirty-some year of good reputation is lost. One lone Lee Feng-jii killed and wounded twelve of our men in two days. If Gi Kon-jii had not come to our aid in time, we probably would have more casualties. How can we keep our security business going?"

Uncle Lu said, "It's no use to dwell on the defeat. In the world of martial arts, there will always be someone who will win. We still have to run our business and deal with our friends or enemies as the occasion arises. If and whenever Chiang Shiao-ho shows up, we'll have to fight him. That is more important."

Feng said, "Don't talk about that renegade. Right at this moment, I'm too ashamed to face anyone!"

Lu sighed, "But I will say that Chiang Shiao-ho is the real problem. Gi's skills seemed to be superior to Lee Feng-jii's. Knowing that we were wrong to gang up on Lee, Gi still came to our aid. I'm convinced that young Gi is heroic in heart. I suggest that we be friends with him. He could help us if Lee Feng-jii comes back for a fight, and he could also come to our aid whenever Chiang Shiao-ho comes back to seek revenge. What do you think?"

Feng disagreed adamantly, "I don't agree, and I don't think our proud Master Bo will agree either." Suddenly, his eyes lit up, "Wait! Gi Kon-jii could marry May-lin. Didn't Master Bo send her out to see the world and to find herself a husband?"

"Gi Kon-jii is a good match. The only thing that bothers me is that Gi Kon-jii seems to be arrogant and showy. I have considered at first that Lee Feng-jii might marry her. That's why I wanted to duel with him to solve our differences. Anyway, Lee is very young and he is also too scholarly to tolerate our ill-mannered and spoiled niece. Lee's family must be of the upper class and he obviously does not like May-lin. Gi Kon-jii is a better match."

Feng said, "Gi Kon-jii is young and he is entitled to be proud. I think Master Bo would be thrilled to have the famous Dragon's grandson in the family."

Lu Zhi-chun said, "May-lin's father should be here soon. He could make the decision of his daughter's marriage."

Feng said, "We don't have to wait for her father. We are her uncles. We could arrange her marriage."

Gi's uncle managed a small, crowded shop. Gi Kon-jii and a clerk had to sleep on a platform behind the counter after the shop closed. Gi was not happy about it. When Feng came to visit, they went to a teahouse where Uncle Feng inquired about Gi Kon-jii's family.

Gi Kon-jii told Feng, "My father passed away at a very young age. My grandfather, the one known as Dragon Knight, was disappointed with the constant killing and revenge business of the world of martial arts. He encouraged my father to study the literary arts only. Unfortunately, my father died right after he passed the second level of the civil services examination. Grandpa realized that merely studying literature arts would weaken the body. I'm his only grandson. He taught me both the literary arts and martial arts. He wanted me to have a strong body, and he also wanted me to be able to make a living with martial arts in case I failed the civil services examinations. I passed the first level of the examination but failed the second level twice."

Uncle Feng said, "I hope you'll stay in town longer so that we can get better acquainted. Master Bo, our teacher, will be here soon, I'm sure that he would like to meet you. You know that your fame has reached far." He continued, "We're all grateful for your help. May-lin is Master Bo's granddaughter. She praised your superior skills and said that she would like to meet you and compare martial arts learning with you."

Gi Kon-jii said happily, "Really! Can I visit you soon?"

"Of course! You're most welcome. Come have supper with us."

Feng immediately ordered a banquet and a guest room to be prepared for Gi. Many guards from other stations came to visit, he told them that he had met Gi Kon-jii before, and that Gi's grandfather and Master Bo had been longtime friends. Most of the visitors had been at the duel, but they gracefully acknowledged Feng's face-saving boast.

Feng told May-lin, "My good niece, Master Bo and your father will be here soon."

May-lin said, "Good. Grandpa and I will go to the East together and I don't suppose that any of you dare to stop us from going." Then she asked, "Where is that little rooster Gi Kon-jii? Didn't he declare that he would like to challenge us? I'm ready and willing."

Uncle Feng smiled, "We should not listen to rumors. Gi Kon-jii wants to be our friend. He is a young accomplished fighter and a scholar, too. He's twenty-four years old, and his uncle has a shop here. I'm inviting him to stay with us for a while. I ask him to show us some of the legendary Dragon Knight's skills. He'll come to dinner tonight and you'll have a chance to talk to him."

May-lin pouted, "I don't want to talk to him."

"May-lin, now you're out to see the world, it's not necessary to stick strictly to Confucius's rules of propriety. It's all right for you to talk to Gi Kon-jii's. His grandpa and your grandpa were old friends. You and he are almost like siblings and it's appropriate for you two to get acquainted. Gi Kon-jii asked me about you, and I told him that you're Master Bo's granddaughter. He said right away, with admiration, no wonder you fight so well."

May-lin was happy to hear that. She shook her head, "No, I don't want to talk to him unless he would want to have a match with me. Grandpa had never mentioned that he knew some famous Dragon!" She noticed Uncle Feng was somewhat a braggart, just like his son.

"Yes, he did. You're too young to know."

Gi Kon-jii came to the station wearing a formal long robe, proper thick white-soled boots and held an expensive scholar's fan in his hand. He tucked his sword, with the red silk cord, at the waist.

It was custom to have a friend present when one invited an important person over for a formal dinner. Feng, Pan, Lu and their friend Chu, formally welcomed Gi Kon-jii to a spacious dining room with a banquet already laid out.

Gi Kon-jii looked around and awed at the wealth on display. The intricately carved windowpanes, the polished heavy red wood and oak furniture, the exquisite table settings and everything else he looked at told him that there was plenty of silver here. *'They are rich. Feng asked a lot of questions about my family and Bo May-lin wears her hair in two braids. She is not married. Am I dreaming that they want me to marry her? She is not very beautiful but not ugly either. Also, she is the first young woman I know that has excellent martial art straining. We'll be a formidable team. I think I like the idea, yes indeed, I like it very much.'*

Gi Kon-jii said politely, "I did not expect to come to a formal dinner."

Lu Zhi-chun thought, *'you sure did. You dressed for it.'*

Feng said, "This is our first meeting and it should be formal. Later when we see each other every day like a big family, there will be no more fussing."

Gi smiled and took off his formal long robe. He did not hesitate when he was asked to take the seat of honor. He told them in detail about his famous grandfather's heroic deeds. He also told them how he won his duels with a famous sword master, Master Lin, and with the well-known *'Tien Hsueh'* expert, Master Kac, at Kaifeng. When Feng asked him about Lee Feng-jii, he said, "I've heard a lot about him. It is said that Lee is also a scholar who failed the civil examination and that he is Szechwan Dragon's student. Lee Feng-jii indeed fights well with a sword and he had accomplished quite a few heroic deeds in the East."

Feng said angrily, "Brother Gi, it's all right that you didn't want to injure Lee Feng-jii and let him walk. Somehow we have to find him and fight him. He wounded my son and a few others, and killed my sworn brother Miu. I've sent word everywhere to request aid from my friends. All of my sworn brothers will be here to attend the funeral of our deceased Brother Miu. We'll fight him again."

Gi thought, *'So you can gang up on him again.'* He said instead, "When the time comes, I'll help you."

Uncle Lu asked, "Brother Gi, when you were in the East, did you ever hear something about a young fighter by the name of Chiang Shiao-ho?"

"The name sounds familiar. What is this Chiang to you?"

Feng sneered, "Chiang is an enemy of our Kung Lung School. We were told that he had a great teacher. He might come to fight us."

Gi said, 'When he comes to fight you, I will be on your side."

When Feng offered him the guest room for a long stay, Gi Kon-jii accepted without hesitation. He was disappointed that May-lin did not come out to meet him.

Lee Feng-jii moved out of the inn after he paid for the damaged window. He stayed at the library of one of his teacher Dragon Du's friends. When he heard that Gi Kon-jii had move in with the Kung Lung's. *'It is no fun and no purpose fighting with the Kung Lung gang and now Gi Kon-jii.'* He left Xian for the historical famous Middle Peak.

One afternoon when May-lin back from her afternoon ride, she heard her Grandpa's thunderous laugh.

"Grandpa, you shouldn't have traveled in this heat!" May-lin rushed to him.

"May-lin, I'm so angry that Lee Feng-jii killed your Uncle Miu and ruined the sound name of my Kung Lung School. I rushed here to challenge him. Where have you been? I don't like you going out alone."

"I went out for a ride. And I heard that coward Lee Feng-jii had run to the East. Grandpa."

Master Bo sighed, "Shame on us. Lee Feng-jii humiliated us and we had to have Dragon Knight's grandson repel him for us," He continues, "I worry about you, you are so young and you don't have any experience. Then your Uncle Yu came to fetch me. May-lin, you should listen to your uncles!"

"Grandpa, did you have lunch? I have not even had breakfast yet." May-lin changed the subject.

"Greeting! Honorable Master Bo." Gi Kon-jii walked in.

The stout Master Bo stood up laboriously and greeted Gi, "Thank you for helping us, Mr. Gi."

Gi Kon-jii bowed low and said respectfully, "Please call me Kon-jii. It's my honor to meet you, Master Bo."

Master Bo talked noisily with Gi. The news of Master Bo's arrival spread and many guards came to greet him. Some of them stayed for the inevitable banquet and listened to Master Bo's reminiscence of his past adventures, and Gi's anecdotal stories of his grandpa, the famous Dragon Knight.

Master Bo told his pupils that he intends to arrange the marriage between Gi Kon-jii and May-lin. Carrying out Master Bo's orders to be the middleman; Pan Zhi-sam talked to Gi over drinks in a tavern. Gi agreed readily.

Master Bo walked into May-lin's room. She greeted her grandpa with a lovely smile, "Grandpa, it's so hot! Did you have a nap?"

"No, the heat does not bother me. I have not left home for twenty years. Now I'm out, and I feel young and energetic." He sat, stroking his white beard and smiled, "May-lin! I've come to tell you the good news."

"Tell me. Are we going to the East soon?" May-lin had not seen her grandpa so cheerful for a long time. She pouted, "Don't make me wait."

"May-lin, you remember how I told you to come out to see the world, and also to meet a suitable young man to marry? Now I think that young Gi Kon-jii is every bit qualified to be your husband. You'll marry him as soon as possible." May-lin lowered her head cheerlessly with tears swimming in her eyes. She was just ready to protest when her grandpa continued, "May-lin, don't be shy. Listen, I have something to tell you and it's for your ears only. You know that I'm getting old. Your father and all your uncles do not fight well. We have made countless enemies through the years and now we have new ones. Lee Feng-jii's skills are superior to ours. If Gi Kon-jii had not come to our aid, the Kung Lung School would be finished. Besides, rumor has it that Master Hsu from Szechwan wants to challenge us again soon. If we cannot find someone with better skills to help us, we soon will be humiliated. This young Gi is good at both literary and_martial arts. He may be a magistrate or a governor someday. Besides his admirable skills, his family name is to our advantage too. I also think that his looks and his age are your match. If I had such a young master to be my grandson-in-law, no enemies of ours would dare challenge us. May-lin, I know it's a hasty decision." He looked at May-lin with sad, old pleading eyes. May-lin sobbed a while, and she tried a couple of times, but she could not tell her Grandpa that she loved Chiang Shiao-ho, a family enemy. Finally she wiped her tears and agreed.

Master Bo said happily, "Good. I'm seventy-six now. Your future is a big worry on my mind and now, even if I were to die this minute, I could breathe my last breath in peace knowing your future is settled."

Uncle Feng ordered an elaborate banquet for the announcement of their engagement. Gi Kon-jii kowtowed thrice to Master Bo and once to each uncle. The guests congratulated Master Bo and him in unison.

The jubilant Gi Kon-jii visited Master Bo and Uncle Feng's friends in Xian every day, and fully enjoyed his newly acquired affluence. On the contrary, the usually lively and boisterous May-lin became quiet. She stayed in all the time now. Master Bo and the uncles did not pay too much attention to the sudden change. They thought that she was shy. The maids and Feng Junior's wife noticed that May-lin wept often. They could not imagine why she should be sad. It was a wonderful marriage. They talked about it, but none of them knew May-lin's dilemma. They could not tell Master Bo and Feng about their concerns.

May-lin missed her mother. She was too young to really understand her feelings toward Chiang Shiao-ho before her mother died. But she believed that her mother knew, or at least guessed, about her feelings. Her mother often told May-lin to be submissive and to accept what fate would bring. May-lin recalled that once she had argued with her mother about her uncle's abusive behavior. Her mother said something like this, *'we, women, are expected to be submissive. Anyway, we have very little say about our future, and about the way we live. Many women carried their dreams to their graves.'*

Uncle Lu sensed that May-lin was not happy about the marriage. More than once he noticed that May-lin was both sad and angry whenever Shiao-ho's name was mentioned. He wanted to have a talk with May-lin but he knew he had no right and no way to influence Master Bo's decision. Besides, it's not proper for him to talk to a grown-up niece alone.

Most of Master Bo's students came to attend the funeral of Uncle Miu whom Lee Feng-jii killed. Bo Zhi-an lamented the deaths of his sworn bother but rejoiced at his daughter's good marriage.

The evening after the funeral, they all sat around a big banquet of four tables. Master Bo, his elder son, the young couple, two guests, Feng and his wife sat at the head table. After a couple of rounds of toasts, Uncle Lu expressed his concerns about the possible confrontation with Lee Feng-jii and Master Hsu of Szechwan.

Gi Kon-jii declared with a toast, "Toast! Grandpa and Uncles, please let me handle Master Hsu and Lee Feng-jii. I'm confident that my sword will repel them both and any other enemies. May-lin and I will glorify the name of Kung Lung School."

"Bravo! Let's drink to that!" Uncle Feng stood up and cheered aloud, "Let all of us respectfully propose three toasts to Master Bo, two toasts to Brother Bo, the lucky father of the bride, and one toast each to the young couple.

"Congratulation! Good Fortune!" Everyone stood and joined the jubilee. The beaming Master Bo accepted the full cup from Feng, emptied it promptly for Feng to fill it again.

Lung Zhi-chi, the one who killed Chiang Shiao-ho's father, came in with his traveling clothes covered with dust. "Teacher, I have urgent news..."

Master Bo stood up nervously and demanded, "What? Tell me!"

Lung Zhi-chi took out an envelope and said somewhat disjointedly, "It.. It's Chiang Shiao-ho! I got a letter from him. He is on his way here to avenge his father's death."

Pounding the table, Master Bo demanded, "Read it to me."

Uncle Pan read it aloud, "This letter is to ask the Lung brothers of Zie-Yin City to notify Master Bo of Chengba my intention of revenge. I, Chiang Shiao-ho, have not let a single day pass by without having the bitter memory of your cruel killing of my father. Ten years ago, I was too young and too weak to resist your treachery and almost died at your hand. Now I'm grown and I'm confident that I can complete my revenge. You killed my father, split my family, and exploited my youth. With the exception of two, the rest of you Kung Lung gang are all my enemies. This letter is to warn you that I'm on my way and offer you ample time to prepare your defense against me. I promise that I will only kill my father's murderers. Signed, Chiang Shiao-ho." Pan noticed that the writing was rough and the words were simple ones. A hired letter writer did not write it. Chiang Shiao-ho probably wrote it himself.

Master Bo's face turned from deep red to a deathly pale. Gi Kon-jii unsheathed his sword and pounded the table top with it. He yelled, "Grandpa and Uncles, I beg you not to worry. I don't think too highly of that damned Chiang Shiao-ho. I promise you that I'll slay him within five sword strokes!"

Only a few applauded Gi Kon-jii. Everyone was nervous.

"Who delivered this letter?" Uncle Lu asked.

"An herb merchant from the South. He told me that Chiang Shiao-ho has made quite a name for himself there along the Yangtze River. Someone said that Chiang Shiao-ho might challenge Gi Kon-jii.

Gi sneered, "Not Bad! He knows my name! I'll teach him a lesson with my sword." He was puzzled to see May lin's expression, and could not tell whether she was angry or sad. May-lin stood up and left, with an excuse that she had a stomachache. Watching her melancholy retreat, Master Bo suddenly remembered a trivial incident more than ten years ago. He remembered a snowy night when the fourteen-year-old Shiao-ho dueled with the twelve-year-old May-lin. On that cold snowy night, Chiang Shiao-ho failed in his first attempt of revenge, and May-lin tried to punish him. Master Bo had kept Shiao-ho at his home as a servant for a while and even contemplated letting him marry May-lin with the hope that the animosity between the two families would be resolved. But his son abused Shiao-ho and the boy fled.

Master Bo pulled his thoughts back to the present with an effort and wondered whether Gi Kon-jii could really fend Chiang Shiao-ho off. The sorrow, the worry, the drinking and the heat finally got to him, Master Bo collapsed.

He came to a while later and told his anxious pupils, "I'm fine. Don't be afraid of Chiang Shiao-ho. When he comes, I'll meet him and let him kill me only to settle the score. All of you please listen carefully to my words of advice: don't ever be too ruthless, be kind to your opponents, lest you have regrets in your old age. You're still young. Please take my words to heart." He turned his head to face Gi Kon-jii, "You're my future grandson-in-law and one of my families. I want you to hear what I have to say. If Chiang Shiao-ho comes before my death, let me face him alone. If he comes after my death, promise me that you will reason with him politely first before fighting him. Otherwise...."

Gi interrupted indignantly, "Grandpa, you worry too much! Chiang Shiao-ho can't be so omnipotent, can he? Could his teacher's skills be superior to the Szechwan Dragon's and my grandfather's? I don't think so."

Master Bo sighed deeply, "You are all too young to know that thirty years ago, the two Dragons were called the two Zeniths in the world of martial arts. Dragon Knight, and Szechwan Dragon Du retired suddenly at the same time. Not many people knew why. The truth is that there is another master, superior to both the Dragons, who would punish the two haughty Dragons and Steel Rod Monk at will with his phenomenal skills. I was young and had full capabilities, I was defeated completely when I met this short scholar. You may not believe, but I, Bo Kung Lung, was as powerless as an ant in front of him...."

"Is he Chiang Shiao-ho's teacher?" Gi Kon-jii asked anxiously.

Master Bo sighed, "If Chiang Shiao-ho had any other teacher, and I wouldn't have been worried and scared to death for all these years."

Uncle Feng told everyone what happened ten years ago when the scholarly old man rescued Shiao-ho. He had seized Uncle Feng's extra heavy Kung Lung saber with two fingers and broke it into pieces with one foot. Uncle Feng's voice shook as he vividly remembered the humiliation he suffered that day.

Total silence. Finally, Gi Kon-jii said, "Grandpa, you don't have to fight him yourself. Let me go to the East to meet him." He continued, "But I do not know him. I'd like to go with someone who knows him well enough to point him out to me." It was decided that Uncle Chen, who knew Shiao-ho very well, and the one-eyed Uncle Yu would accompany Gi Kon-jii on his mission to seek Chiang Shiao-ho. Master Bo and May-lin would go to Uncle Lu guard station at Da-Sam Fort to wait.

6

It was a hot summer and the Yellow River puffed out hot steam. The thick forest and a clear creek at the foot of the Middle Peak had kept the unbearable heat away. Lee Feng-jii had a room at the White Pin Temple. He was a born poet and he managed to live comfortably with his beautiful calligraphy. His great-grandfather was a high ranked official of the Ming Dynasty and died fighting the Manchu. So his grandfather and father were all very good at literary arts but vowed never work for the invaders, the Chin Dynasty. Lee Feng-jii's father and his wife died together in a boating accident when Lee was only three years old, and his baby brother was one. Lee was twelve years old when his grandparent died and his uncle abused them. His older brother took Lee Feng-jii with him and left home with a trusted old servant. Not far from Beijing, they were robbed. The bandits killed his brother and the servant. When they tried to rape him, Lee Feng-Jii struggled wildly. An old Tao priest came, 'Tien Hsueh' (attack vital points) the bandits, and saved him. In Beijing, the Tao priest taught Lee Feng-jii martial arts and literary arts. Two years ago, the Tao Priest died. At his death, He gave Lee a manual of advanced Martial Arts, some silver certificates and told Lee Feng-jii that he was Szechwan Dragon Du. "I did not get the silver the honorable way but I want you to use it wisely. My teacher was a renegade Tao Priest from Wu-Ton Mountain. I had bad company, so I did a lot of senseless killing. I want you to remember that there always is someone who has better skills than you. Don't ever be conceited. Thirty years ago, a short scholarly looking super master caught me in my atrocity act, punished me severely, and forced me to retire. Five years ago, steel bit me Steel Rod Monk chased me out of Szechwan. I want you be kind. You could disable your enemies but maim and kill them only when it is unavoidable."

Szechwan Dragon Du only taught Lee the rudiments of the '*Tien Hsueh*' technique. He said, "'*Tien Hsueh*' is a deadly technique. Not many people know how to do it, and the one who knows how to do it eventually will make more enemies. I'll only teach you the basics; you can use it to cure the sick and, if necessary, to make a living. Of course, you also need to know enough to avoid being killed or crippled by someone who knows '*Tien Hsueh*'".

On this beautiful summer morning, Lee wandered down the hill to the almost finished rooms that he and a half-witted man nicknamed Big Fool had built. In two days, he would marry the maiden he had rescued from some roughnecks. Her widowed grandma was dying and she wanted to see her granddaughter married to Lee right away. Lee heard the pleasant sounds of a bell. The small bell was tied to the neck of a horse and the rider was a tall young man with a heavy long sword hanging from the saddle. '*This is no ordinary temple worshipper. and I bet he is very good at martial arts.*'

It was lunch hour. Big Fool was biting into a huge piece of coarse wheat cake. He called, "Master Lee, have a cake!" Big Fool He pointed to a huge bundle of firewood he collected and continued, "I sold the first one and bought some meat. Stay here and have lunch with us." Big Fool was a good son to his blind and crippled mother.

The tall young rider whom Lee had seen earlier came down from the temple. He seemed to be lost.

"Friend, can I help you? It's easy to get lost around here." Lee Feng-jii asked.

"Yes, friend! Can I ride down the valley on this narrow path?"

"It's too rocky and narrow for a horse. Friend, there are few houses down there. are you looking for someone?"

"I am looking for an older scholar living in this mountain. My teacher asked me to deliver a letter to him."

"You can keep your horse here and pick it up later."

"Thanks. How do I address you?"

"Lee Feng-jii here. What's yours?"

"Chiang Shiao-ho." The name sounded familiar.

"I'm from Beijing. Brother Chiang, you talk like a Southerner." Lee asked.

"Brother Lee, I'm originally from the North and I've been in the South for ten years."

"You carry a heavy sword; you must be very good at martial arts. Who's your teacher?"

"My teacher is an old scholar from the South."

Lee thought, '*so you do not want to tell me your teacher's name yet, I will not impose.*' Chiang said, "Brother Lee, I know it is odd but I really do not know my teacher's name. He does not talk much. I lived with him for ten years but he never told me his name."

Ten years ago, the old scholar saved Shiao-ho from the Kung Lung gang. The old scholar applied the '*Tien Hsueh*' technique to stop the boy's bleeding and put the boy to sleep on the horse's back and he himself walked. He bought some herbs and treated Shiao-ho's multiple wounds at night in the inns they stayed on their long journey south. They crossed the mighty Yangtze River and finally reached the old scholar's home in a deep recess on the high Joe-hue Peak. A few acres of tea crops surrounded a small house. A mute kept the house and tended the tea trees.

The mute could not talk and the old scholar never did tell Shiao-ho a thing about his identity, but Shiao-ho knew that the old scholar possessed the highest martial arts skills. Shiao-ho was determined to learn well, but the kind old man did not teach him any martial arts even after his wounds were healed completely. At first he merely ordered Shiao-ho to gather firewood and to tend the tea crops. Half a month later, he told Shiao-ho to gather rocks, small or big, from near or far. Shiao-ho worshipped his teacher and he was so grateful that he would do anything to please him. His teacher gave him a place to live, to have plenty of rice and fish to eat and decent clothes to wear. After his father's death, it was the first time Shiao-ho was safe and had a home. His teacher had never once lost patience to listen to Shiao-ho's telling of his sorry past. Somehow, Shiao-ho did not tell him about May-lin. He was shy. His father was killed for his trouble with a woman. Shiao-ho was afraid that his teacher would condemn him and not accept him anymore if he told him his strong feelings for May-lin.

He obediently gathered rocks and considered it a test like lifting the steel rod at Master Hsu's place. He had strong arms from his blacksmith training and in two months, he almost cleared the surrounding areas of rocks and piled them mountain high behind their hut. The old man, sometimes with the mute, would leave the peak for days. Shiao-ho had never been lazy when there was no supervision.

When his teacher saw the two high piles of rocks, he simply told Shiao-ho to empty it out. "Shiao-ho, get rid of all the rocks in ten days. Ten Days! Don't throw them in the ravine. Don't block the creek and the mountain paths."

Now Shiao-ho could hold two huge rocks in his hands or two baskets full of smaller ones and carried them to the top of the mountain easily. He worked hard and completed his mission in less than seven days. The old scholar praised him, "Good, you have a strong mind and you have the determination to succeed. I will teach you now."

The first things he taught Shiao-ho were 'breathing and concentration' and some simple boxing and jumping exercises. He stayed home for a year and half to teach Shiao-ho and he also taught him how to read and write.

For jumping exercise, he ordered the boy to hop up the high peak or down to the deep ravine at all hours. In the beginning, besides teaching and demonstrating, his teacher often worked out with Shiao-ho, his movement was ever so graceful and Shiao-ho tried to emulate him. In the spring when the tea flowers were blooming, he wanted Shiao-ho to catch butterflies alive and not damage any flowers and leaves. The exercise Shiao-ho liked the best was to catch small finches alive and then set them free.

At the beginning of the third year, he handed Shiao-ho a book of boxing styles and walked the boy through all the steps a few times before he left for a long trip. Shiao-ho stayed behind and he practiced diligently. The forms and styles were not many but very difficult. A few months later, Shiao-ho found that he could block and defeat the boxing styles that he had learned from his father and Uncle Ma very easily with this new form. *It's just great. Now I can beat the Kung Lung students in boxing.*

His Teacher came back and handed Shiao-ho an extra heavy sword and a few books on swordsmanship. He ordered Shiao-ho to memorize the instructions by day and practice at night. In less than a month, Shiao-ho could recite every line, and then the old man took the books back and left again.

Shiao-ho continuously practiced by memory arduously regardless of whether his teacher left home with the mute or not. Every month or two, the old scholar would check up on Shiao-ho's progress or to correct his mistakes. He also urged Shiao-ho to practice swimming in the ice-cold mountain creeks at all hours. The eighth and ninth year, the old man stayed home to teach Shiao-ho '*Tien Hsueh*' and other sophisticated skills. He also taught Shiao-ho geography with a map. Sometimes teacher and student would have a long discussion about any subjects. He treated Shiao-ho as an equal and encouraged Shiao-ho to express his own ideas. They also talked about ethics and code of behavior. Shiao-ho learned the value of morality and good manners first from Master Hsu when he was in Szechwan and now from this great teacher. He learned self-respect and also the value of genuine respect for others. His teacher seemed to be pleased with Shiao-ho's progress.

He thought about his family and Bo May-lin often. In the first two years, Shiao-ho cried often when he thought about his unspeakable sufferings at the hand of Master Bo and his son. The old scholar always listened and let him cry and talk and then consoled him. When he got older he was ashamed of shedding tears in front of his teacher and the mute. He would go up the high peak or go down the deep ravine to let out his grief. He wept when he thought about his mother's soft hands and her singsong voices to lure him to sleep at night. He grated his teeth when he remembered the abuses he had endured at Master Bo's place. The few trees on the high peak would shake their leaves and the grass spurting between the rocks would weave to accompany his ranting. The creek in the deep gorge would also sigh along with his heart-wrenching yell or soft sobs. The wild flowers would look extremely pretty through his tears when he thought about May-lin. Somehow his teacher and the mute knew that he had been sad and they would be extra nice to him. The mute would give him some delicacies to eat. He liked the way the mute ruffled his hair and his teacher's soft tone.

Three months ago, the old scholar asked Shiao-ho, "You've been with me ten years now. Do you think you have learned well enough to face your enemies now?"

He was anxious to go home and to fight the Kung Lungs, Shiao-ho replied, "Teacher, I believe that I have learned well all of the skills that you have taught me."

"Oh! No. Far from it. You may have learned almost one half of my skills, less than the mute. He is your classmate, your brother. He probably has learned sixty percent of my skills."

Shiao-ho broke out in a cold sweat. He could not believe that the mute actually knew any sophisticated martial arts skills. He thought,

"Ah! The mute. It seems to me that he can't even move a heavy rock." He sat rigidly in awe when he thought, *'I am too blind to see it. Didn't the mute carry huge bags of rice and walk up the mountain so fast that I had to do my best to follow him? Didn't we always have wild birds he caught to eat? Didn't he always catch more fish when we fish together? and didn't..."* He heard his teacher said, "Shiao-ho, you're right. He is highly skilled. He is your big brother, and a good example of modesty for you to emulate. We, the Wu-Ton School of martial arts, concentrate on inner strength and mind training. We strive for harmony and moderation, not the outward show of skills and strength. In your case, it calls for some allowances. You have suffered so much at a young age, and you're entitled to avenge your father's death. Listen carefully to my instructions: First, you can only kill your father's murderers and you must harm no others. I prefer that you forgive them but I know it will be difficult for you to forgive and forget. They did mistreat you. Second, you can challenge other martial arts masters for a match so you can learn different skills, but you must not injure your opponent needlessly. If you must fight your enemies, you can only maim or kill when it is absolutely inevitable. Third, you have to help the weak and subdue the evil. You have to help the young and old and women. In one word, the martial arts skills are designed to protect you and enable you to help others, NOT for self-indulgent material gains and fame. You may meet some other warriors of Sho-Lin School and Wu-Ton School of martial arts. Treat them as your brothers. A monk from India founded the Sho-Lin school, and Wu-Ton School's founder was the legendary Taoist Chang, and we're a branch of the Wu-Ton School. Both schools emphasize inner strength training for the purpose of self-defense and obtaining harmony. The inner strength increases our capacity of endurance and also our capacity to resist the temptations of greed and other bad desires. Remember my words well and OBEY them. You can leave any time. You have the gold and silver you had before and I'll give you some more and a letter of credit for you to get silver from some tea companies doing business with us. There are frequent natural disasters in the North, you can help them with some silver and also Uncle Ma and others in need."

Shiao-ho knelt and begged, "Can I stay with you longer to learn more?"

The old scholar laughed, "Oh, no! If you learn more, no one could curb you. Now you can defeat the two Dragons at will, if they were still alive. Master Bo will be an infant in your hands. All the others, they are less than worms to you. Are you not satisfied? I would have let you leave a few years earlier, but you were young and your enemies, the Kung Lung, are strong. Now is the time for you to go out in the world to start some real learning. You better leave soon. I hope you will forgo your revenge. But I also know that you will have to do what you think is right by you. I suggest that you inform Master Bo of your intention of revenge ahead of time, so he could be prepared. He might have repented and changed."

Shiao-ho kowtowed thrice to his teacher, once to the mute and started going down the mountain. Half a *lee* (about one half mile) later, the mute soundlessly appeared in front of the startled Shiao-ho. The mute handed him two letters for him to deliver. Then the mute smiled and rubbed his chin, pointed two fingers skyward and shook his head vigorously. It meant his teacher forbade him to use the deadly 'Tien Hsueh' technique. He nodded. The mute took Shiao-ho's sword and taught Shiao-ho a round of swords fighting styles, which Shiao-ho had not yet learned.

It was late spring and many peasant girls worked hard in the fields. Shiao-ho thought about Bo May-lin. He wondered if May-lin was married already and whether she forgot all about their innocent pledge of marriage under the big willow tree. He thought about his mother and speculated about how tall his baby brother had grown. He was happy that he could read and write, could now fight well with prominent martial arts skills. He also had silver and he definitely was not the same destitute orphan boy of ten years before. He regretted that he did not tell his teacher about May-lin and he almost doubled back up the peak but he was shy and so he didn't.

A huge boat took him across the mighty Yangtze River to Nanjing on the north bank and he delivered one letter. Then Shiao-ho bought a horse and hung a small silver bell to the horse's neck. Master Hsu had given him the silver bell ten years ago when they were on their way to challenge the Kung Lungs. '*I was so hopeless after Master Bo had wounded Master Hsu. All the Kung Lung members wanted to kill me and luckily I met my teacher and here I am.*' Shiao-ho was so happy and wanted to sing. '*I wonder if I could lift the heaviest steel rod at Master Hsu's place with ease now.*' He smiled because he knew he definitely could. However, his heart ached when he thought, '*what am I going to say to May-lin that I will kill her grandpa*'

On his way to the North, Shiao-ho had won many friendly matches with well-known martial arts masters. He heard about Lee Feng-jii and he wanted to meet him some day. At Kaifeng, he defeated the famous 'Tien Hsueh' Master Kac, and he also met his old friend Nan who had helped Shiao-ho a lot when Shiao-ho was in Szechwan ten years ago.

"Shiao-ho! I know that you have suffered gravely at the hands of the Kung Lung gang, but I would not like to see you become merciless and bitter. You know that harboring hatred and thoughts of revenge can only bring us sorrow at the end. I hope you can forgive that old man; he must be almost eighty now. Come back again and for now, have a safe trip." Nan advised him.

A sudden summer shower came when Lee Feng-jii tried to fix an old table.

"Ahe! Ahe! Master Lee Quick.. help!" Big Fool shouted.

Lee rushed outside and saw, through the mist of the curtain-like heavy rain, a woman with a baby in arm and a little girl were falling fast to the ravine from the slippery winding path above. It was a hopeless situation. Then a huge form flied through the mist, Bid Fool yelled "Ahe!". Chiang Shiao-ho, holding the woman and bay in one arm, the girl in the other, landed in front of Lee's hut. Lee Feng-jii was speechless and the little girl was too scared to cry.

"Brother Chiang, Your martial arts skills are super!" Lee Feng-jii said.

"My classmate the mute and I did something like this kind of rescue before. Brother Lee, I have a super teacher. But I really don't know his name. He did not tell me himself and my classmate is a mute."

Lee thought, 'so, he is not conceited. *He had not many people to talk to for ten years. No wonder.*'

It was dark and cold. Lee took out some silver and asked Big Fool to buy some supper. Chiang Shiao-ho watched the rain and frowned.

"Brother Chiang, it's raining hard. Let's talk and drink all night long, how about it? I'd like you to stay for my wedding, the day after tomorrow."

"Thanks, but I'm anxious to go to Xian."

"You won't go far today in the rain. It may be clear tomorrow and you can ride fast."

There was a rough bench and a table in the grass hut. They both sat on the warm *kon (bed)* and drank in turn from a cracked bowl and ate peanuts and coarse rice balls.

Lee said apologetically, "I did not know you'd be here today. I sent Big Fool to get us some supper."

"Brother Lee, this is good enough for me. Besides the old scholar, and the mute. I have been alone for a long time. I'm glad to have a friend. Ahe! It's warm and comfortable sitting on the *kon* (bed) during a raining day like today. I've been in the South too long, I almost forgot about the warm '*kon*'. It's warmer down South and we don't need it."

"It's the first time I let the hot air and the smoke from the kitchen fire go through the hollowed out part of it. The earthen '*kon*' actually is cool in the summer and warm in the winter. We must have some very clever ancestors to build it. Brother Chiang, you don't look like a Southerner to me. You are too tall. Where do you come from?"

"You're right. I'm not a Southerner. I came from Chengba Town, at the south end of the Shaanxi Province."

Lee was startled. "You're Master Bo's neighbor. You know some Kung Lung members."

Shiao-ho pounded the table so hard that the wine spilled. "Don't mention that Bo Kung Lung," he continued, "Brother Lee, ten years ago, I stabbed Lung Zhi-tin, one of the old Bo's students. I was fourteen."

"What? So you're not on friendly term with the Kung Lung guards."

"Absolutely not! Besides Uncle Ma and Uncle Lu, the Kung Lung members are my enemies. My father was Master Bo's student. Master Bo and the Lung brothers killed my father and forced my mother to remarry. That's why I did not want to stay here too long. I want to complete my revenge quickly. I did not go to Chengba directly because I want Master Bo to hear about me first. I sent him a letter. I want him to be prepared and to gather all his students and friends to his aid. I don't want the others to think that I'd take advantage of Bo's being an old man without any help."

"I fought the Kung Lung gang alone in Xian last month. I killed one of Master Bo's students and wounded six or seven others. It's true that I did not fight Master Bo himself, but I have fought Feng and Lu. They do not fight well and their so-called Kung Lung saber system is clumsy. The only ones that count are Gi Kon-jii and a young woman."

"A young woman? What's her name?" Shiao-ho asked anxiously.

"I don't know, but I'm certain she is one of them. She fights better than all of the other Kung Lung members."

"How old is she? What does she look like? What is her hairstyle?"

"Come on, Brother Chiang, I did not pay close attention and I was too busy fighting all of them. I guess she is about twenty-something. She had a scarf on. I couldn't tell whether her hair was in braids or not. But I do know she is conceited and obnoxious." Lee Feng-jii told Shiao-ho what had happened between him and the Kung Lung gang. Shiao-ho gulped down the wine fast. '*It must be May-lin.*'

It rained even harder. Shiao-ho said, "Rain or shine, I must leave tomorrow."

Lee Feng-jii agreed with sympathy, "A father's death must be avenged. I can see that you're eager to go. I want to fight Gi Kon-jii again, I'll go with you."

"How could you? You're getting married. If you want to go after Gi, you better wait until I have finished my business. You see, if we go there together, no one will say that I could win without your help."

Shiao-ho browsed a page of one of Lee Fong-jii's anthologies.

"Brother Chiang, do you like poetry?" Lee asked.

"No. My teacher taught me how to read and write the simple stuff. I only know enough words to get me by. I'd like to learn more. It's very important to know more words."

Lee said, "There are definitely benefits of knowing how to write. I don't want to be a security guard fighting roughnecks and I don't want to be an official working for the Manchu, the Chin Dynasty either. I make a living with writings. I write deeds for the locals, copy lists of herbs for the doctors, and religious doctrines and prayer scrolls for the monks and Tao priests. There are many temples around here."

"My late father did that. Uncle Ma, my father's sworn brother raised me after my father's death and he taught me the trade of blacksmith. I guess later I can be a blacksmith. But, first, I have to take care of the business of revenge."

They talked more about the eccentric Master Bo. Shiao-ho told Lee that Master Bo had defeated the conceited Master Hsu. Lee thought, '*Master Bo defeated the famous Master Hsu. He must be hundred times better than his students. I wonder whether Shiao-ho can match up to the old but experienced Master Bo, with Gi Kon-jii and that young woman to help him.*'

A neighbor came and told Lee that Big Fool was in trouble in the village and Lee took an umbrella and went to get Big fool home.

It stopped raining. Shiao-ho went out for a walk around the seemingly deserted village because of the cold rain. His mother always told him stories on a rainy day to keep him in. The memory of it made his chest hurt and he silently renewed his oath of revenge. *I just have to kill the old Bo, but what will May-lin do?*'

An old man pointed to a shabby hut nearby and said, "Miss Chen lives there with her grandma. Her father was a hunter. He died two years ago from a fall. Now, Master Lee will marry her and everything will be fine."

"Master Lee is a good man," Shiao-ho said. Then he suddenly thought that he should at least buy Lee Feng-jii a wedding present. He asked for directions to the nearby town, and rode slowly there while considering what he should buy. He could not buy any cosmetics since he knew nothing about it and it was also not proper for him to buy anything for the bride. He could not buy books for Lee either, because he really did not know the words enough to buy a good book. Finally he decided that he would buy some chickens. Lee could use them for the wedding feast or raise them.

Chiang Shiao-ho bought two fat hens and one rooster. He saw a lively gander stand tall in a cage, Shiao-ho liked the look of it and bought it as a sign that Lee would have a strong boy soon. *There must be some snakes in the hill, a goose will eat the small snakes and it can also guard the yard.*'

He tied the chicken, their legs and wings bound up, to his saddle. Because the goose's legs were too short to tie, Shiao-ho had to hold the struggling animal with one hand and hold the rein with the other. The noisy birds made the horse jittery and it was hard going through the crowd.

A short dark form moved out of a corner. The startled horse bolted and galloped away with the chickens. Shiao-ho jumped free holding the bellicose goose.

It was a short monk, wearing a cone-shaped straw rain cape. He stood there and laughed at Shiao-ho holding tight to a flapping and honking goose.

"What's the matter with you? Don't laugh! You scared my horse away! Ah! You know how to '*Tien Hsueh*'." The short man swiftly closed in and suddenly pointed his two fingers at Shiao-ho. Shiao-ho pushed the monk away. The monk fell onto the muddy street.

"You! Get up. Wait!" The monk looked familiar, "Do I know you?"

"I know you, too! You are a renegade. Master Hsu did not want to teach you and...." The short monk ran away when someone led Shiao-ho's horse back to him.

Chiang Shiao-ho tried to remember where he met the monk. Lee and the indignant Big Fool were at home when he got there.

Lee said, "Why? You bought chickens? Thanks."

"These are your wedding presents. Is your big friend here alright?"

Lee laughed, "He is big, isn't he? Call him Big Fool, he doesn't mind. He beat up some one, he himself got beaten up too. Anyway, we brought supper home.

"I met a nasty short monk in town. He attacked me." Shiao-ho said.

"A monk from the White Pine Temple uphill?"

"I don't think so. He knew me and I knew him from the past too. But I can't remember who he is. He fights well, and he also knows '*Tien Hsueh*'."

"He knows '*Tien Hsueh*'? That's strange. Besides my teacher and Gi Kon-jii's grandpa, Master Kac of Kaifeng, I do not know anyone else who knows '*Tien Hsueh*'. I only learned some of the basics to cure but not enough to fight with. Gi Kon-jii did not use it so I don't think he knew how to. I wonder who else knows this deadly technique." Shiao-ho did not want to tell Lee that there were even more secret, more advanced and more deadly skills unknown to the masses.

Big Fool ate and drank with them, and asked for some food to bring back to his mother. Lee lit a makeshift oil lamp.

"A toast, Brother Chiang. I'm glad to know you. You're highly skilled and you're modest, not like that braggart Gi Kon-jii who tells just about anyone how great his grandpa was. The Kung Lung guards are even worse. I can't understand how they earned their name."

The mentioning of the Kung Lung gang saddened Shiao-ho. He thought, '*that young woman Lee told me about must be May-lin. Is she married? Does she hate me? I'll be sad if she is married but somehow I'll let it go. But if she is not married yet, it will be a dilemma for me. How can I want to kill her grandpa and, at the same time, want to marry her? What can I do?*' He sighed, pushed his drink away and said, "Brother Lee, I can't drink any more. Tomorrow I'll go even if it pours. I may not live up to my act of revenge."

"Why? If you really think you are not Gi Kon-jii and Master Bo's match, I will go with you and help you. The wedding can wait."

"Eight Bo Kung Lung, sixteen Gi Kon-jii, I can beat them all. There is something else, in some way connected with the revenge that has worried me all these years. It's more difficult than killing my father's murderers."

"Tell me your problem. I'd like to help, I lost my older brother years ago, and I'd like to have you as a brother."

Shiao-ho said happily, "I'd like that very much. I'll be twenty-five soon."

"I'm twenty-two now. So you are elder brother, and I'm younger brother."

Chiang Shiao-ho almost blurted out that May-lin was also twenty-two.

On their knees, they recited a simple oath of brotherhood, and then they kowtowed once to the sky, once to the earth and once to each other. At last, Shiao-ho stood solemnly to receive Lee's, the younger brother's, kowtow.

"I'm glad that we do not have to drink the ceremonial wine mixed with our blood. Sincerity is good enough. I have a younger brother, although I've not seen him for eleven years but I'll tell him to honor you."

"I also have a younger brother at home and he should be nineteen now. I have not seen him since the day I ran away from my abusive uncle and was saved by my late teacher. We have a lot in common."

"Now that we're sworn brothers, I don't want to keep anything from you. But I can't tell you my trouble in a few words and I don't believe you can help me even if you knew. I promise I will tell you the whole truth later. Please forgive me. Right now I'm too troubled to be pleasant. Let us sleep," Shiao-ho said.

Lee sensed that Shiao-ho's trouble must have something to do with that Kung Lung woman. He figured that they must have loved each other ten years ago. 'No. It's not possible. Both of them were very young then.'

He cleared the food when Shiao-ho whispered urgently, "Blow the light out! Someone is out there!"

"I heard nothing. It's just the leaves," Lee said, he grabbed his sword.

"It's nothing serious. The monk I met today has come for me."

"Are you sure? I heard nothing but the rain drops on the leaves."

"I heard someone push the gate open slyly. I'm confident to say that I can hear a needle being dropped ten steps away."

It might be a dog pushing against the gate." Lee was not convinced.

Shiao-ho said, "Go to sleep. It's nothing to worry about at this moment. I may catch the short monk tonight."

"Good. It's your show." Lee wanted to see how good Shiao-ho's skills were.

The nervous Lee waited for something to happen; all he heard was Shiao-ho's soft snoring. Then Lee heard footsteps outside. He sat up and Shiao-ho said, "Stay. It's Big Fool."

Big Fool yawned loud. Lee laughed, "You're right! Let him be the watch dog." No reply. Lee finally closed his eyes. Suddenly, Shiao-ho jumped out of the room and started to fight someone even before Big Fool's yell stopped. The intruder had applied 'Tien Hsueh' on Big Fool.

Lee knew how to reverse the technique. He patted Big Fool's leg hard a couple of times. Big Fool stood up.

Chiang Shiao-ho was dueling empty-handed with a short man brandishing a steel rod fiercely. The monk tried vainly to attack Shiao-ho with 'Tien Hsueh' twice. He was ready to run away again. Shiao-ho caught him and said, "Friend, you don't have to leave in a hurry. You shouldn't use 'Tien Hsueh' freely, for that alone you should be punished. Who are you?"

"Chiang Shiao-ho, let go of my arm. I admit that you're better than me."

"You know my name. Ahe! You're Brother Yuan. I met you ten years ago when Master Hsu took me to your home. We were both children then. Your father was very kind to me." Yuan was the skinny boy he had met ten years ago when Master Hsu took him to challenge Master Bo.

Shiao-ho continued, "Brother Yuan, did you go to Master Kac to learn how to 'Tien Hsueh'? At that time I was so jealous of you."

"My teacher is Steel Rod Monk. Nine years ago, bandits killed my father and burned down my home. My teacher saved me. You're the cause of my father's death. I came to fight you."

"How could I be responsible? I was a homeless boy then."

Monk Yuan said, "Everyone knew that Master Bo defeated Master Hsu. Master Hsu kept his promise and stayed away from that area afterward. Without his protection, all the bandits had a free run and they robbed the rich and you know my family was rich." The Monk continued after they went into the room and sat down, "A faithful servant saved my mother and me and hid us in his home. My father had always been generous with his donation when Steel Rod Monk came around. So when he heard that we had been robbed, he killed a couple bandits and got back some silver for us. I became his student and he called me 'Monk Pure'."

"Monk Pure, why didn't you tell me that you knew me earlier? You didn't have to come here like a thief."

"I just wanted to challenge you and see how good you are. Everyone knows that you have a super teacher. Chiang Shiao-ho, I better tell you that Gi Kon-jii came to the East to apprehend you for Master Bo."

"Arrest me. I'm no criminal. Is Gi Kon-jii a law officer? Who told you that?"

"He posted posters of '*Chiang Shiao-ho – wanted*' everywhere. He's in An-Yin town now. Two men are traveling with him."

Lee Feng-Jii said, "That's Gi Kon-jii's way of forcing you to come out in the open."

Shiao-ho told Lee, "younger brother, I'm going to find Gi Kon-jii now. I can't wait."

"Chiang Shiao-ho, I can understand that you want to go after Gi immediately. I want to warn you. Gi indeed fights well; he is the famous Dragon Knight's grandson and he is cunning and unscrupulous. Please don't take him lightly." Monk Pure said.

7

Shiao-ho resented Gi's posters. *'How dare he blemish my reputation? I'm not a criminal and he is not an officer."* His teacher told him to think through the cause and effect of a problem first. An understanding of the 'why' is helpful in finding the right solution. *'The posters are Gi Kon-jii's odd but effective way of forcing me to fight him first. He is a buffer. Ahe! It's so true; the posters have angered me so much that I'm actually trying to find him. Gi is cunning and he is winning because I'm compelled to seek him. Monk Pure said that Gi Kon-jii might be at An-Yin City. An-Yin City is in Henan Province and I have to go south again. I really should go to Xian to find out where old Bo is. May-lin is in Xian. Ahe! May-lin, how can I face her?'* Shiao-ho rode to the south. *'Certainly old Bo should have received my letter by now and he is not stupid enough to stay in Chengba. I better go to Xian. And…and…the posters might be Gi's trick to draw me away from Xian!'* He turned around and rode to the west. *'Oh no! What if my teacher is out on a trip? He would hear about the posters and he might think I'm a thief. I must stop Gi Kon-jii.'* He rode to the south again.

His teacher wanted him to be on friendly terms with the two Dragons' students. They were also the students of the Wu-Ton School of martial Arts. *'If you ever meet them by chance, you should consider them as your brothers and schoolmates,"* his teacher said.

'Teacher, you *also said that the disciples of the Wu-Ton School should be modest. Gi Kon-jii is not. I think that he is younger than me and I have the right to discipline him.'*

Lo-Yang, a magnificent capital of the Chou and Han Dynasties some fifteen thousand years ago, was the biggest city Shiao-ho had ever been to. The wall of the city gate was at least ten feet thick. There were more than ten gates. He entered the Northwest gate and went to the first security station he saw to get some information about Gi Kon-jii.

"Master Gi is not here. A few days ago, Gi Kon-jii and two Kung Lung guards came..."

"Where are they now? Tell me!" Shaio-ho demanded.

"Gi Kon-jii stayed in town for two days and he put up the "Wanted" posters everywhere."

"Where did Gi Kon-jii go? Do you know?" Shiao-ho asked politely. He was ashamed of his bad manners.

"Someone said that he headed south to Nan-Yin City."

On the route to Nan-Yin City, a huge wanted poster was chiseled deeply, probably by a sword, into a section of the ruins of the old Great Wall. Shiao-ho had to stop and scrape the words off one at a time with his sword. His wrath toward Gi increased a notch each time when he obliterated a word.

An innkeeper informed him, "Three chaps stopped here for lunch yesterday. The short one wrote the wanted poster on our wall. We thought that he was an officer and dared not stop him. But we scraped it off after he left. You can still see the traces of it."

Shiao-ho stopped frequently to ask about Gi's whereabouts. Once he felt a lump in his throat at the sight of a huge willow tree adjacent to a creek. "*Good Shiao-ho! Please go up and get my kite down for me. Please! Please...*" He could almost hear May-lin's sweet little voices and see her standing under the tree. But when he rushed over, there was no one. '*May-lin! May-lin!*' he murmured in a trance and almost fell off the horse. '*what am I doing here? I should go to hunt Master Bo. But the posters..*' Now he decided that he would kill Gi Kon-jii. For once he would disobey his teacher's order that he cannot kill anyone but his father's murderers.

Riding through the night, Shiao-ho arrived at Nan-Yin City at early dawn.

There was a crowd of poverty-stricken farmers, children and feeble elders everywhere: on the street, at someone's door... All of a suddenly, every one ran to the southern part of the city. Afraid his horse would bump into them, Shiao-ho dismounted and asked one of them, "Where are you going?" The stranger shouted an answer and did not stop. It was a different dialect, Shiao-ho did not understand.

He found an eatery to have breakfast.

The owner of the eatery told him, "They are refugees from the North, Shandong Province. The Whe River flooded and washed away homes and crops. Yesterday, a kindhearted guest of an inn gave some of them a bit of silver. That's why they were rushing there today to beg for more." *Didn't my teacher tell me to help the weak and the poor? I can help them with some silver too. Of course, I will keep enough for my mother.* Another customer sighed, "It's so true that it's not easy to be benevolent. Yesterday, that kind young man had changed five ounces of silver into small cash to give to the refugees. Now all of them rush to him to beg. He does not seem to be rich; maybe he knows how to magically create inexhaustible amounts of silver. Now even if he had five hundred ounces of silver, it won't be enough!"

He paid the owner to keep his horse and started to follow the crowd. "Buddha! Merciful Buddha! Please give me some coins too! My eighty-year old mother is dying of hunger! Please..."

"Save my son! Please! We have not eaten for two days..."

The hungry crowd amassed at the gate of an inn. The scared innkeeper kept the gate closed. A short young man stood upon the wall and shouted, "I have no more silver. Sorry! I have given away all of my silver and also my friends' yesterday."

This man knows martial arts well. Looking at the young man's fine clothes, Shiao-ho thought with admiration, *He must be rich, and he's kind also. I can give him my silver. He looks like a scholar, is he...?* Two middle-aged men jumped upon the wall, stood on each side of the young man. One wore an eye patch and the other, a heavy-set one, shouted down at the crowd, "Go! You hear! Go now and come back tomorrow morning!"

Ahe! I know both of him. aren't they Master Bo's students? Uncle Chen and one-eyed Uncle Yu. Ahe! the young man must be Gi Kon-jii! Shiao-ho walked away, *Oh! No. I can't kill him now. He is kind.*

Later at the restaurant, Shiao-ho heard, "That benevolent young man must be an important detective incognito. He and his assistants post wanted posters everywhere. The criminal is someone surnamed Chiang."

Now what am I going to do? I can't beat the kindhearted Gi now. If he defends the Kung Lung gang, I will have another dilemma.

The talkative waiter told Shiao-ho, "Mister! I wouldn't go out after dark. There are refugees sleeping on the streets. They are waiting for the morning to beg for silver from that generous young man."

Shiao-ho wondered from where Gi Kon-jii could have gotten the silver tonight. From what Lee Feng-jii had told him about Gi, Shiao-ho did not have the impression that Gi was very rich.

When the hotel clerk lit the oil lamp in his room, Shiao-ho asked, "Are there any millionaires around here?"

"Yes. Ku of the Ku's Village to the west has more than a million ounces of silver."

"Why does this rich Ku not help the refugees?"

The clerk sneered, "If he's not a miser, how can he be rich? Ku won't give anyone even the smallest coin. Everyone calls him Miser Ku." Shiao-ho thought for a while and said, "I'd like to pay you now. I may leave very early tomorrow."

Shiao-ho squatted among the sleeping refuges on the street across from the inn where Gi Kon-jii was staying and waited. When the night-watcher sounded the midnight call, Shiao-ho saw Gi Kon-jii, dressed in a short, tight black set and pair black cloth-soled shoes, walked fast to the west. He grinned knowingly and discreetly tailed Gi.

They were close to a high-walled villa. *'I have guessed right. The righteous Gi Kon-jii is going to steal from the rich to help the poor. I may give him a hand but first I want to see how good he is.'* There were prickly throne branches and pieces glasses on top of the high stonewall. Gi walked along the walls and it looked like he was trying to find a lower part to jump over. Shiao-ho tied his straw sandals and jumped over the wall, landing soundlessly on the roof. Most of the rooms in the sprawling complex were dark but one. Shiao-ho went to it and hung himself, bat-like, from the roof. With a moistened finger, he punched a hole through the paper windowpane and looked in. *'I am lucky that I have learned this kind of skill from the guards in Szechwan when I was fourteen. Thankfully, my teacher is not here to scold me.'* An old, fat, richly dressed man, who must be the millionaire Ku, called out the quantities of various piles of silver and bills on the desk. A weary-looking clerk tallied the sums up with a weathered abacus. They were recording the daily account. *'He is indeed a miser, and a loan shark too. One third of his daily income will be enough to feed the refugees. I guess since he won't part with his silver voluntarily, I'm willing to give him a hand.'* He obeyed his teacher's taboo of not hurting and scaring ordinary folks with the martial arts, so Shiao-ho waited. Finally Miser Ku and the clerk finished their accounting and stored the bags of silver and bills in a chest with a heavy lock. The yawning pair blew out the lamp, chained and locked the door.

No locks could stop Shiao-ho. He twisted the locks off the chest, and took three bags of silver and a bundle of bills, assuming they were signed notes of loans. He hopped over the wall and waited for Gi outside the high walls. He did not wait too long when he heard loud alarms sounded and men shouting; the whole villa was lit with torches. Gi Kong-jii had been sighted. Gi ran quickly past Shiao-ho's hiding place, turned back to parry with two armed guards.

Shiao-ho watched them fight for a while and saw that one of the guards was very adept with the saber. Gi seemed to have a hard time getting free. He wanted to rescue Gi first, but then he thought, *'It is just great. Gi wants to arrest me. It will be a laugh when he gets caught for stealing.'* He threw all the loan contracts into a deep, rushing creek and went back to Gi's hotel, sat on the roof and waited.

It was quite a long time before Gi Kon-jii came back. He looked tired and carried no bags. He was just ready to jump over the wall and into the yard of the hotel. With precision and a low laugh, Shiao-ho threw the heavy bags at the exact spot in front of where Gi would land. Gi immediately jumped upon the roof, but Shiao-ho had already left.

At dawn, Shiao-ho heard the refugees babble on cheerfully on the streets. He knew that Gi Kon-jii had indeed distributed the silver that he had stolen for Gi last night. He quickly dressed and saddled his horse just in time to catch the gloomy-faced Gi, Chen and a one-eyed Yu riding fast to northwest.

Shiao-ho rode after them. *'They are heading to Xian. Why should I follow them? I was angry at Gi for posting the wanted signs and wanted to beat him, but now I know that Gi is an eccentric but kind man, and I should not think about beating him anymore. It's better for me to go to Xian to have a talk with May-lin. How can I tell her that I have to kill her grandfather and, at the same time, I want to marry her? What should I do? I wish I told my teacher about May-lin. That was the only thing I held back, I was too shy to tell him. Maybe I should go back to ask my teacher's advice before I go to Xian. I know for sure that my teacher will want me to be forgiving. My friend Nan at Kaifeng also wanted me to be forgiving. But, how can I make my father's soul be at peace? How can I forget about the abuses I had when I was young? They had hunted me down mercilessly. Ahe! May-lin, tell me what I should do. And also, why does the heroic and kind Gi Kon-jii want to help the Kung Lung gang? What's the catch? For silver or . . . no! Gi is after May-lin.. Maybe May-lin wants to marry Gi Kon-jii. I need to find out. I should be happy for her. Gi Kon-jii is a scholar and if he passed the examination, May-lin could be a lady. But what could I do?'* Shiao-ho was confused.

At noon, he stopped at a roadside eatery.

"Whose horse is this?"

Someone shouted with an air of authority. Four horsemen, two of them uniformed officers, stood around Shiao-ho's horse. Chiang Shiao-ho recognized the two guards who fought Gi-Kon-jii the night before.

"My horse, officer."

"Sergeant, Not him, he is too tall," one man said.

They got on their horses and were ready to leave.

"Wait. I was having a meal when you called me out to ask me. I think I deserve an explanation," Shiao-ho demanded.

The short guard, the one fights well, replied apologetically, "Sorry! We saw your horse and a sword so we thought that the thief Gi was here. Gi Kon-jii is a thief. Last night, he stole more than seven hundred ounces of silver from my employer Master Ku. I'm one of Ku's hired security guards. My name is Yan Hen. My colleague and these two officers are after the thief Gi. Sorry for bothering you."

Shiao-ho thought, '*This man Yan fights well. With two officers to help them, they could arrest Gi. But I'm the real thief. I better go after them and see to it that they will not arrest Gi for a crime I have committed.*' He followed them discreetly.

At the next town, he spotted more wanted posters.

"Pardon me. Who wrote these posters?" Shiao-ho asked a storekeeper.

"A Mr. Gi. He paid for the right to write on the walls everywhere."

'*Gi kept some of the silver which I stole for him, and used it to insult me. Somehow I'll find a way to punish him. I'll tease him.*'

The Guard Yan saw him and stopped him, "You, my young friend! You thought that I did not know you were tailing us. Why? Are you Gi's friend?"

Shiao-ho said, "No. I'm just curious to see if you can catch Gi Kon-jii."

One officer accused, "Are you his accomplice?" We better arrest you first."

"How could I not know the famous Buddha Gi? I did not know he was a thief. I'm just curious, that's all!"

Yan held his angry colleague and the two officers back. He glanced at Shiao-ho's sword, and said, "My young friend, you can watch us fight with Gi as long as you stay aside and don't help him."

He turned and whispered to his companion, "He must be Chiang Shiao-ho. I heard that Chiang is tall and carries a sword."

Shiao-ho heard it and he sneered, "So what? I'm Chiang Shiao-ho. I better warn you that Gi Kon-jii is Dragon Knight's grandson."

The other guard was angry. He said, "You must be a thief, too. I'll fight you." He chopped at Shiao-ho savagely. Nobody had time to see how and when Shiao-ho caught the saber and broke it into two pieces with one hand. He laughed and galloped away.

Next day, he followed Gi's group to the Province of Hubei through heavy fog. A talkative hotel clerk told Shiao-ho, "Everybody here knows about the famous Master Gi. We heard that he had helped the refugees. He offered a reward for any information about a criminal named Chiang and posted the wanted posters everywhere. Oh, yes. He is famous."

"Where is this Hero Gi now?"

"He left earlier with two Kung Lung guards. They wanted to visit the famous Wu-Ton Mountain. They are probably staying at the small town at the foot of the mountain. You see, he does not know that he has to wait for a clear day to go up the mountain. The god will seal the passes with dense fog for days. Sir, do you know that fellow Chiang? Mr. Gi also told us to inform Chiang that he can find him at a famous Kung Lung security station in Xian."

"I know about Chiang Shiao-ho. He is not a criminal." Shiao-ho said.

His teacher once told him, "Wu-Ton Mountain is where the Wu-Ton School of martial arts originated. The Tao priests there know martial arts. If you have to pass there by chance, be extremely respectful and careful."

Shiao-ho asked the clerk, "How far is Wu-Ton Mountain from here?"

"Sir, not far at all. Less than a day's ride to the north from here."

"I'd like to visit the Wu-Ton Mountain and to light a stick of incense for the legendary Master Chang."

"Sir, I advise caution and sincere reverence lest you be severely punished."

"How? What are the taboos?" Shiao-ho asked.

"Sir, first and foremost, you have to leave your sword behind."

"Why?"

"That's the rule. There is a "Swords Depository Pond" at the entrance from this side. Everyone, even the most prestigious general, has to throw his sword into the pond. If he does not do it, the spirit of Lord Chang or the Tao priests there will punish him severely." The waiter lowered his voice and continued conspiratorially, "Once, a most powerful general refused to give up his sword. He kept on going up the mountain, wearing his sword and..," the clerk stopped for suspense.

"What happened?" Shiao-ho asked with feigned anxiety.

"Why, a huge boa constrictor appeared miraculously, and literarily scared the general to his deserved death. Sir, you see, the snake is Lord Chang. You know, Sir, even on the portrait of the Lord Chang, he is holding no sword but a long handled broom. How can anyone else be allowed to carry a sword? All the Tao priests there carry a sword though."

"How many skilled priests are there? Do you know?"

"There are at least a hundred armed ones plus the famous seven sword masters. Sir, please remember to leave your sword behind if you want to visit the mountain. Otherwise the least of your troubles will be suffering a case of bad diarrhea."

"Of course. Thank you for your advice. I'm here to show my respect. How can I not obey the rules?" *'I wonder the conceited and arrogant Gi Kon-jii knows about the business of leaving his sword behind. If he goes up the mountain with his sword, it would be fun to see how the great seven sword masters punish him. I better go to the same village and wait to follow Gi up the mountain. Ahe! A good opportunity to tease him.'*

The small village seemed to have a good business from the worshippers. It had three inns and two restaurants. He inconspicuously followed the impeccably dressed Gi, on a white silk top and black silk pants, to the biggest restaurant.

Shiao-ho sat in a dark corner and waited for an imminent fight with Gi if Chen came in later and pointed him out. Gi Kon-jii drank alone and murmured something that sounded like a verse.

"Waiter! Bring me a pen and ink! I want to write a poem on the wall," Gi called.

"But, my Lord! The wall is newly white washed and it would not look nice with writings on it. I can bring you paper and then I can paste your poems on the wall. How about it my Lord? Sometimes other guests will buy a well-written verse from us. We surely will appreciate the opportunity to earn some coins."

Gi sneered, "Are you afraid that you will not earn some silver if I write the poem directly on the wall? Here is one ounce of silver. You don't have to wait for someone to come along to buy it. Go and fetch me the writing tools, I'll even pay you a bit more if you prepare the ink for me."

Shiao-ho swore silently, '*Damn you, you're certainly very generous with the silver I stole for you.*'

Gi Kon-jii wrote "Chiang -- Wanted" on the wall. Gi had a flair for calligraphy. Shiao-ho looked on with admiration. He thought, '*Gi sure writes well. I don't know enough to make a judgment, but I think Gi writes better* than *my teacher and Brother Lee. Ahe!. My father wrote beautifully, too.*' Sadness and hatred washed over him, and Shiao-ho renewed his determination for revenge.

He did not fully understand the three lines Gi had written, but he knew enough to tell it was something about Gi's heroic deeds. '*He is a braggart all right*' He chuckled and praised aloud, "Great. fit for a hero!" annoyed at the interruption of his flow of thoughts, Gi turned around and looked at Shiao-ho angrily. He saw that Shiao-ho was poorly attired, bare-footed with a pair of straw sandal and carried no sword. Gi decided that it would not be worth his effort arguing with an ignorant simpleton. He paid for his drinks and left, not knowing that Shiao-ho had followed him.

Gi lit the oil lamp on the wall in his room, and he began to compose the fourth line to complete the poem. He wanted to use this poem as his "morning after" poem to impress Bo May-lin and show he was good at both martial arts and literary arts. He could not concentrate. He thought, '*I had never dreamed about marrying a rich woman when I left home. If I could capture that damned Chiang Shiao-ho and take him to Master Bo, May-lin and the others will praise me to no end. I have written so many wanted posters in many towns, but I cannot find him. He must be afraid of me and keeps hiding. But I don't understand why Chen and Yu changed their attitude and refused to sleep in the same room with me now. Ever since that night someone delivered the silver to me to help the refugees, both of them are jittery. Chen is probably too scared to identify Chiang Shiao-ho for me even if we come face to face with that rascal. There's no point in prolonging my search and keeping May-lin waiting. I will go back to her after I visit the famous Wu-Ton Mountain and see how good the famous seven sword masters are. I may even challenge one or two. After the wedding, I will have May-lin accompany me to look for Chiang and the unknown person who stole the silver.*'

Gi did not even bother to wash the ink off his favorite pen brush. He blew out the light, and slept fully clothed. It was bright when Gi woke up. He noticed the ink spots on the bedding and thought, '*I was too tired to wash my hands last night. The ink on my fingers stained the bedding. I better remember to wash the ink off before I sleep every time from now on.*'

"Waiter! Fetch me water!" Gi opened the tightly closed door and called.

The waiter put down the washbasin, and just stood there staring at Gi's back.

"Fetch me breakfast. What are you looking at? Are you stupid or deaf? This is the second time I'm telling you."

"Nephew Gi, do you still want to go up the Wu-Ton Mountain today? I...." One-eyed Yu said as he walked into Gi's room. He stopped talking and stared at Gi's back, "Why did you write the wanted poster on the back of your nice white shirt? You've ruined a nice shirt."

Gi broke out into a cold sweat, and quickly took off his white top and looked at the writings on it. '*Who dares write on my top while I'm sleeping? I did not feel a thing. Ahe! This man could have killed me.*' His forehead dampened suddenly. However, Gi said with a forced nervous laugh, "I write them again and again. I must have written them last night after I had too much to drink. I'm tired of this business of catching Chiang Shiao-ho."

"It's a useless chase, let's go back to Xian and wait for him there. Who knows what will happen there if we stay out too long. The Kung Lung School need your help to defend us from that renegade," Yu agreed.

"Let me think about it. I'll talk to you later," Gi dismissed Yu impatiently.

Gi examined the writings on his white top closely. They were poorly written. '*The write is no scholar. That tall young man whom I met last night might have written it. When he praised my verses last night, I thought he was pretending that he knew the words. Maybe not so. Didn't they all say that Chiang Shiao-ho is tall? I'm going back there to have a drink, and maybe I can find out something about that young man, I need a drink anyway.*'

"You braggart! I spared your life." Someone had added a line to the poem he wrote yesterday with these words.

For the second time, cold sweat rushed over him. Gi yelled at the waiter, "How dare you let someone else ruin my poem? Who wrote this?"

"Sir. I don't know how to read. He gave me two ounces of silver to write it. More silver than what you gave me. Mercy! Don't hit me. Please."

"What does he look like?"

"A tall young man, he was here yesterday when you were here." Then both of them heard the shouting. "Gi Kon-jii, shame on you!" Gi Kon-jii rushed downstairs and caught sight of a tall man on a black horse galloping toward Wu-ton Peak. He went back to the inn to fetch his own horse.

"Kon-jii, where are you going?" Yu and Chen asked.

"Wait for me here!" Gi rode toward the mountain. He did not spot Chiang Shiao-ho hiding behind the trees waiting to make sure he was going to the Peak. Now Shiao-ho turned his horse around and rode back to Gi's hotel.

"Chen Zhi-pi. Come out!" Shiao-ho shouted.

Chen and Yu had come to the conclusion that there must be a highly skilled martial arts master who had followed them. Yu said, "you know, I don't think that mysterious master wants to kill Gi. But, from the way he humiliated Gi last night, he is not Gi's friend either. Someone is calling you."

"I'm Chen, young friend. Why? .... Hay! Are you...?"

"Right on, I'm Chiang Shiao-ho! I just want to talk to you."

"Shiao-ho, you surely are grown. You are even taller than your father. We have heard that you have learned martial arts well."

"Right on again. Let's find a place to talk. Follow me! And relax! You know I could have killed all of you last night or at Nan-Yin City.

Shiao-ho took Chen to an empty field. A barrel-thick stone post was half buried.

"You know that Master Bo and the Lung brothers killed my father, and you also know Bo's second son abused me when I was a helpless youth. Although you did not torture me, you did not help me either. I think you're neither my enemy nor my friend. I will show you a bit of my strength now and you can tell the others. I don't want to wound anyone lest he's in my way." Shiao-ho pulled the half buried stone post out and threw it about thirty feet away with ease.

"You ...you indeed learned well. Shiao-ho, please understand that One-eyed Yu and I did not come with Gi willingly. We dared not obey Master Bo's order.."

"I do understand. Don't worry! My teacher instructed me that I can only kill my father's murderers: Master Bo and the Lung brothers. I only come to ask you not to identify me to anyone," he then sneered, "not that I'm afraid. I just want to tease that braggart a bit longer."

"You could have killed Gi Kon-jii many times. I will not point you out."

"Good! I'm sure that braggart is provoking the wrath of the famous Wu-Ton sword masters now, I better go up to rescue him."

Through the lingering dense fog, Gi Kon-jii entered the Wu-Ton Mountain first, followed by Chiang Shiao-ho. Gi Kon-jii galloped through the mountain pass. He thought furiously with a bravado he did not feel, '*who dares tease me? I'm the grandson and the successor of the famous Dragon Knight. I will teach this person a lesson.*' Actually Gi Kon-jii was scared. He knew that he could have been killed twice already. Once by the person who stole the silver for him, and then by the young man who teased him last night. Was there only one man, or two men? Anyway this man, or two men, definitely was no friends. '*Is he afraid of the power of Master Bo and the Kung Lung School? Or is he afraid that I might have some highly skilled classmates?*'

He came to a waterfall. The words "Remove Swords Pond" were carved into the cliff. He did not remove his sword. A tall Tao priest with a black beard, standing beside an old pine tree on a high ridge, looked down at him and shouted something, but Gi could not hear him over the sound of the cataract. He hopped over a few rocks and heard the Tao priest shouted angrily, "No sword is permitted here! Drop your sword. If you don't, Lord Chang will punish you. Didn't you see the sign 'Remove Swords Pond'?

"My name is Gi Kon-jii. My grandpa was the famous Dragon Knight Gi."

"Your grandpa visited Wu-Ton Mountain several times. Every time he removed his sword reverently."

"Oh! Time changes. no need to follow the antiquated rule." Gi refused to remove his sword.

"No one has dared to come here carrying a sword, you are the first one to break the rule in two hundred years. I'll arrest you." They fought. The Tao priest was going to lose. Another Tao priest came out to help. Gi was too strong and pretty soon there were five priests fighting him. Gi was still winning then another three priests entered the melee. Gi wielded his sword into a big arc, forcing the eight priests back. He ran uphill and hopped on a huge rock and fought them from his advantageous higher position. None of the panting priests could get close. Somewhere, two or three bells sounded urgently and Gi heard more priests coming. He brandished his sword and retreated higher.

A graybeard priest called a halt and said, "Ten years ago, Steel Rod Monk came to provoke trouble here and we repelled him. Since then, no one has dared to come here to give us trouble. Did your grandpa tell you that? There are seven superior sword masters here. I'm the fourth one."

Graybeard alone fought him and Gi Kon-jii soon found out that graybeard was no easy opponent. Gi's arm was sore from blocking the graybeard's powerful thrusts. He jumped upon a higher huge rock and fought down while mouthing insults. Faraway another bell sounded. Gi knew that more priests were on the way. He fought and retreated backward toward the cliff and fell backward down the deep ravine.

When Gi Kon-jii came to, he was being held head down. The tall young man was washing his head with cold water. Gi slapped the young man hard and_shouted, "You tricked me. You knew the Tao priests are too many for me to fight." Chiang Shiao-ho dropped Gi into the rushing creek. Gi Kon-jii was floundering in the swift current. Chiang Shiao-ho fished Gi out.

Gi asked, "Friend? Foe? Who are you?"

"I'm Kao Joe-hua." Kao means high, Joe-hua was the name of the peak where his teacher taught him.

"I have never heard about you. You must not be famous. I thought that you were Chiang Shiao-ho, the one I want to catch."

"If I were Chiang Shiao-ho, you can bet I wouldn't save you, and you'd still be hanging from the tree up there," Shiao-ho laughed, and pointed up. Gi looked up and thought, '*He must be very good. It's not easy to get up there and fetch me down.*'

"I followed you all the way from Nan-Yin City. I wanted to see how good you are, that you think you can catch Chiang Shiao-ho. you're just a braggart."

Gi Kon-jii retorted angrily, "There were too many damned Tao priests." He continued conciliatorily, "You stole silver for me and now you save me. If you're not Chiang Shiao-ho, I'd like to be your friend. Let's go back to the hotel to have a drink. How about it?"

"Good. I'll meet you at the restaurant."

"Where is my sword?" Gi said.

"There!" Gi looked up at the sword caught in between the tree branches. Shiao-ho climbed up and got it. He threw it down to Gi and shout, "Catch!" He jumped away swiftly like a monkey. *'He has followed my every step and I knew nothing about it. He is so much better than me. If he is Chiang Shiao-ho, I don't think I'll have a chance. Why did he tease me? He is no friend.'* Gi thought.

Chen was worried about whether Shiao-ho had killed Gi Kon-jii. Gi and Shiao-ho walking in.

"Nephew Gi, what's the matter? You're injured!"

Gi ignored Yu and started the introduction. "Brother Kao, please meet Yu and Chen, two famous Kung Lung guards traveling with me."

"Nice to meet you, Brother Kao."

Gi Kon-jii watched carefully when Chen and Yu greeted Shiao-ho. There was no sign of recognition. Gi relaxed and thought, *'so, this Kao is indeed not Chiang Shiao-ho. And that damned Chen even afraid of his own shadow now.'* He did not notice that Chen was very nervous.

Gi said cheerfully, "Brother Kao, it's cool out in the yard. I'll wash up and be back." Chen got up and wanted to accompany Gi, but Shiao-ho held his arm and said, "Let's wait here. It's cool here. I am flattered to meet two famous Kung Lung guards." He slightly increased his hold.

"Yes! Yes! It's cool. Cool here...." Chen stammered. Chen was sweaty and pale from the pain.

Yu asked with concern, "Chen, does the heat ill you? Sit and try to relax."

Yu then politely asked Shiao-ho, "Brother Kao, where do you come from? Are you new to this area?"

"I came from the South. I'm a vagabond. While I was visiting Wu-Ton Mountain, I saw Tao priests fighting Brother Gi. Brother Gi fell and I saved him." Gi claimed indignantly, "Brother Kao, there were too many of them fighting me. Let's go back and demand a fair one-to-one duel. I'll show you that I can beat any one of the so-called seven sword masters."

"Bravo! But it won't be easy. The Tao priests are not braggarts." Shiao-ho laughed. Yu and Chen agreed, "They must be good. They are very famous."

Gi sulked a while and then asked, "Where are you going?"

"Xian."

"Business or sightseeing? We have friends there, maybe we can help you." "You could say it is business, there are a few people who owe me a lot ten years ago. I am going to call in the debt, principal plus interest."

"We'll go to Xian together. I'd like you to meet my newly acquired family. Did you ever hear about the famous Kung Lung School? They're my family now.

Shiao-ho laughed, "If I want to challenge someone, I'll surely choose Master Bo. I don't want to take advantage of his old age; I'll fight his heavy Kung Lung saber with my bare hands. If I cannot grab his saber in three passes, I'm no winner."

Gi smirked, "Do not brag. I bet his granddaughter Bo May-lin can beat you easily." Hearing May-lin's name, Chiang Shiao-ho's face turned red and then pale. He sipped some tea and asked, "Is she in Xian now?"

"She will be there soon."

"Brother Gi, does she fight better than you?"

"We did not have a match. But I assume that her training is a bit inferior to mine. For instance, she fought Lee Feng-jii but she didn't win. I did. Lee is Szechwan Dragon's successor," Gi gloated.

Chiang Shiao-ho tried hard to control his mixed feelings of enmity for Master Bo and his longing for May-lin. His facial expression kept changing and his hand holding the teacup shook. Yu and Chen thought that Shiao-ho seemed_suddenly older. Finally, thinking he had his emotion in check, Shiao-ho asked, "Is she promised to be married?"

Like most self-centered man and a bully, Gi Kon-jii did not pay attention to Shiao-ho's changing countenance. He was excited about his upcoming marriage to Bo May-lin. He said, "Indeed. She is promised."

Chiang Shiao-ho asked hastily, "To whom?"

Gi Kon-jii roared, "It is not your business. How dare you ask about her affairs. You're neither her brother nor her family. All right! If you must know, she is mine. We'll be married in the fall. Damn you!" Gi hurled the teacup at Shiao-ho. Chiang Shiao-ho dodged and pointed two fingers at Gi's chest. Gi slumped to the ground.

"Did you kill him?" Yu yelled.

"Shiao-ho, you promised that you wouldn't harm Gi. Brother Yu, he's Chiang Shiao-ho," Chen shouted.

Shiao-ho thought, *'what have I done? Teacher forbade me to use 'Tien Hsueh' I better get hold of myself.'*

"I did not kill him. Is it true that May-lin is going to marry Gi?"

"Yes. Shiao-ho, please be merciful." Chen pleaded.

Shiao-ho freed Gi Kon-jii.

Chiang Shiao-ho wanted to be in Xian fast; however, he was hurt all over. Somehow he managed to get on his horse, and let the horse canter ahead by itself. His chest hurt and he was confused and dazed. He did some deep breathing exercises to steady himself.

"Chiang Shiao-ho, you coward! You even dare not use your own name. Do you dare fight me squarely with your sword? You...," Gi caught up with him.

"Gi Kon-jii! I don't want to fight you. Sorry, I should not have used 'Tien Hsueh' on you. I have no grievance against you. We are both students of the Wu-Ton School. We should be friends and brothers, not enemies. I could have you killed. You must know that, don't you? My enemies are Master Bo and the Lung brothers only. I would kill no one but them to avenge my father's death."

Gi thrust his sword forward, "I, Gi-Kon-jii, won't allow you to harm anyone affiliated with the Kung Lung School."

Shiao-ho raised his sword seemingly lazily only to block Gi's thrust. His strength numbed Gi's arm. Soon Gi's arm was too sore to apply the superior styles anymore; he could only thrust wildly and haphazardly.

"Stop! Gi Kon-jii! I don't want to harm you." Shiao-ho retreated.

Gi came after Shiao-ho ruthlessly. Shiao-ho pierced at Gi's chest lightly, not to kill but only to draw blood. He said, "Gi Kon-jii, go back home. Go back to your grandpa's tomb and learn more before you fight me again."

The white-faced Gi stood there paralyzed. He looked down at the tiny cut between his breasts. There was a small bloodstain. He thought in shame, 'Why! Chiang Shiao-ho could have killed me again. He controlled his sword and pierced me with such meticulousness.' He recalled the numerous reprimands from his grandpa whenever Gi beat up some one and then bragged about his skills.

"Remember! Kon-jii, martial arts is for self-defense. I'm sorry that your mother and I spoiled you. Learn to be modest. I cannot live forever to protect you when you offend someone better than you. Don't you know that there will always be someone who is superior to you? I want you to copy this every day for a month until you remember it well."

Dragon Knight continued, "There are some deadly techniques - 'Tien Hsueh' is one which can inflict or delay death at will. I'm not going to teach you now until you shape up your manners and behavior."

Gi remembered that he wrote the following sentences many times: 'Both the Sho-Lin School and Wu-Ton School of martial arts equally emphasize pacifism over violence. Both schools teach the most refined self-defense, unarmed or armed, fighting techniques. Martial arts' philosophical essence should be: Learn the ways to preserve rather than destroy life. Avoid rather than check; check rather than hurt; hurt rather than maim; maim rather than kill. For all life is precious and cannot be replaced.'

Dragon Knight died soon afterwards, and Gi Kon-jii never learned 'Tien Hsueh'. 'That damned Chiang Shiao-ho obviously knows all of the other techniques too. How can I fight him?" Gi Kon-jii was fumed with frustration and humiliation and took his anger out on Chen. "I took you along because you know him and you can identify him, but you pretended that you didn't know him. Are you conspiring with him, and let him play a dirk trick on me?"

One-eyed Yu intervened, "Nephew Gi, you can't blame Brother Chen. He knew Chiang Shiao-ho when he was a boy. It's been ten years. How can Brother Chen recognize him right away?"

"Nonsense! I know you, all of you so-called mighty Kung Lung guards are afraid of Chiang Shiao-ho. Master Bo, would faint whenever Shiao-ho's name is mentioned. If it were not for May-lin's sake, I wouldn't help you."

Yu retorted, "Gi Kon-jii, that's not true. My Teacher is now old and feeble; he also has regrets. Brother Chen must have known that the three of us together, have no chance of surviving if we were to fight Shiao-ho. That's why he did not identify him."

"Chiang Shiao-ho could only harm me when I'm not prepared. Oh! Well! He must have escaped quickly, I did not catch him." Yu and Chen stared at the now spreading bloodstain on Gi's beige colored top and said nothing.

Gi continued, "Chiang Shiao-ho must be on his way to Xian now. He does not know that Master Bo and May-lin are staying at Uncle Lu's. We should go and warn Master Bo. It's best that Master Bo find a place to hide for a while; we'll fight Shiao-ho in Xian. Get ready to leave now!"

Yu agreed, "Exactly! We better be on our way before it's too late."

Yu counseled the dejected Chen, "At least Gi is still willing to help us to fight Chiang Shiao-ho."

"Are you completely blind? Even with one eye, you must have seen the blood stain on Gi's chest. Shiao-ho did not intend to kill Gi Kon-jii. That's all. Last night and this morning, Shiao-ho had many opportunities to kill Gi. Shiao-ho is not conceited like his father. He is better than his daddy." Looking at Yu's eye patch, Chen continued, "You know, it's true that old Master Bo was cruel, ruthless and stupid. He should not have had Shiao-ho's father killed in the first place. After that mistake, he should have killed Shiao-ho when he was young and not '*Let the root grow*'. But Shiao-ho's father, Chiang Zhi-shen, was to blame too. He was very conceited about his own agility, and he did insult Master Bo. Shiao-ho must have a good teacher who taught the boy well, not only skills but good manners too. Shiao-ho wants only to kill the Lung brothers and Master Bo. Twelve years ago, Master Bo and the Lung brothers hunted Shiao-ho's father down and killed him. The supreme god does have eyes."

Yu advised, "Let's hurry. Maybe we can all go into hiding. We can convince Master Bo to lead us into hiding in Szechwan."

Chen said, "You forget that Master Hsu's there. Master Hsu surely is not Master Bo's friend."

Gi Kon-jii rode fast ahead, but Yu and Chen dwindled. They were afraid of catching up with Chiang Shiao-ho soon. Gi became very impatient. At the next town, Millionaire Ku's guards and the officers caught up with them. Gi fought them and got away. They arrested Chen and Yu.

8

Uncle Lu was surprised to see that Gi came back to Da-Sam Fort alone, "Nephew Gi, did you meet Chiang Shiao-ho? Where are Yu and Chen?"

Gi shouted, "They are slow. I must see Grandpa Bo and May-lin at immediately." He dashed to the inner court where May-lin, in a pretty pink silk short set, practiced her Kung Lung saber skills diligently. "May-lin, I caught Chiang Shiao-ho at Wu-Ton Mountain. We fought and he jumped into the creek and escaped." Gi Kon-jii bragged.

Master Bo was not pleased that Gi joked with his granddaughter before the formal marriage. He coughed to show his disapproval and asked, "Kon-jii, tell me everything."

"Grandpa, I posted *"Chiang Shiao-ho -- Wanted"* posters everywhere. He avoided me. A few days ago I met him at the foot of Wu-Ton Mountain. He fooled me with a feigned name and wanted to be my friend. Uncle Chen wouldn't identify Chiang Shiao-ho for me, even though he obviously recognized the culprit. I almost fell into the rascal's trap. I wounded him. He jumped into the creek and swam away. I suffered a slight wound on my chest too. Chiang Shiao-ho said that he is coming to Xian to kill you only. Grandpa, I suggest that you find somewhere safe and go into hiding for a while. May-lin and I will fight Chiang Shiao-ho at Xian, I need her help."

Master Bo hid his fear and sneered, "I'm not going to hide. Where? My tomb? I'll wait for him at Xian and fight him. He can only kill me once. Get my horse ready!"

May-lin begged, "Grandpa, you cannot go! I'll go. I want to talk to Shiao-ho first before I kill him. I want to know whether he still remembers..." May-lin cried.

Lu Zhi-chun said, "Teacher, It is better that yourself and May-lin wait here a few days. Kon-jii and I will go to Xian, and have a council with Brother Feng. Besides, I may be able to talk Shiao-ho into his senses."

Master Bo thought, '*Yes, I always knew that you had helped him to escape.*'

Gi Kon-jii opposed adamantly, "Not good enough! I'm not afraid of Chiang Shiao-ho if I can fight him face to face, but I'm no match for his trickery. His swordsmanship is just so-so, but he's very good at leaping and wall climbing. At night, I cannot beat him. He will be in Xian soon. If he knows that Grandpa is here, how can we prevent him from sneaking in here at night to assassinate Grandpa? I insist that Master Bo should go into hiding for a while. May-lin and I, together, will beat him in Xian."

They had a lengthy discussion. Uncle Lu summarized, "Nephew Gi's idea seems to be the only solution for now. I will accompany Master Bo to hide at a trusted friend's villa in Henan Province. Chiang Shiao-ho cannot find us there." Master Bo seemed to be swayed at first, but he objected, "No. I can't go there myself and let Shiao-ho kill all my students; I won't be able to live afterwards."

Gi Kon-jii insisted, "If Grandpa not here, the rest of us will be safe. In his letter to you, and he told me again in person, that he won't kill anyone but the Lung brothers and… and Grandpa."

Old Master Bo recalled the pitiful scenario of when Shiao-ho's father was killed. '*His clothes were torn, his feet were bleeding, and Chiang Zhi-shen was a pitiful sight. He had left his young family behind. I was cruel to have ordered him killed. Now, his son comes back to avenge his death. I do deserve to die.*" Huge tears rolled down his wrinkled checks, he said, "I was merciless. Shiao-ho has the right to kill me."

They discussed more and finally Master Bo agreed, "Zhi-chun and I will go to hiding. Get someone to warn the Lung brothers. I don't want anyone of you to fight Shiao-ho. I'll ask my life-long friend Master Lee to help. Master Lee has a lot of students."

Gi said, "I'm certain that I can curb that rogue all by myself. I'm only afraid that Lee Feng-jii, will come to fight us too. I'm sorry to say that none of your Kung Lung guards can be of any help. I need May-lin to be at my side and to help me to fight him, only she can help me."

Master Bo agreed, "Of course, she will go with you, but…" he hesitated and continued, "Without a proper marriage, it won't be fitting for you and May-lin to be traveling together… It's still early. If we hurry, you can be married tonight."

May-lin sobbed and went to her room. Master Bo followed her into her room and said, "Don't feel sorry for me. It's my fault. I am too cruel to be forgiven. I'm only sorry that my students and you, Gi Kon-jii, are all going to suffer because of that. To tell you the truth, I truly admire Chiang Shiao-ho; he is determined, brave and resourceful. Tomorrow I'll go into hiding. If we can live though this, we'll see each other again. Otherwise...."

"I'm going with you"

"No! Gi Kon-jii will need your help to fight Shiao-ho, and probably Lee Feng-jii, in Xian. For you two to travel together properly, you'll marry him tonight."

"No! Grandpa, No! ...I don't want to...I like...I love..."

"I know you love me and don't want to leave me. Please obey me. Otherwise, I won't be able to die in peace ...You're the one I worry about the most. Knowing that you have a good husband, I'll feel better...even if I die."

Uncle Lu's wife was not at the station. The wives of his assistants and friends all eagerly pitched in to help. They worked diligently to decorate the bridal suite in the frontcourt. A few younger women crowded into May-lin's room to help her into a borrowed wedding gown. They undid May-lin's maiden-styled braids first, and then piled her black glossy hair high to form a woman's hair-do held with gold and silver combs. Everyone said the necessary good wishes. May-lin kept on sobbing.

One woman said with a trace of envy, "Why, isn't it grand that you're going to marry a good-looking scholar who fights well too? Don't cry. You don't want your handsome groom to see that your eyes are red and swollen tonight, do you?"

Others joined the teasing. May-lin could not endure it any longer; she pushed them away, tore free her elaborated hair-do, threw her red embroidered jacket away and wept.

Master Bo came in and asked, "My precious May-lin, what's the matter? It's a hurried wedding, and I don't like it either. I'd like you to have a grand wedding, too. But now we don't have time. May-lin, you know that I'm forced into marrying you off without a well-planned ceremony; you don't even have a new gown made. But I insist on having a proper marriage. Before my departure, I'd like to see you happily and formally married. I know you're sorry for me, and it's not fitting to marry you off in haste, but...."

"Grandpa, I'm sorry. I don't like.. I only love... It's just that they are making such a fuss. I..."

"But, a wedding is supposed to be noisy and festive. Besides, laughter and noise are supposed to repel the evil spirit. We're so unfortunate now; we need a noisy one, *Ha! Ha!*" He sounded nothing but cheerful, "My good May-lin, let them help you get dressed up again."

He asked the women, "Please help her dress up again. My family is facing a very difficult time. Please pardon my granddaughter's bad temper." The women dressed May-lin up in silence.

Gi Kon-jii appeared to be electrified. He repeated his victorious fight with Lee Feng-jii and Chiang Shiao-ho to the visitors. With each subsequent telling, he would add on more details. To the listeners, it was a matter of fact that Gi Kon-jii, successor of Dragon Gate Gi, should beat the obscure Chiang Shiao-ho easily. But Uncle Lu was uneasy, '*a cut on his chest! Shiao-ho did not want to kill Gi Kon-jii.*' He wondered why Gi Kon-jii had not come back together with Chen and Yu. Gi's excuse of wanting to be here fast seemed flimsy. Besides, Lu Zhi-chun noticed that Master Bo looked over every younger visitor with apprehension. Master Bo did not quite believe Gi's telling either.

At the wedding ceremony, the pair kowtowed to the symbolic nameplates of Gi Kon-jii's ancestors first, to Master Bo and Uncle Lu second, and to each other last, to complete the ceremony. A big square of red silk covered May-lin's head and face. Nobody could tell whether she was pleased or not, but the two now subdued women, on each side of May-lin to guide her, saw tears dropping down onto her red wedding slippers. They all wondered why and hoped that their husbands would take them home quickly, away from this seemingly doomed family.

Gi drank and talked about his victories throughout the hasty wedding banquet. Then Lu Zhi-chun announced, "Thank you all for coming. By now I expect that everyone here knows that we are preparing to repel an enemy, or enemies. Tomorrow morning, the newlywed couple will go to Xian to intercept the enemy. Master Bo and I must leave early tomorrow to make necessary arrangements too. Thank you all for coming." Lu also forbade the three younger assistants to play the customary pranks on the newlyweds.

It was dark and quiet. Only the pair of huge red candles in the temporary ceremonial hall, and a small oil lamp in the bridal suite kept burning. They were supposed to burn all night long as the customary token of a long and happy marriage.

Gi Kon-jii, freshly groomed in his pajamas, coughed aloud to announce his entrance to the bridal suite. Suddenly, the lamp of longevity went out. In pitch-dark, Gi nervously laughed to repel his superstition, "Don't be bashful! May-lin, don't you think we have seen each other often enough....Ouch!" he bumped his head on a heavy chair barring the door to the bedroom, and said, "Oh! My precious May-lin, you're teasing your bridegroom before..."

Clang... Gi then tripped on a basin half-filled with water. He pushed the closed bedroom door hard and shouted, "It's too much. May-lin, don't spoil our wedding night. Open the door NOW!"

May-lin shrieked, "You dare come to my room? If you dare push again, I'll...."

"What's the matter with you? Of course I'll come to OUR room. Are you not my bride? OPEN THE DOOR!" Silence.

Gi Kon-jii stooped down, pushed the bedroom door at the bottom. The door gave in and two chairs leaning against the door inside collapsed. But he jumped aside free, barely avoiding May-lin's saber. He laughed tensely, "Duel first before...."

He gripped May-lin's wrist, trying to relieve her of the saber, but a vicious kick to his eye numbed him. He hit his head on the corner of a heavy dresser. May-lin chopped at him again and somehow he managed to back out the wedding suite.

"Why, do you want to kill me? I'm your husband."

May-lin cried, "Get away. Get away. I don't want...."

Gi Kon-jii stood dumbfounded and at complete loss of what he should do next. Lu Zhi-chun came out holding a lamp and said, "Kon-jii, please be patient. May-lin indeed has a bad temper. Now her grandpa is forced to hide, and she may not be able to see him again for a long time. It's too much for her right now. She will come to terms soon."

"Uncle Lu, I understand. But she should not...." Gi intended to say that May-lin should not chop at him so viciously, but he only said, "All right. I'll be patient." Gi's new pajamas were wet and dirty, and he had one swollen and blackened eye. It looked funny. Lu Zhi-chun smothered a laugh. Master Bo was drunk and exhausted from worry. He did not hear the commotion from his room at the inner court. Others kept quiet even they heard it.

Gi said to the closed door, "May-lin, your grandpa wanted us to get married. Why do you reject me? Besides, you don't think that I, Gi Kon-jii, could find a wife? You're not the only young woman I have met. I do admire you and your skills. I understand your dilemma and I'll be patient." May-lin sobbed even harder. Gi Kon-jii pulled two chairs together to make a temporary bed in the front room and slept.

When he saw May-lin next morning, Gi forgot all his trouble from the night before. He looked at her fondly when Master Bo sent for them.

Master Bo told them, "Now you two, as a young couple, will face the enemy for me. I'm worried about your safety too. By the blessings of the gods, I wish we will see each other again soon."

"Grandpa, don't worry. Don't think that you'll have to hide for long. Think of it as a vacation and have a good time. Don't worry. May-lin and I will win."

Master Bo sighed and handed Gi Kon-jii two sealed envelopes. "The letter writer wrote these two letters for me. This one, you'll give to Uncle Feng. That one...you keep it. When and if he defeats you, GIVE Chiang Shiao-ho the envelope."

"I'll obey your order. Good luck and good-bye."

May-lin said in tears, "Grandpa, Uncle Lu, good-bye. We'll see you soon." She turned back again and again on horseback until she could not see the dejected old man any longer.

9

May-lin had traveled on the same route alone two months ago, and now she rode behind Gi Kon-jii as a wife should. She thought, *"I will see Shiao-ho soon. I will fight him to the death if only he insists on killing grandpa. He can kill the Lung brothers. They are wicked anyway. Somehow I have to let him know how much I miss him yet hate him. I am married now, how can I talk to him alone? How can I tell him I'm not really married yet, it was only a ceremony? How can I tell him something like that? Will he or any other man believe me if I tell him that? What am I going to do?"* Her tears came.

Gi Kon-jii said, "May-lin, why? You're a crying baby. Are you afraid? Honestly I'm afraid, too. You have to be strong to help me fight Chiang Shiao-ho. Now that we are married, I'll tell you the truth that I, alone, can't fight him off. I need your help." no reply.

Gi sighed, "Last night should have been our memorable wedding night. You spoiled it. If I was not patient, we would be eternal foes instead of a newlywed couple. You must understand that I'm not afraid of you. I care for you very much. Now that we are traveling together, I expect you to behave as a wife should, I don't want you to fight me every night and make us laughingstocks. We must be a team when we fight Chiang Shiao-ho. I'll take you to my home and present you to my mother later. Oh! How she wishes to have a grandson soon. I'll go to Beijing to take the civil examination. I promise that you'll be a lady soon."

May-lin pouted, "No more nonsense! You better hurry up." Gi Kon-jii smiled happily at the way May-lin addressed him as "YOU".

At dusk, May-lin insisted that they keep on going. Gi said, "We better find a hotel for the night. We have to cross the Wei River and I'm not sure how late the ferry will run. Besides, even if we could reach

Xian tonight, we have to wait for the city gates to open in the morning."
Reluctantly, May-lin agreed. A raised earthen *kon* (bed), but no table, in
their room. May-lin sat on the bed with her Kung Lung saber beside her.

The innkeeper brought them basins of water to freshen up with. Gi
Kong-jii ordered a meal and wine.

He handed May-lin a cup of wine and said cheerfully, "A toast, and
my precious. Let's have a new beginning." May-lin pushed it away, the
wine spilt all over the bed and Gi's new clothes. He protested, "What's
the matter with you? You could have told me that you don't want it.
You treated me with no respect. Do you loathe me? Do you not want
to be my wife? You know that you don't have to marry me, and I am
sure that I can find another young woman to marry."

May-lin reached her saber and shouted back, "Who's your wife?"

Gi laughed, "You! You're my wife. We were properly married
yesterday. You are my wife, consort and lover." He leaned forward,
wanting to kiss her. But May-lin unsheathed the saber and Gi ducked
immediately, barely having time to avoid his head being chopped off.

'*How dare she treat me this way? I'm going back to Master Bo to
demand an annulment.*' Gi Kon-jii rushed to the stable and started to
saddle his horse. As soon as he put the saddle on, he took it off again.
'*No! I can't do that. We will really be foes. It's true that there are other young
and prettier women who also know martial arts, but where can I find one
as rich and skillful as May-lin. Besides, I can't back out now. All of them
will think that I'm too afraid of Chiang Shiao-ho to marry into Master
Bo's family.*' He went back to their room.

Pushing the door open slowly, Gi told the sobbing May-lin "I know
now that you don't like me, but I don't understand why you married
me. Marriage will not buy my loyalty. It's not only for you that I
voluntarily help the Kung Lung School to fight off Lee Fong-jii and
Chiang Shiao-ho. I do it because I think it is not fair to let some young
upstarts humiliate Master Bo at his age. To tell you the truth, Chiang
Shiao-ho is very good at the deadly '*Tien Hsueh*' skill. I am not. His
running, leaping, and wall climbing skills are all superior to mine, even
though his swordsmanship is not as good as mine." Gi felt his face hot,
he was bragging, "The outcome of the impending fight to the death
between Chiang Shiao-ho and me is anybody's guess. Who knows
which one of us will be killed? If I'm the one to die, I'll have no regrets
since I died for a good cause of defending Master Bo. If by chance I live,

I will go away and grant you the freedom of marrying someone else." May-lin whined, "Who grants you the right to kill Chiang Shiao-ho? He's my family's foe; no need for you to kill him. If you kill him, I'll kill you. I don't want to talk to you."

Gi chuckled first and said seriously after a long sigh, "I don't want to talk to you either. Let's be husband and wife in name only for now. Someday you'll know that I, Gi Kon-jii, am a champion and you're not the only one who is proud." He ate in silence and then slept on the bed apart from May-lin. At midnight, he woke up and saw that the oil lamp was almost out of oil. In the flickering light, May-lin looked extremely attractive and seductive. Gi's heart pumped fast and he reached out his hand ever so slowly, wanting to take May-lin's saber away first and then overpowered her. At that moment, May-lin opened her eyes. Gi pretended that he was dreaming and shouted, "Chiang Shiao-ho!" while moving closer to his unapproachable wife. By then, Gi's head was very close to May-lin's red-embroidered socks and his fingers nearly touched her saber. May-lin moved farther away.

The next morning, Gi deliberately ignored May-lin, but his heart kept pounding at the sight of her grooming with a small mirror. All the way to Feng's guard station at Xian, Gi suppressed his urge to talk to May-lin. He wanted to find a way to make her long for him.

May-lin wore the new matron styled hairdo and a red silk outfit. Uncle Feng welcomed them as a couple. "Congratulations! Now we're truly a family. Good Nephew Gi, did you meet Chiang Shiao-ho? Where are Yu and Chen?" Gi bragged again how he indeed defeated Chiang Shiao-ho and how he rushed to Da-Sam Fort alone to inform Master Bo of Shiao-ho's impending arrival.

Gi complained, "Uncle Chen would not identify him for me. They are afraid of that renegade, and they probably won't come to Xian soon. Uncle Feng, here is a letter Grandpa wanted me to give you." However, Gi Kong-jii did not tell Feng about the other one addressed to Chiang Shiao-ho.

Inside the thick envelope, Feng found a short letter and another unsealed envelope addressed to Chiang Shiao-ho. It briefly stated the hasty marriage that was necessary so that Gi Kon-jii and May-lin could come to Xian together to fight Chiang Shiao-ho. Master Bo also stated that he was not afraid of Shiao-ho's revenge but Lu Zhi-chun and Gi Kon-jii insisted that he should hide somewhere temporarily. Uncle Pan also read the unsealed letter addressed to Shiao-ho. It read, "Shiao-ho, I truly regret killing your father twelve years ago, even though your father did covet his neighbor's wife and deserved to die. Shiao-ho, now you're grown. If you can be understanding and forsake the act of revenge, we can be friends. Otherwise, if you insist on revenge, I am willing to surrender myself if you promise not to harm my students and family. I'm not afraid of fighting you and of being killed."

"We must not give Shiao-ho this letter... We'll...."

"We'll fight Shiao-ho until the very last one of us dies. We will never give him this letter!"

All the uncles and their students shouted in unison their willingness to defend Master Bo. May-lin started to weep.

Feng calmed everyone down and said, "When that villain shows up, we will not fight him at once, we'll let him read this letter...."

Uncle Pan interrupted, "You want our reverent teacher to surrender without a fight?"

Feng argued, "Of course not! We would rather all be killed first before he can reach Master Bo...."

"Why do we have to give him this letter first?"

Feng continued, "It's an order and we must obey. As soon as Shiao-ho comes, we'll show him this letter. Lieu Zhi-an, you are the only one here who knows the past. You tell Shiao-ho the details: his father's immoral behavior, sacrilege and the intolerable insults to Master Bo. I expect that the grown-up Shiao-ho would be reasonable and understanding."

Lieu shouted, "He should remember that Master Bo was kind to him and fed him for a while." May-lin cried, "But Shiao-ho was abused. Whenever he shows up, let me talk to him first. I want to ask him...." Gi Kon-jii wondered, 'May-lin is on his side. Is this why...' he knew that May-lin could not repel his advance in front of all the uncles. He put an arm around her and hugged her.

Feng Zhi-pan said, "Not to worry! I'm very well prepared. I have many friends in high official positions. If Shiao-ho comes, the net will be tight; he'll have no way to escape."

May-lin pleaded urgently, "We should not ask the officials to arrest him. It's not fair."

Gi Kon-jii also argued, "We should not get the law involved."

Feng said, "We're not going to get him arrested right away. We'll talk to him first. But, if he's not reasonable, I'll have to ask for the officials' help. Indeed I value my thirty years of reputation of not involving the officials. But, if it's the last resource to save our Kung Lung School, I'll arrange to have him jailed. If I can't have Shiao-ho beheaded, at least he'll be jailed for life. You'll see."

Pan said, "Put him in jail for a year or so, and he will lose most of his training without proper daily work outs."

Gi Kon-jii said angrily, "Uncles, we can't do that to him or anyone in our circle of martial arts brotherhood. It's not fitting. I will fight him and win or lose the honest way."

May-lin looked at her new husband and thought, *He is righteous. He is better than Uncle Feng and Uncle Pan.*

Feng quickly changed the subject and said, "First, let's celebrate and congratulate the newlyweds. It's a happy event."

All the uncles joined in on the teasing and well wishing. May-lin's cheeks turned flamingly red and she ran to the women's quarters. The usually talkative Gi Kon-jii had something else on his mind. He thanked the uncles and talked excitedly for a while then said he would go to see his uncle. He did not go to his uncle's shop, instead, he went into a blacksmith's with a sign advertising all sorts of weapons that can be forged to specifications. There were sabers, swords, and daggers hanging on the walls of the shop.

"What do you want us to make for you, a sword or a saber?" The storekeeper asked Gi

"Do you have any steel darts?" Gi Kon-jii asked

"No. We don't have steel darts on hand. You have to order them. Which security company sent you to us?"

"Feng's."

"I know everyone who works at Feng's. Oh! You must be the famous Gi Kon-jii. Didn't you go to the East to catch Chiang Shiao-ho? Did you catch him?"

Gi Kon-jii said, "I'm in a hurry. If you don't have steel darts, I'll go somewhere else."

"For you, we have, Master Gi. Please wait. We have some in the back."

He showed Gi a box of assorted steel darts and said, "We forged these twenty years ago. Twelve years ago, Master Bo's son lost a convoy to the bandit Dart Hu Li. All the blacksmith shops in Xian were ordered not to forge and sell any darts." Gi thought, *'he is talking about my father-in-law'*.

He said, "My grandfather, Dragon Knight, was famous for his swordsmanship. Not many know that he was also very good at throwing darts. The darts we use are much better than these. I don't have any with me."

"If you give us the specifications, we can forge them for you."

Gi drew the specification and ordered twenty. He paid the deposit, bought five better darts and a leather-carrying pouch.

There was a huge half-buried stone column with words chiseled on it at an empty lot next to Feng's station. Gi Kon-jii picked up a stone, aimed at a stroke of a word and threw the stone at it. The rock hit the target. He picked other marks and again he hit the target squarely. A crowd gathered to see him throwing stones and cheered every time he hit the target. So he announced his target before each throw and gained more cheers.

A formal banquet was laid out to honor the newly wed. Gi laughed happily, but he was puzzled by May-lin's attitude. She just sat there silently, ate and drank nothing. She looked sad.

Feng's daughter in-law looked tired. She was heavy with child. She tried to be cheerful and congratulated the bride, "Congratulations, Sister Bo," then she whispered, "How was it? If I were you, I would train him to be more considerate of you when he is most mellow now. Give in a little and control a lot. Ah." Red-faced May-lin said, "Please don't tease me. You know that my grandpa arranged this marriage. I'm not...." Barely halting her tears she continued, "Because it's convenient for us to fight Chiang Shiao-ho together."

"You know, it's convenient now but not for long. We women just cannot go out to fight enemies as freely as men can. There will be times when we're just not available." May-lin guessed that her sister-in-law was talking about having a child. She blushed. Somehow, she did not want to go back to their room lest the loathsome Gi would be there. All of a sudden, she sobbed.

"Why? did I say something wrong? Sorry, I'm just joking. I didn't mean to upset you," Feng's daughter-in-law apologized.

May-lin said hurriedly, "No, it's not you. Sorry. It's just that I don't want to marry...." A maid called, "Mistress Gi, Master Gi wants to take you to visit his uncle. The carriage is waiting."

Gi Kon-jii told May-lin, "We're going to visit my mother's only brother, our uncle." Gi's uncle and aunt welcomed the bride and Gi was proud. May-lin remained unapproachable in their room.

Feng invited two officials to dine with him and told them that Chiang Shiao-ho was a thief and asked their help to apprehend him. Chief Ting offered the assistance of his whole detective force and declared, "Unless this Chiang Shiao-ho has six arms and eight legs, he can't get free. I'll have my men ready to come in whenever you sound the alarm." Gi Kon-jii did not agree; he thought a hundred soldiers would not be enough to catch Chiang Shiao-ho. He alone knew Shiao-ho's ability. His only hope lay in the few steel darts he carried. He thought, *'If Chiang Shiao-ho could be here a few days later, I will have my specially ordered darts ready on hand. I'm confident of my accuracy and speed and I'm sure that he can't escape if I had the chance to surprise him.'*

May-lin sat on the bed and brushed her shiny black hair cascading over her shoulders, Gi Kon-jii watched her with aching longing. He dared not make a pass lest May-lin would fight him and make him a laughingstock again. But when May-lin changed her hair back to two thick braids, the style of a maiden, Gi Kon-jii protested, "May-lin. What's the meaning of this? Why did you change your hairstyle? Do you deny that you're married? I demand you to change it back...." but upon seeing the girl's breasts partially revealed through her sheer undershirt, the mesmerized Gi continued, "Well, you sure look pretty this way. I guess it's all right at night when we're alone, but you should wear your hair in the matron style during the day. Otherwise, we'll be laughed at." No reply.

Gi Kon-jii tentatively reached out, took May-lin's hand and asked, "Please tell me why you don't like me. We're married, are we not?" Breaking the silence, Gi continued, "I don't think Chiang Shiao-ho will be here tonight. If he does show up, I won't let him get away again."

May-lin, saber in hand, went out and jumped upon the roof. Gi followed her and they landed on the roof simultaneously.

"Thief! Thief!" an assistant guard on watch duty yelled and struck a gong.

"You fool! It's us. Didn't you see us come out?" Gi slapped the offender. The whole household aroused, and all the guards, Feng, Pan... were out fully armed. Also the town detectives rushed in to help.

"Where's the thief?" "Is anyone injured?"

Feng did not want to admit that it was a false alarm. He told the soldiers, "We heard someone on the roof, but we did not see him. The thief must have run away. Thank you for coming."

Back in their room, Gi Kon-jii opened Master Bo's sealed letter addressed to Shiao-ho, the one he did not give to Feng earlier. It read, "Chiang Shiao-ho, if you would insist on taking revenge, I'm at Ho's farm in Nan-To town, Henan Province. I'm willing to give you my white-haired head if you spare my family and students."

Gi explained the message word by word to May-lin. He said, "Grandpa ordered me to give this letter to Shiao-ho if I am defeated. I won't hand him this letter even if his sword pierces my chest. I'll never reveal grandpa's whereabouts. To tell you the truth, I'm no match for Chiang Shiao-ho. I promised to help you Kung Lung School, and I'll defend you to my death whether you love me or not." He tore the letter into pieces and then burned it, turned around and slept without saying another word. May-lin was touched. Looking at the sleeping Gi, her husband in name only, she thought, '*Why, he meant it. He would fight Chiang Shiao-ho to the death to shield Grandpa and me. Without him, Lee Feng-jii would have injured more Kung Lung members. I'm married to him, but I treat him as an enemy. It's not right.*' She moved closer to Gi, wanting to pour her heart out to him, but a fleeting remembrance overtook her. She sat and wept. Gi Kon-jii heard her but did not comfort her. If he had, she would have succumbed and cried on his shoulder.

A "boom" sounding like a ton of rocks startled everyone. Gi rushed out, sword in hand, ahead of May-lin and the others. A huge stone pole dented the hard packed earthen floor. It was the same one that Gi had practiced throwing his darts on earlier. Gi shouted, "It's him! Chiang Shiao-ho is here!" Everyone could jump were on the roof, Chief Ting and his detectives rushed in to help but found no trace of any intruder.

May-lin noticed that the front hall was dark. '*That's strange!*' She knew that the room stored important document and was always lit and guarded. She entered the room cautiously with her saber ahead of her, but she did not sense any danger. She lit the lamp and started to search under the table with a sense of uncertain and urgent anticipation. No one there.

"What's amiss?" Gi followed in with a torch.

May-lin spotted a long strip of paper with words on it hanging down from the ceiling, and jumped up to reach it. Gi Kon-jii grabbed it first and they each had half of it. She threatened Gi, "Give me the other half! Now!" Gi ran out to the yard with his half. May-lin's half read, "May-lin. Ten years…we ..talk…tomorrow…Shiao" Chiang Shiao-ho wanted to meet her tomorrow, *'But where and when?'* She burned it. Gi's half read, "... morning at Ba Bridge. miss ... ho".

"May-lin, how could you burn it? I'm helping you Kung Lung School to protect Grandpa... Anyway I think that Chiang Shiao-ho wants to fight me tomorrow morning at Ba Bridge." The uncles crowded into the room. Gi Kon-jii quickly tucked the note in a fold of sash tied his pajama.

"Uncles, Chiang Shiao-ho invited me to a duel tomorrow morning at Ba Bridge. He left a message."

"Where's the message?" Uncle Pan asked.

"It sounded rude, so I burned it."

"Too bad! It's a piece of evidence."

Gi said, "Never mind. Chiang Shiao-ho's night skills are truly incomparable. I will depend on my steel darts to defeat him; Too bad. I don't have my special designed ones at hand yet."

"Let's plan then, we could search for him and arrest him for breaking in," Chief Ting continued, "But Chiang Shiao-ho did not commit any major crime. After we've caught him, we can't put him to death legally."

Feng agreed, "Of course we can't hang him. We'll just have to jail him for a few years. He'll lose his skills and strength. That stone post must weigh a ton. He was able to pull it out of the ground, carry it and hop up the roof, and throw it down. His strength alone is frightening enough."

Gi Kon-jii protested strongly, "We can't do this to him. It's cruel. It's not honest. It's against the code of integrity. How could you even think about it? Are we not all brothers of the circle of martial arts warriors?"

"Nephew Gi, you're right. It's just that I am too angry now to think clearly. We'll catch him and then persuade him to forget his revenge. It's getting late. By the way, better keep May-lin out of it. Kon-jii, you should be with May-lin now. Don't let her go out tonight to seek Chiang Shiao-ho on her own," Feng wanted get Gi out of the way so he and Chief Ting, Uncle Pan could plot.

"May-lin, don't cry and don't worry about the duel," back in their room Gi said, "If Shiao-ho defeats me tomorrow, I don't think he will kill me. I think I can talk him out of hurting Grandpa. You stay home tomorrow, and let the Uncles and me handle him." No response.

It was drizzling early next morning. May-lin pretended to be sleeping when Gi Kon-jii covered her with a blanket and left with the Uncles.

It was at Ba Bridge that Gi Kon-jii helped the Kung Lungs repel Lee Feng-jii not too long ago.

It was misty at Ba Bridge, only a few pedestrians holding umbrellas. Uncle Feng said, "We're here too early."

Lieu said, "It might be a trick to get us here, or he's afraid to come."

Pan said, "He is not afraid. If Chiang Shiao-ho could throw that heavy stone post last night, he's not afraid of us. Let's wait at tea house over there." The teahouse was crowded with husky farmers, fishermen with long hooks, and armed travelers. They were Chief Ting's detectives and solders in disguise. Feng and Pan exchanged a knowing smile. Gi Kon-jii did not notice it. He touched the pouch containing the five steel darts. His eyes were glued on the two ends of the Ba Bridge and he was ready.

Chief Ting dressed as a rich merchant carrying a birdcage. He whispered to Feng, "The net is complete and the surrounding area is all covered. The renegade can't get away unless he has wings. Chiang Shiao-ho checked in a hotel in the west section of Xian, but he did not go back to his room last night. We'll catch ...."

A tall young rider with a wide-brimmed hat got on the Ba Bridge from the east. "It's him. It is Chiang Shiao-ho!" Lieu recognized Shiao-ho. Gi Kon-jii was already on the bridge. Chief Ting slipped away. Gi Kon-jii told Feng urgently, "Be careful and don't make a hasty move. Chiang Shiao-ho swims well, if he jumps into the river, there are no way we can ever catch him."

"Brother Gi, nice to meet you again," Shiao-ho greeted Gi Kon-jii friendlily.

"Brother Chiang, let's start the duel right away. We could fight on horseback or on foot. You choose."

"A duel? Who set it up? Ah, that's why you came with bodyguards."

"You did. You left a note last night, did you not? Don't pretend that you did not, coward!"

"I did, but I did not invite you."

"Did you not write the message to invite me here to fight? Don't lie."

"I certainly did write the note and it's not for a fight, and I did not invite you!"

"Whom? Whom did you invite?"

"Bo May-lin. I invited her here today. It's not your, or anyone else's business."

"Of course it's my business. She's my wife." Gi Kon-jii advanced and slashed at the suddenly paled Shiao-ho furiously. Shiao-ho blocked Gi's thrusts, and then Feng, Pan and the whole Kung Lung gang joined in to fight Chiang-Shiao-ho.

May-lin was on the bridge from the west. Shiao-ho saw her and called, "Stop, all of you! I'll fight you all after I have a talk with Miss Bo." He blocked Gi's sword thrusts and forced back all his attackers.

They met at the middle of the bridge. Shiao-ho's cracked voice trembled when he greeted May-lin, whose hair was in braids, "Miss Bo, ten years is a long time. Do you still remember me?" The drizzle turned into rain. May-lin was pale, her eyes wide with tears, but she could not cry. Her mouth was agape, her lips quivered, but no words came. She sat stiffly on the horse and her whole body tensed. The rain poured down her hair, her face, but she did not move. She just stared at Shiao-ho and he stared at her. Gi Kon-jii and the others were there in between them. Their silence and their grief-stricken looks mesmerized everyone around, for a while no one moved.

Then Gi Kon-jii thrust again but Chiang Shiao-ho blocked it. The sound of the two swords clanging together broke the spell. All of the Kung Lung gang and soldiers ganged up and charged at Chiang Shiao-ho with all kind of weapons. May-lin's shrill voice pierced the air. "Stop! All of you! Uncle Feng, Gi Kon-jii...stop! I'll ask him."

"Yes, May-lin. We have to talk. It's between our families. It has nothing to do with the others," Shiao-ho blocked the attacks from all sides.

"May-lin is my wife. Chiang Shiao-ho, it's not fitting for you to talk to her. You can't insult me. She is my wife. I'll kill you, or I'll die first," Gi Kon-jii shouted and attacked savagely.

"But... your hair... May-lin, is it true? You're married? But you wear your hair in braids. You and I better have a talk first and sort things out. It's been ten years and I've a lot to say. After you hear me out, then we can decide whether I should seek revenge or not," Shiao-ho said coarsely.

"Shiao-ho, I want to talk to you about...the past ten years. Let's talk. Let's go there." She turned her horse around and rode to the grassy field under the bridge. Chiang Shiao-ho rode behind her. No weapons could stop him.

"May-lin, YOU are my wife. I forbid you to talk to him. Chiang Shiao-ho, you are morally wrong" Gi was furious and he kept on attacking Chiang Shiao-ho.

"Wait, Let them talk, we'll...." Feng Zhi-pan held the enraged Gi back with force. "Let them have a talk." He signaled everyone with his eyes.

"Miss Bo, don't talk to him. It's not fitting. You have a husband," someone shouted. Chiang Shiao-ho and May-lin rode fast. Gi Kon-jii aimed and threw a steel dart at Shiao-ho's back but Shiao-ho dodged it. Gi threw another dart, Shiao-ho caught it with two fingers. When the third dart sped toward him, Shiao-ho tossed the dart in his hand and knocked the third dart down.

"Gi Kon-jii, you have more?" Shiao-ho did not slow down.

Chief Tong's men waited. They let May-lin's horse pass and attacked Shiao-ho from all sides with long sharp hooks. Three of them hooked onto the legs of the horse and one hooked onto Shiao-ho's right arm. With his left hand, Shiao-ho pulled the hook out. It came out with a chuck of flesh and a stream of blood. He jumped free from the falling horse, dodged two rapid darts. The Kung Lung gang now surrounded him for the kill.

"No!" Gi Kon-jii shouted. He slashed at the hooks and cut a few in half.

May-lin heard the noise and turned around and saw that wounded Shiao-ho was in danger. Shiao-ho had already chopped down Lieu and Pan. He ran toward May-lin on foot, Gi was in hot pursuit on horseback.

"Uncle Feng, Please stop the soldiers! Don't you see that he is injured? Please stop," May-lin pleaded.

"It's an ambush. I despise you," Shiao-ho shouted and he pierced Gi Kon-jii, knocked Gi down from the horse, he then jumped onto Gi's horse and galloped passed May-lin's horse. He looked at her with anger and accusation, since he thought that she was a part of the plot to trick him. "Shiao-ho, wait!" May-lin kept on calling. She cried.

Shiao-ho shouted back, "You, you set up an ambush to capture me. May-lin, you forget our pledge. You help them to trap me. You are the bait...."

"Shiao-ho, I swear I did not know about the ambush. Wait! Come back! I swear."

Chiang Shiao-ho spurred Gi's horse, and overran all of his pursuers.

They gathered around the three wounded: Gi Kon-jii, Lieu and Pan. None of the three had serious wounds. Gi Kon-jii suffered a bloody flesh wound inside his left thigh. He shouted, "May-lin, why do you want to talk to him? See, my blood is red like the color of your wedding robe. But, I have no regret. I'll defend you and the Kung Lung School again; someday I'll cut and wound Chiang Shiao-ho deeper."

"Kon-jii, take it easy. Chief Ting and his men will surely catch Chiang Shiao-ho. He is bleeding, and his wound might be serious. He can't run too far." May-lin worried about the injured Shiao-ho, and at the same time, she worried about Gi Kon-jii's wound, too.

"Kon-jii, we'll seek the best doctor," May-lin comforted Gi Kon-jii.

"It's nothing. It's just a flesh wound. Don't worry. But May-lin, why did you want to talk to him?" Gi moaned. No reply.

Then Gi Kon-jii blamed Uncle Feng, "You set the ambush, a dirty trick. shame on you Kung Lung school." Feng Zhi-pan said nothing.

Chief Ting came to Feng's at lunch hour. "Did you catch the renegade?" Feng asked.

"No way! He is the most cunning and slippery man I've met in my twenty years on duty. He is a master of horsemanship. Gi Kon-jii's horse is an ordinary one, but Chiang Shiao-ho turns it into a champion. We chased him through forests, across rivers yet somehow he shook us off and disappeared in thin air. How could he know this area better than my men? Don't worry, we'll catch him tonight if he shows up." Chief Ting reported.

"Ahe! He's free! We'll have endless trouble now. I'm sure of it," Feng whined.

10

Feng asked Uncle Lieu, "Lu is not here. Only you and Chen know about the past. Was there anything between Shiao-ho and May-lin ten years ago?"

"I'm not sure. But, it sure does not look right the way they looked at each other on the bridge this morning. Ten years ago, Shiao-ho was fourteen and May-lin was twelve. They played together often."

"Ahe! They were not adults, but they were not children either."

"They were very young. Ahe! I remember now. May-lin hates Chiang Shiao-ho. She gnashed her teeth and cursed him when Chiang Shiao-ho led Master Hsu to challenge Master Bo. I saw it with my own eyes. It also seems to me that May-lin and Gi Kon-jii is a loving couple. You worry too much."

"I hope you're right," Feng was not convinced.

In the evening, Feng went to Gi and May-lin's room. He stood outside the window and asked, "May-lin, is Kon-jii better? Dr. Lee's preparation should help. Don't get up and open the door for me. I won't stay."

"Uncle Feng, Gi's sleeping. Is there something important?"

"I'm coming to tell you and Kon-jii not to worry; there are a dozen soldiers here to help us tonight. Besides, Chiang Shiao-ho was injured and he lost a lot of blood. He dares not come tonight."

"Uncle Feng, come in. I'm awake. I'm waiting for Chiang Shiao-ho. He'll come tonight, wounded or not, because he has to find out whether May-lin and I are married or not. A hundred detectives can't stop him, or an ambush. I'm ready to fight him again. May-lin, I order you to put your hair up right now!" Gi Kon-jii pretended he was not in pain and continued, "When he comes, I'll deal with him."

Uncle Feng was surprised to see May-lin started to change her hair style. And thought, *'She did obey Gi's order. Maybe she will be a good wife from now.'*

May-lin actually worried about both Gi Kon-jii's and Chiang Shiao-ho's injuries. She felt wretched with regrets that she had treated Gi Kon-jii like dirt. She respected Gi's gallantry to defend her family even though he knew he would be wounded or even killed. She also noticed that Gi Kon-jii actually fought against the soldiers with the hooks. It was obvious that Gi strongly disapprove Uncle Feng's treachery. He was righteous. She truly worried about Gi's wound, and decided that she will be nice to him from now on. *'We are women and we don't have any say about our future, about how we want to live or to whom we want to marry. Some women will take their wild dreams and wishes silently to their graves,"* her mother told her before, and now she must accept this arranged marriage. But she also kept seeing Shiao-ho's bleeding right arm with a chuck of dangling torn flesh. She thought, *'It's his right arm. Is he disabled? He was mad at me. He thought I played a part in the ambush. He probably hates me now. I know he has not forgotten our pledge under the willow tree. He obviously did not know that Grandpa coerced me to marry Gi. Besides, how could he know that Gi and I merely completed the ceremony? I am not Gi's wife in reality. How can I tell him...?."* She wept.

Feng inspected the security everywhere. He felt a rain drop and wished that it would pour so that Shiao-ho wouldn't come. With a yawn he told Lieu to take over the watch and retired to the room he used as an occasional bedroom in the frontcourt. Sitting on his bed, he took off one shoe and saw a hand holding a sword reach out from under the bed. Feng yelled and tried to run but Shiao-ho pushed him back on the bed.

Lieu heard Feng's shouts and asked, "Brother Feng, is something wrong?"

Shiao-ho's sword was at Feng's throat. Feng called, "It's nothing. I'm all right. Good Night."

"Feng Zhi-pan, I don't want to hurt you or anyone else. I only want some information. Then I'll leave." Shiao-ho said.

"I'll tell you, but you will have to free me first."

Feng got up and sighed, "Shiao-ho, you don't have any grievance against me...."

"No grievance against you? If my teacher had not rescued me and scared you stiff ten years ago, you would have me dead. Never mind, it's not important now. I'll only kill my father's murderers. That's all. Tell me now! Is it true that May-lin is married? Where is Master Bo? Chen lied to me; he said that Master Bo is here, but he isn't. Tell me the truth now. Where are old Bo and the Lung brothers? Tell me NOW!"

"The younger brother is at home. The older one-Lung Zhi-chi, he is the real killer, was here a few days ago; I don't know where he is now. That's the truth. Master Bo is in hiding at one of his old friends' place. May-lin is married. She said that her Grandpa did not want her to know where he went. That's the truth."

"How convenient. Feng Zhi-pan, I'll...."

"Wait, Shiao-ho! There's a letter from Master Bo addressed to you. I kept it in the front hall. I'll get it for you."

"I want to read it. We'll go together. You're my shield. You should understand that I'm not afraid of however many fighters you have out there, but I don't want to harm anyone unnecessarily, especially the soldiers. Let's go!"

There were many soldiers on the roof with long hooks, and guards with weapons crowded the courtyard.

"Feng Zhi-pan, don't worry! You're the buffer. They dare not attack me, and I promise that I won't harm you. Go!"

"Everyone listen to me! Listen! Chiang Shiao-ho only wants to read Master Bo's letter," Feng handed a string of keys to Lieu, "It's in the big chest. The front hall. Hurry!"

May-lin hid behind a door and watched the unruffled Shiao-ho and decided, '*Grandpa's pathetic letter begs for Shiao-ho's forgiveness. I'll wait and see. If Shiao-ho is moved and forsakes his revenge, I will go to him and pour my heart out to him. I'll even tell him that I'm still a maiden.*' she forgot her resolution to be nice to Gi Kon-jii a moment ago.

"Chiang Shiao-ho, here it is. I'll ask Pan to read it aloud."

"Please do! I have to guard against any contingent ambush or steel darts." Master Bo's plea in his letter moved May-lin to tears. From the mist she saw Shiao-ho's expression change from melancholy to anger.

"Master Bo is cunning, isn't he? Now he begs for mercy. When my father sneaked back home and gulped down cold rice before his escape, Master Bo did_not pity him and hunted him down like an animal. Twelve years ago, he did not pity my father. How can he ask me to forgive him now? No! I won't. Master Bo made me and my infant brother orphans, used me as a servant and allowed his son to abuse me.

He also waited in the wheat field to kill me. How can I be forgiving? No way!" Shiao-ho's hatred was naked for everyone to see.

"Chiang Shiao-ho, I'll kill you first." May-lin rushed in and slashed at him.

"Wait. You helped them to ambush me this morning and now you want to kill me. I can't believe that you have turned into such a fraud. I don't know you anymore." Shiao-ho blocked her saber.

Gi Kon-jii rushed to fight Shiao-ho, and all of them joined the melee. Shiao-ho wounded a few and seized the sabers from May-lin and Pan, and also the sword from Gi' Kon-jii. Then May-lin rushed at his sword hysterically. Shiao-ho repelled the others with his injured right arm and swept up the struggling May-lin with his left arm and jumped upon the roof.

He shouted, "Stop! I don't want to hurt anyone unnecessarily. I'll...."

"Chiang Shiao-ho, set my wife free, I'll...." The wounded Gi tried to leap onto the roof too. He couldn't and fell.

"May-lin, I'll take you somewhere. I know you're married now and I just want to talk to you for the very last time. Ough, . Don't...."

May-lin bit down hard on the arm holding her and cried, "Let me go! How dare you insult me like this. I don't want to talk to you. I hate you. You want to kill my grandpa. How can I not hate you? Let me go!"

Shiao-ho released the girl and escaped through a maze of hooks and throwing darts.

Feng Zhi-pan gathered everyone two days later and said, "It's no use to keep up the tight security anymore. Chiang Shiao-ho could come and go at will. Now I know why Master Bo is afraid of him. However, he did make it clear that he'll kill no one but Master Bo and the Lung brothers. We will thank Chief Ting and make sure that his soldiers are compensated properly."

Uncle Pan said, "Now Shiao-ho knows that Lung Zhi-chi was the killer and Brother Lung probably found a safe place to hide already. I suggest that we let May-lin lead us to see Master Bo. If Master Bo wants to fight, all our Kung Lung members will fight Chiang Shiao-ho to the death. If Master Bo wants to hide, we'll accompany him to Beijing. The Manchu Emperor won't allow anyone to get away with killing. We will be safe there,"

Uncle Feng disagreed, "No, we can't go to Master Bo's hiding place. What if Chiang Shiao-ho follows us there? I bet that bastard is just waiting for us to lead him to Master Bo. It seems to me that Chiang Shiao-ho is not short of silver; he can afford to watch us and wait. We better stay put for a while and let him search for Master Bo. China is a big country." Feng did not tell them that he had asked a friend to offer Shiao-ho a lot of silver and a top paying guard position. Chiang Shiao-ho politely refused but said again that he would only kill his father's murderers.

Gi Kon-jii's injury worsened. The continuous rain and his impatience were no help either. He loathed the way Feng had bribed the officials to help, and he could not make anyone believe that he honestly did not know the plot. *'Now everyone, especially Chiang Shiao-ho, will certainly despise me. All of them will think that I'm a deceitful coward. I have blemished my grandpa's good name. This marriage is a sham and my greed had led me blind into it. Every one of the Kung Lung school, except Uncle Lu Zhi-chun, had convinced me that Chiang Shiao-ho is truly a villain. But now I think he is a man of standards. He could have killed me over and over again but he only teased me. He definitely has the right to be angry with me because of these stupid 'Chiang Shiao-ho -- wanted' posters. On Ba Bridge, he could have easily cut off my whole leg in anger when he had thought that I was a part of the ambush. If I had not gotten mixed up with the Kung Lung gang, I may have had the opportunities to make two new friends: - Lee Feng-jii and Chiang Shiao-ho.'* He moaned and cursed in pain.

May-lin now acutely felt Gi Kon-jii's pain as her own pain. She resented that Chiang Shiao-ho had insulted her in front of the others and wrongly accused her of participating the ambush at the Ba Bridge. *'He took advantage of me when I was twelve. He knew then that I wanted the kite, and tricked me into calling him 'my husband'. That's blackmail."* She felt that her anger and hatred toward Chiang Shiao-ho was justified. Somehow her justified anger did not last. She couldn't get him out of her mind. She missed his sad look and the feel of his arm holding her. *'Why did I bite his arm? He said that he wanted to take me somewhere to talk and it will be the last time. Didn't I want to talk to him, too? I wanted to tell him my feelings and that I'm not really married. He would believe me. Maybe I can talk him out of revenge and then I'll go away with him. Oh! I missed the opportunity to talk to him. No! How about Gi Kong-jii? I could not do this to him. Gi is a good man, a little flamboyant perhaps. He yelled at Feng for setting up a wicked trap to catch Shiao-ho. I wish someone could tell me what to do."*

Gi Kon-jii groaned in his drugged sleep. She went closer to him and Gi Kon-jii jerked himself awake to subdue a moan.

"Kon-jii, do you feel a bit better now? Does the medicine help?"

"Don't worry. I won't die, and I'll fight him again. Now I understand that you and he were sweethearts. You stared at each other at the Ba Bridge, and he carried you up to the roof tonight. I'm a fool. I'll go and ask Master Bo to release me from this miserable false marriage. I come from a good family, and I'm sure that I can find another wife. But, I will fight Chiang Shiao-ho. He insulted me and I cannot live with the shame."

May-lin wanted to tell Gi Kon-jii the past - how her uncle abused Chiang Shiao-ho, and how the proud boy had silently taken it all, how her pity gradually turned into love and their childish pledge of marriage. But she could not bring herself to tell Gi Kon-jii or anyone about it. *No, it's too embarrassing to tell anyone my deepest feelings. Besides, Grandpa adamantly prohibited an affair between a man and a woman. Isn't it the very misconduct that caused Shiao-ho's father be killed? Grandpa will die from fury if he knows that I secretly love Shiao-ho, an enemy. Now he thinks that I'm truly married and he will consider it as adultery. He might kill me. No, I can't tell Gi Kon-jii or anyone else.*

"You're wrong. How could I love an enemy? I cried this morning because I was angry and ashamed that I couldn't beat him off. He insulted me tonight and I can't do anything about it. He is tougher and stronger than all of us. That's all."

"He is super, isn't he? I admit that his leaping skills and strength are superior. If I'm well and I have the specially designed steel darts, I believe that I might have a better chance of winning."

"You can't spread rumors that I love him. I forbid you."

"I won't, May-lin. It's too shameful for me to mention it. If it's true like you said, that you don't have any feelings for Chiang Shiao-ho, I want to know why you don't love me as your husband. Many marriages are arranged and most brides never met their bridegrooms. After they are married, the wife will love her husband any way. We knew each other a while before we're married. After the ceremony, you have never allowed me to be close to you and to be your husband. I want to know why you dislike me that much. If I had not been injured today from defending you Kung Lung School, would you still ignore me and not talk to me. Why?"

"Grandpa coerced me to marry you. I did not want to marry anyone, and I just want to stay with Grandpa. My mother died when I was fifteen and since then I have been very close to Grandpa. That's all."

"It's too bad. Chiang Shiao-ho won't let your Grandpa live. Besides me, you can't find another fool who is willing to die to defend you. We may as well consider each other strangers from now on. Good night."

Gi Kon-jii's biting remarks infuriated May-lin. *'It's no use to depend on Gi Kon-jii, an outsider. We have to face our problems ourselves. Grandpa's cruelty deserves retribution anyway. It's not worth living under the constant fear of Chiang Shiao-ho and now the contempt from Gi Kon-jii.'* She decided that she would go to her grandpa's hiding place alone the next day, and then together they would face their peril and death honorably.

It drizzled again early next morning when May-lin wanted to leave before the others were up. Gi Kon-jii was not awake, but he was frowning and moaning in pain. Looking at him, May-lin hesitated. *'Whether I like him or not does not change the fact that he's my husband, and he was injured because he wanted to protect my family. I can't leave him without having a discussion with him first. Besides, if I go to Grandpa alone, he will be angry with me, and he will order me back here.'* She dawdled a while, and then the whole household woke up.

"May-lin, a cup of tea," Gi Kon-jii murmured.

"Here it is." May-lin carefully put the cup close to Gi Kon-jii's mouth and waited on Gi tenderly.

"Thank you. May-lin, please forgive me. I shouldn't have made those awful remarks last night. I love you so much and I'm afraid of losing you. I let jealousy get in the way. Now I think the way you stared at him was because you wanted to accuse him for your family's peril. Chiang Shiao-ho has been your family's enemy for a long time. He induced Master Hsu's attack on your family ten years ago and Grandpa beat Master Hsu. You know what I believe? I think that Grandpa's skills could be actually higher than that renegade's. Master Bo's fear is from his old age, and he is actually afraid of Chiang Shiao-ho's omnipotent teacher, that's all. With help and encouragement from both of us, Grandpa may very well defeat Chiang Shiao-ho. Last night, I was out of my right mind. I was frustrated, and I was rude last night. I'm sorry."

May-lin blushed and felt wretched that she simply couldn't forget Chiang Shiao-ho and be Gi Kon-jii's wife. Ten years ago when Chiang

Shiao-ho and Master Hsu came to challenge Master Bo, she truly hated him then. Later, she missed him and pitied him all the time. Yesterday morning when she and Chiang Shiao-ho had their painful reunion, their longing for each other overwhelmed her. She knew that she loved Chiang Shiao-ho and she was sure that Chiang Shiao-ho truly loved her. Her anger at Chiang Shiao-ho's improper action was real but short lived. Chiang Shiao-ho's sad expression and his handsome face haunted her, and her feelings for Chiang Shiao-ho have become a permanent barrier between Gi Kon-jii and her. She felt guilty, and so she talked extra nicely and tenderly to Gi Kon-jii.

May-lin wished that Uncle Lu were here in Xian. She would tell Uncle Lu the strong love between Chiang Shiao-ho and her without any reservation. She would even boldly tell Uncle Lu the fact that she had never gone to bed with Gi Kon-jii. Uncle Lu might find a way to end this phony marriage. Uncle Lu might be able to convince Chiang Shiao-ho that killing the Lung brother would be enough to avenge his father's death. Then she and Chiang Shiao-ho could get married and live happily ever after like a happy ending of a story.

11

Chiang Shiao-ho was thinking and wishing Uncle Lu was here, too. Uncle Lu and Uncle Ma had protected him and in many ways had kept him alive ten years ago. Sometimes, Uncle Lu would slap or yell at him first in Bo Zhi-lin's presence. Chiang Shiao-ho hated Uncle Lu then until one day Uncle Ma told him, "Shiao-ho, Bo Zhi-lin was very jealous of your father. He insisted that you be killed lest you would avenge your father's death when you grow up. We all knew that your life was in danger. Uncle Lu hit and punished you whenever you did something wrong. He wanted to protect you whenever there might be a cause for the sadistic Bo Zhi-lin to severely punish you or kill you. He tried his best to make sure you weren't alone with Bo Zhi-lin." Chiang Shiao-ho will never forget how Uncle Lu had helped him to escape. Now he thought, '*I could tell Uncle Lu of my love for May-lin. Not a day has gone by in the last ten years that I did not think about May-lin and our secret pledge of love. It hurt so much when I knew that Gi Kon-jii married her. I was so jealous and I had behaved improperly. Now I cannot talk to May-lin anymore and I'm sure that she must hate me now since I wounded her husband. I can ask Uncle Lu to tell May-lin that I'm truly sorry. Uncle Lu can tell her that I won't bother her any more. I can also seek Uncle Lu's advice on the matter of revenge.*' Chiang Shiao-ho stayed in his hotel room all the time. He could not eat and he could not sleep. May-lin was forever lost to him. This kind of pain felt even worse than his injured arm and all the beating he got ten years ago.

Nothing happened for a couple of days and Feng Zhi-pan relaxed a little. A friend of Feng's brought him some of his family's secret preparation to treat Gi Kon-jii and Pan. This friend also mentioned that he had information that Lee Feng-jii might be back in Xian soon.

Gi Kon-jii collected his specially ordered steel darts and started practice before he was fully recovered. He was happy that May-lin was finally nice to him.

Feng visited the young couple one evening. He told them, "Lee Feng-jii and Chiang Shiao-ho marred Kung Lungs' reputation. Lately, we have had hardly any customers come to buy our protection. Everyone knows that Master Bo was forced to hide from Chiang Shiao-ho. How can anyone trust us to escort their valuables? We may as well close our business.

"Uncle Feng, you're right. Grandpa should not hide. Now we don't know whether he's well or not. Sooner or later, Chiang Shiao-ho will find him. It will be better if I go and ask him to come out. We will fight that renegade together," May-lin said.

"No, we should not let Master Bo face the danger. His hiding place is very secure and it won't be easy for Chiang Shiao-ho to find him," Feng said.

Gi Kon-jii said, "All of us will stand and help Grandpa to fight Chiang Shiao-ho. But his hiding from Chiang Shiao-ho is not good for business. We can't let this affair drag on too long. Uncle Feng, you're rich, but a lot of your employees will starve if all the Kung Lung Security Stations close their doors."

"Right! Uncle Feng, you can't close your station. We just can't let Grandpa's thirty years of accomplishments fade away." May-lin said.

"I don't really mean that I'll close the security station. I just want to be fully prepared to face Chiang Shiao-ho. There is no information about his whereabouts lately. We're not sure the elder Brother Lung is still alive, or Teacher Master Bo... I'll go to Han-Chun City soon," Uncle Feng said.

May-lin asked, "Why?"

"I'd like to ask your father to be our leader. We'll gather all the Kung Lung members and friends together to fight Chiang Shiao-ho."

Gi Kon-jii said, "Bravo! My father-in-law should be the one to lead us to fight. We'll go with you"

Gi Kon-jii was riding in a carriage at the beginning of the trip. He was impatient with the slow pace and insisted on riding. The almost healed wound on his inner thigh ruptured. When they stopped at an inn on the first night of the trip, Feng had to help Gi Kon-jii dismount and get to bed.

May-lin's mind was in turmoil. She started to get used to being married, and they would be a real couple when Gi Kon-jii got fully recovered. But she was not sure that she could ever forget her first love and the pledge under the willow tree.

"May-lin, don't worry about my wound. It will be healed soon. You look tired. Don't fuss about me. I'm fine. You better go to sleep. We will get up early tomorrow," Gi Kon-jii said. He looked at May-lin with all the love he could express. He was happy and he did not know anything about May-lin's troubled thoughts.

"I'm not sleepy yet," May-lin said and rearranged Gi Kon-jii's pillow.

She heard someone outside the window sigh softly. She opened the door quickly. Gi Kon-jii struggled to get up, readied his sword, stood beside her protectively. They only saw some other travelers sleeping on the ground under the bright moon. It was cooler outside.

"May-lin, did you see someone? Hear something?"

"I'm not sure."

Gi Kon-jii spotted a black form on the roof across from where he stood. He threw a dart at it. "Mew!" He hit a black cat and the dead cat fell off the roof and landed on the ground. Someone cursed. With difficulty, Gi Kon-jii walked over and collected his dart from the dead cat. He apologized sincerely for the disturbance. Gi did not know that he had changed and now he was nicer and more considerate to others.

They reached Lu Zhi-chum's security station at Da-Sam Fort two days later.

"Uncle Lu how is Grandpa?" May-lin asked anxiously.

"Let's get Kon-jii comfortable first. I'll tell you after supper," Lu said.

"How is Grandpa? I want to know now," May-lin once again asked as soon as they had helped Gi Kon-jii to bed. She sat beside Gi on the bed and the uncles sat around the table.

"May-lin, promise me that you won't cry. Master Bo and I got to Ho's ranch safely. Mister Ho is over eighty. Ho prayed to the Buddha all day long and his two sons were in charge. There are grandchildren too. They were all rude to us. Master Bo decided to leave and ordered me not to follow him. I tried, but he insisted that he would go to Szechwan alone to visit his old friend Master Lee. I got back two days ago."

"But, Master Hsu is in Szechwan. He's no friend of ours," May-lin sobbed.

"I don't think Master Hsu will harm Master Bo. I believe Grandpa wants to fight Chiang Shiao-ho alone. That damned Chiang Shiao-ho has forced Grandpa_become homeless. We'll...." Gi Kon-jii said. He struggled to sit up and put his arm around May-lin's trembling shoulders.

"I can't take it any longer! I'm going to find Grandpa and we'll fight Chiang Shiao-ho together. Kon-jii! Sorry, I can't wait for you to get well," May-lin shrieked. Gi Kon-jii held May-lin's hand.

"May-lin, calm down! Master Bo knows Szechwan well. He...." Lu Zhi-chun said.

"Grandpa has not set foot there for thirty years. He is too old to travel alone. Besides, Master Hsu is Chiang Shiao-ho's first teacher. He'll detain Grandpa for Chiang Shiao-ho."

"May-lin, Master Hsu won't do something like that. He was grateful that Master Bo had spared his life ten years ago."

"I will fight Master Hsu if he would act against us." Gi Kon-jii said.

Finally May-lin stopped crying, but Uncle Lu and Feng were afraid that May-lin would leave alone during the night again, and they dared not sleep until just before dawn. May-lin sneaked out at dawn and rode fast on the deserted mountain pass.

"May-lin! May-lin!" Uncle Lu caught up and said, "Let's go back. You can't travel Tu-Nan Mountain Range alone from this side. So many trails branch out from the main one, you will get lost and you may wander a month and still cannot find your way out of the mountains. Besides, Dart Hu Li and his two sons have been very active lately. They knew that we Kung Lung had met defeat."

"Please don't force me to go back, Uncle Lu. I'm worried to death about Grandpa. He is old and should not be alone."

"I'm sure Master Bo is safe. Please come back with me. When Gi Kon-jii's leg is better, I'll go with you two."

"Uncle Lu, I know you care about my safety. Why can't you accompany me?"

"I have no weapon and no silver. You wait here! I will go back to get them."

"I'm not a child anymore. Don't think you can stall me. Besides, if you go back, Gi Kon-jii will insist on coming, and he will slow us down. I have some silver. When we get to my father's place, we'll have more silver."

"Let's hurry then. May-lin, when we meet with Chiang Shiao-ho, I can talk him out of wanting revenge. Ten years ago, I had pointed out the right route for him to escape. You see, May-lin, I'm his father's sworn brother, and I did not think that his father deserved to be hunted down and killed like an animal. I did not want Chiang Shiao-ho be killed when he was only fourteen years old. Later, I helped him to escape from Lung Zhi-chi again. I have saved Chiang Shiao-ho twice. He will listen to me." They rode through increasing heat until they were almost out of the mountain range.

"Uncle Lu, where can we find some water?"

"Not so loud. Soon we'll be at my friend's place. We can rest a while there. I'm going to ask my friend to send a message to Feng and Gi Kon-jii. They must be worried about us.

When they were close to the check point where Dart Hu Li's bandits guarded the pass to the next peak, Uncle Lu warned, "May-lin, be careful now! Our arch enemy Dart Hu Li controlled this mountain area. He's deadly accurate at throwing darts and he wounded your father twelve years ago." May-lin thought Uncle Lu was too cautious. She was not afraid of the bandits, but she did not want an encounter that might delay them. So she kept quiet and followed Lu obediently. Lu was both amazed and sad to see that the once spirited yet spoiled May-lin had suddenly matured. *'Poor child, she has gone through a lot lately. I wish that she could confide in me and tell me her true feelings about Shiao-ho. Feng told me what had happened when Shiao-ho and May-lin met at Xian. It's the first time they saw each other in ten years. I had my suspicions when I noticed that she honestly did not want to marry Gi Kon-jii. She rejected him on their wedding night. Oh, that's something even a father cannot ask his own daughter. If she had told me the truth, I might have talked to Master Bo about it. A marriage between Shiao-ho and May-lin will absolutely dissolve the animosity between them. Then the Kung Lung School would be number one again for sure. Ah! It's wishful thinking. Anyway it's too late now. May-lin is married. I noticed that she's quite attentive to Gi's wound.*

Hu Li's second son ogled May-lin openly and blocked the narrow passage with his men. He said, "Bo May-lin is gorgeous, I only want to ask her to have a drink with me. Is anything wrong with it? It does not mean that I want to bed her...." May-lin cut off his right shoulder and arm. Hu Jr. died instantly. She also killed Black Bear, another Bandits leader. Uncle Lu urged, "Hurry, the whole gang will be here soon." The dead man's brother threw steel darts at May-lin and Lu but missed, Uncle Lu slashed off his two fingers. Dart Hu Li came and the first dart he threw lodged in May-lin's right shoulder. Dart Hu Li threatened, "Lu Zhi-chun, I order you to fetch Master Bo and May-lin's father here to see me in five days. On the sixth day if they are not here, I'll cut off this wicked woman's head and send it to her father."

"Your son insulted my niece first. She's Gi Kon-jii's wife. Your son should not have insulted a married woman," Lu Zhi-chun argued.

"Don't threaten me with Gi Kon-jii's name. I'm not afraid of Dragon Knight Gi's grandson. I demand that Gi Kon-jii accompany the Bos, father and son, here with one thousand ounces of silver and kowtow to my sons' caskets. Black Bear was also a son to me. I'll extend the time to ten days," Dart Hu Li continued, "Hurry! It's good enough that I spare your life." Lu watched helplessly as the bandits dragged May-lin away. He met Gi and Uncle Feng.

"Where's May-lin?" Gi Kon-jii shouted from afar; he could not ride fast.

"May-lin killed Dart Hu Li's son and a lieutenant. Hu Li wounded her with a dart and captured her. They took her up the peak."

His defeat at Chiang Shiao-ho's hand, his wound and now his wife's capture drove Gi Kon-jii mad.

"Nephew Gi, be patient! They've got May-lin and they may kill her," Lu Zhi-chun warned Gi Kon-jii, "Hu Li's darts are deadly accurate."

Gi Kon-jii said angrily, "Who's afraid of his darts. I have darts too."

It was decided that Uncle Feng and Gi go up hill with no weapons to negotiate, not fight. Uncle Lu would wait.

They rode up the winding path. Feng whispered, "This peak is named Hawk Fall, meaning even the hawk can't fly up to its top. With his unerring darts, Hu Li and his men have held it for over thirty years. Even the Manchu Army could not dislodge him. More than two hundred desperadoes are up there. If a fight begins, the two of us won't have a chance to survive and May-lin will die for sure." He continued, "Don't worry! Nobody dares touch May-lin, or even look at her for now. Dart Hu Li and Master Bo both respect a married woman and hate 'lust and adultery' Master Bo ordered Chiang Shiao-ho's father killed because Shiao-ho's father committed adultery."

Gi Kon-jii argued, "Hu Li might not know his students' insolence. His son ogled and insulted May-lin." They left the horses and walked up on foot.

A piercing whistle signaled dozens of men to circle tightly around Gi Kon-jii and Feng. More were coming out from the caves like mice. "Gi Kon-jii!, Bo May-lin's life or death is in my hands. You, Master Bo and May-lin's father must kowtow to the two coffins. Give me five thousand ounces of silver and a hundred good horses." Hu Li hissed.

"I'd like to see my wife."

"Come with me!"

All the caves, resembling mouse holes, were carved into the mountain. Some of them were very deep with windows. Two caves with rusted iron bars were prisons and they were darker than the other caves. May-lin was in one of them. Her right arm was caked with dried blood.

"Uncle Feng, Kon-jii, you are here!" May-lin sobbed.

"We're here to save you." Gi Kon-jii said, "Master Hu, release my wife now, and I promise that I'll deliver the silver."

"I will hold her as a hostage. No ransom, she'll be killed. These are my final words. You see this huge padlock here and the thick bars on the door. Even a leopard couldn't get free; if you come back at night to save her, you'll be killed. I warn you."

Gi Kon-jii reached for his concealed darts, but the experienced Hu Li had noticed the slight bulge around Gi Kon-jii's waist earlier. He was prepared, and he dodged in time to avoid Gi Kon-jii's two darts. His men rushed at Feng and Gi Kon-jii at once. Feng Zhi-pan was down immediately, but Gi Kon-jii snatched a saber and cut down four bandits. Hu Li aimed well and threw his dart, hitting Gi Kon-jii's wounded leg. Gi Kon-jii stumbled. The bandits tied up Gi Kon-jii, and dragged him past May-lin's jail.

"Kon-jii let them kill us together now. I'll be your true wife in the underworld," May-lin sobbed. "May-lin, I've no regrets. I'm only sorry I could not kill Chiang Shiao-ho to keep Grandpa safe and to restore the Kung Lung School's glory." Gi Kon-jii and May-lin looked at each other.

"Master Hu, please kill us now, or put us together in one cell," Gi Kon-jii said.

"No way. I will lock you in a cave close to hers. You may not be able to talk to each other, but I'm sure you'll hear her screaming. *Ha!*

Ha! I have captured Dragon Knight's grandson. My sons' souls will be pleased," Hu Li laughed, but tears welled in his eyes and his voice cracked.

Hu Li told his men, "We'll not kill them or starve them. Treat their wounds. Gi Kon-jii is Dragon Knight's grandson. Dragon Knight may have other students. The Kung Lung gang is not completely sunk yet. Fetch Feng Zhi-pan here."

"Brother Feng, we don't have any grudge against you. Gi Kon-jii is cunning. You did not know that he had two darts hidden when he came up here with you, did you?"

"He told me that he was empty-handed. From now on, I will not be part of anything between Bo Kung Lung and you," Feng said.

"Good! You better keep your word. You're free to leave."

Hu Li ordered his men to send Feng downhill to where Lu Zhi-chun was waiting. Feng told Lu what had happened up there and then he said, "I told Hu Li that I will be neutral from now on. I hope I can live my old age in peace."

Lu argued, "You cannot quit on us! We have to stick together to help Master Bo. You know the saying; *'one day teacher-father, lifelong teacher-father.'* Besides, our oath is that we are to be loyal to our teacher and each other forever."

Feng sneered, "You do that. For me, I don't want to stay on a sinking boat."

Lu hired a carriage to take Feng back to Xian. Then he hurried to deliver the bad news to May-lin's father. He felt sorry for old Master Bo. *'Master Bo does not treat his pupils equally. He was merciless when he ordered Brother Yu to cut off one eye, and got Chiang Shiao-ho's father killed. Master Bo falls for flattery. He is blind to the corrupt Feng Zhi-pan and the Lung brothers. Feng got his wealth through embezzlement and Lung Zhi-chi had many women and he is nothing but evil behind Master Bo's back. Master Bo needs all of his students' help and support now. Feng quits and Lung Zhi-chi had escaped. I can't complete Hu Li's demand in ten days and I don't even know where Master Bo is at the moment. I think the only one who can save May-lin and Gi Kon-jii is Chiang Shiao-ho. He will definitely save May-lin. But how about Gi Kon-jii? Yes, Shiao-ho will save him too simply because he is May-lin's husband. He must love May-lin a lot. From what Feng Zhi-pan told me, Shiao-ho could have cut off Gi's leg and killed more people when he was ambushed at Ba Bridge.*

Gi Kon-jii's wound was not fatal. In the heat of the fight, he controlled his anger and used his sword just to pierce but not maim. It's not easy. He could have killed Gi-Kon-jii when they met at Wu-Ton Mountain. As far as I know, Shiao-ho did not kill anyone yet. His teachers taught him well, not only martial arts, but also the true meaning of 'right' and 'wrong'. I'm sure he had trailed after May-lin and the poor black cat was a victim. He might have wanted May-lin to take him to Master Bo or simply because he wanted to have a look at May-lin. He is around this area. He is famous after what he did in Xian. I will ask around and I hope I can find him.'

Dart Hu Li and his men controlled three peaks. Hu Li ordered White Tiger to take over his late son's position.

"Teacher, I don't think that Master Bo will come. He's still in hiding somewhere from Chiang Shiao-ho. Old Bo killed his father twelve years ago. Now Chiang Shiao-ho wants revenge. I heard that Chiang Shiao-ho's is superior to Lee Feng-jii, Gi Kon-jii's and Master Hsu,"

"Can we kill Gi Kon-jii. I also think that we should hold Bo May-lin, and allow Master Bo to come here to see his granddaughter only. Lest the Kung Lungs will come back later to have revenge," Red-faced suggested.

"Let's think about it," Hu Li said. Hu Li and Master Bo were alike in their strong belief of the worst evil is 'lust'. His men could rob but not rape. He did not kill May-lin because he was told that his dead son was in the wrong. The only women in the camp are the wives of some older bandits. Red-faced was thinking about Bo May-lin, the first young woman he had met for a long time. He wanted to take advantage of her. He did not have the key of the heavy padlock to the jail and he decided that he at least could talk to her and tease her a bit. He dismissed the two bandits on watch and whispered, "Bo May-lin" May-lin!" No reply.

"Bo May-lin, I'm the third-ranked man here. I can save you and your husband if I can have you for one night. Only one night. I'm young and strong and I'll make you happy. *Ha! Ha!*"

"Get away, Scoundrel!" May-lin shouted.

"I promise I'll save you and your husband and send you home after you bed me. Ahe! Who is..?" Someone choked him from behind and smashed his head against the iron bars.

May-lin tried to find something in the cave to hit Red-faced with. There were ants and centipedes crawling on the damp ground and she dared not to search the ground in the dark with her bare hands.

Suddenly, she heard muffled sounds and watched Red-faced slump down. Then, someone tall twisted the lock and opened the door.

"Who... who goes there?"

"Hush! It's me. Chiang Shiao-ho. May-lin, come with me quickly."

"No, I'm going nowhere with you. It's your fault that I was captured. Go away!"

"May-lin, there's not a moment to spare. Hurry! I'll save you first and rush back here to save your husband. Sorry, I won't hold you too tight." Shiao-ho seemed to be able to see in the dark like a cat. He swept May-lin up and said, "Hush! May-lin, don't cry! If the bandits awaken, it'll be difficult for me to save Gi Kon-jii. They may kill him." He kicked the inert Red-faced away, and jumped nimbly over the rough terrains, peaks and ravines. May-lin held tight and closed her eyes a couple of times when she thought that they would fall. In his arms, she felt his warm body and she knew that she loves no one but Chiang Shiao-ho.

"May-lin, sit here and wait! I'll bring Gi Kon-jii here soon." Chiang Shiao-ho left May-lin sitting on a big rock surrounded by tall trees.

By now torches shone all over the camp and hundreds of bandits searched everywhere like an army of ants. Chiang Shiao-ho knew that they must have moved Gi-Kon-jii to another cave. He stood on a rock halfway up the peak and watched. Soon he spotted Red-faced, with a bandage wrapped around his head, and a few others standing afar beside an obscure niche. He disabled them.

"Chiang Shiao-ho, cut me loose and I can escape myself. They tied me extra tight after you saved May-lin. Too bad I was sleeping when you came to save her," Gi Kon-jii shouted. He was bound tight like a cocoon and now Shiao-ho held him under his armpit.

"Maybe they've drugged you. Brother Gi, there is no time to untie you, and you can't move very fast anyway," Shiao-ho shouted amid the uproar. More than a hundred bandits fought them. Shiao-ho held Gi Kon-jii with one arm and cut down several bandits with quick sword thrusts and swiftly jumped upon a rock halfway to a peak. Neither he nor Gi Kon-jii was hurt. While catching his breath, he dodged a few steel darts thrown up at him. He looked down and spotted a grey-bearded man aiming another dart at him. He knew this man must be Dart Hu Li. He held Gi under his left arm; Shiao-ho tucked the sword into the sash at his waist to free his right hand. He caught one of Hu Li's darts, and threw it back. His aim was good and he killed Hu Li.

They got to the rock where he had asked May-lin to wait. She was not there. Shiao-ho set Gi on the rock and quickly searched around. Nothing.

"May-lin! May-lin!" Shiao-ho shouted and the mountain echoed. He untied Gi, and continued calling May-lin and so did the echo.

"Where's May-lin?"

"I told her to wait for us here. It did not take me long to save you, but she is gone! May-lin!...."

"May-lin, don't be afraid. I'm here. I'm your husband, Gi Kon-jii." Both of them searched and kept calling. No reply.

"Did they capture her again?"

"No, that's not possible. There are no easy paths up here. No one but me can climb so high.!"

"But...a tiger? A leopard might have snatched her. Are there any huge animals up here?

"I don't know," Shiao-ho's voice trembled.

They tried to search for any trace of blood and paw prints, but they could not see very well in the dark.

"Let's go down and have a look. She might have thought that it's not safe here and went down. She may be waiting for us down there," Gi said.

"No! Impossible. In front of us is a deep ravine full of spiked rocks. Behind us is a rushing creek. Either way is a long drop. She could not manage it."

"Chiang Shiao-ho, it's all your fault. If you had not come to save us, somehow I would have found a way to escape with her. It is not your business any way. How did you know that we were captured?"

"I shadowed you from Xian at first. I know I shouldn't have done it, but I thought that you will lead me to Master Bo. I went to Su-An town after you killed the black cat. There I met Uncle Lu. He told me that May-lin and you were captured and asked me to save you. Uncle Lu had saved me twice when I was running away from the Kung Lungs ten years ago," Shiao-ho sighed.

He did not want to talk about how he had spied on and followed Gi Kon-jii and May-lin when they left Xian. He could not help himself from wanting to have a glance at his love. He told himself, '*I just want to have a look at her, that's all. I want to find out whether she loves Gi or not. If I see that she is not happy as Gi's wife, I may have another chance to win her over.*' He knew this was wishful thinking and he behaved foolishly, but he could not stop it. That night he saw through the window that May-lin was very attentive to Gi's need. He was so disappointed and gave up the impossible hope.

"Why? May-lin is your enemy's granddaughter, why do you want to save us?" Gi asked.

"Uncle Lu asked me to save both of you. Brother Gi, I don't consider you my enemy. Yes, I was furious when you posted the ridiculous thief-wanted posters everywhere. I wanted to kill you then. I changed my mind because of the refugee business. I even stole silver for you."

"Chiang Shiao-ho, who is your teacher? I heard that he is an old skinny scholar. What's his name?"

"I don't know his name. Honestly. He does not talk a lot. He is a good listener and I cannot even begin to tell you how superior his skills are. I'm a little afraid of him and I never asked him about his identity."

"Chiang Shiao-ho, May-lin is my wife. Are you after my wife?"

"May-lin and I liked each other a lot when we were young. I was hurt when I knew that you two are married and I was very jealous. Now I respect the fact that she is your wife. But I feel that I'm responsible for her being missing. I'll find her for you. You're not capable of searching for her among the high peaks and deep ravines here. It's not an insult. It's the truth."

"I'm injured now. When I'm recovered, I'll come back to punish the bandits and I'll challenge you again, Chiang Shiao-ho."

"That's up to you. Now I'll carry you down to where my horse is. Actually I should say 'your horse', the one I had snatched from you at Ba Bridge. Go to Su-An Town. Uncle Lu is there. After I find May-lin, I'll send her to Su-An town, too. Please don't be suspicious. May-lin is your wife and that's that. I'll never be infatuated with a married woman. If I did, my teacher would punish me severely. Besides, you're a scholar and May-lin could be a lady someday."

"I see; you do care for her a lot, Brother Chang."

Gi Kon-jii let Chiang Shiao-ho carry him over precarious ravines and helped Gi to get on the horse. Gi Kon-jii said, "You need a horse too."

Chiang Shiao-ho chuckled, "I'm a wanted thief, am I not? I will steal one." Shiao-ho handed Gi Kon-jii his own sword and said, "Take it! You may need it to fight off bandits on your way out. I'll pick it up at Su-An town or later at Uncle Lu's guard station."

Now Gi Kon-jii was truly moved, he said, "Brother Chiang, I would be honored to be your friend. I'll try to get you and the Bos to reconcile and dissolve your animosity. No matter what, I'll never help the Kung Lungs fight you again. By the way, I would like you to know that I knew nothing about the ambush at Ba Bridge."

"I never thought you did, Brother Gi. You're a braggart but you're a man of integrity. If I thought you had been a part of the dirty plot, you wouldn't be alive. Brother Gi, you better hurry. It will be dawn soon."

"Brother Chiang, if you find May-lin, you must tell her to come to Su-An town. She did not... We're not.... I must talk to her. It's important." Chiang Shiao-ho did not understand what Gi had intended to say.

Back at the peak, Chiang Shiao-ho searched again but found no sign of May-lin. He thought that either a huge animal had mauled her or May-lin had committed suicide. He did not find any traces of blood or paw prints the next morning. So he jumped down to the rushing creek and found it was not deep. Then he waded downstream and found one of May-lin's red embroidered slippers jammed between two rocks and he scrutinized everything along the creek for miles. He was elated at first that he did not find a body, and thought that May-lin probably was alive. Then he started to think that her body might have been eaten or she might have been captured again.

"May-lin! May-lin!" he kept calling when he met two hunters.

"Did you see a young woman around?" he asked.

"A young woman? Here? What does she look like?"

"About twenty. She probably wore something blue. She only had one shoe on." Shiao-ho was wet through, moss covered his hand, and his left hand grabbed onto one red woman's shoe. The hunters thought Shiao-ho was deranged and tried to get rid of him quickly.

"We hardly ever see any women around here. Men don't walk around here early in the morning either."

"Are there dangerous animals?" Shiao-ho asked.

"Oh yes, all kinds - rabbit, fox, wolf, tiger, leopard." They left with a smirk on their face, but the troubled Shiao-ho did not take notice. He thought, *'May-lin must be dead. She was wounded and she did not have any weapon to fight off an animal. A tiger or a leopard must have dragged her to its lair and that's why she lost one shoe. Gi Kon-jii is right. She's my enemy's granddaughter and Gi's wife. It's really not my business to save her. It's no use to search for her any longer. I better concentrate on the revenge business.*"

He met White Tiger who gave him a horse and said, "We know all about you. Master Bo killed your father and forced your mother to remarry. You should go after your father's murderer. That's a son's duty. Instead, you rescued your enemy's granddaughter. I'm sure you can kill all of us easily, but I don't think you can hold your head up high for too long. Did you accomplish anything regarding a son's duty to avenge his father's death? I don't think so. We're afraid of you. We'll give you anything: a horse, silver…"

"A horse will do, thanks. *'White Tiger is very cunning. He wants a clash between the Kung Lungs and me and hopes that both parties will suffer. But he is right; I should take care of the business of revenge first.'*"

At Su-An town, he told Uncle Lu that he could not find May-Lin, "An animal probably got her. I loaned my sword to Gi, please get it for me." Shiao-ho did not want to face Gi Kon-jii because he wanted to keep May-lin's shoe, and he knew very well that it should be handed to the husband.

Uncle Lu handed Shiao-ho the sword and then said, "Shiao-ho, I'm repeating myself again. Master Bo is old now. I beg you to forgive and spare him. Lung Zhi-chi was the real murderer; you have the right to kill him."

"But…All right, Uncle Lu, I'll try to be merciful." Shiao-ho had told Uncle Lu about the past ten years and his love for May-lin. Uncle Lu had told him, "Shiao-ho, you should have come to me earlier, I could have ….any way it's too late now. Brother Feng should not have enlisted the official's help to ambush you. And that braggart Gi Kon-jii also made things worse. By the way, May-lin told me that Gi Kon-jii had nothing to do with the ambush. Shiao-ho, go home! Go home to see your mother and Uncle Ma. Your young brother was sold to be an apprentice somewhere in Shandon and your mother is not well. Uncle Ma has a hard time, too."

"Uncle Lu, I will go home. Gi Kon-jii is not that bad. He likes to brag, but he is kind and generous." They laughed when he told Uncle Lu the silver he had stolen for Gi Kon-jii to give to the refugees.

On his way to Xian a month ago, at Su-An Town, he met Black Leopard whom had saved him when he escaped from the jail ten years ago in North Szechwan. Black Leopard had suggested that Master Bo must have hidden somewhere close to home. Now Shiao-ho knew that Master Bo was travelling somewhere in Szechwan from the conversation between Uncle Lu and Feng. He did not like to admit that he had done some eavesdrops.

He had promised Uncle Lu that he might spare Master Bo's life. However, he was not sure that he could contain his hatred and be truly merciful when he finally caught the old man. The closer he came to his hometown, the more he recalled Bo's cruelty. His heart hardened again. He wanted revenge.

Chengba town looked dilapidated and small to Shiao-ho now. His legs leaden, his chest ached and his eyes misted...when he led the horse through the streets Many people crowded the narrow streets, some of them must have been Shiao-ho's friends, but none seemed to recognize Shiao-ho.

His hands trembled when he tied his horse to a post in front of Uncle Ma's shop. No one was forging and the shop stood dark and old.

"Uncle Ma! Uncle Ma!" Shiao-ho called.

"What do you want to buy, a pot?" a sleepy apprentice asked. The sight of the young boy reminded Shiao-ho that he had once been an apprentice. He was suddenly hungry as he was back then when Aunt Ma never gave him enough to eat.

"Will you tell Master Ma that Chiang Shiao-ho is here?" There were only a few dusty pans and pots hanging on the wall in the shop. Business was not good.

"Shiao-ho! Shiao-ho! Is that really you? Stand up! You are tall." Uncle Ma was thin and old. He coughed and pulled the kneeling Shiao-ho up.

"Uncle Ma, how are my mother and my baby brother? How are you?" Shiao-ho sobbed.

"Come inside. Shiao-ho let me have a closer look at you. You've grown." Uncle Ma coughed again and then led Shiao-ho to a thin woman and said, "Woman, do you know who this young man is? He's our Shiao-ho!"

"Aunt, greetings!" Shiao-ho kowtowed.

"Shiao-ho, you've grown. Sit, your daddy would have been proud. Your mother is sick. Ton does not treat her well. I'll go and get her. She misses you."

"Uncle Ma, how is everything?"

"Not good. We had famines and drought, and business is poor. I'm a night guard for a rich landlord. My two boys are apprentices and their masters feed them. Oh well, at least we are not starving." Uncle Ma coughed again and then whispered, "Who's your teacher? Did you fight Gi Kon-jii? Master Bo is in hiding. He hopes that Gi will beat you."

Shiao-ho told Uncle Ma everything.

"I'm so proud. You're the number one now, Shiao-ho!"

"I heard that Master Bo is in Schwann. I will beat up that mean son of his."

"Shiao-ho, be forgiving! You cannot revive the dead no matter what. Your mother has a hard time too. Ton lost his business, and he blamed your mother for bringing him bad luck. Your brother, Shiao-leo (Little Loon) is about twelve years old now. Two years ago, a merchant from Shandon province took him away to be an apprentice. Your mother had three more children. Two died. The young one is not well."

"Shiao-ho! Oh! My Shiao-ho! It's really you, not a dream. You must avenge your father's death. He came to my dream often and asked for cold rice..," Shiao-ho's bony mother coughed and cried, "I should have remained a widow. Ton cursed me every day and said that I brought him bad luck. He abused your brother. Two years ago he sold Shiao-leo to a merchant from Shandon. That kind man gave me his address; you must go to Shandon to see your brother. I don't have long to live now, but I'll die in peace knowing that you'll kill your father's murderers, and find your brother. Your poor father came home that night to eat some cold rice and then he was killed."

"Mother, I promise I'll kill my father's murderers. Here! I have some silver for you to see a good doctor. Mom, you will get well soon. My teacher owns a profitable tea farm. You'll never be impoverished. I can't wait any longer; I'm going now to Bo's village to beat up Bo Zhi-lin." Shiao-ho cried and kowtowed to them and said, "I'll be back soon."

"Shiao-ho, wait! Your mother just got here, and I want to talk to you, too!" Uncle Ma shouted, but Shiao-ho rode off fast toward Bo's village. His chest hurt so much that he almost fell off the horse. *'If I cannot find Master Bo, at least I can kick Bo Zhi-lin. He kicked me every day when I was fourteen.'*

Bo's village was also dilapidated. Shiao-ho's old home was a relic now. Master Bo's training field was rough and uneven. Its topsoil had been washed away. However, the enclosing wall was reinforced, built higher and the side door through which Shiao-ho had escaped was sealed. Shiao-ho pounded on the tightly closed gate.

"Who's there?"

"I'm Chiang Shiao-ho. Open the gate! I'll kick it open or jump over the wall. You think the high wall can stop me?"

"*Master Bo* ordered me here to guard his home, Chiang Shiao-ho, I could call the officials and have you arrested. You have to fight me first," Master Bo's latest student Su Zhi-mi shouted.

Shiao-ho jumped over the high wall. Su Zhi-mi fought him, Shiao-ho blocked Su's heavy saber and wounded him just enough to immobilize him.

"Bo Zhi-lin, come out!" Shiao-ho shouted.

"Shiao-ho, please spare him. I was nice to you and I always begged him not to abuse you," Bo Zhi-lin's wife begged.

"Aunt Bo, I won't hurt you. You know how mercilessly he had abused me. He treated the dogs and pigs better than me. I won't kill him. Bo Zhi-lin, come out! No use to hide behind a woman."

No reply. Shiao-ho dragged Bo Zhi-lin out from under the bed.

"Shiao-ho, please forgive me. I beg of you. I was evil to abuse you before, please spare me." Shiao-ho halted his sword. He could not kill a cripple. Bo Zhi-lin's back was permanently hunched. Shiao-ho's teacher disabled him with '*Tien Hsueh*' ten years ago. Shiao-ho kicked Bo Zhi-lin once and sent him rolling.

"Aunt Bo, you know that I have the right to kill him. Master Bo and he wronged me cruelly. But, I cannot kill a cripple. Bo Zhi-lin, tell me the truth! Who killed my father?"

"Shiao-ho, be merciful, don't kill your Uncle Bo." Uncle Ma rushed in. He coughed and tried to catch his breath.

"He is no uncle of mine." Shiao-ho sneered.

"Brother Ma, ask him to spare me. He'll obey you. Shiao-ho, Everyone said that it was Lung Zhi-chi who killed your father. But Lung Zhi-chi told me later that it was my father who killed your father."

"That's not true. Shiao-ho, Lung Zhi-chi killed your father. Master Bo had a stroke when your father insulted him and fought him. If he was well, he did not have to order me to fetch the Lung brothers here to do the killing. He could easily do the killing himself," Uncle Ma said.

"I won't exonerate Master Bo and Lung Zhi-chi," Shiao-ho said.

"Shiao-ho, I beg you not to kill your Master Bo! He's old. Your father won't revive even if you kill all the Kung Lung members. Do you want to kill me, too? By oath I have to defend my teacher Master Bo. By oath, Bo Zhi-lin is your uncle. He and I, your father, Uncle Yu, Lu Zhi-chun, and Feng Zhi-pan are all sworn brothers. Do you want to kill every one of us? We all are under oath to obey and to protect Master Bo with our lives. If I had to fight you, would you kill me? Would you kill your Uncle Lu, too? He saved you and helped you to escape and I raised and sheltered you because we are your father Chiang Zhi-shen's sworn brothers. You see, we are all connected. I don't think you want to kill me but I'm obliged to fight you," Uncle Ma said.

"But, Uncle Ma, you heard my mother..." Shiao-ho argued.

"If you kill Master Bo now, someone from the Kung Lung School will take revenge on you later. Why not have mercy and end the animosity. I know you're not evil, you could have killed me or wounded me a lot worse," Su Zhi-mi said.

"My teacher told me that I could only kill the murderers. I'm going now to find Lung Zhi-chi and Master Bo. Uncle Ma, tell my mother I will bring their heads back." Shiao-ho left.

He went to the tall willow tree where he and May-lin had pledged their young love. He heard young girls' singing. For a split moment, he thought May-lin was among them. The girls stopped singing and were ready to run when they saw Shiao-ho on his big horse.

"Don't be afraid, little ladies. I'm from this village too."

"No! You're not. We don't know you," a bold one said.

"I left home ten years ago. Do you know old Master Bo?"

"We don't want to talk about the Bos," one said angrily.

"Master Bo is not here. His granddaughter left a while ago too. We don't like Master Bo's son. His granddaughter is nice," the bold one explained.

Two other girls nervously looked around and said, "Say no more, we don't want trouble." It was obvious that the Bos were feared and hated.

"I knew Bo May-lin. tell me how nice she is?" Shiao-ho asked, but the girls just stared at him and followed him to the willow tree.

"Don't be afraid. My name is Chiang Shiao-ho. I grew up here. Your brothers and your uncles may know me."

"You? You're Chiang Shiao-ho?" The girls came closer.

"Yes. Your elder brothers probably played with me before."

"We heard about you. We all hoped that someday you would come back to punish Master Bo' son, the Hunchback. He's evil."

"Especially his student Terror Lung Zhi-chi, Master Bo backed him up all the time. Last year, Terror Lung crippled a farmer, yet nobody dared to tell the officials."

"Terror Lung beat my father up pretty bad. When Master Bo asked my father why he was limping, my father dared not tell him."

"Girls, go home and tell your folks that I'll kill the Lung brothers. What happened to this tree? Who has chopped it again and again?"

"Miss Bo did. She rode every day and she came here often. She cried and chopped the tree, sometimes twice or thrice. See, how many cuts? They looked like scars. My brother said that the tree may die soon."

"Why? Why did she cut the tree?"

"She told my elder sister that she hates this tree. Why? Are you ill?"

"Look at his face. He's whiter than my Grandma when she was dying. He must have seen a ghost."

"A ghost? Let's get out of here."

The girls shrieked and fled like a pack of birds. Shiao-ho quivered and leaned on his horse. *'May-lin really hates this tree. She has hated me since that day. She hates me and she hates the time we spent together. Ahe! I'm a fool. How can I care whether she's alive or not anymore? Poor Father, his soul must be in agony. Mom said that his spirit came to her in her dream to ask for cold rice. Father, I'll kill your murderers.'*

Shiao-ho rode listlessly across the Ba Mountain in the dusk. He lingered at the rushing creeks and waited for any signs and signals from his father whose body was found at the bottom of the creek. He also remembered that twice he had dashed across this mountain to safety. The second time he was with Master Hsu's group. His first desperate escape came the night after he stabbed Lung Zhi-lin. Uncle Lu caught up with him and pointed out the correct route for him. He had ravenously gobbled down the dumplings that May-lin had stolen for him. Ah! May-lin! Everything led back to her. Her image and words came flashing back.

"Shiao-ho, please! Get my kite down for me."-- A sweet little girl so long ago.

"Shiao-ho, wait! I'm not a part of the ambush."-- At the Ba Bridge at Xian.

"Shiao-ho, put me down! You want to kill my Grandpa! How can I not hate you?"-- On Feng's roof at Xian.

"I'm going nowhere with you. It's your fault that I was captured."-- At Hu Li's camp.

'*She does not hate me. From the way she stared at me at Ba Bridge, I know she remembers our pledge of love very well. But now that I have to kill her beloved Grandpa. she's trapped in the dilemma and so am I.*' Shiao-ho thought.

Shiao-ho wanted to rush back and look for May-lin again. Then he realized that even if he could find her, she was forever out of his reach. She was married and she won't forgive him for wanting to kill her Grandpa.

Ten years ago, Master Hsu had taken Shiao-ho to Zie-Yin City. He was young and scared. Now Shiao-ho walked directly into the Lung brothers' security station.

"Stop right there, you! You cannot go in," Lung brothers' student shouted.

Shiao-ho pushed him away and other guards came to fight him. Kao came out. Shiao-ho remembered that Master Hsu had stabbed Kao ten years ago.

"Uncle Kao, do you remember me?" Shiao-ho said.

"Ahe! It's Chiang Shiao-ho. All of you stay away! Don't come close. Don't fight him! It's no use to fight him, We cannot win. Get back and put down your weapons! Now!" Kao ordered the armed guards not to fight Shiao-ho.

"I won't kill the innocent. Better stay out of my way," Shiao-ho laughed.

"Chiang Shiao-ho, you must be a reasonable man. Your Daddy Chiang Zhi-shen was my sworn brother, too."

"It's true that Lung Zhi-chi killed my father?"

"Yes, they searched everywhere in Chengba for three days and could not find your daddy. Bo Zhi-lin must have watched your home because he knew your father came home one night. The impatient Lung Zhi-chi killed your father before Master Bo could stop him. That's the truth, Chiang Shiao-ho!"

Lung Zhi-tin rushed out from the living quarters and shouted, "Damn you, Kao, you're a coward. You betrayed us. You're afraid of Chiang Shiao-ho, and now you try to make us the killers." Lung Zhi-tin charged at Shiao-ho.

Chiang Shiao-ho simply forced Lung Zhi-tin back.

Kao shouted, "Stop, Shiao-ho, go after Lung Zhi-chi. He's the real killer. Master Bo did not have the heart to kill your father. Now Lung Zhi-chi escaped to North Szechwan. Shiao-ho, leave now before the officials come here to arrest you," Not wanting to hurt anyone, Shiao-ho brandished his sword in a tight arc to force everyone back and rode away.

12

Officials were on alert to catch a middle-aged, fat, beard and brutish bandit name Chiang Shiao-ho in North Szechwan. Lung Zhi-chi had robbed, raped, and called himself Chiang Shiao-ho. Lung Zhi-chi was Master Bo's most favored student. Behind Master Bo's back, he committed adultery, snatched pretty married women. Kao knew some of it, but he bullied Kao into secrecy and threatened to kill Kao if Kao dared to tell Master Bo. In front of Master Bo, Lung Zhi-chi was ever so obedient and righteous. Master Bo did not even know that he terrorized his neighbors at Bo's village.

Chiang Shiao-ho's imminent revenge tore Lung Zhi-chi away from his new seventeen-year-old concubine. He feared and hated Chiang Shiao-ho. When he heard about Gi Kon-jii's 'wanted....' postcards. He thought, *'great, I will get Shiao-ho arrested and hanged.'* He started to steal and rob and told his victims that his name was Chiang Shiao-ho. He robbed a rich merchant's wife while she was on her way to join her husband. Lung Zhi-chi killed two of the hired guards, and boasted, "You know who I am? I'm Chiang Shiao-ho. The famous Master Bo is afraid of me." He then forced the carriage driver to drive the woman to an inn and pretended that he was the husband of the woman. But before he could rape the woman, she hanged herself. He ran away and hid from the law in the hills for a few days and escaped to another town. When he was low on silver, he paid a letter writer to write home for some silver. Kao sent him a small amount of silver and the news that Master Bo might be travelling alone to an old friend Master Lee in South Szechwan. Lung Zhi-chi went south to join Master Bo.

Master Bo was glad to see him and told him, "I will stay in hiding no more. I'll go after Shiao-ho and fight him to the death. An honorable death is better than humiliation. Last month, Lu Zhi-chun accompanied me to my old friend Ho's farm to hide. Ho's children humiliated me. We left together and I ordered Lu Zhi-chun home. I wanted to fight Shiao-ho alone. I had his father killed and now it's my punishment to be killed. I'm not afraid to die. I'll find him, but I'll allow him to kill me only. All the gods and ghosts will not allow him to kill innocent ones." His eyes huge and his white beard spiked. Lung Zhi-chi feared that Master Bo's was losing his mind.

Old Master Lee has many students and many grandchildren. Everyone was courteous, maybe not very warm, to Master Bo and let him stayed in a separate court. Old Bo enjoyed a longer rest ever since he was forced to leave his nest. He had time to think and remember.

Another day, Master Bo sighed, "Zhi-chi, I had his father killed but truly I was not unkind to Chiang Shiao-ho. He was homeless and I took him in ten years ago. I could have killed him ten times over. I should have *weeded the root* to eliminate the potential danger of his revenge. At that time I wanted to be a kind person and I didn't kill him though my son urged me to kill Shiao-ho time and time again. Now Shiao-ho came back and forced me to flee home at my old age. I did not have time to give May-lin a proper marriage ceremony. He forced me to separate from my family and I'm not sure if Gi Kon-jii and May-lin are still alive. Oh! My hair and my beard are all white now and I can't stay at home to enjoy my remaining years."

Lung Zhi-chi thought, '*You deserve it. You're the one who ordered us to hunt Shiao-ho's father down and bring you his head. You're the one who split Chiang Shiao-ho's family and made him an orphan; and you're the one foolish enough to allow a pup become a killer wolf and put all of us in danger.*'

"Teacher, somehow we will trudge through this. The supreme god won't allow a fiend to get his way for long," Lung Zhi-chi feigned sympathy.

When Master Bo heard the news of Chiang Shiao-ho's alleged crimes, He said, "Fighting Chiang Shiao-ho is no longer a personal issue. He is evil. I will fight him to my death to rid this criminal for the innocent people. It might be true that I'm merely afraid of his teacher. I'm old but I still have good skills and strength." Master Bo went out every day to look for Chiang Shiao-ho and he loved to hear the news of Shiao-ho's criminal behaviors. He was in high spirit. His favorite student Lu Zhi-chi hid in his room all the time. Lu worried every day that he would be identified as the one who impersonated Chiang Shiao-ho, and catch him for being the real culprit. He also was afraid that the real Chiang Shiao-ho would come and kill him. *'Master Bo is an old fool. It was on his order that I killed Chiang Zhi-shen. He turned soft and would not kill the son. Now the cub has grown to become a killer. Damn that old fool! It serves him right to be hunted like a homeless dog. Damn old Fool!'*

Master Hsu and his son came to visit Master Bo and declared, "I cannot believe that Chiang Shiao-ho became a low criminal. We will join you to purge Chiang Shiao-ho. My daughter in law is Dragon Du's granddaughter. She is highly skilled in martial arts and she will be back soon from North Szechwan. She will help us." Old Bo was glad and Lu was scared.

Chiang Shiao-ho was not well on route North Szechwan. The constant fighting, the acute misery of losing May-lin, the pressure and the conflicting ideas of revenge…had caused him poor appetite and sleep. At a small town in North Szechwan, he was very sick and fell into a stupor at the first inn. He did not notice the inn keeper's odd expression at hearing his name. The officials arrested him and he would have been jailed if the carriage driver did not clear him. "It is not him. This young man is tall and slim. The criminal is not as tall, fat, almost fifty, dark complexion, has busy thick beard and a big head. Maybe they have the same names. Ahe! I remember that the criminal sometimes call himself 'Lord Lung'". The detective also noticed Shiao-ho's southern accent and found in Shiao-ho's bag a letter of introduction form a reputable tea company in Nanjing. He released Shiao-ho.

Shiao-ho thought, *'Did Lung Zhi-chi use my name? Isn't he in Szechwan.'* He recalled his teacher's words, *'Shiao-ho. Prevent and avoid a danger is important. Think ahead… anticipate…'.* He asked the detective, "Could you write a notice to clear me. I don't want to be arrested again."

"Yes. I will also let all the other detective know the you have been framed. Where are you going?"

"I will go down south to visit Master Hsu."

This incident reinforced Shiao-ho's resolution of revenge. In a few days, he had gain back his health. He also earned his new estimated status for being the hero who killed the notorious Dart Hu Li with one of Hu Li's dart.

Shiao-ho waited his friend Black Leopard and he did not wait too long.

Master Hsu's daughter in-law came home from North Szechwan and told everyone the news that the villain Chiang Shiao-ho was still at large. One of her relative was a victim and she wanted to catch Chiang Shiao-ho.

Master Hsu also heard the news that Dart Hu Li was killed. He wondered, *"Chiang Shiao-ho cannot be both a lowly villain and a hero. Not my Shiao-ho!, the courageous boy I knew ten years ago.'* He went to visit Master Bo one evening. While they were drinking and talking, a screaming and bloody Lung Zhi-chi ran out to the yard. Someone had cut off Lung's left arm and half of the left shoulder. A small person dress in black escaped from the roof. Master Hsu made a half-heartedly chase. He recognized the killer was his daughter-in-law.

Six officers with lanterns came. One asked excitedly, "Is Chiang Shiao-ho caught? Where is he? Someone told us that we can capture Chiang Shiao-ho here."

"It's him. Ah! He fits the description perfectly; tall, fat, a bushy beard and a big head." One of them looked at the inert Lung Zhi-chi.

"He's not Chiang Shiao-ho. He's my pupil, Lung Zhi-chi," Master Bo shouted angrily.

"No mistake. The robber sometimes called himself 'Lord Lung' and sometimes said his name was Chiang Shiao-ho." Master Bo kicked the chain out of the detective's hand and aimed his saber at them.

"Halt! You dare attack the law? Captain Fee, should we chain this old rascal up, too?" the sergeant yelled.

"It's outrageous. Lung Zhi-chi is my best student." Master Bo said.

"Lung Zhi-chi called himself Chiang Shiao-ho, committed all the crimes. The real Chiang Shiao-ho was framed. My colleague up north had arrested and released the real Chiang Shiao-ho." Captain Fee deduced.

"If anyone dares insult me and my student, I will kill him. My student would never rob and lust after a woman. You hear?" Master Bo roared like an enraged lion.

"Shut up, old man!" The detectives wanted to arrest Lung Zhi-chi.

Master Hsu quietly handed the captain some silver and asked that they do not take Lu away. He said, "He is dying anyway. Please let him stay. Maybe there are two impostors. We need a witness."

"Master Hsu, we will put him in your custody for now"

Master Hsu loathed Lu Zhi-chi and he knew Lu is truly wicked. He pitied the old homeless Master Bo. *'When Chiang-ho comes, he can have Lu's head'*

Master Bo stood there, a sad and hopeless old man.

"We cannot be responsible for our students' evil doings. When I see Shiao-ho, I will talk him out of taking revenge. Take care." Master Hsu left.

Master Bo knew that Shiao-ho would be here soon, he was on alert. He tore a pair of pants into strips to bind tight his flabby stomach and thick thighs. He practiced and worked out more. He was waiting for the imminent fight with Chiang Shiao-ho. *'Did May-lin and Gi Kon-jii fight with Chiang Shiao-ho already? Did Chiang Shiao-ho spare their lives? I have taught so many students and now I'm alone at my old age.'* Master Bo held his tears back with tremendous effort.

Master Lee's students and family did not want to get involved, but Master Hsu almost came to be with old Bo every day. He invited the detectives to a dinner, trying to get them not arrest the wounded Lung Zhi-chi. The banquet was on the second floor of the biggest restaurant in town. Master Bo arrived and carried his Kung Lung saber. He insisted that Lu was innocent.

"My student would not rob and steal. You should not accuse an innocent man." Old Bo roared.

"Master Bo! There is no mistake. The witness, the carriage driver, had met the real Chiang Shiao-ho and said Chiang was not the robber. The real Chiang Shiao-ho is young and tall. He is not fat. He does not have a beard and his head is not big. If you offer some silver...." The corrupted detective said.

"I swear it with my life. I guarantee it with my reputation. My student Lung is innocent," Master Bo shouted again. Nobody listened; they were all staring at the tall young man just coming upstairs.

"Shiao-ho, be merciful. Master Bo is old," Master Hsu called.

"Master Bo, it's between you and me. Let's go somewhere else to...." Chiang Shiao-ho said.

"Enemy!" Master Bo chopped savagely at Chiang Shiao-ho, and Chiang Shiao-ho's sword blocked it. Bo's heavy saber dropped on the floor.

"Shiao-ho! You cannot kill him!" Master Hsu and his son rushed in to intervene. Master Bo took this opportunity to run to the stairs.

Chiang Shiao-ho dodged Master Hsu's and his son's swords, he ran down and caught Master Bo. He threw the heavy old man onto the horse's back and ran with the horse in a flash to the waiting Black Leopard.

"Brother Wu, don't hurt him. I'll go now to finish the other business." Shiao-ho said. Master Bo struggled; Black Leopard hit his head with a rock and tied him up.

"Bo Kung Lung, you old bastard! All these years you permitted your students to terrify us. You'll pay for their wickedness now." He dumped Master Bo roughly on the cracked floor of a shabby temple and waited.

Chiang Shiao-ho returned soon and handed Black Leopard a bloodstained bag and said, "Please tie it to your horse." He put old Bo on a horse and called, "Let's go. I'll bring Lung Zhi-chi's head to the place where my father was killed. You don't have to slow down your horse. I walk fast."

Master Bo looked Chiang Shiao-ho over and saw that Chiang Shiao-ho was taller and more muscular than his father. He sighed when he recalled that once upon a time he had wanted to see him and May-lin get married.

"Shiao-ho, I'd like to see my two sons and May-lin once again before my death. Did you, tell me the truth, did you kill them all already?"

When he heard May-lin's name, Chiang Shiao-ho sighed. He cut loose the cord that tied the old man and helped Master Bo sit straight on horseback. He replied, "No, I did not kill them."

"Shiao-ho, you.. you are not going to kill me? I regret...."

"Of course I'll kill you, Master Bo! Ten years ago, I was a boy and you plotted to kill me in the wheat field. You killed my father. How can I let you live? But you're old and alone, so I won't kill you right here. I'll take you home and give you plenty of time to gather your sons and students. Then I'll duel with you and kill you squarely in front of your sons and students."

"Very well! I do regret. It's no use to say any more."

"Listen, old monster! You indulged Lung Zhi-chi; you let him terrorize your own neighbors. Don't you know that they call him 'Terror Lung'? Lung Zhi-chi committed crimes and wanted to get me arrested. If the witness had not cleared me, I would be jailed now. I will bring his head to my father's memorial. Don't you dare attack me! I'll tie you up again!" Black Leopard laughed. Black Leopard led them north on some less traveled roads and stayed in some meager village inn. The dejected Master Bo kept quiet but sighed often. They hardly ever met other travelers.

Black Leopard said, "We better kill the old rascal now. There was a mean Tao priestess in Win Town. We have to pass there to enter the mountain path. Master Bo might call for help and we'll have trouble."

"A Tao priestess who knows martial arts? I'm not afraid. Let's cross the mountain before nightfall. Master Bo, I'll kill you the minute you call for help, you hear!"

"Shiao-ho, I am not a coward, and I won't call for help. My Kung Lung School is down in luck now, and everyone jeers at us. As long as one member lives through this catastrophe, someday he will take revenge on you."

"I've told you again and again that I'll only kill my father's murderers," Chiang Shiao-ho said furiously. Actually, he was angry at his own indecision. He should kill Master Bo now. Instead he delayed with the excuse of wanting to take Master Bo home first. The truth was that he simply could not kill this old man whom he used to call Grandpa Bo. His heart squeezed and hurt whenever Master Bo sighed. Besides, every hair of Master Bo's white beard seemed to beg him to be lenient. Uncle Ma and Uncle Lu had asked him to be merciful. His teacher advised him to be forgiving. May-lin's tearful face mirrored in Master Bo's unyielding but pathetic old eyes.

"Bo's village is just on the other side of the mountain. I'm not afraid of their future revenge, but you may want to avoid it. Let's part here." Chiang Shiao-ho told Black Leopard.

"No, Shiao-ho, I hate the Kung Lung gang and I want to see the end with pleasure."

Black Leopard led them astray; he was trying to avoid Win Town and the Tao priestess. It was pitch dark, yet they still rambled along the curvy, rocky route. The horse slipped and threw the heavy Master Bo off. Chiang Shiao-ho caught the falling old man but not his bag of clothes. He hastily gathered the scattered articles up. He did not see May-lin's shoe. When Black Leopard hit the old man, he said, "Leave him alone, it's not his fault. We better find shelter for the night," He wanted to walk back to find the missing shoe.

"Look! A shed with light on over there! Let's go, Shiao-ho! It's dark. Can you wait till tomorrow morning? What did you lose?"

"It's nothing important. You take him up there first. I'll have another look," Chiang Shiao-ho said. He did not want to tell Black Leopard that he must find May-lin's shoe. He had carried it all the time. It was the only tangible article connecting him to May-lin.

"Look, this nice hunter's wife has a pot of millet cooked."

"I'll be back." Chiang Shiao-ho traced back along their trek but found no shoe. He hated himself for the absurdity of looking for a shoe; but he was compelled to find it. He bent his head and strained his eyes in the dark till his back and eyes hurt."

Two horses were tied to a tree with their bags on it. *'Black Leopard should take the bags in'* Chiang Shiao-ho searched his bag one more time and found no shoe. He took the bags and walked up to the faintly lit shed.

"What?" Black Leopard, the hunter and his wife all-dead. Someone cracked their skulls. Blood everywhere, but no Master Bo, only a pot of millet steaming.

"Old Brute, you killed them all!" Chiang Shiao-ho cursed. His heart pounded, and hairs on his arm stood up and vomited. Two horses were still tied up. *'old Bo cannot escape far on foot'*. He dodged just in time. The end of a heavy steel rod had stroked the spot where Chiang Shiao-ho was, and a towering monk attacked him with a heavy steel rod. Shiao-ho met the famous Steel Rod Monk.

Chiang Shiao-ho threw his sword away and used his two hands to grab the steel rod. The monk could not free his rod, and neither could Chiang Shiao-ho gain an inch. Chiang Shiao-ho had met his match.

"You captured a feeble old man, and you robbed and nearly raped a woman in Szechwan. You're evil. I will kill you," Steel Rod Monk roared. The mountain echoed back evil ..evil .. kill .. kill.

"Lung Zhi-chi committed the crimes, not me. He told everyone his name was Chiang Shiao-ho. I almost got jailed, a witness cleared my name. Your student Monk Pure is my friend. Please hear me out. Master Bo and Lung Zhi-chi killed my father ten years ago. I caught Master Bo, but I don't want to kill a lone old man on the run. I'm taking him back home to his sons and pupils...."

"Don't beg for mercy! Are you afraid of death? *Ha! Ha!* I won't spare you tonight."

"Who is afraid? I just want you to know the truth. That's all," Shiao-ho shouted back.

Chiang Shiao-ho was too smart to fight Steel Rod Monk with strength alone. He let go of the heavy rod and fought with agility, and jumped free whenever the monk's rod struck at him. They fought quite a while and Shiao-ho pushed the exhausted Steel Rod Monk, holding the heavy rod, down the hill. He heard a piercing shriek. *'He must have cracked his head on the rocks and died'.* Shiao-ho gulped for air when he heard a horse neigh, and found one horse, the one with Lung Zhi-chi's head on it, was gone. He wondered, *'It's possible that Steel Rod Monk did not die and he took the horse. Master Bo might have had stolen the horse when I was fighting Steel Rod Monk. Or the frightened horse broke the cord and ran away. None of these reasons good.'* Chiang Shiao-ho was also exhausted. He was afraid that some other warrior might be lurking in these unknown hills; he hid between two rocks and slept.

Chiang Shiao-ho woke up and found his sword among the bodies. *'I should have listened to Black Leopard and killed Master Bo yesterday. The hunter and his wife, Black Leopard all died because I hesitated.'* He sighed and walked down the hill. When he took a closer look at the huge body, he found that Steel Rod Monk did not die from the fall. Someone had slit his throat with a sword or a knife. Who? Chiang Shiao-ho did not have his sword last night. Another scare awaited Chiang Shiao-ho when he found the cord that tied the horse had been cut. He knew that someone with even higher martial arts skills was around last night. This person was neither a friend nor an enemy. If he were a friend, he would have helped him fight Steel Rod Monk. if he were an enemy, he could have killed the exhausted Chiang Shiao-ho. However, this person must have saved Master Bo.

Not far from Steel Rod Monk's body, Chiang Shiao-ho spotted the red embroidered shoe. He stared at it for a long time, hating it. His compulsory search for it last night had caused three persons' lives. He decided not to pick it up and ride away quickly. The hungry horse, Black Leopard's old mount, would not move fast. Chiang Shiao-ho's resolution weakened. He blushed and felt like a fool when he doubled back and picked up the red shoe.

He found the path to Win Town, and eat at a crowded noodle shop.

"Mr. Wong, did you feed Steel Rod Monk today?" someone asked the owner. Chiang Shiao-ho strained to hear the answer above the noise. "Not today. I hope he will go to Lee's shop to beg. Yesterday he ate eleven bowls of noodles here. He eats so much. He'll ruin my business at this rate; I may as well close the door," the owner complained.

"Why? He does not pay you enough?" Chiang Shiao-ho asked.

"Pay? Not even a small coin. He just bars the door with that heavy rod of his, and demands to be fed. He has been around here a month now. I heard that he stays at a monastery up the hill, but they can only afford to feed him one meal a day," the owner grumbled.

"I bet you don't mind offering a meal to the Tao priestesses when they come to beg. A couple of young ones are pretty," another customer teased.

"Don't blaspheme! It's not funny. The Tao priestess only asks for a little," the owner rebutted.

Chiang Shiao-ho concluded that whoever had saved Master Bo must have sent him to a monastery or a temple. It was also possible that an enemy of Steel Rod Monk waited and killed the monk and stole the horse last night. The other possibility is that Master Bo might have known this area well, and escaped to a temple on his own.

On his way uphill, he met two young boys herding pigs and sheep. They seemed to be afraid of telling Chiang Shiao-ho anything about the temple and convent. Chiang Shiao-ho recalled that Black Leopard had mentioned a mean Tao priestess was around here. 'The monks and Tao priestesses here might have harassed the farmers.'

He felt that he could smell the odor of pig shit on him again. The memory of his suffering at Master Bo's ten years ago came back vividly. Through his tears he saw himself, as a young boy, with pig waste all over him again. The young boy held a kite and looking down at May-lin's small lovely face from a high branch of the willow tree.

In this dream-like mist, he let his horse trample through the hills and woods. When he had a glimpse of the frightened Master Bo on the run around the corner of a convent, he was not fast enough to catch him. It was a big convent with many courts. Chiang Shiao-ho pounded on the closed gate, but no one answered. He then jumped upon the wall and saw a young woman, wiping the tears from her face with a scarf, was on her way to open the gate for him. Chiang Shiao-ho did not want to be caught watching a woman; he jumped down from the wall and waited at the gate. He wondered whether this convent might be a corrupted one that would hold ordinary women hostage. The gate opened. When the woman took away her tear-soaked scarf, Chiang Shiao-ho was speechless to see May-lin's sad and bitter face.

"May-lin, is that you, am I dreaming?" Chiang Shiao-ho murmured.

"It's you. You drove me here. You want revenge? Good! But you cannot kill my old Grandpa. You can only have one life." She rushed at the paralyzed Chiang Shiao-ho and held onto his arm. The numbed Chiang Shiao-ho lost all his strength.

"May-lin, please hear me out. I. I'm so confused. I don't know what to do any more."

"My family wronged you and abused you, you had suffered a lot. You must have revenge. But you can only kill one of us. One of us is enough to compensate your father's death. One to one! You hear!" With tremendous strength, May-lin pulled Shiao-ho's sword hard against her chest. Her blood gushed.

"May-lin! May-lin! You mustn't die…"

"I have to die. It's for the best. It's my homage to Gi Kon-jii, Grandpa and YOU… Are you not satisfied, Chiang Shiao-ho? You are the cold and heartless one. I waited for you ten years. Grandpa forced me to marry Gi Kon-jii but I'm not his wife in reality. You know, Shiao-ho, ten years ago I promised to marry you and I have never forgotten it…" her voice weakened. Chiang Shiao-ho wept.

"Chiang Shiao-ho, you can kill my granddaughter but you can't embrace her. She's not your wife. It's sinful and unethical. Put her down! I'll fight you," Master Bo roared.

"Grandpa, you're cruel. I have loved Chiang Shiao-ho since I was twelve. If you had been kind … If you had not allowed my uncle to abuse Shiao-ho, we would be a happy family now. You're very cruel.…Why did you force me to marry Gi Kon-jii…Ah! Shiao-ho! Hold me! Let me die in your arms. I love you…. Shiao-ho."

Master Bo stared at the wounded May-lin and the weeping Chiang Shiao-ho. Ten years ago, he had wanted them to get married once. The memory of Shiao-ho's father died terribly flashed vividly back. He truly regretted his cruelty now, but he shouted with added venom, "May-lin, I renounce you. You're no longer my granddaughter. Chiang Shiao-ho, I know you can kill me at will. But let me tell you that Lung Zhi-chi killed your father before I could stop him, and I gave your mother the silver that I found on your father body. Everyone else advised me to kill you, but I did not. I'd like you to know the truth. That's all. I'm going to find Gi Kon-jii to nullify the marriage." Master Bo walked away without a second look at the heart-broken couple.

13

An elderly Tao priestess bandaged May-lin's chest.

"Reverend Mother, when did she come here?" Shiao-ho asked.

"Steel Rod Monk and his student took her here. He knows our Head Priestess Keen. He told us that a bandit was chasing her and her Grandfather. She had wounds on her shoulders and legs when she first came. Yesterday, Steel Rod Monk took her grandfather here. We cannot have a man live here, so he stayed at a shed where we kept some deer. Poor girl."

"Shiao-ho, you better leave. We're doomed. I don't want to see you or my cruel Grandpa anymore," May-lin whimpered.

"I'm so sorry. I...I'm wicked and I don't deserve your forgiveness. Please get well. I...." Shiao-ho sobbed. No answer. Shiao-ho waited a while and then said, "I'm going to get some medicine for your wounds. I'll be back soon." May-lin had a deep cut on her chest. It was a tricky place to use 'Tien Hsueh' technique to stop the blood. A wrong move might kill her, Shiao-ho was afraid to apply it. He wished his teacher were here.

He scooped some dirt to cover the bloodstains near the gate and he could not find his sword. He left it at the gate when he carried May-lin to her room. He did not want to look for it further so he ran downhill and his horse was missing, too. There was only a pile of droppings. 'Master Bo must have stolen my sword and the horse.' Shiao-ho ran to Win Town.

No doctor specializing in cuts and no adequate medicine was available at Win Town. He bought some mint-like herb and hoped it could at least reduce the pain. Then he thought about May-lin's husband Gi Kon-jii. He wondered, 'what should I do now? May-lin told me that she always loved me. If May-lin gets well and marries me, how *could I face Gi Kon-jii? My Teacher will certainly punish me. I won't have a leg to stand upon; everyone will loathe me. I can't marry her. Now I can't kill Master Bo either. How can I face my mother and my dead father's soul? What shall I do?'*

The gate of the convent was bolted from inside. Shiao-ho did not want to wait, so he jumped over the wall. When he landed, something hit his left elbow; he fell and dropped the package of medicine. He stood up at once and dodged the second and the third egg-sized iron balls rapidly hurled at him.

"Who is it? Come out! No more dirty tricks!" Chiang Shiao-ho shouted.

"Bastard! You killed my sworn brother Steel Rod Monk. Now I'll kill you!" A tall and malicious looking middle-aged Tao Priestess charged at Shiao-ho with a curved saber.

"Steel Rod Monk killed my friend, an innocent hunter and his wife. He fought me, and I won."

"They are not hunters. They are bandits and they deserved to die. You tortured old Master Bo."

"Master Bo killed my father, split my family and abused me ten years ago."

He evaded the Tao Priestess's lethal saber thrusts, but another iron ball from her bow almost hit Shiao-ho on his head when he tried to pick up the package of medicine. No longer defensive, Shiao-ho seized her steel bow and used it as a sword to fight. The Tao priestess had great strength and she fought better than Gi Kon-jii. Shiao-ho wanted to end the fight quickly, he applied the '*Tien Hsueh*' (vital points press) technique and disabled her, left her sprawling on the ground and yelling obscenities.

He put some medicine on May-lin's wound and hoped it would work.

"Shiao-ho, you should not hurt Priestess Keen. Steel Rod Monk saved me and she is very kind to me. I....." May-lin closed her eyes and the tears came. She told Shiao-ho her story between sobs and moans. When she was sitting on the big rock waiting for Shiao-ho to save her husband Gi Kon-jii from Hu Li's camp, her thoughts were so tangled and jammed even the finest comb could not detangle them. She could not be a good wife to Gi Kon-jii because she secretly harbored her unquenchable love for Shiao-ho. She could not truly love Shiao-ho knowing that he wanted to kill her grandfather. There were no feasible solutions. Only death could set her free. She wanted to die, so she threw herself from the cliff down into the rushing creek.

It was a long drop but she did not die. Her years of martial arts training and her survival instinct saved her. She landed on the rocky river bed with a twisted ankle, torn clothes and bleeding knees. She waded and got on the bank, lost one of her shoes. She hopped and crawled to a nearby mud house and knocked on the closed door. A woman pulled her in, pushed her to the corner and whispered, "Silence."

A man knocked on the door and shouted, "Did you see any strangers, a man and a woman, around?"

"No."

The woman handed May-lin some old clothes and a pair of shoes. She told May-lin, "Dart Hu Li is dead. A young man saved your man and killed Hu Li. Somehow they knew that you're still in the mountain and they are searching for you. Hurry, walk to the back of the house and turn to your right. You can get out of the mountain through the trees. Good luck."

Some bandits saw her, she fought them but they were too many and she had a bad ankle. At the crucial moment, Steel Rod Monk came and saved her. Monk Pure, Steel Rod Monk's student, carried her first on his back, and then hired a carriage for her to come to this Taoist convent.

Monk Pure said, "I know you are old Bo's granddaughter. Last night Chiang Shiao-ho killed Hu Li and saved your husband, too. Now he probably is hunting for your grandfather. Your grandfather cannot hide forever; sooner or later Shiao-ho will kill him. I met Chiang Shiao-ho ten years ago when Master Hsu took him to fight your grandpa." May-lin cried, she needed someone to talk to so she told Monk Pure about the past and her dilemma.

Monk Pure blamed her, "You should have insisted on marrying Chiang Shiao-ho. Then, he definitely would not want to kill Master Bo."

Steel Rod Monk and the skinny Monk Pure would come and go. From their conversations, May-lin learned that her grandfather was at Szechwan, and she also guessed that Lung Zhi-chi, not Chiang Shiao-ho, was the criminal. She tried to explain, but Steel Rod Monk would not listen and vowed to save Master Bo and kill Chiang Shiao-ho.

May-lin's talk of wanting to die knifed Shiao-ho's heart. *She is right about us being doomed. I wished that I had told Teacher about May-lin. He would tell me what to do.*

He told May-lin, "I met Monk Pure about a month ago. I'll release Priestess Keen now. She and Steel Rod Monk saved you, but they are not authentic clergymen and they are ruthless. They have the same teacher. And I don't know why one is a monk and one is a Tao priestess. Once, my teacher told me that Buddha and Taoism are two different religions. I'm sorry that Steel Rod Monk is dead, we fought but I did not kill him. It's all very complicated."

"Shiao-ho, go and release Priestess Keen and I want you to tell her that you are sorry. Please. Do it for me. Then come back, I have so much to tell you."

"I want to talk to you, too. I want to tell you all my dreams and longings for you ten long years."

"Shiao-ho, I missed you and worried about you every day after you escaped ten years ago."

Shiao-ho apologized and told Priestess Keen again that he did not kill the Steel Rod Monk. He freed Priestess Keen. Unexpectedly, Priestess Keen jumped up the minute she was free, and tried vainly to 'Tien Hsueh' Shiao-ho. He pushed her away.

"Chiang Shiao-ho, do you dare go up to Wu-Ton Mountain to fight me there? I don't think you have the guts to go."

"You have friends there? Don't scare me with the Tao priests. I'm not afraid of the famous seven sword masters and all the armed priests. I've been there."

"I'll wait for you there. We'll see whether you're a coward or not." She left. Chiang Shiao-ho thought, 'She fights better than Steel Rod Monk and she is very powerful. She is a woman and she is older, but I had a hard time to defeat her.'

The same elderly priestess came out with a meager supper for May-lin.

She told Shiao-ho, "Sir, you mustn't mind Priestess Keen. She looks mean, but she's not all bad. We're all afraid of her but we have to obey her. She is not an authentic Tao Priestess, and she does not know the doctrine well. But she is rich. She had the convent repaired and she subsidizes us. She also protects us."

"No wonder she swore. Was she here last night?" Shiao-ho asked.

"No, she came back this morning and told us that you killed Steel Rod Monk. Sir, you can stay here a little longer but you can't stay here overnight. No man can stay here overnight."

Shiao-ho wondered who the mysterious stranger out there last night was. He thought, '*I was lucky. If she were there and helped the Steel Rod Monk to fight me, I would have had a hard time to escape or be alive...*'

"Shiao-ho, you better leave. It's late, come back in the morning," May-lin said.

"Can I stay with you a little longer? Now I hate my father too. If he had not deliberately broken Grandpa's Bo's rules, we might be happily married now. It's fate. Gi Kon-jii is a good man. It's not proper that we are together, but you're not safe here, that vicious priestess might come back tonight. Let me carry you downhill to Win Town. After you're well, I promise you that I'll find Gi Kon-jii...."

May-lin interrupted, "No! Don't. I.. ten years ago, I hated you when you brought Master Hsu to fight my grandpa, but I could not hate you for long. I missed you and I never forgot our secret marriage vow under the willow tree. I told you before that I did not... I'm not truly... Gi Kon-jii's wife yet. Although I can't forget him, I don't want to see him again. Shiao-ho, I want..I want...ten years ago, when my uncle kicked you and abused you, my heart ached. Every day and every night, I was worried. I knew that my grandpa wanted to kill you. They all wanted to kill you and I was afraid for you. I missed you all the time after you escaped," May-lin moaned.

"May-lin, you see, I found your shoe. I searched and searched up and down that creek when I tried to find you. I found one of your shoes. I did not want to give it to Gi Kon-jii, your husband. Because of you, I did not kill your Grandpa, and I did not let my friend Black Leopard whip him. I want..."

"Shiao-ho, it's late. You better leave. I understand everything now," May-lin sobbed

Halfway to Win Town, Shiao-ho thought, '*May-lin said that she is not, in fact, Gi's wife. Gi Kon-jii hesitated to tell me something like that, too. Ah! They are married in name only. I pierced Gi Kon-jii's thigh and he couldn't.. I guess I can marry May-lin.*' He rushed back excitedly to May-lin's room. It seemed that she was waiting for him.

"May-lin, I have had only two wishes on my mind the last ten years. One was revenge and the other was to marry you. Master Bo told me that Lung Zhi-chi killed my father. Now that I have killed Lung Zhi-chi, I think my father's soul should be satisfied. Yesterday, your grandpa said that he would find Gi Kon-jii to end your marriage. I think we can keep our vow and get married after you're well. Your grandpa would give us his blessings eventually. Please say yes...I won't blame you if you say no, May-lin!"

"Shiao-ho, you know that I have always wanted to marry you."

"Good! Good! I'm going to Win Town tonight to hire a carriage. I'll get the seat well padded. May-lin, I'm so happy."

"Shiao-ho, don't cry. I'm happy, too. Hold me! I wish you could stay with me," May-lin sobbed also.

"I'll be back with a padded chair to carry you downhill early tomorrow morning." He did not want to go but he had to. He was excited and also very tired; he did not detect two pairs of eyes watching him as he ran downhill.

May-lin was excited too. Their sweet young love in the past and a happy future kept her awake. She worried for Shiao-ho when she remembered that Monk Pure had told her both Steel Rod Monk and Priestess Keen wanted to kill Shiao-ho. Now Steel Rod Monk was dead, but Priestess Keen wanted to kill Shiao-ho even more.

Priestess Keen was Steel Rod Monk's classmate of the Sho-Lin School. They could not stand anyone who fought better than they do. They fought the aged Szechwan Dragon Du twenty years ago, and forced Du into hiding in Beijing. Dragon Knight Gi retired and he was also a student of the Sho-Lin School. They left him alone. Steel Rod Monk shamed Master Hsu, and demanded silver when Master Hsu could not lift the heavy steel rod. Only Shiao-ho's teacher and the mute punished them frequently. They hated and feared Shiao-ho's teacher intensely. Of course they wanted to kill Shiao-ho.

Steel Rod Monk asked old Bo, "Old Bo. Chiang Shiao-ho captured you and you've been on the road with him for a few days. Do you think Chiang Shiao-ho's skills are higher than mine? If I fight him, which one of us will win? Tell me!"

Old Bo hesitated for a while and then said, "Chiang Shiao-ho's strength might be comparable to yours, but he is more agile. If you two fight, Chiang Shiao-ho probably will win. That's the way I see it."

Steel Rod Monk roared furiously. He then sent Monk Pure to fetch Master Bo's students from Chengba to take Master Bo home.

May-lin knew Shiao-ho had killed Steel Rod Monk and overpowered Priestess Keen. She was worried that her friends, the militant Tao priests at Wu-Ton Mountain, would harm the lone Shiao-ho. She also thought about Gi Kon-jii and her Grandpa and finally she moaned and slept.

Someone walked into her room. May-lin asked sleepily, "Shiao-ho, you're back already? Don't worry; I won't change my mind again. I'll marry you."

"Gi Kon-jii is your husband, whore! Now you want to marry your enemy," Priestess Keen sneered.

"Reverend, you don't know that Shiao-ho and I had a promise of marriage ten years ago. Don't hurt me. Please!"

Priestess Keen tied May-lin up roughly. The coarse straw rope cut deeply into May-lin's chest wound, and she fainted. Keen carried her downhill.

Priestess Keen hid and watched Shiao-ho after she was released. She already stole Chiang Shiao-ho's sword. She watched Chiang Shiao-ho went downhill and came back. She waited until she was sure Shiao-ho would not return again, and snatched Bo May-lin. For a long time, she wanted to have a female student with a sound martial arts foundation. In this area, only two young women knew martial arts well: Fairy Du and Bo May-lin. She could not snatch Fairy Du, Master Hsu's daughter-in-law. She had the homeless May-lin until the damned Chiang Shiao-ho showed up. Now they wanted to get married. She would not allow it. She must take May-lin to somewhere remote to teach May-lin all her skills.

May-lin came to and realized that Priestess Keen was carrying her on her back. Keen's every step jerked May-lin's abrasion and caused her excruciating pain. She moaned. However, Keen ran even faster as though someone was chasing her. May-lin hoped that Shiao-ho was pursuing them.

The sound of a horse came from behind when they came to a bridge. Priestess Keen jumped down from the bridge and stood in the knee-deep water. She warned May-lin, "Don't you dare moan. I'll kill you."

The pursuer went over the bridge. Priestess Keen waited for a long time and then crossed the bridge too. May-lin assumed happily that Shiao-ho must be the one who chased them. She was too sick to yell or even to whine. She fainted again.

At daybreak, Priestess Keen stopped when she saw a horse with no rider at the roadside. She looked around cautiously and then slung May-lin roughly on the horse's back. Before she could mount the horse, a man came out of the high grass and charged at her. She recognized the mute, her feared enemy.

The mute snatched Chiang Shiao-ho's sword from Keen's hand, and kicked Priestess Keen away. He held May-lin in one arm, mounted the horse and rode fast.

May-lin asked her middle-aged rescuer, "Who are you? Did Chiang Shiao-ho send you here to save me?" No reply. However the rider dismounted a short distance away and gently cut May-lin loose, and then put her back on the horse. With one hand he steadied the girl, ran alongside the horse until they reached a grand villa. Servants and maids hastened to put May-lin on the bed and a doctor was called.

"Where am I? Who saved me?" May-lin asked.

"Is she your wife?" different voices asked.

May-lin's rescuer tapped her shoulder first and then pointed to his own nose, pushed a thumb up, flapped his arms like a bird and wiggled his little finger.

Someone told May-lin, "He's a mute. Only the master understands his signs."

A richly dressed old gentleman exchanged a few hand signals with the mute first and then told May-lin, "Miss, my name is Cus. He is a mute, his teacher and he saved me twice. From his signs I gather that his younger brother's name means a bird. You're his brother's wife. A bad woman wounded you. He wants me to take care of you while he goes to get your husband. He's very smart. He can read facial expressions."

"I see, thanks." May-lin was too weak to explain that she is not Shiao-ho's wife yet. They moved her to a nice room and laid her down on a well-padded bed. A maid served her and a doctor tended to her wounds. Mister Cus's wife and her daughter-in-law came to stay with May-lin for a while. They make May-lin comfortable and helped May-lin into clean clothes. The maid combed her hair, too. The doctor's medicine soothed her pain a little and May-lin fell into a drugged sleep.

Mister Cus wondered, '*how could the mute know that his brother's name means "a bird"? he does not know how to read and write.*' Indeed the mute was illiterate. But he was very smart. Once when he and Chiang Shiao-ho tended the tea plantation together, Shiao-ho pointed to the soaring eagles and then pointed to his own nose. That was how the mute knew that Shiao-ho's name had something to do with a bird.

Shiao-ho's teacher found the baby mute in a deserted shed, hired a woman help him to raise the mute. When the mute was five years and very intelligent, the old scholar started to teach him martial arts and sign language. The mute accompanied the old scholar on frequent trips; he remembered every route, every place they had traveled. A month ago, the old scholar mapped out a few routes, marked a few places for the mute, and sent him to trace Chiang Shiao-ho. The old scholar knew that Shiao-ho's skills were good enough to beat most adversaries. However, he was worried that no one could curb Shiao-ho if he would commit any evil.

The mute went to Bo's village, the first location his Teacher marked, and could not find Shiao-ho. He could not ask anyone but he spotted Steel Rod Monk and Priestess Keen. It seemed that they were also looking for Chiang Shiao-ho. too. These two were highly skilled and cunning, and the old scholar made sure the mute understood that Shiao-ho might not be able to defend himself against them. He followed them to the Taoist Covent and found a secular young woman staying there and decided to stay around. One night he followed Steel Rod Monk and spotted Shiao-ho and his prisoner; Old Bo. He watched Shiao-ho desperately search for something in the dark. He was too late to save Black Leopard, the hunter and his wife. He watched Shiao-ho fight Steel Rod Monk, pushed the Steel Rod Monk downhill. The mute killed Steel Rod Monk, stole a horse and threw the bag containing Lung Zhi-chi's head away. Later, he watched the blushing Shiao-ho picked up a woman's red shoe. He watched Shiao-ho and May-lin and assumed that the young woman must be Shiao-ho's wife. The mute also spotted Priestess Keen stealing Shiao-ho's sword, and was in hiding after Chiang Shiao-ho defeat her. When he woke up from a short sleep, and saw that Priestess Keen had kidnapped the young woman. He then follower the Tao Priestess, used the horse as bait to trick Priestess Keen, and saved May-lin.

The mute knew that Chiang Shiao-ho would definitely go back to the Tao convent to look for May-lin. So he hurried there after he deposited May-lin at the Cus's. When he got there, the quiet yard of the convent was full of men.

Lu Zhi-chun, Ma Zhi-min, Gi Kon-jii and Bo's two other students were all there questioning the elder priestess about Master Bo and May-lin's whereabouts. Monk Pure was ordered to bring Ma Zhi-min here to take Master Bo home. On his way there, he spotted Gi Kon-jii. Gi and Lu Zhi-chun were also looking for Master Bo and May-lin.

The mute found no Shiao-ho, he tapped Uncle Ma's shoulder first and then imitated a bird flying. He was asking, "Where's Shiao-ho?"

"Get out, you crazy! Are you a bird? A butterfly? Get out! You hear!" Gi Kon-jii tried to push the mute away.

"Wait! I think he is a mute. He wants to tell us something. Don't hurt him!" Ma shouted.

The mute did not budge, instead, he snatched Gi Kon-jii's sword and threw it away. He also kicked Gi.

"How dare you kick me? Who are you? Ah! You have Brother Chiang's sword." Gi Kon-jii recognized the sword and he wanted to charge at the mute again. Lu Zhi-chun held Gi back and said, "He's a mute, Nephew Gi, and I think he's also highly skilled. Let me try to guess what he wants us to know."

Lu Zhi-chun smiled at the mute friendlily. The mute pointed to the elder Tao priestess, imitated someone carrying something on the back, and then imitated a woman's walk.

Lu thought a while and then Uncle Ma said, "I think he's telling us a Tao priestess carried May-lin away."

"Where? Can you ask him, Uncle Ma?" Gi Kon-jii asked.

Monk Pure walked in, his eyes were tearful. He had just buried the Steel Rod Monk's remains. As soon as he saw the mute, he wanted to escape. But the mute grabbed him, patted his shoulder and smiled. He was saying, "I came as a friend."

"I know him. He's a mute. He is Chiang Shiao-ho's classmate. He fights almost as well as their Teacher," Monk Pure said and everyone was scared speechless. The mute drew a bird, a few lines on the ground with Shiao-ho's sword.

"He's asking us where did a bird…an eagle…a crane… Ah! Shiao-ho (Little Crane) goes. Before you came, he tried to tell us a priestess carried May-lin away. Chiang Shiao-ho must be on the chase now, but where?" Lu Zhi-chun guessed.

"Priestess Keen and my Teacher, Steel Rod Monk, were taught by the same teacher. She fights better than my Teacher. I just can't imagine that she would run away from Chiang Shiao-ho. She wanted May-lin to be her student. If she kidnapped May-lin, she would take her to Wu-Ton Mountain. She knows many militant priests and the seven famous sword masters there."

"I've been there. I'll challenge the swords masters again. Let's go," Gi boasted and gave the mute a friendly pat. He then pointed to the picture of the bird and nodded. He was telling the mute that he would lead the mute to Shiao-ho.

"Uncle Lu, Master Bo must not have gone far. You will find him. I'll take the mute to Wu-Ton Mountain," Gi said.

"Brother Gi, when you meet Priestess Keen, please be nice to her. If you're rude, she might kill Bo May-lin. By the way, please tell Chiang Shiao-ho if you meet him, that I'm still his friend even though he killed my teacher. I'm going to retreat to a monastery to study Buddhism."

The mute was a Southerner. He was even shorter than Gi Kon-jii. On their way to the Wu-Ton Mountain, the usually dominating Gi Kon-jii found that he had to obey the mute. If the mute wanted to stop to eat, he simply dragged Gi Kon-jii off his horse. If the mute wanted to go, Gi was not allowed to sit. Gi Kon-jii cooperated. He knew that he had to depend on the mute's help to fight and to get May-lin back. He missed May-lin. He thought often of what May-lin had told him when both of them were captured by Hu Li. *"I will be your true wife in the underworld."* He wanted to ask May-lin whether she still wanted to be his wife, now that both of them were alive. *'May-lin loves me, at least a little. If not, she won't say something like that.'*

They met Lee Feng-jii at the foot of Wu-Ton Mountain. Gi told Lee Feng-jii everything. Lee said, "I'd like to joint you. Chiang Shiao-ho is my sworn brother."

The clerk of the inn served them dinners and advised "Young masters, No one is allowed to go up there now. A tall young fellow is raising havoc up there. He killed one of the seven sword masters, one guard leopard and at least wounded five others."

"Bravo! Brother Chiang is great," Lee Feng-jii said excitedly.

"We, the folks around here, all know that one of the famous seven sword masters is a bad lot. He knows a mean-looking Tao Priestess. Behind the back of the noble Abbot and the other good Tao priests, the two of them had done crimes. The Tao priestess must have kidnapped a young woman. This young man came to find the woman. The innocent good Tao Priests really did not know about the kidnapping. The young man did not believe them and argued with them first and then fought them. I heard now the Abbot began to investigate the case. I hope he'll get rid of the evil pair."

14

There was dense fog when Chiang Shiao-ho reached Wu-Ton Mountain. The Tao Priests were annoyed when Chiang Shiao-ho asked them again and again about a missing woman. They fought and Shiao-ho killed a leopard, its owner fell off a cliff and died. The priests ganged on him, Shiao injured a few more and escaped to the woods.

Priest Quey stopped Shiao-ho and said, "Brother Chiang, I am not a local. I killed someone and came here to hide three years ago. I tell you this because I want you to believe me. I know of Priestess Keen. She indeed comes here once in a while but not lately. You can find her at Uennan Province down south or at Chin Mountain Range at Shaanxi up north."

"I just came from Shaanxi. She kidnapped a young woman and challenged me to be here." Shiao-ho had the impression that Quey was not telling the truth and trying to send him on a wild goose chase.

He was very hungry and smelled cooking. An old Tao Priest at a shabby temple offered him a meal and told Shiao-ho that not all the Tao priests at Wu-Ton Mountain know martial arts. He also told him that Quey was a bad lot and he indeed had some shady deals with a Tao Priestess. Another priest told Shiao-ho the location of the village where he thought Priestess Keen might be hiding. "Get rid of her, We want to get the peaceful mountain back soon. You may stay here tonight."

It was raining and the mountain paths were dangerously slippery. Shiao-ho found the village. It was a hard and lengthened fight. He finally pierced the Priestess Keen with the skills which the mute taught him on the day he left his teacher.

"Tell me where May-lin is. Quick! I won't kill you."

"Your ..the mute grabbed May-lin...I...."

"My brother the Mute! Where?" Priestess Keen died.

All the bells of every Taoist Temple on Wu-Ton Mountain were ringing again to alert the priests of intruders. He half dragged, half carried the dead Priestess Keen to the center court. '*This is the proof, Maybe the Abby can force Priest Quey to tell...*'

All the priests stood with their mouth-open, eye bulged, and Gi Kon-jii and Lee Feng-jii were there also. The mute and the Abbot, number one sword master, were engaged in a duel. The two combatants slowly circled each other; their two swords moved slowly and never came close to each other. Shiao-ho knew that it was a hair-raising, to the death duel.

"Chiang Shiao-ho, where is my wife?" Gi demanded.

"The mute knows where she is. Watch! We have to wait,' Chiang Shiao-ho said. His mouth opened as he watched intently. Just when he thought the barefooted mute was going to win, the white-bearded Abbot fell.

Most of the Tao priests went to the wounded Abby and some priests looked at Tao priestess's body.

"Ya Ya..." the Mute hugged Chiang Shiao-Ho and handed over Shiao-ho's sword, which the Priestess Keen had stolen. Then he reached up and slapped the puzzled Shiao-ho hard, pointed out his two fingers. Shiao-ho understood that he was being punished for applying the '*Tien Hsueh*' technique to Priestess Keen. Now everything came to him clearly and he knew that the mute had killed Steel Rod Monk, stole the horse, watched his every movement and saved May-lin.

"Brother Chiang, Priest Quey is under house arrest..." Lee Feng-jii said.

"Where is my wife?..." Gi Kon-jii demanded.

"My brother the mute saved May-lin. He'll take us to her," Shiao-ho told the impatient Gi Kon-jii. The mute pulled Shiao-ho to the horses.

When Shiao-ho was locked in the critical fight in the village with Priestess Keen. Gi Kon-jii, the mute and Lee Feng-jii wanted to search the mountain with the accusation that the Tao priests had hid Bo may-lin. The two sides decided to have a duel and the winner will have the last word.

The mute impatiently wanted take Shiao-ho to Master Cus's villa. He did not understand why Gi-Kon-jii insisted on going. He pull Gi Kon jii off the horse and threatened Gi with fists. Shiao-ho repeated talked with his hand and finally the Mute allowed that Gi joined them.

When they reached Cus's villa, they were informed that May-lin died two days ago

Mister Cus took them to the elaborate coffin and said, "Poor Miss Bo, the cuts on her chest were deep and extensive. Two doctors tried very hard, but they could not save her. Which one of you is Shiao-ho? She called 'Shiao-ho' often and with her last breath."

"I'm Chiang Shiao-ho. But her husband is Gi kon-jii...." Shiao-ho sobbed.

"Stop it, Chiang Shiao-ho! I'm leaving. Your dead father must be proud of you. You forced an old grandpa homeless, caused his granddaughter's death. *Ha! Ha!* May-lin called your name with her last breath. I was never really her husband. I am just a clown playing the role of her husband. That's all. I'm leaving. It's your turn to be her husband now. Bye!" Gi Kon-jii left with a deranged laugh. Mister Cus, the mute and the maids stood stunned.

Shiao-ho managed to stop crying long enough to draw a route and ask the mute to go to Bo's village to fetch Uncle Ma. Mister Cus was a good listener. Between sobs and over drinks, Shiao-ho told him everything.

Mister Cus sighed, "It's all predestined. The three of you are bound into an eternal triangle. There is nothing more to say. But I wish to see the practice of 'revenge' comes to an end. You should have listened to Uncle Ma and Uncle Lu and be forgiving. They were right to say that even if you kill all the Kung Lung members, you cannot revive your dead father. I wish that all the warriors learn a valuable lesson from your tragedy and no more acts of revenge. The vicious circle of killing for revenge must be stopped. Shiao-ho, you killed Lung Zhi-chi because he killed your father He was evil and your revenge was justified. Are you not afraid that one day Lung's son, if he had one, or a family member of his will try to kill you for revenge?" He then continued, "It is really ridiculous to say that *'it's a son's duty to kill his father's murderer, to please the dead father's soul'*. I would think a dead father's soul, regardless if he was murdered or died in bed, would rather see his sons and daughters have a good life. A son's primary duty to his parents should be to have a successful life, to have a loving family. I think that is the wish of any parent."

Uncle Lu and Uncle Ma arrived at Cus's villa with the mute. They consoled Shiao-ho, "It's fate. There are only two persons to blame:

Master Bo and your father. But it's useless to dwell upon it any more. You are young and you have a bright future to look forward to. We'll take care of everything."

The mute pulled Shiao-ho aside, pointed to the sky and imitated the action of stroking one's beard. He was saying, "Shiao-ho, go home, go to see our teacher now. He'll take care of you." The mute understood Shiao-ho's pain.

Shiao-ho used all his strength to resist the mute who pulled him, wanting him to go. He shook his head, touched his little finger and made other signs. He was saying, "I'll be back home later. Now I want to see my little brother."

The mute nodded. He walked like a woman, waved his hand, and wiped his eyes. He was saying, "I know your wife is dead. Please don't cry any more. It's no use to cry." He then reached up and ruffled Shiao-ho's hair fondly and left.

On the way to Bo's village with the coffin., Uncle Ma told Shiao-ho that his mother died.

"Shiao-ho, your mother hired some Buddhist monks and Tao priests to conduct a memorial for your father with the silver you had given her. Her husband, Ton, repeatedly accused her of wasting silver. Then your stepsister died. Shortly after, your mother died. She told me to tell you that you must find your brother and take care of him," Ma continued, "Shiao-ho, you should have come home directly to see your mother. You should be frank about your wish that you want to marry May-lin. Master Bo would gladly have you marry May-lin, and dissolve the animosity. It's too late to be sorry now. Go to see your brother and look after him. I know you will."

"Thanks. I'll see to it." He did not say that he would look after Uncle Ma and his family too.

He went to the big willow tree. The village girls said, "Mister Chiang, you're back with your big horse. Miss Bo likes to ride too. She is not home yet." Shiao-ho said nothing.

He went into town and lay on a lice-infested bed for three days without eating. On the fourth day, he went to Uncle Ma's shop to find out where his mother's tomb was and his younger brother's address.

"Shiao-ho, have you been sick? Don't be too hard on yourself. Life has to go on, and it's no use to weep over the past. Will you stay for the double funeral?"

"Double funeral? Who else died, Uncle Ma?"

"One-eyed Yu and Feng Zhi-pan brought Master Bo's casket back. He killed himself." Uncle Ma sighed.

Master Bo was too ashamed and remorseful to go home to face his students.. He found a Buddhist monastery. There he repented. He regretted that he had killed so many persons, sometimes with no reason to kill. He regretted that he had indulged and spoiled the Lung brothers while he punished other students harshly. He regretted that he let his second son abuse Shiao-ho. He regretted a lot and he wanted to see his crippled son one more time before he became a full-pledged monk. When he found out that he had no more silver and he was too old to rob, steal...and he hanged himself.

After the funeral, One-eyed Yu told Shiao-ho that he and Chen had been tried for the crime of stealing silver from Miser Ku. Luckily the security guard Yan cleared their names. Shiao-ho shamefully admitted that it was he, not Gi Kon-jii, who stole the silver to help the refugees.

Yu laughed, "Chen and me knew. Gi Kon-jii could never steal or carry nearly seven hundred ounces of silver and jump up a roof. You should see how unhappy and nervous he was when he distributed the silver to the refugees the next day. You should see how scared he was when he found out that you wrote that ridiculous 'Chiang Shiao-ho -- wanted" poster on his back."

Then Yu told Feng, Lu and others in detail how Chiang Shiao-ho had teased Gi Kon-jii. They talked about the past and the tragedy. No one condemned Shiao-ho and they all agreed that it was predestination.

Feng and May-lin's father were shrewd businessmen. They wanted to have Shiao-ho as a friend. Shiao-ho also knew that his beloved Uncle Ma and his family would need to have the Kung Lung member's good will. They parted amicably.

Shiao-ho burned incenses and paper silver nuggets, for the deceased to use in the underworld, at the site where his father was killed, at his mother's tomb and under the dying willow tree for May-lin. He cut off a piece of the tree bark as a keepsake.

His younger brother was a well-liked and very honest twelve-year-old apprentice at a fabric shop. The owner liked him and treated him like his own son. The boy cried at their mother's death, but Shiao-ho did not tell him the details of their father's death.

He told his Teacher everything. His Teacher listened to him with patience and consoled him with a long philosophical talk. "Shiao-ho, there are two equally cruel and unreasonable traditions. All the women are the victims of the foot-binding custom and you are a victim of the tradition that all sons must avenge their father's death. We were told and taught to follow them. I was to blame, too. I could not break off from this evil tradition otherwise I would have forbid you to do it. It's no use to regret it now." In the following days, Shiao-ho did his chores, practiced martial arts listlessly and lost weight. The mute looked at him with concern and coerced him to eat more.

Teacher said, "Shiao-ho, don't live in the past. I know you cannot forget your painful past. But, life goes on. No one can turn back the time to correct the wrongs. You owe it to yourself and to the people who care for you, deceased or alive, to be happy. Nobody said life is fair. We have to grasp the beauty, the pleasure, and the joy of being alive. Your late parents and May-lin would be disappointed if you let the bitter past prevent you from enjoying any small doses of happiness you can get out of life. Shiao-ho, be happy for me, for the mute, for your brother, for Uncle Ma and Uncle Lu. You are fond of martial arts so learn it well. Put your passion into it." Teacher taught him the highest martial arts skills. Teacher also agreed that he would help Uncle Ma with the proceeds of the tea plantation.

His Teacher passed away five years later, Shiao-ho wore a white armband as a true son would, and he also wore white as a true son for Uncle Ma and Aunt Ma.

Every three or four years, Shiao-ho would repeat the same trip. He would visit his brother and return to his hometown to see Uncle Ma first and then burn incenses at his mother's grave and the site where his father was killed. He would stand a long time besides the site where the big willow tree was. It was there under the big willow tree where he and May-lin pledged their love. A piece of the tree bark and one of May-lin's red shoes accompanied him everywhere.

-End-

Epilogue

Chiang Shiao-ho compiled the martial arts skills his teacher taught him into a two-volume manual with few simple words and many detailed pictures for the mute to review. Years later, he and the mute went to Szechwan to visit Master Hsu. Then he himself went to visit Uncle Lu and taught Lu's grandson martial arts for a while. The mute disappeared with the manuals. Shiao-ho traveled near and far, but he could not find the mute and the manuals.

One of Uncle Ma's sons and his family managed the tea plantation for Chiang Shiao-ho. He teamed up with Lee Feng-jii repelled the bandits along the Yangtze River. Many grateful travelers praised their efforts. Gi Kon-jii, Hawk Hsu and his wife did more or less the same thing along the Yellow River. Travelers enjoyed bandit-free journeys.

He visited Lee Feng-jii's family often at Nanjing and he taught Lee's youngest boy Lee Mo-bai martial arts and swimming. One day Lee Feng-jii suggested that Chiang Shiao-ho change his name to Chiang Nan-ho. Lee said, "You're a big tall balding old man now. You cannot be called Shiao-ho (little Crane) any more. You've spent most of your life in the South. Chiang Nan-ho (south crane) would be more appropriate."

Chiang Nan-ho and Lee-Feng-jii often reminisced about the past with sighs and over drinks.

Once, Lee Feng-jii quoted a well-written verse:

'The mighty green mountains stand solid year after year.
Our short lives are a few sunup and sunsets.

Lee Mo-bai (李慕白) and a living widow

1

The birds were quarreling and the dew on the leaves was sparkling. Lee Mo-bai finished the morning workout and murmured,

'In the big gradual and turbulent world,
where can I use my talent to achieve?

He felt the same frustration that a demoted minister wrote two hundred years ago. "Young master, should I get a carriage?" A servant who brought him water for him to wash and shave asked. "No, I will stay home." He used up his allowance and did not want to ask his uncle for more silver.

Lee Mo-bai was depressed. He was twenty-four years old, taller than average, and lived comfortably as the nephew and heir of a landowner. And he also was an expert at both the literary arts and martial arts. His idea and dream of how to live his life and whom he wanted to marry clashed with his uncle's. The burden of being the only heir made him feel trapped like a caged tiger. He wanted win himself fame and fortune with his martial arts skills; he wanted to see the world and rid it of bandits. Doing anything was better than staying home and getting served, literally, from mouth to foot. His uncle wanted Lee Mo-bai to pass the second level of civil services examination and be an administrator. He wanted to keep Mo-bai safe. His own son was robbed and killed and left no child.

His aunt said after breakfast, "Mo-bai, the matchmaker found you a good wife. Miss Pu is seventeen and her feet are tiny." She understood Mo-bai's restlessness and thought a good wife would keep him happy and she wanted to have grandkids soon.

His uncle said, "Her family is very much like ours. You're a scholar with a promising future; she would bring us a good dowry. It's a good match. You've rejected two marriage proposals. Don't you know how much it cost us to pay that greedy matchmaker?" Lee Mo-bai said nothing.

His aunt pleaded, "We want to have a grandson soon to carry on the bloodline. Her sister had two sons in four years; Miss Pu is likely to have children soon. I was told this girl has tiny feet, true *'golden lilies.'* Think it over." No reply. His aunt sighed, "Maybe we should not be afraid of letting you leave home, you may find a wife yourself." His uncle said in a conciliatory tone, "Mo-bai, I know you want to have a wife who knows martial arts. Where could we find someone like that? Maybe we can make an arrangement for you to have a look at Miss Pu."

"Let us wait for a while. I will try hard to pass the examination in the fall." Lee Mo-bai said, Both his uncle and aunt smiled.

Lee Mo-bai thought, 'who *cares whether she has tiny feet or not. My mother had tiny feet, but my father always wished that her feet were bigger, so they could go to places together.'* He missed his parents and Uncle Chiang, his father's sworn brother. His parents died when he was eight years old.

His classmate Tu came, "Mo-bai, you better thank me first. I have found you a perfect wife."

"I'm in a bad mood. My aunt is trying to arrange a marriage for me again."

"It's for real. This pretty maiden knows martial arts well."

"She knows martial arts? Who is she? Tell me."

"*Ha Ha*. I bet you're interested. Be patient. I'll tell you in my own time. The famous Master Yu, nicknamed *'Iron Wings'*, has a pretty daughter."

"Our late Teacher Gi praised him highly. He must be close to seventy now."

"He's old. His daughter is about seventeen years old and very beautiful"

"The folks of a small town like to exaggerate. Besides, a proper maiden hardly ever shows herself in public. How do you know that she is pretty and knows martial arts well?"

"It's true. On Spring Memorial Day, Master Yu and his family went to visit their ancestors' graves. On their way back, four young men attacked them. Yu Ceo-lian seized an attacker's saber and wounded one. That's why the folks know that she is pretty and fights better than men."

"Ahe! She's truly one in a thousand," Mo-bai praised.

"I told you so. She also beat up Brother Lu pretty bad."

"Why? She likes to fight?"

"Brother Lu was there when Yu Ceo-lian and her father fought off the enemies. He was obsessed with her. Lu went to Master Yu's house at night to peep at her. He got caught, and she nearly killed him."

"It served Brother Lu right. But, his defeat will certainly tarnish our Teacher's reputation."

"Only you can fight her and let folks know that Master Gi's students are good. You can kill two birds with one stone, be famous and fulfill your dream of marrying a pretty girl who knows martial arts well."

"How can I bluntly go there and challenge a maiden? Besides, Master Yu must have arranged a marriage for her already." Lee Mo-bai sounded disappointed.

"She is not promised. You fight her, you win and you will have a wife. Master Yu pledged that whoever could beat his daughter in a friendly match, would be his son-in-law. With your good looks, Yu Ceo-lian might admit defeat. *Ha! Ha!* Mo-bai, you're not afraid, are you?"

"I told you twice already that I'm in no mood for jokes."

"I swear it is true. If you don't believe me, go ask Master Yu yourself. I want you to gain back our teacher's good name."

"You want me to fight her. That is it."

"I got it from a reliable source that Master Yu truly wants to find a capable son-in-law who can help him to fight off his enemies. He did say that his intended son-in-law has to fight better than his daughter. You just have to challenge her; you may very well win a wife with your sword."

"Four young men attacked an old man! Master Yu may have more enemies. I would help Master Yu. I don't want to see a true hero suffer defeat at old age."

"That's the spirit. Do you want to have a look at her? The day after tomorrow, the seventh day of the Fourth Month, is Buddha's birthday. Everyone will go to the temple to ask for blessings. Tomorrow we can stay overnight at my father's shop in town. Then we can go to the temple to have a look at her." Mo-bai agreed.

Tu rushed home and sent a servant to town with a letter to his friends. He wanted his friends there to help him play a trick on Lee

Mo-bai. Though Tu and Lu were also Master Gi's students, only Lee Mo-bai learned well. Tu and Lu were jealous of Mo-bai's achievement, and they thought Lee Mo-bai is conceited.

The next day, Mo-bai told his uncle that he wanted to go to Lu Town to buy some books and stay overnight. His uncle agreed readily. His uncle always wanted Mo-bai to be friends with the well-to-do Tu and Lu.

Tu took Mo-bai to dine at a teahouse. They met two friends of Tu's. One said, "Brother Tu, did you know there are a few young martial arts fighters in town already. They came to challenge the pretty Yu Ceo-lian."

Tu said, "Has anyone won the trophy yet?"

"Not yet. Someone mentioned that Master Yu would rent the field behind the temple for the match after tomorrow. Tomorrow is Buddha's birthday."

"I think that Master Yu wants to save a dowry for his daughter and get someone to help him to fight off his enemies. He probably will want his future son-in-law to move in and live with him. He even might hope the young chap will reopen his security company. I think it's a kind of wishful thinking of his." another friend of Tu's said.

Tu said to Lee Mo-bai, "You may have to forgo the whole thing. Your uncle wants you to earn an office with your pen."

Lu's friend asked, "Brother Lee, do you really want to challenge her? She is very pretty."

Lee Mo-bai blushed and said, "I don't want anyone to think Teacher Gi has no good students."

Tu said, "Brother Lee sure will win and get a pretty wife."

"Really? He better fight better than Lu. Miss Yu is not easy to win."

Lu said, "Brother Lee will win. Let's have a toast." They all wished Lee Mo-bai good luck.

A crowd gathered at the temple; slender maidens wore new pastel-colored outfits, portly matrons dressed in somber colors. Many idle young men walked around to watch the pretty girls. Tu pointed out Yu Ceo-lian for Lee Mo-bai, and it was love at first sight. They rode behind Yu Ceo-lian and her mother's carriage and followed her to her home.

Su, Master Yu's student, wielded a heavy saber at Tu and Lee, "You rascals. Get away!" Tu got scared and walked away. Lee Mo-bai said to Su, "I came to visit Master Yu."

Su sneered, "No you're not. You followed Miss Yu all the way from the temple. Get away from here, you hear!"

They fought. Su could hardly defend himself and then Yu Ceo-lian came out. She had on a short outfit and a pink scarf covered her two braids. She shouted, "You rascal, I won't fight you on the street. You dare come inside?"

"Certainly"

The robust Su insisted on helping Yu Ceo-lian to fight Lee Mo-bai, but he could not keep up with the fast moves and withdrew reluctantly. Carrying a birdcage, Master Yu rushed home at a neighbor's urging. He saw right away that his daughter was not the young man's match, and the young man fought in defense only.

"Stop!" Master Yu ordered. Lee Mo-bai obeyed instantly but not the girl. She advanced and slashed, scissors-like, at Lee Mo-bai with her two sabers. Lee Mo-bai jumped free with her scarf on the tip of his sword. Yu Ceo-lian cried and rushed inside.

"Teacher! He and another young rascal followed Sister Ceo-lian all the way from the temple." Su said.

Master Yu asked, "You don't look like a rascal. Why do you come to fight my student and my daughter?"

Lee Mo-bai sheathed his sword, bowed respectfully low and said, "Reverent Master Yu. Please forgive me. I behaved impulsively. I'm Lee Mo-bai of Nan-kon Village."

"You fought with genuine Wu-ton style. Ahe! You must be the late Master Gi's student."

"Yes. I am."

"Oh! You must be Master Lee Feng-jii's son. Once I had a drink with your late father and Master Chiang. You're almost a nephew to me. Come in, we will talk over a cup of tea."

"May I ask why do you come here to fight us, Mo-bai?"

"I won." Lee Mo-bai bowed, with the girl's scarf in hand. He blushed and wishfully thinking that Master Yu would accept him as his son-in-law.

"Indeed you have. Master Gi taught you well. I want to know why you came to fight us. I don't think we've offended you. And, what do you want to do with my daughter's scarf?" Master Yu tried to hold his anger in check.

"But...But Uncle Yu, didn't you..." Lee Mo-bai stuttered at first and then his words gushed out, "didn't you say that whoever could beat your daughter in a match, could marry her?"

"Ha Ha! You were duped. Someone played a dirty trick on you. You're a fool." Su laughed. Master Yu also chuckled and said, "I've never said such a thing. Your young friends played a prank. Ceo-lian's marriage was arranged five years ago. She is promised to marry my good friend Master Mon's second son. This fall, I will take her to Da-ton, Shanxi Province to be married. Nephew Lee, you're welcome to come to visit us any time. If I know of a suitable maiden, I'll be the middleman."

Lee Mo-bai's face turned red first and then pale. His flame of hope a moment ago turned into ice. He managed to murmur, "Reverend Uncle, I'm sorry. Please forgive me."

"Let's forget it. I'm glad to meet you. Come to see us again."

Lee Mo-bai thought about nothing but Yu Ceo-lian's pretty face and her graceful, agile movements. He composed verses and verses praising her beauty and lamenting his misfortune. Sometimes in his dreams, he would fight a faceless young man or rescue Yu Ceo-lian from a brutal husband and a mean mother-in-law. He was lovesick and getting thinner, and decided that he would find an excuse to leave home soon. *'There are many martial arts masters out there, and they must have daughters who are good at martial arts. If I stay home, I would never find another one like Yu Ceo-lian.'*

His servant suggested that he could copy Buddhism scriptures and verses for devotees and earn some silver. They paid him well for his beautiful calligraphy. His writing style was a perfect mix of his father's graceful strokes and Master Gi's powerful ones. Once when he was mechanically copying the religious verses, his mind wandered from Yu Ceo-lian to Teacher Gi and Uncle Chiang. *'Were they ever enchanted by pretty girls when they were young? Have they ever been brokenhearted like me? Daddy used to brush my mother's beautiful long hair tenderly. From reading the poems my father had written, I knew he must have adored my mother. Teacher Gi married and had children though he hardly talked about them. How about Uncle Chiang? Why wasn't he married?'*

His aunt noticed his melancholy and thinning face. She worried and she knew that Mo-bai was bored at home. She sent a letter to her cousin in Beijing and asked him to find a position for Lee Mo-bai.

Yu Ceo-lian was worried because her father was worried. She noticed it even before she had to help her father to fight off the attackers. Ever since her father's student Wei from Henan Province came to visit during a blizzard two months ago, her father started to practice and teach her martial arts in earnest. He even brought a horse and rode often. She knew something was up so she practiced more. When these four vicious men attacked them, she was scared at first. When she saw her father in danger, she jumped in and helped. That night when a young man came to her home, she chased him away. Since then, she had been on alert, and she knew that she needed to practice more after Lee Mo-bai took her scarf away. *'Ahe! He could have killed me. Luckily, he is no enemy'* Her face felt hot whenever she thought about that incident.

Then Wei came again. Their enemies were closing in. Su suggested, "Teacher, I'll go to Nan-kon Village to fetch Lee Mo-bai. We don't have to worry about anything if we have him here to help us."

"No, we cannot. It's not fitting for Ceo-lian to meet him again. Ceo-lian is promised. Lee Mo-bai's uncle wants him to be an administrator and he certainly won't want his nephew to marry the likes of us. I heard that Lee's uncle is greedy and he probably wants to have a huge dowry." Master Yu said.

"But, he wants to marry Ceo-lian very bad."

Master Yu prepared to take Ceo-lian and her mother to her betrothed's.

A letter came from Lee's uncle saying there would be an opening for a minor clerk, Mo-bai should be in Beijing soon. His uncle and aunt thought that if Mo-bai could find a job there, he could stay there and then take the civil services examination in the fall. Mo-bai was elated and he promised that he would study hard for the examination.

His aunt supervised the tailor to make new clothes for Mo-bai. His uncle hired a reliable long-distance carriage to take him to Beijing. They consulted a fortuneteller to pick an auspicious day for his departure. Lee Mo-bai gladly set out in the increasing summer heat. He secretly took his father's sword with him. He had three swords: his own, his father's and Teacher Gi.'s.

At the first town north, Lee Mo-bai dismissed the carriage and bribed the groom not to tell his uncle. He brought an inexpensive horse, a used saddle and a wide-brimmed straw hat. He loved to ride and he could ride very well when he was five years old. His uncle did not want to have a horse around and this was the first time he rode after Teacher Gi's horse died. Now, he had a horse and felt free like a released caged eagle and the dirty hotel room and coarse meals did not bother him at all.

"Mr. Lee, Nephew Lee, where are you going?"

Master Yu was riding alongside a carriage. Mo-bai caught a glimpse of Yu Ceo-lian and her mother inside the carriage before she closed the curtain. He blushed.

"Greetings, Uncle Yu. I'm on my way to Beijing."

"We're going to Da-ton. Glad to see you again. Have a nice trip. Nephew Lee..." Master Yu seemed to want to talk more when his daughter called from inside the carriage, "Daddy, can we go now? It's hot."

Mo-bai said, "Goodbye, have a safe trip."

Mo-bai thought, *'the whole family is going to Da-ton. Isn't that where Yu Ceo-lian's husband-to-be lives? Master Yu is anxious to see his daughter get married. I hope his decision has nothing to do with my ridiculous behavior a month ago. What did he want to tell me? They have to turn to the west after two or three stops. I'm going straight to the north. If I slow down and stay behind a bit, I won't meet them again. This is an embarrassing situation.'*

His meager fund got low after buying the horse. He remembered that Teacher Gi had told him about how to earn a free stay at the temple. So he found a Buddhist temple and copied some scriptures for the abbot. He earned a two-day stay and meals. On the second night at the temple, he thought wishfully, *'Maybe the old man changed his mind about his daughter's marriage. He called me in the middle of the road and tried to tell me that I may marry Yu Ceo-lian. She was too shy to let him finish telling me. I'd better try to catch up with them and find out.'* Another thought chased him on the road before dawn. *'Maybe he is afraid of his enemies. He wants to send his family to the in-laws to be safe. What if the enemies attack him now? I better hurry up to help them.'*

Four riders, three men and a woman, passed him in a rush and their horses kicked up enormous dust. Lee Mo-bai's horse bolted and he had a hard time getting the jittery horse under control. *'They might be Master Yu's enemies.'* He hurried.

When he was close to the next town, Lee Mo-bai saw a crowd and heard shouting and the sound of weapons clashing. Master Yu and his daughter were fighting the four riders who had passed him on the road. The woman shouted obscenities while fighting Yu Cco-lian and the other three men circled the old Master Yu. Lee Mo-bai dashed in with his sword; he injured one tall man and the other two men fled. The crowd cheered when Yu Ceo-lian wounded the malicious woman. At the sight of blood, Lee Mo-bai turned pale and his hands shook when a good by-stander brought his horse to him. It was his first real fight and his sword had drawn blood. '*Taste the blood once, you sword would forever be thirsty for more*' he seemed to hear Master Gi's words. He knew that he could no longer keep his promise to his dear aunt that he would not fight, and his promise of passing the examination.. He was no longer living in a sheltered and pampered world anymore but he actually did not mind it very much. '*This is real life.*' He felt good.

Soldiers came. They dragged the wounded man and the screaming woman to court. The Yu family and Lee Mo-bai was ordered to follow them to the court. Some by-standers followed them and told the magistrate that the four riders attacked the Yu family first. Lee Mo-bai came later and helped them.

"My lord, this man killed my father. We want revenge," Ho Su-an, nicknamed '*She Devil*' said.

"Silence! You cannot take the law into your hands. You're injured so I won't order you to be clubbed. Put these two in jail. Sergeant, take the Yu family and the young man to a hotel and have them wait for further investigation." They were dismissed. On their way out, a fancy-dressed young man ogled the pretty Yu Ceo-lian.

Mrs. Yu was sick. They found a doctor, bought the medicine, and borrowed a small charcoal burner and a medicine bowl for Yu Ceo-lian to brew the herbs for her mother.

Master Yu came to Lee's room and explained, "You must have heard about the saying of '*weed out the roots*'; a person killed someone has to kill the victim's children too, lest they perform their duty-bound revenge on their father's killer. I don't blame them for wanting to kill me. I killed their father. I was anxious to send my family to my in-laws and then I can fight them alone. I knew they were after me. When I met you the other day, I wanted to ask you to help me then."

"Uncle Yu, you know I would help if I only knew." Lee Mo-bai refrained from asking the details of the animosity. His looks betrayed his curiosity.

"I and their father, Master Ho, were professional guards when we were young. We were good friends first and later sworn brothers. Right from the beginning, Master Ho's unscrupulous ways bothered me. We parted. I was poor then and I had to move to where the jobs were. I lost two boys since we did not have a steady home. Gradually I made a name for myself and had my own security company. When Ceo-lian was five years old, that was eleven years ago, a young scholar and his pretty bride bought my protection for a trip. The convoy carried the flags that identified my security company. I did not have to escort them myself; most bandits would honor the flag. Master Ho, by then a bandit leader, led his men to rob the young couple and he himself raped the bride. She killed herself. I went to challenge Master Ho and I killed him. I took enough silver from his estate to compensate the unlucky scholar's family. However, I spared his children and his students. Then I started teaching Ceo-lian martial arts. Two months ago, Master Ho's two sons, two students came to kill us. Ceo-lian helped me to repel them. I know they will come again soon."

"Uncle Yu, I will go to Da-ton with you lest they attack you again. I don't have to be in Beijing soon."

"Thank you, but no. Da-ton is not that far. By the time they could return with extra help from Kaifeng, Ceo-lian and her mother should be settled. My in-laws will stand by me."

Lee Mo-bai's heart felt like it was stabbed by a sharp dagger, he thought, '*Oh yes, she will be married,*' he said, "They may have more help nearby. Please let me accompany you."

"That's not their style. If they were more, they would gang up on me already. Master Ho's children are mediocre. The woman is the most capable one and Ceo-lian wounded her. The only one who might be difficult to fight is her husband Jao, nicknamed '*Golden Spear*'. Jao's uncle Mew's steel darts are deadly accurate. Mew was the late Dart Hu-Li's student. I'm telling you this so you will be prepared. You are their enemy now. Mo-bai, is this your first real fight?"

"Yes." Mo-bai admitted, "I was scared at first and I was clumsy."

"Master Gi taught you well, you have strength, skills and speed, but you don't have enough experience. That will come. When you have to fight your enemy, you should not hesitate. Remember your enemy intends to kill you…"

A sergeant walked in, "Master Yu, I have good news for you…"

"Are we free to leave?"

"Soon. The bystander's report cleared you. The Ho woman admitted that they wanted to kill you. I'm bringing you great news. The magistrate's only son wants to take your pretty daughter for a second wife, not a concubine. His first wife did not have children. If your daughter has a son soon, her position will be equal to the first wife. Magistrate Feng will pay you three hundred ounces silver. You need not to worry about the dowry. You're in luck, old friend."

"Sergeant, my daughter is already engaged to be married. We are on our way to her new home. Please thank Magistrate Feng for me."

"Master Yu, don't ruin your luck. You should think it over."

"My daughter is indeed to be married to Master Mon's second son. I can show you the marriage contract. Please intercede for me. Sergeant, here is some silver for your trouble."

"I'll try. But if I were you, I would reconsider it seriously." The sergeant accepted the silver and left. His threat lingered in the air.

Master Yu sighed and whispered, "It's preposterous. My Ceo-lian is not going to be some wealthy scoundrel's second wife. I'd rather marry her to…" he did not finish his statement, Lee Mo-bai's hope started to rise again.

"Uncle Yu, please don't be angry. The magistrate must be a corrupt one. My Teacher always said that no honest men want to work for the Manchu. I'm afraid that he will find a way to detain us somehow."

"Don't voice your opinion in public. The walls have ears. The Manchu have occupied us, the Han, over a hundred years now; they were still weary of the resistance. Be careful."

Lee Mo-bai thought angrily, *'Beauty surely tempts evil'*. He remembered that his Teacher told him how to gather information. He put on his scholar's garb and went to a crowded teahouse and sat at a dark corner. His keen hearing picked up segments of conversation above the noises.

--*'That woman bandit is surely vicious. Lucky for the old man and the pretty girl, a young chap came to their rescue just in time…'*

--*'That young man looks like a weak scholar, but he sure know how to wield the sword….'*

--*'The fighters of the internal Wu-ton School of Martial Arts never appear tough outward. You remember that Master Gi and Master Lee, before them the two Dragons, all look like weak and soft scholars. Rumors had it that they composed poems when they fought. Ha.Ha…'*

Lee Mo-bai thought, "They are talking about my Teacher and my father."

--'I'm sorry for that pretty girl. She won't be safe now. Magistrate's son gaped at her..'

--'Oh. That devil won't leave any pretty young woman alone. ...I heard.. Chen's wife..." Lee Mo-bai strained to hear more of the whispering but he could not. He suddenly was afraid for Yu Ceo-lian, and left without touching his tea.

As soon as he stepped into the hotel, a tearful Yu Ceo-lian met him and pleaded, "Brother Lee, please help us. The soldiers arrested my father. Please go and find out why."

"Yes, I'll go. Miss Yu please stay in your room and wait."

He adjusted his scholar's cap and robe, asked a guard at the gate while he inconspicuously handed the guard some silver. The guard told him that Master Yu was arrested because someone had reported that Master Yu is a bandit.

"Go to Captain Ta-di, he will help you," the guard whispered.

"The last name is Ta-di. A Manchu?" Lee Mo-bai also whispered.

"Captain Ta-di is indeed a full-blooded Manchu, but he is just. It was on his order that old Yu was put in a cleaner cell. He knows the magistrate's son is a bad lot and he will help you. Not all the Manchu are cruel and not all the Hans are nice either. Go to ask him quickly," the guard whispered. Lee Mo-bai had to bribe another guard again before he was presented to Captain Ta-di.

"Master Lee, don't worry. They cannot hold him long. The woman insisted that she would not lie. She said, "Of course we want him dead. But it's against our ethics to indict him when he is truly not a bandit." I know that Magistrate Feng is very corrupt. I have sent a report to a very just high rank minister. Our Emperor is trying to get rid of the corrupt officials now. Master Yu will soon be released. You can visit him."

"Mo-bai, I'm grateful you are here. I'm jailed because…"

"Uncle Yu. Take it easy. Captain Ta-di said.…. I'll look after your family. I will bring you meals, too." They whispered through the barred window.

"Mo-bai, I don't know how to thank you…"

A guard came and said, "Visiting time is over," and told Lee to leave.

Lee Mo-bai bought a meal and he had to bribe the guard to let him take the meal to the Master Yu. He started to worry that he would not have enough silver to keep going like this. Yu Ceo-lian handed him some silver and said, "Brother Lee, we're very grateful that you are here to help us. I don't know what we would do without you. I don't know how to thank you...," she wept and so did Mrs. Yu.

Master Yu was released two days later. He looked a lot older. Two days in jail with constant worry and rage seemed to be longer than a year. He ordered his daughter to pack their belongings, paid for Lee Mo-bai's fare with extra if Lee wanted to stay another day.

"Aunt Yu is still not well enough to go in the heat yet. Besides, you need rest, too. Why not stay one more night? We'll leave tomorrow morning."

"Mo-bai, we're not safe here. The Magistrate can easily find something else to detain us with. Besides, you're right about how my enemies may have some help nearby. Someone visited the jailed 'She Devil' and her brother. I overheard that someone is on his way to fetch her husband *Golden Spear* Jao from Kaifeng. I'm not afraid of them, but I want to send my wife and daughter to Da-ton. They will be safe there," Master Yu whispered.

"Let me go with you. What if they attack you soon? I'm not in a hurry to go to Beijing," Lee Mo-bai argued.

"No. Mo-bai, your position in Beijing awaits you. I'm sorry I delayed you already. I also don't want to drag you into this deeper. Master Gi told me that your uncle wants you to be an administrator. Ceo-lian and I can repel them before Jao arrives. Thank you again for everything. You can mention my name to Master Lieu. He is my friend and the owner of Grand Security Station in Beijing. I'm sure he will help you if you ever need help. Safe trip."

Yu Ceo-lian and her mother waited in the carriage and were ready to go.

Master Yu almost could not mount the horse if Lee Mo-bai had not helped him with a push. The old man was pale and sweaty. Lee Mo-bai pleaded again, "Uncle Yu, please wait. I'll pack and go with you."

"No, I said no. Thank you, we can manage. Bye."

Lee Mo-bai did not want to insist on accompanying them again lest they think that he wants to go after Yu Ceo-lian. He stood there and watched them leave. The hotel owner overheard the exchange and said, "Young Master Lee, I would follow them discreetly. Master Yu is in no shape to travel in this heat. If something happens to him, how could that young girl manage? Her mother is not well, too."

"Yes, I will follow them. If I leave tomorrow morning, I can still catch the slow-moving carriage."

'They are traveling west. I would go north first and then west. You know, young man, you might be watched," the hotel owner whispered.

2

Lee Mo-bai watched the Yu family check in at an inn. He had a swim at a creek and stretched out on the grassy bank. The bright stars of a clear summer night blinked at him like Yu Ceo-lian's sparking eyes. *'She is lovely but is off limit to me. How can I forget her?'*

At midnight, he jumped upon the roof of the inn where the Yu family were staying and scanned the area. No sign of enemies. He deliberately made a noisy landing. No one came out to check it out. He sighed, "Master Yu must be tired and Yu Ceo-lian's a young girl. I better keep watch.' His Teacher told him about the unscrupulous trickery that one's enemy could do in the dead of the night.

It was very hot the next day. Lee Mo-bai's sweat dripped down his face and his top shirt was drenched with sweat and sticking to his back. Through the mist of the hot air, he saw that Master Yu's group kept on going. *'Master Yu should not ride in the heat, he will soon be sick...'* Master Yu's horse slow down suddenly and the heavy old man was just about to topple. Mo-bai galloped ahead and jumped down from his horse to intercept the old man's fall. Both of them fell to the ground with Lee Mo-bai on the bottom.

"Ahe! You caught him, he did not break his neck." the carriage driver yelled and rushed over to help them up.

The impact of the old man's fall knocked the wind out of Lee Mo-bai. The groom pulled Master Yu's limp body away and Lee rose shakily. The fall gouged his back and it started to bleed. He said to the weeping mother and daughter, "Don't. Worry. Everything will be all right." He asked the groom, "Help me carry him into the carriage. He should be out of the sun.

"Thank *Lou Tien Yeh* (God). You're here," Master Yu came to. White foam and blood covered his white beard. He closed his eyes and breathed hard.

The groom said, "I know a doctor who lives two miles from here, Master Lee."

"Let's go there." Mrs. Yu sat on the footboard and sobbed silently. There was no room for Yu Ceo-lian to sit in the carriage. Lee Mo-bai brought Master Yu's horse to her. She cried, "I don't know how to ride. It's so tall. I'm...scared." Her tearful eyes were full of fright. Lee Mo-bai had to bite his lips to stop the impulse of holding her in his arms.

He said, "Miss Yu, don't be afraid. You know martial arts well and you'll learn how to ride very quick." He bent down and cupped his hands together and told her, "Step on my hands, I'll help you get on the horse. I promise that you won't fall." He gave her a hoist, and adjusted the stirrups. With one hand, he steadied the girl, and with the other hand, he held the rein.

Dr. Ma took charge. Lee Mo-bai went to unsaddle the horses. The groom said, "Dr Ma is very good, but I don't like the look of it. He may not pull through." Lee Mo-bai said, "It's bad. We'll wait and see."

Dr. Ma said to Lee Mo-bai, "I don't think you're his son, but I have to tell you that it's bad. His vital signs are very weak. He must have been extremely worried and anxious lately. I can only make him comfortable. You should prepare for the worst. What's your relationship to him?"

"We are not related. He knew my Teacher, I met them..." Lee explained.

"He is lucky to have met you. We will have to see to things then," Dr. Ma sighed and continued, "I'll get my men to prepare everything. You had a nasty fall; I'll treat it later. You go in now, he wants to see you."

Master Yu told his wife and daughter between breaths, "I know the end is coming. Luckily we have Lee Mo-bai here to help you..."

He told Lee Mo-bai, "My good nephew, I cannot repay your kindness in this life anymore. I want to be your..horse to serve you ...in the next life. Promise me..."

"Uncle, you'll get well soon. Tell me what you want me to do."

"Ceo-lian, kowtow twice to him. From now on, Lee Mo-bai is your brother. You'll obey and respect him as you will obey me."

Lee Mo-bai stood rigidly and accepted. Then he kowtowed to Master Yu once, to Mrs. Yu once. Kneeling, he said, "Please order me!"

"Mo-bai, promise me that you will escort your aunt and sister to the Mon's. She is almost seventeen now. I want her to get married right away, no need to observe the customary twenty-seven months long mourning period. Please don't refuse a dying man's request."

"I, Lee Mo-bai here solemnly promise that I'll escort my aunt and sister to the Mon's. I'll see to it that my sister Ceo-lian will have a proper wedding."

"Good," Master Yu coughed, spat blood and died.

They buried Master Yu besides a grove of willow trees behind the villa. Lee Mo-bai wrote a tombstone tablet to be chiseled and erected later.

When Mo-bai offered Dr. Ma silver for the expenses, Dr. Ma refused, "I'm glad to be able to do a good deed and hope it will please Buddha. Mo-bai, Buddha will bless you, too. You wrote beautifully, would you please indulge me and copy a couple lists of herbs for me?"

"I'd be honored." They stayed two more days there.

"Mo-bai, may I be blunt? You are depressed, are you not? Whatever it is that's eating you does you no good. Please let it go and learn to enjoy the precious small pleasure that our hard living brings us. Look after yourself; you're thin for your height. You have a bright future ahead of you."

"Thank you, Dr. Ma. You're right. There is a big world out there, I'll make new friends and enjoy my stay in Beijing."

That evening Mrs. Ma complained to her husband, "Master Yu was a fool. He should let Lee Mo-bai marry his daughter right away. Her mother told me that they heard nothing from the Mons for three years now. Who knows what has happened; the groom-to-be might be sick, might be ugly and rude. Young Lee helped them so much and he is good-looking, polite and a scholar. If Lee passes the examination and gets a position, Yu Ceo-lian would be a lady then. Instead, Master Yu made them sworn siblings. He was an old fool."

Dr. Ma said, "Master Yu loved his only daughter and he wanted her to be happy. She is a simple country girl and Lee Mo-bai is too sophisticated, too well educated for her to marry. You are right that Lee Mo-bai will be somebody someday. But Yu Ceo-lian is not groomed to be a lady. She would be completely out of place among the highborn, well-versed wives of other administrators. Lee Mo-bai could only be happy if his wife can compose a poem or at least read and write well. Yu Ceo-lian cannot read. Master Yu had to make them sworn siblings so that Lee Mo-bai could escort them to Da-ton."

Dr. Ma did not know that Master Yu said the same thing when his wife and his student Su suggested that he should let Lee Mo-bai marry his daughter.

Mrs. Ma sighed, "Poor Lee Mo-bai! He adores the girl and he can't marry her."

"Yes, Lee Mo-bai is a born poet and now he is bleeding inside."

"I think Ceo-lian loves Lee Mo-bai, too."

"I don't think so. Right now she is in shock. She worships Lee with deep gratitude. I'm afraid she will be hurt also when she realizes that she loves Lee later on. I just hope that her husband will treat her well."

His concubine chuckled, "Master, you're so wrong. I was only sixteen when you took me. She is seventeen and she sure has feelings. From the way they looked at each other, both of them have feelings, and strong feelings, too."

Early morning they set out for Da-ton. Mrs. Ma had packed boiled salty eggs, steamed buns filled with meat fillings, bottles of tea and pears for them to eat at noon hour. Dr. Ma advised that they travel in the morning and in the evening, but take a rest at noon. Lee Mo-bai attached a loop to the foot-stirrups for Ceo-lian to mount the tall horse. He walked along side her horse for a while to make sure Yu Ceo-lian had learned enough to ride on her own.

At noon they rested at a thick grove of trees off the main road. While they were eating, Lee Mo-bai politely answered Mrs. Yu's inquiries about his family. Then Lee told Yu Ceo-lian, "You know that the 'She Devil', her husband Jao and the others are now your enemies. If you don't mind, I'll teach you martial arts."

Yu Ceo-lian said excitedly, "Yes. Please teach me. You've taught me how to ride already. Thank you." Mrs. Yu also agreed, "Mo-bai, teach her. She must be well-prepared for the impending troubles."

"The first thing you have to learn is how to control your breathing and the flow of your energy. It'll take time to achieve any noticeable progress. But, gradually you will learn how to use your energy economically, how to conserve energy, and how to utilize your total reserved energy at will. A master of the internal martial arts can reach the stage of *'quiet like a maiden, fast like a dashing rabbit.'*"

Yu Ceo-lian interrupted, "Is that why you could recover from the fall so quickly when my father fell on top of you? You looked so white, I was afraid that you were sick, too."

"You have a keen sense of observation. This is very good. At that moment, I spent all of my reserved energy. I'm not fully recovered yet." Lee scrutinized the forest carefully and then continued, "I will teach you the technique of how to breath effectively now. While you're practicing, I want you to be my guard even though I think we are safe here. I need one more session of meditation in the open air to be fully recovered."

Lee Mo-bai showed her the proper sitting position and demonstrated deep breathing a couple of times and then said, "You keep on practicing now, and it will help your sore leg. It's common the first time you ride. Watch over me, wake me up only when you need help."

Yu Ceo-lian watched the eye-closed and seemingly breathless Lee Mo-bai with awe and she saw a light sheen of sweat covering the thin face. Meanwhile, she tried to practice deep breathing. Her mother dozed sitting against a big tree.

It seemed a long time before Lee Mo-bai opened his eyes; he looked refreshed and smiled at the obviously relieved Yu Ceo-lian. "Thank you, I feel better. Dr. Ma's *ginseng* pill helped too. I hope the breathing exercise does some good for your sore legs."

"Yes, it did help. But, I did not see you take any pill."

"Dr. Ma made some for Aunt and he gave me two of them and said they will help restore my energy and lift my spirit. I took one before I started to meditate." Lee Mo-bai took out a small ball of herb to show her.

"I did not see you take it. I was watching your every move." Yu Ceo-lian blushed and continued, "Is this another magic trick of yours like the one when you took my scarf off?"

Lee Mo-bai said, "No magic tricks, just *'speed'*," He stood up and stretched his arms. Ceo-lian was up too and she asked, "Are we leaving?"

Lee Mo-bai opened the palm of his right hand and laughed, "Sorry, little sister, you have to retie your hair." In his palm lay a strip of white cloth with which Yu Ceo-lian had tied one of her braids.

"How did you get it? I still have my scarf on. Daddy warned me that I should be wary of skinny Taoist priests or scholars. He said that they might be superb martial arts masters. Is that why you're so thin?" Yu Ceo-lian said with admiration.

"I'm only a beginner. I lost weight lately because of…a family problem. Aunt is awake. It's time to go," Lee thought, '*Because of you, Yu Ceo-lian, no food tastes good any more to me, and sleep evades me most of the time. Now you're beyond my reach forever.*'

Next day when they stopped at noon, Lee Mo-bai told Yu Ceo-lian, "Uncle told me that one of the enemies, Dart Mew, can throw deadly accurate darts. I'll teach you how to avoid, throw and catch darts. Most honest fighters despise the throwing darts. My Teacher insisted that I learn it well. He and his wife were wounded and captured by a bandit who was good at throwing darts. It is a good technique to learn, especially for a woman. Throwing darts, or pebbles, can repel several enemies rapidly. Some one used a small bow and arrows, but throwing darts only require one hand and pebbles could be found everywhere."

They practiced with pebbles. Lee Mo-bai showed her how to hold a handful pebbles and to throw one at a time at different targets with quick succession. He stood still and asked Yu Ceo-lian to throw pebbles at him and he caught every one. He said seriously, "I should not show you how to catch it. Learn how to dodge and not to catch the darts that your enemy throws at you. The darts might be poisonous. Try to remember NOT to catch the darts with bare hands when you're in a real fight. I regret that I had showed you how to catch it."

Yu Ceo-lian learned eagerly and laughed every time she hit a target. She did not know that the sound of her innocent laugh pierced Lee Mo-bai's aching heart just as badly as her tearful looks whenever she mourned for her father.

Lee Mo-bai also taught Ceo-lian throwing and dodging pebbles while riding at high speed. He taught her the almost soundless leaping skills in the evening. He behaved most properly and Yu Ceo-lian simply worshipped him and she also learned to be quiet whenever she sensed that Lee Mo-bai was sad.

One night Yu Ceo-lian wanted to practice her newly learned jumping skills. She opened the door of the room she shared with her mother and walked by Lee's window as quietly as she could. Through the rice paper window panels, she saw Lee sit and read. She jumped. Just as she was about to land upon the roof, she was pulled down the roof and was pushed into a room, and she heard Lee whispered, "Stay in the room and close the door. There is danger out there. I'll be back soon." She was in the pitch-dark room alone and her heartbeat was so fast and loud that she could hear it. A low cough, she heard, "Come out and let me walk you back to your room."

She also whispered, "The enemies?"

"No. only two clumsy thieves. I'll tell you tomorrow. No need to be afraid. Good night."

The next day Lee Mo-bai told her, "I heard you last night the moment you opened your door. I was not going to stop you, but then I heard a low whistle, a common signal among the thieves. That's why I pulled you down and pushed you into my room. I'm sorry. I found out there were two thieves, they did not see me. Miss Yu, we have to be on our guard at all hours. From the books I read and also from what my Teacher had told me, I learned that there are wicked men, who are good at night leaping skills, out there looking for maidens to ra...to hurt. A woman has to be extremely careful." Lee Mo-bai changed the word 'rape' to 'hurt'.

Yu Ceo-lian sensed that he was going to say at first something more sinister than 'hurt' and she was scared. Noticing her suddenly paled face, Lee Mo-bai apologized, "Don't be scared. Sorry, I did not mean to scare you. I just want you to be cautious."

"My father used to tell me to be alert, too. Thank you. My father's spirit would be at peace knowing you are taking good care of us."

"It's my duty and I'm honored." He thought, *'I'm glad that I can be with you, to hear you laugh, talk and sob. I do wish this trip would never end. You'll be another man's wife soon when we reach Da-ton. I don't know how I can carry on without you.'*

Noticing Lee's melancholy, Yu Ceo-lian kept quiet and they rode in silence.

Two days later, Lee Mo-bai said, "Aunt, Ceo-lian rides well now and we can sell Uncle's horse at the next big town before we reach Da-ton. That way, you'll have some silver at hand."

"Let's sell the horse. You will need some silver to go to Beijing."

"Aunt, I have some silver. You and Ceo-lian should have some silver of your own. We also need silver to move Uncle's casket back to Lu Town." Lee sounded sad and the women started to sob.

Next day they checked into a hotel before noon at a big town. Lee Mo-bai sold the horse and changed the silver into amount bearing certificates for Mrs. Yu.

Riding ahead of the carriage, Lee Mo-bai dismounted at the gate at Mon's security company and told a guard, "We are here to see Master Mon. I'm Lee Mo-bai of Nan-kon Village. I escort ..."

A white-haired man came out and called, "Oh! Sister-in-law and Ceo-lian are here, but where is Brother Yu? What happened?" Master Mon asked when he noticed the women wearing white armbands; white strips of clothes tied their hair, the attire of mourning. Lee Mo-bai had on a black armband.

"Ceo-lian's daddy passed away on the way up here." They sobbed. Mrs. Mon and other women took them into the women's quarter.

Lee Mo-bai took the bags out of the carriage and paid the groom generously. The groom said, "May all the gods bless you. Master Lee, you're a righteous and brave man, one in ten thousand. Good luck and good bye."

Master Mon noticed that Lee Mo-bai had a black armband on. He said, "Master Lee, I did not know that Brother Yu had a nephew? Why did he have to travel in the heat?" Master Mon sighed and continued, "I was going to visit him and tell him the problem myself, and now... let's discuss it over drink."

Something was wrong. Lee Mo-bai felt it. He replied, "Master Mon, I am not related to the late Master Yu. My Teacher and Master Yu were friends. Last month, I met..." He detailed the incidents leading to Master Yu's death and continued, "On his death bed, he asked me to escort Aunt Yu and sister Ceo-lian here to marry your second son. I'll be on my way to Beijing as soon as Ceo-lian is wed. Uncle Yu said that she should be married now, no need to wait for the twenty-seven months long mourning period to end. I'm her sworn brother."

Master Mon exclaimed in agony, "That's the problem. There cannot be a wedding soon because.." It was Lee Mo-bai's turn to exclaim, "No wedding soon? Why! Uncle Yu told me that the marriage between your second son and Ceo-lian was arranged five years ago. Is your son sick? I can wait for a while."

Master Mon shook his head hard and said rather too fast, "My second son is not sick. He is missing. He ran away eight months ago, all my inquiries have failed. Nephew Lee, let me explain."

"Please do. Your son did not want to marry my sister?" Lee Mo-bai's heart skipped a beat. His wild hope rose high again.

"He knows Ceo-lian is a pretty girl and he wants to marry her. My second son, Mon Zhi-an, is twenty-one years old. He always is a difficult and mischievous boy. His older brother and I tried very hard to discipline him. Maybe we were too hard on him. He ran away the first time when he was eight years old. Miraculously, he came back on his own six years ago and changed completely. He also learned martial arts very well. But, he still could not get along with his elder brother and wanted to leave home again. Then Master Yu came to visit us and mentioned that his daughter Ceo-lian learned martial arts, too. I asked her hand for my second son and a marriage contract was sealed. Mon Zhi-an knew about the betrothal and he was happy about it. He stayed home and all was well. Eight months ago, millionaire Ting, who had a relative held high position in Beijing, raped his servant's pretty daughter. Both father and daughter hanged themselves. It was bad and it was not my second son's business. He went there and chopped both of Ting's legs off. Ting did not die. His gang and the soldiers came to arrest Zhi-an. He fought them off and ran away. We have not heard from him since then." Master Mon sighed and continued, "I'll raise Yu Ceo-lian as if she were my own daughter. Zhi-an probably dares not come back. I'll take Yu Ceo-lian to him as soon as I know where he is. What else can I do? I wish to see my Zhi-an before I die."

Lee Mo-bai was dumbfounded at this unexpected twist of fate. He knew the rigid custom would demand that poor Yu Ceo-lian be a '*living widow*'. Without the news of the certainty of her fiancé's death, she could not, bound by custom, marry another man. The only hope for her was that Mon Zhi-an could be found quickly, living or dead. Even if the death of Zhi-an could be confirmed, it would still be a problem for Yu Ceo-lian to marry someone else. Not many families would be free of superstition to marry a girl whose karma was so bad to have a fiancé dead. Lee Mo-bai mused, '*But, if I know for sure Mon Zhi-an is dead. I'll marry her. I'm not superstitious. To be with her one day is worth more than living a long lonely life. I better leave tomorrow morning. It's not proper for me to see her or talk to her anymore. I can only imagine how hard Aunt Yu and her are crying at this moment. It's fate.*"

A short man came to the guest room and introduced himself, "I'm Hsu Mo-ti of Lu Town. I was an assistant guard at Master Yu's security company. Master Yu recommended me work here after he closed his security company. Miss Yu used to call me 'Short Brother'. Poor girl. Mrs. Yu told me everything. Thank you." Hsu tried to kneel, Lee Mo-bai pulled him up and said, and "I only did what a decent man would do. Brother Hsu, please tell me everything you know. What does Mon Zhi-an look like? I'll make inquiries in Beijing. I hope I can find him for Miss Yu. You know I'm her sworn brother."

"Mon Zhi-an is of medium height and thin with a sallow complexion. He is not the sort of man whom folks would notice and remember. Wait, his eyes are big. His eyes are big but not very bright. It won't be easy to find him, like a straw among a heap of hay." Short Hsu sighed and continued in a sad tone, "Mon Zhi-an's mother was a concubine. Mrs. Mon abused her; she died. The first son, Mon Zhi-chi, is greedy. He coveted the family wealth, charmed his father and forced his younger brother out of the family. The greedy elder son controls everything, now even his father is afraid of him. His wife is a mean woman, too. I'm afraid that they won't treat Ceo-lian and her mother nicely. I'm worried. I know you cannot take them back to Lu Town. Could you send ward to Brother Su to come here to take them home? At least they will have their own home and Brother Su will look after them."

"I'm in a very awkward position here. Master Mon told me that his second son is a wanted criminal and he dares not come back. Please tell me more. I need to know the whole truth to help Ceo-lian"

"It's a common story, the wicked elder brother forced the younger one out. Mon Zhi-chi dared and manipulated his younger brother to go after the vile millionaire…." Hsu filled in the details.

"Now we have to find her fiancé and then bring Yu Ceo-lian to him as soon as possible. I'll ask Aunt Yu whether they want to go back to Lu Town or not."

At the dinner in honor of Lee Mo-bai, Mon Zhi-chi subtly belittled his younger brother. Lee Mo-bai in turn also subtly praised Mon Zhi-an for his heroic deed and stated that he, as Yu Ceo-lian's sworn brother, would ask for a share of the family wealth for Yu Ceo-lian later. He told them that he would leave for Beijing early next morning."

In the evening, Lee Mo-bai asked the middle-aged Short Hsu to accompany him to visit Aunt Yu and Yu Ceo-lian. He handed Mrs. Yu the remaining silver and told them that he'll leave for Beijing the next day. Their swollen eyes pained him. He asked, "Aunt, do you want me to send a message to Brother Su and tell him to escort you back to Lu Town?"

"Let's wait for a year or so and hope they will find him," Aunt Yu said. Le Mon-bai handed her a piece of paper, "Here is my Uncle Kao's address in Beijing. I'm going to ask around and try to find Mon Zhi-an in Beijing. I'll come back to see you next spring." Lee Mon bai signaled Yu Ceo-lian to follow him to a corner and whispered, "Continue to exercise the breathing technique but do not practice your saber fighting and jumping skills when everyone is around. You can go over the steps in your head. Find something heavy to lift to pump the iron in your arms. It's not fitting for me to talk to you like this. I know your difficult situation. Be strong and be careful."

Yu Ceo-lian cried and begged, "Can you stay a few days? You're the only one we have."

"No. It's not fitting for me to stay. My staying would cause scandal. If I travel, I can make inquiries about your fiancé. Uncle's friends at Beijing might know something."

Whenever Lee Mo-bai passed a security company, he asked around. Most of them knew about the crime, but they didn't know where Mon Zhi-an is. He would copy some scriptures to earn free meals and a night at a temple often; it saved silver and made it easy for him to do the required morning workout. The change of scenery and the freedom of being able to travel fast lifted his spirit and stimulated his appetite. He harbored a secret hope, *'If Mon Zhi-an cannot be found for a year or so, or his death can be confirmed. I might have a chance to marry Ceo-lian after all.'* He was ashamed to have the thought of wishing someone died. No matter how hard he tried to forget, the image of Ceo-lian tantalized his mind day and night. In his agony, Lee Mo-bai wanted to provoke a fight with anybody and he did just that when he had to go through the Gu-bai Pass of the Great Wall.

The number of travelers dwindled at the entrance of the mountain road before the pass. He rode alone for a while and soon he caught up to a convoy carrying a security company's triangular banners. A guard who sat on the back drop of a cart, called, "Hi, young fellow, you have the nerve to travel alone. Don't you know that Bandit Wu's gang controls this mountain area? Come along then, you'll be safe traveling with us. My master's name card will see us through."

"There are bandits around? I'm not afraid of them. I'll beat them all off."

"Wu has more than two hundred braves, and Wu is famous for fighting with a heavy steel rod. But he respects my boss Master Yan." The guard said proudly.

"Friend, do you know Mon Zhi-an, he is twenty-one, of medium height.

"Sure we know him. Wasn't he on the run from the law? His brother tried to force him to leave home. His father Master Mon is blind."

"Ahe! That's the one. Do you know where he is now?"

"I don't, but my master may know...."

"Stop!" twenty-some rough young men rushed toward them.

"Brothers, we are Master Yan's party. Here is Master Yan's calling card and some silver for you to buy a drink." The guard greeted the leader. "I'll signal ahead and you'll not be stopped again." The leader whistled for his men to leave.

"Wait! I did not give you silver and my calling card yet. I travel alone and I have silver if you dare rob me." Lee Mo-bai shouted. The bandits rushed back and surrounded them.

The guard cried, "Are you crazy?" Turning to the bandit leader, he pleaded, "He is not one of us." The bandit leader ordered, "Let the convoy go, but not this crazy bastard. He has eaten a tiger's heart and thinks he is brave. Get him!"

Lee Mo-bai called, "Come! All of you. No need for me to draw my sword." He scooped a handful of pebbles and threw at them. Every one of the bandits yelled with pain. The bandit leader, his forehead bleeding, ordered, "Get him. All of you!" He wielded his saber at Lee Mo-bai. Lee Mo-bai laughed, "Come on! All of you! I'll fight you with my fists." He jumped around and punched this one and that one. They all got hit and fled. Lee Mo-bai called after them, "My name is Lee Mo-bai, and I'll wait for your leader Wu at the first town the other side of the pass." He laughed and somehow he felt better. He deliberately rode slowly, but he met no more bandits. Black clouds gathered and soon a sudden summer rain poured. He was drenched through and the horse nearly slipped. He thought, *'I better get down and pull the poor old horse through. It is my only valuable possession.'* Leading the horse, he sloshed through the mud and puddles and checked into the first inn. It was a huge establishment with three courts. The room was comfortable with nice, clean bedding. He knew the price would be high, but he was too miserable to find a cheaper one.

It was early, he had a plateful of steamed dumplings, and he saw the tearful face of Yu Ceo-lian on each one. He sighed, *'Poor Ceo-lian and Aunt, they must cry a lot.'* He did not feel like eating, but he forced himself to eat all the dumplings and a bowl of noodle soup. Then he took out a damp anthology to read. He found the one that the famous Madam Lee of the Sung Dynasty (12th century) wrote:

You, my dear husband, reside at the head of the Mighty Yangtze River,
And I, your wife, live at the end of the same river.
Every day and every night I miss you, but I can't see you.
Although we drink the water from the same river.

Lee Mo-bai closed the book and thought, '*did it rain also at Da-ton, where Yu Ceo-lian is? Which are more? The rain drops or her tears?* He woke up to angry voices.

"I can't wake every customer and ask him his first name. 'Lee' is a common last name. We have more than seven customers with this last name," a hotel clerk said. Customarily, the hotel register only listed the surname.

A guttural voice snarled, "This Lee is a tall, thin young man who looks like a scholar. He has a horse. He said he would wait for me at this town. I have checked all the other hotels. Wake them up and ask before I beat the shit out of you."

Another voice, "You can't harass a hotel clerk. You hear!"

The same guttural voice, "What if I do? What can you do?"

Lee Mo-bai said, "Are you looking for me? I'm Lee Mo-bai. I beat up your men yesterday. Are you the bandit leader 'Wu'?"

"No need to know my name, I'll punish you."

"I have nothing to do with the law. I want to know the name of the persons whom I will beat up. fight me!" The stout Wu hit Lee Mo-bai with his steel rod.

Lee did not want to have his father's sword damaged, he avoided direct confrontation and slashed at Wu's hand holding the rod. Wu laughed, "You weakling, you're afraid, are you not? Ouch." Wu dropped the rod and both of his hands were bleeding. He called menacingly, "We will meet soon again. Next time I will not be fooled by your soft scholarly looks."

"I'll be in Beijing soon. You can find me there."

Someone knocked at Lee's door and asked politely, "Master Lee, may I come in?"

"Please."

The middle-aged, portly man said, "I watched the fight and I admire your martial arts skills. You must be a student of a top-notch teacher of the Wu-ton school?"

"You, my friend, have good judgment." The stranger looked like a Manchu, Lee did not want to tell him more.

My name is Dae-ti Fu. In Beijing, folks called me Dae Wu (five). I'm the fifth son in my family. I would be honored to be your friend. I know Beijing well and I'd be glad to be your guide."

The name is a Manchu name. Lee said politely, "Master Dae-ti, I'm honored to make your acquaintance."

"Master Lee, are you coming to Beijing to take the triennial metropolitan-level of civil services examination next spring? I'm sure you will pass it with flying colors."

"No, Master Dae-ti, I'm ashamed to admit that I failed the provincial-level. I'll try it again this fall. A relative of mine might find me a clerical position in Beijing. I should have been in Beijing a month ago. I had to go to Da-ton first. I will set out soon."

"I was hoping you could stay another day and we'll go to Beijing together. I lived there. I hope you will have a good position and I'm sure we'll meet again soon."

Early that afternoon, Lee Mo-bai entered the mighty capital Beijing. The grand buildings and the crowd intimated him; he dismounted and walked besides the horse until he saw others, even a few women riders. He rode again.

Uncle and Aunt Kao welcomed him warmly, but he was told the position was taken. "You should have been here earlier. What was the delay?"

"I was sick. I'm sorry." He lied.

"Look at you. You are thin. Your aunt should have found you a wife to look after you long time ago. I know a couple of nice maidens. I'll find you a good wife," Aunt Kao said. Uncle Kao said, "Mo-bai, come back tomorrow afternoon. I'll ask around. There will be other positions."

Lee Mo-bai went to Grand Security Company to see Master Lieu. He told him about Master Yu's death and asked him to make inquiries about the whereabouts of Mon Zhi-an.

"Ahe! That's bad. Where is his family now? I know that they have a daughter."

Lee Mo-bai replied, "Yes. Mrs. Yu and their daughter are staying with Master Mon at Da-ton."

"Mo-bai nephew, Master Yu would not recommend just anybody. If you want to be a guard, I would be glad to have you work for me here. Your Teacher's fame is far reaching." Master Lieu also told Lee that he would find a buyer for Lee's horse.

"Mo-bai, your Uncle Kao may introduce you to Master Dae Wu. Although he is a Manchu, he is very friendly and helpful to us, the Hans. He knows many people who are good at martial arts. He may help you. If this Mon Zhi-an had been caught and jailed, Master Dae Wu would know, and he may extricate Mon, too. Dae Wu is very resourceful."

"I have met him already. I don't have his address."

"Dae Wu is well liked and well known. Everyone knows where he lives."

The next day, Uncle Kao handed Lee Mo-bai twenty ounces of silver and a few books. "Mo-bai, I heard that you wrote beautifully. It won't be difficult for you to pass the provincial level of examination this fall and then the highest level next spring. Don't be idle. The Manchu court is in need of talented young scholars." Lee Mo-bai thought, '*I should really try to pass the examination. With a position and the authority that comes with it, I can help Yu Ceo-lian to get her entitled share of the family wealth. But why, every thought of mine turns back to her. Can I ever forget her?*'

He tried to study, every page he opened to read, showed only Yu Ceo-lian's tearful face. Finally he gave up and went out for a walk. He wondered absently into a section with fancy bungalows and many carriages parked alongside. It was the district of prostitutes and wanted to leave when he heard, "Master Lee, I did not expect to see you so soon. Beauty sure draws young heroes. *Ha Ha*."

It was Dae Wu. Lee Mo-bai blushed.

3

"Brother Lee, don't be bashful. It is normal for an elegant and romantic scholar wants to meet a pretty lady. I'm surprised that you found your way here so soon." Lee Mo-bai blushed likes a petty thief who just got caught.

Instead of offering an explanation of how he had absentmindedly walked into this district, he asked, "Brother Dae-ti, when did you get in?"

"Late last night. Call me Dae Wu. I'm so glad that I have run into you. I forgot to ask you where you would be staying in Beijing. Brother Lee, may I introduce you my good buddy Master Yong? Call him Fatso Yong." Turning to the rotund, well-dressed Yong, Dae Wu said, "Lee is the young martial arts master I told you about."

"Nice to make your acquaintance. Brother Lee, take us to meet your favorite."

"I don't know anybody."

"Brother Lee. How about come with me to meet my good friend?" Dae Wu suggested. Lee Mo-bai took the term 'friend' literally and presumes that they were going to meet another man. To his surprise, a heavily made-up, luxuriously dressed woman welcomed them into her parlor and immediately starts to flirt with them. Lee Mo-bai was embarrassed and he felt completely out of place. He awkwardly accepted a cup of tea and kept quiet.

"Don't tease my young friend. He is new and he is shy," Dae Wu told the woman and then asked Lee, "Where do you stay?"

"At Restful Inn, not far from here."

"I will visit you soon. Brother Lee, I'm outspoken, and I want to be your friend very much. Please don't mind my forthright manners."

"Please call me Mo-bai, I'm but a poor rural student. I'd be honored to be your friend, Brother Dae Wu."

"Mo-bai, I know you're not comfortable here, let's get out of here."

Dae Wu insisted on taking Lee Mo-bai back to the hotel in his personal carriage. He said, "Now I know where I can find you. We'll meet soon."

The oil lamp in his room attracted many mosquitoes. Lee Mo-bai blew it out, and sleep evaded him again. The guest of the room next to his was singing a popular Chinese opera about a young woman lamenting her husband's death at the Great Wall two thousand years ago. The sad tone increased his melancholy. *'If I meet another woman, prostitute or not, she might free me from the thought of Yu Ceo-lian. A prostitute would be good-looking but she would not know martial arts. It's my misfortune to know Yu Ceo-lian; I love her but cannot have her. How can I forget her and find someone good enough to replace her?'* He thrashed around on the hot bed for a long time. Finally he stood on his head, feet up and meditated to clear his tormented mind and then slept. Next morning he woke up refreshed and felt he could start life anew. Unfortunately his head did not stay clear for long when he realized that he had written Yu Ceo-lian's name again and again instead of composing an essay of current affairs. He tore the paper into pieces and used them to practice the darts throwing skills. He had a hard time throwing the flimsy paper far or hitting on the target, but he was getting better. He was proud of himself and exercised more when the hotel clerk led Dae Wu to his room.

Dae Wu saw the pieces of paper flying around and said, "A new martial arts technique? I hope that I'm not your target, Mo-bai." He took in Lee Mo-bai's scanty luggage and knew at once that Lee was far from rich.

"It's a stupid game. I'm bored."

"How are you getting along? Did you get the position?"

Lee Mo-bai sighed, "The position had been filled."

"Never mind. Other positions will come along soon. You can't study all the time. we will keep each other company. My office work is not demanding, and I'm free before noon every day. We can have a game of *Wei Qi* (chess) or go to the theater in the afternoon. Boredom and the heat will make you sick."

"Honestly, I'm all right. I'm not distressed. I'm debating with myself whether I should work as a security guard or wait to take the examination."

"Mo-bai, it's all written on your face. You have to be patient. Don't worry about silver. I have enough for both of us providing you're not a spendthrift. If you're happy and not worried, you will pass the examination easily with your beautiful calligraphy."

"You're right! Uncle Kao said so too. He wants me to study hard."

"Yes, you should, but not today. It's too hot. Let's have lunch first and then go to the theater later. You're welcome to my home to study in my library any time." Mo-bai missed his own room a t home with bookshelves lined along the wall.

Everyone at the theater knew Dae Wu, they were offered very favorable seats at the front. Lee Mo-bai asked, "Brother Dae Wu, you're well known in Beijing. Master Lieu, the owner of the Grand security Company suggested that I ask your help to find the missing fiancé for a relative of mine. The young man's name is Mon Zhi-an." He told Dae Wu the situation.

"Mo-bai, I will try my best. But if this Mon Zhi-an does not want to be found, no one can find him. China is a big country and Beijing is a big city. It will be very difficult to find one person. Poor young girl, I feel for her. She cannot marry another man until her fiancé's death is confirmed. She is what you Han people called 'a living widow'. It's an unreasonable and cruel custom. If she is a Manchu, it won't be too bad, she only has to wait for a few months for his return, and then she can marry someone else"

Lee Mo-bai's heart started to ache again. On the stage was the opera of the legend of 'Sister Thirteen'. It is the story of a girl who is good at martial arts, who fights off a group of bandits and rescues a scholar in distress. The actress moved gracefully and her small feature also reminded Lee Mo-bai of Yu Ceo-lian. Dae Wu noticed his melancholy and tried to draw him out of it. He asked, "Mo-bai, do you have a theater at your home town?"

"It's a village. We have no theater. Every year after the harvest in the fall, a troupe will come and play at a crossroad or in front of a temple for two days. I hardly ever watch the show."

"Mo-bai, it sounds like you were bored at home, too."

"Indeed. My Teacher passed away three years ago. I don't have anybody to talk to about martial arts and poetry anymore. My Teacher was good at both martial arts and literary arts. He taught me calligraphy."

"Mo-bai, how many children do you have?" Lee Mo-bai did not want to tell him that he was not married lest Dae Wu would try to find a wife for him, so he simply replied, "None."

Noises and loud quarreling sounded at the back of the theater. A fight.

One man said, "Be quiet, Master Dae Wu and his friend are sitting in the front. Be quiet. Go out and fight outside."

An angry voice, obviously not a native Beijing resident, shouted, "I don't care about this Dae Wu. Even the high judge himself is here; I will insist on having the right to be respected. This Dae Wu better mind his own business."

Everyone looked at Dae Wu, waiting to see his reaction to the insult. He stood up and walked to the back. Five robust young fellows, not locals, encircled a junior office clerk whom Dae Wu knew well.

"It's too hot to fight. Friends, please indulge me and break this up so we can watch the show. I'm Dae Wu." Usually a fight would cease when Dae Wu spoke. But one tall man of the five yelled, "I don't care who you are. Who gives you the right to protect one of your Beijing folks when he is unreasonable? I don't have to obey you. What are you going to do about it? Shut up and mind your own business. you hear?"

Dae Wu shouted, "You rascals. All of you." He dodged in time to avoid the teakettle hurling at him and continued, "You dare? Let's go out and fight."

"Brother Dae-ti, let me fight them," Lee Mo-bai said.

"Master Dae Wu, no need for you to fight them. Just give us orders." More than ten bystanders volunteered to fight for Dae Wu.

"Friends from out of town, there are five of you and I'm alone. But I can gather more than ten men at once. You better choose one-to-one, one of you will fight me."

The tall one challenged, "It's between you and me. Only a coward will need help from others. Come on!"

Dae Wu stopped Lee Mo-bai and said, "I don't need your help to beat up a worm." Their fists joined. The tall man hit Dae Wu a couple of times and then Dae Wu's palm struck flatly on the stranger's bare chest hard and left an impression of his whole hand. The stranger faltered backward and vomited blood.

"Bravo! Master Dae Wu. No wonder you are called *'Iron Palm,'*" someone praised. The five troublemakers left and Dae Wu laughed. However he did not look too happy when he was told the one whom he wounded is one of the Feng Brothers of Ba-tin Town. The five of them were guards working for Universal Security Company.

Lee Mo-bai said, "Brother Dae, you're a true hero, not a showy one. I did not know you fight so well. I really have to emulate your modesty. I'll always be on your side whoever you have to fight." He noticed Dae Wu's apprehension.

"Everyone can praise me but you. I know you're an expert. I think you can scale a three-story building easily. I don't think you have much experience of real fighting. Am I right?"

"You are right. This is the first time I left home. The first time when I wounded a man, I was almost sick from the sight of blood. I had only fought a real fight twice in all my twenty-four years of life. I'm only a beginner. Please don't think too highly of me."

"Mo-bai, a young warrior like you should have someone like the famous 'Sister Thirteen' for a wife. Is that the cause of your sadness?"

Lee Mo-bai sighed again, said nothing but he looked very miserable. Dae Wu thought that he guessed right. A woman was at the root of the problem.

"Cheer up, Mo-bai. Let's have supper first. Then I'll take you to meet a heroic prostitute. She does not know anything about martial arts and can't fight, but she is courageous and generous. I think only an elegant young man like you could win her affection and friendship."

"Brother Dae-ti, be serious. I don't have a job and I don't have silver. How can I afford to pay for her services?" Lee Mo-bai protested.

"Just indulge me. She is indeed someone special. For instance, one of the prettiest call girls spent more than she could earn, and was deep in debt. She wanted to kill herself. Our heroine heard about it and paid off all the debts for the poor girl and then helped her to find a decent man to marry. Another time, she heard that a malicious pimp abused three young apprentice call girls. She gathered all the other righteous prostitutes and went to the law to get the pimp arrested. Then she found a rich family willing to take the three young girls in as maids. Not a heroine? What else we call her?"

"Where did she get the silver to help others? Does not her pimp control her income?"

"She is an independent prostitute. She and her own mother run the business very well. She keeps the earnings. She also holds high standards. I heard a lot of rich men want to pay a lot to bed her but she won't sell herself to just anyone. Rumor has it that so far she likes no one enough to let him bed her."

The so-called heroic prostitute picked her own artistic name 'Violet'. She likes the color purple and all her clothes are in different shades of purple. She and her mother have been in Beijing for two years. With her beauty and artistry, she would be the number one flower in Beijing if she were not so proud and extremely choosy about her clients. Only a selected group, mostly the literary class, would seek her out and pay highly for her favors, which she does not grant lightly.

Dae Wu and Lee Mo-bai found her place tastefully furnished. An old woman asked them to be seated and offered them tea. She told them, "Violet is changing, and she'll be out in a minute. Can you tell me your names?"

"My name is Dae Wu. This is my friend Lee Mo-bai. Mister Lee wants to meet Violet." Lee Mo-bai scanned a few paintings and a poem artistically decorating the walls. The paintings and the poem all bore the signature and stamps of 'Violet'. Lee Mo-bai knew she was indeed not an ordinary ignorant prostitute.

Dae Wu whispered, "Mo-bai, she does have a haughty air. She lets us wait. This is the first time I encounter one in her trade that lets the customer wait."

Le Mo bai whispered back, "The famous poet Bai Jiu-ee of the Tang Dynasty wrote in the poem about the *Pi Ba* (guitar) player; '*thousands calls and thousands pleas before she shows herself.*'"

They were not disappointed though. Twenty-five-year old Violet approached them gracefully. Her beauty and sophistication mesmerized Lee Mo-bai. Suddenly he was tongue-tied. This was another first for him.

Violet glanced at Lee Mo-bai, and asked with a pleasing tone, "You're Master..?"

Red-faced Lee Mo bai found his voice and said, "Lee Mo-bai."

"Welcome, Mister Lee," Violet looked Lee Mo-bai over imperceptibly and then asked Dae Wu, "And you're Master..?"

"Call me Dae Wu. I'm here today to accompany my friend Brother Lee to visit you." He saw the by-play between the girl and Lee Mo-bai. He smiled and thought, "*No more sadness. Mo-bai.*"

She said, "Welcome Master Dae Wu, your fame is far reaching. We're honored to have your patronage."

"Brother Lee is new in Beijing. I dared not take him anywhere else. I know you're nice and you won't take advantage of my shy and honest young friend," Dae Wu said.

The old woman, her mother, chuckled, "My Violet is also shy and honest."

"That is why I bring him where. They are a pair. *Ha Ha.*" Lee Mo-bai blushed, but Violet chatted with complete ease and grace. At the beginning, Lee Mo-bai could only reply whenever Violet asked him something, but gradually he asked a question or two. He asked, "Violet, would you please tell us your real name?"

"Chi Mi-neon. I'm from Kaifeng." Violet replied. She thanked Lee when he praised her paintings and poems. Nevertheless, Dae Wu subtly signaled a stop when he sensed that young Lee Mo-bai wanted to inquire about her background.

A servant delivered a note written on a strip of elaborately decorated red paper. Lee Mo-bai did not know what it was, but Dae Wu knew that it was a note to summon Violet's services somewhere else. He said casually, "Mo-bai, it's late. I don't want to face a complaining wife." He put some silver beside the teacup quietly.

Violet said, "Sorry, I'm asked to be at the Grand Inn. Please come by tomorrow?"

Dae Wu stood up and said, "I can't. I promise you that Brother Lee will visit you tomorrow and the day after. I'm sure of it."

Back in his shabby hotel room, a feeling of emptiness weighed him down. Lee Mo-bai thought, '*How could a beautiful classy lady fall so low to become a prostitute? Violet must have had some unspeakable experiences. That's why Dae Wu did not want me to probe further. She and I have something in common. Both of us are talented but not successful. Is it fate or a flaw of character that made us this way, who knows?*' He paced and finally went to a nearby tavern to drink himself into a stupor to block his mind of two images; an innocent pretty girl and a beautiful mature woman.

He was still asleep next morning when Dae Wu's valet, Tan, delivered a letter.

It said, '*Mo-bai, I'm not well today. I cannot come to visit you. Mo-bai, you're talented but at the present have met with difficulties which life itself has the habit to grant us once so often. Please indulge me with a little pleasure and accept the enclosed silver certificates. I'm looking forward to seeing you soon. Be happy.*'

His eyes moistened and thought, '*I have only know him, a Manchu, a few days and he is so understanding and caring. Besides my Teacher Dr. Ma and Dae Wu are two of the kindest friends I have met.*' The thought of Dr. Ma brought his thoughts back to Yu Ceo-lian again. He wrote two letters: one to Mrs. Yu and one to Dr. Ma. He took the letters to Grand Security Company and asked Master Lieu to deliver them whenever there is a convoy going there. Master Lieu welcomed him and they chatted about his teacher Master Gi and Master Yu over drinks and lunch. Master Lieu asked him again whether he wanted to be a guard. He said he would consider it. He did not like the sight of blood and he preferred finer things of life. He thought that he should study more since he had help now.

He walked slowly and tried to spot a medium height young man with big eyes among the crowd. A carriage stopped besides him. Violet invited him, "Will you come visit us tonight. I'll be waiting."

"I will be there."

Lee Mo-bai stared at the leaving carriage and thought, '*why did I promise her that I'll visit her tonight? I need to study. What would my Aunt Kao, Uncle Kao and Yu Ceo-lian think if they knew that I visit a prostitute? I'm not going. That kind of woman would not mind if I don't go.*' His empty hotel room and boredom sent him to Violet's parlor that evening.

Violet felt an unusual sensation of waiting and anticipation of Lee's visit. She thought, '*Lee Mo-bai does not look like a man who could afford to visit me. He may not come.*' Lee Mo-bai's thin face, modest clothing, and especially the deep melancholy of his eyes, touch somewhere deep in her. She thought about her painful past and the constant fear she has and her tears came. Her tears stayed on her long dark eyelashes like tiny crystals.

The doorman announced Lee's visit. Violet quickly retouched her hair and went out to welcome Lee warmly, "Master Lee, you're really here."

"I said I would come."

Violet poured him a cup of tea. Lee Mo-bai noticed that Violet dressed her hair in a different style. Her snugly fitting light purplish outfit with black trimmings showed her tall, willowy figure to perfection. He blushed and he couldn't take his eyes off her.

Violet also had a pinkish glow as she asked, "Master Lee, you said you're staying in a hotel. Is your wife with you?"

"No" Lee replied but did not mention that he was not married.

"Are you a colleague of Master Dae Wu?"

"No. I'm still looking for a position. A relative told me there was a position a while back. I did not arrive in Beijing in time and the position was filled. I'm not sure what I want to do next; to prepare to write the civil services examination in the fall or go down South to seek Uncle Chiang. But I have to find my sworn sister's missing husband for her first." Lee Mo-bai stopped and he was surprised that he talked so much to a new acquaintance. He was embarrassed and picked up the teacup.

Violet thought, '*He is indeed an honest man. It's refreshing to hear someone talk candidly when all the other clients of mine only brag.*'

"Master Lee, you're very young. A setback at the present does not mean much. I know you'll be successful in the near future."

"Thank you. This is the first time I have come to a prost..a nice place like yours."

Violet laughed, "I don't mind. I'm a prostitute. But I have conscience. I don't want to see a young scholar like you to fritter away time and energy in a place like mine." She sighed and continued with a low laugh, "But, on the other hand, I would like you to visit me often, Master Lee."

"Call me Mo-bai."

"Oh! It's not fitting. I know my place."

He looked gloomy and she tried to cheer him up. She pulled Lee up to look at the bright moon out of the window. "Tomorrow we will have a full moon and one month from now we'll eat moon-cakes and celebrate the Moon Festival. By then, you'll be an important official and you will forget poor Violet completely."

He appreciated her effort to bring him out of the blue. Lee Mo-bai forced himself to be cheerful too.

Lee Mo-bai was not quite sure of where Dae Wu lived. When he went to visit him the next day, he hired a carriage thinking the groom might know where the well-known Dae Wu lived. He was right. The carriage took him across town to a well-kept residential area with many grand mansions. They stopped at a mansion with two huge stone lions guarding a redwood gate. A uniformed servant came to answer the door and asked him his name.

"I'm Lee Mo-bai, I come to visit Master Dae-ti." Dae Wu's valet, Ton, rushed out to welcome Lee and escorted him to an elegantly furnished parlor, "Master Lee, please take a seat. I'll notify my master."

Dae Wu welcomed Lee Mo-bai, "Glad to see you. Mo-bai." He had on a comfortable silk short set. "Brother Dae-ti you look well. Thank you for the ..."

"Don't mention it. I had a slight case of diarrhea. did you go to see Violet?"

Lee Mo-bai blushed, "Yesterday, she invited me and I paid her a short visit."

Dae Wu laughed, "No need to explain. You can't sit in your hot hotel room alone all the time. I honestly think that Violet likes you. She was cheerful that other day when we visited her too. These are signs that she values your attention. I heard that many rich men paid her a lot of silver and still did not get any good words from her. You're lucky."

"I don't think I should go to that kind place often," Lee Mo-bai said.

"I agree. No matter how nice and graceful she is, she is still a prostitute. You have a bright future to look forward to. I'll take you to do some sightseeing and then we'll come back here to have supper with my family. I'd like you to meet my wife and my mother."

They met many of Dae Wu's acquaintances at the famous Yuan Ming-Yuan, Everywhere they stopped to rest, the waiters would offer come to greet Dae Wu them the finest seats, and others would greet Dae Wu warmly. Dae Wu was proud of his popularity. Dae Wu greeted a thin, well-dressed man, "Master Hwang, a pleasant afternoon." Master Hwang kept on walking and ignored him. Dae Wu was very embarrassed.

Lee Mo-bai asked angrily, "He is rude. He has no manners. Who is he and what make him think he is better than you?"

"Master Hwang, nicknamed '*Thin Buddha*' is a philanthropist in Beijing. He knows martial arts very well. I'm neither rich and or very good at martial arts, but I'm more popular and he cannot take it. You could say that he is jealous of me."

"So he is narrow-minded and conceited. He has no right to humiliate you openly today. He deserves a beating."

"No, Mo-bai. He and I have mutual friends. Viscount Chiu is a good friend of mine, so somehow we have to get along and keep peace."

"The surname '*Chiu*' does not sound like a Manchu name."

No, he is not Manchu, neither is Hwang. They are the descendants of the first group of the Han people who betrayed the last Emperor of the Ming Dynasty and accepted the Manchu. They were rewarded with wealth and position. Viscount Chiu fights very well with a spear and he is Master Yan's student."

"I will challenge Hwang to a friendly match and I will not mention that I'm your friend."

Dae Wu said, "Hwang is very powerful and he has spies all over Beijing. I'm sure that he knows we are friends. It you beat him, he'll find a way to discredit you and make it impossible for you to be successful in Beijing. It's not worth it to make this kind of rascal your enemy." He continued, "Let's go home and I'll treat you to a Manchu-style home-cooked meal."

"If I'm used to eating Manchu-styled meals, what am I going to do when I go back home?"

"It's easy. MB, bring your family here and live with us. I'd be flattered."

"My aunt and uncle won't come."

"Take your wife here then."

"I don't have a wife."

"Really? You told me you don't have children the other day. Mo-bai, be serious. Are you not married? You country folks usually marry at sixteen or seventeen."

"I'm the odd one. That's why I cannot get along with my uncle. He's so angry with me for not wanting to marry the girl he and my dear aunt had arranged for me."

"Ah, you're reticent. I'm your friend, am I? Why can't you tell me?"

"I've learned a painful lesson and I learned to be reticent. You're a true brother and I'll tell you everything."

Dae Wu's mother and wife liked Lee Mo-bai right away. They told him that he is welcomed to visit them at the inner court anytime.

Lee Mo-bai told Dae Wu everything.

"Brother Dae, let me tell you my first and painful lesson. I was so naïve that I honestly believed that I could win a wife with my sword."

Lee Mo-bai told in details that his friend tricked him to win a wife with his sword.

Dae Wu roared with laughter, "That was absurd. Mo-bai, you're gullible. How could you be so stupid?"

"I had a sheltered and pampered life at home. This is the first time I'm on my own. Now I realize that my Teacher Gi Kon-jii was a brag, and…"

"Mo-bai, you never told me you're Master Gi's student. What else did you not tell me? Your surname is Lee, are you Lee Fong-jii's son?"

"Yes. I'm telling you everything. I need to talk to someone."

"That made sense now. Master Gi taught you all his skills without any reservation. Did you know your father and your Teacher were good friends?"

"Yes, I know and Uncle Chiang Nan-ho is my father's sworn brother. Teacher Gi was a braggart. He made me believe that I can win anything with my sword. He taught me for nine years and I was very close to him."

"Wait a minute, there is something missing, Master Gi was from Szechwan. Why did he move to the East to teach you?"

"I don't know. Teacher Gi told me a lot of his heroic deeds and how many fights he had won. He did not talk about his family much."

"Tell me from the beginning. Please."

"My father, Teacher Gi and Uncle Chiang resisted Manchu's rule in the beginning. But when my father realized that only the Manchu Emperor could stabilize the country and let us the Han people have a better life, he offered his service to a famous general. I grew up in an army camp in Nanjing with a sister and a brother. Uncle Chiang visited us often. He and my father taught us martial arts. I learned well and I also rode well. When I was seven, my father's company went to the Southwest to put down the Muslim rebellion. During a skirmish, my father lost a leg, but he managed to put my mother and me on a horse and told me to run. My brother and my sister were on another horse and both of them died. Uncle Chiang saved my father from the enemies' jail. But my parents died shortly afterward. Uncle Chiang took me to my father's only brother's home and asked permission to adopt me as his own son. My uncle refused and kept me. Five years ago my cousin was killed and had left no child. I became the only heir. My uncle wants to keep me at home and get married. But I vowed to marry a girl who knows martial arts well. That's why I fell for a trick."

Lee Mo-bai then told in detail what led him to become Yu Ceo-lian's sworn brother

He sobbed, "I promised her that I'll find her fiancé. I wish that I had never met her. Now I live in a state of perpetual agony. I can't have her and I can't forget her. Sometimes I want to be a Taoist priest if I did not have the obligation to carry on my father's and my uncle's bloodline."

They sat in silence for a long time. Then Dae Wu said, "Mo-bai, if we cannot find Mon Zhi-an in a year, I will go to Da-ton to have a candid talk with Master Mon. He cannot let Yu Ceo-lian be a living widow forever. I'll be the middleman and arrange the marriage for you and her." He then added, "Of course, we'll try our best to find Mon Zhi-an. You're a very virtuous man, one in ten thousand. You are drunk. Stay here tonight. Tomorrow we will bring your luggage here."

"1 don't want to impose on you. Ask your groom to take me back to my hotel. I need to be alone."

The next day, Uncle Kao's valet came to the hotel to summon Lee Mo-bai.

"Mo-bai, it's too expensive and too noisy for you to stay in a hotel. I made arrangements for you to have a room in a temple. The old monk there once told me that someone broke in and stole the silver his devotees donated. He would like to have you there to help him to repel any thieves and also to copy some scriptures for him."

Lee Mo bai could have a quiet court for himself. The room was in need of repair. He could practice martial arts anytime, and he was anxious to move.

Dae Wu was wounded and was in his hotel room. He proudly told Lee Mo-bai, "Remember the fellow Feng whom I had hit the other day at the theater? He and his brother gathered ten roughnecks and waylaid me down the street. They wounded me, but I cut down two of them before the soldiers came."

"Where can I find them? They cannot get away with this."

"The tall one whom I hit the other day is Feng sam (three). There are five brothers. Feng wu (five) is a guard at Universal Security. Feng sie (four), nickname 'Saber King' fights with two heavy sabers superbly. It's said that Viscount Chiu, Thin Buddha Hwang and the bandit Wu whom you had wounded are all not his equal. That's why the other day I started to worry when I was told who they are. For a couple of days, I avoided this section of town."

"Is Feng sie (four) the one who wounded you today?"

"Not him. He is not in Beijing. If he were here today, there would be no ambush. He is just and righteous and he won't allow his brothers to do this."

"I'll go and beat them off. They've gone too far. If I don't punish them now, you will not be able to walk on the streets without fear from now on," Lee Mo-bai said.

"You're right, I'm coming with you."

"Dae Wu, Stop! I'd like to know how tough you are," Feng wu (five) shouted and his long spear, snake like, almost touched Dae Wu's chest.

Lee Mo-bai broke the heavy spear into two, "I won't fight you here on the street, let's go out of town and fight. I'm Lee Mo-bai. Whoever dares harm Brother Dae Wu will have to fight me first. If you're afraid, go home and get *Saber King* here to fight me."

They went out of the city gate. There they ganged up and wanted to upturn the carriage with the wounded Dae Wu inside. None of them was free of some slight sword wounds from Lee Mo-bai's lightening speed sword thrusts. Most of them fled. Feng wu's neck was bleeding and he knew he had been spared. He shouted, "Lee Mo-bai, we'll fight you again."

"You'll find me at Peace Temple on East Street. Tell *Saber King* to come to Beijing soon!"

Lee Mo-bai told Dae wu about the room at the temple.

"Good, Mo-bai, I came to ask you to move into my house, but I think you'll feel less restricted living in the temple. If you don't like it there, you're always welcomed to move into my home."

"Thank you. You're a true brother to me."

4

Tall walls circled the temple. Lee Mo-bai could practice martial arts in the quiet court. there was a well in a corner. The old monk was very pleased with Lee's calligraphy and suggested that they set a table in the frontcourt for Lee to write letters for the illiterate devotees. Lee Mo-bai felt for the first time that his life was somewhat regulated.

The room was in need of repair; the once whitewashed wall had cracks, one corner of the earthen raised *kon* (bed) was potholed. The nice bedroll his aunt prepared for him looked out of place. Dae Wu wanted to send a servant to help him to tidy the room, but Lee Mo-bai refused. He was embarrassed. Thinking of his comfortable room at home, he laughed lest he would cry. He preferred his present rough and adventurous new life. He felt better after he told Dae Wu everything. Now he did not feel that he was completely alone any more. He could talk openly with Dae Wu about his confused thoughts.

"Mo-bai, I was right to say that Thin Buddha Hwang has spies all over. He knows that you helped me fight Feng wu (five). He said he wants to meet you."

"That's preposterous! How dare he summon me? Does he think he is an emperor, a lord? I don't want to meet him."

"Of course you don't have to meet him. Mo-bai, you better stay away from him. He could use his silver to set you up and incriminate you..."

Lee Mo-bai interrupted sarcastically, "You don't mean that silver can do everything."

"Of course silver is indeed power. One of Violet's regular clients is Huge Bo who owns six pawnshops. Hwang and Huge Bo are the wealthiest men in Beijing; even the ministers have to be cordial to them and do their biddings because they owe either Huge Bo or Hwang silver." Dae Wu sighed and continued, "Believe me, Mo-bai, the rich

Hwang can use the weight of his wealth to hire someone to trick you or ambush you. I heard that he is the real owner of Universal Security Company. You've wounded one of their guards, so you've damaged their business standing. Hwang will think of you as his personal enemy. I'll be out of town on official duty soon and I want you to stay low for a while. I want you to be careful."

"I'm not afraid of them. Don't worry."

"Mo-bai, just remember this: *'It's easy to win an open-handed battle but it's hard to avoid a dart coming from the dark.'*

He was mildly drunk when he got to Violet's place.

"Long time no see. I'm glad that you still remember me." Violet said.

Lee Mo-bai stammered, "I. I've been busy. I moved and.." he added quickly, "I have not come to see you for three days, longer than three years to me."

"I just know you won't forget me. It's raining, I'll sing for you." She stood up, reached up to the top shelf and took down a *Hu chin* (two stringed guitar) in one smooth movement and started to play. Lee Mo-bai was puzzled, *'She moves with unusual agility. It almost looks like she has some martial arts training. Is it possible?'*

Violet sang a Sung Dynasty poem about a lonely woman missing her traveling husband during a rainy day. Lee Mo-bai tapped his teacup in harmony with the song. The haunting verses mesmerized both of them. Yu Ceo-lian's tearful face came to his mind, and his melancholy touched Violet. She said, "It's wrong of me to sing a sad song. It's the rain. When the sun comes out tomorrow, everything will be fine. Master Lee, you should not miss your wife in my presence. I'll be annoyed."

"I'm not married. That's part of my problem. I am halfway drunk. The rain and your enticing song made me temporarily forget myself. Sorry."

"Do you want to talk about it, Master Lee? Letting it out will help you feel better. I'm a good listener. It's my job to listen."

"I met the girl of my dreams recently, but she is engaged to someone else already. It's silly of me to pity myself." He thought, *'You're the most beautiful woman I have met. But you are a prostitute. I can't and I don't want to marry you.'*

Violet thought about her past unspeakable sufferings. They sat in silence. The sound of a neighboring prostitute's lamenting singing came through the partially curtained window.

Her mother came in with a note summoning Violet. She said, "Master Lee, don't leave in the rain. There are books and anthologies you may want to read."

"I'll stay for a while. I'll leave when it clears a bit." Now Lee Mo-bai was_alone and he pulled a thin volume down from a shelf on the headboard. A long, thin wooden box fell and exposed a shining eight-inch-long dagger. He put everything back and pondered, '*That's why Violet looks sad. Sometime she has the look that she is ready to flee. She must have an awful past and her enemies are chasing her. I may be able to help her. It's odd that I met another woman who knows martial arts. She is a prostitute, I won't marry her and I can't afford to support her anyway. Besides, I can't forget Yu Ceo-lian.*'

It poured when Violet came back. They talked and read some poems. The half-drunk Lee Mo-bai stayed overnight. He left at dawn and felt miserable and guilty. He wondered now how could he face Yu Ceo-lian? How disappointed his uncle and aunt would be if they knew about his visiting a prostitute? However, he visited Violet almost every day. When he asked her about her past, Violet only sobbed.

Dae Wu asked Lee over for supper and said, "Mo-bai, I know you like Violet very much and she likes you, too. But, please keep in mind that she is a prostitute and silver is important to her. You can't trust a prostitute. I heard either Vice Minister Hsu or Huge Bo will buy her out. Either one can wipe you out at will. Jealousy is a very strong emotion." He continued, "Mo-bai, you're young and you are lonely. I want you to be careful. I will be away for at least two months. Please be careful. *Thin Buddha* Hwang likes to stab you in the back and…"

Lee Mo-bai interrupted, "But, I can't keep quiet and do nothing if someone challenges me to a fight."

"Mo-bai, I'm sure you will win if they fight you openly. I'm not worried about *Saber King*; he is a man of principles. The others may ambush you or frame you. Who knows what schemes they may harbor? Maybe you should leave Beijing and go to the South to seek your Uncle Chiang. You could come to meet me at Yin-kin Town in Shanxi Province two months later. Yin-kin is not far from Da-ton. You can go to visit Miss Yu."

"I can't if I want to write the examination, I'll be careful. Besides I have to wait for *Saber King*. I don't want them thinking that I'm scared and run."

"Mo-bai, here is a passbook of silver for you to draw on. If you refuse, I'll consider that you don't value our friendship."

"Ah!.. thank you and have a safe trip."

Lee Mo-bai was lonely. He did not want to leave Beijing and could not resist the lure of wanting to visit Violet. It was an extremely hot afternoon, Lee Mo-bai sat on a straw mat under the shade and watched the floating white clouds and threw pebbles to knock down a leaf. Three men came into the quiet court, the thin one looked familiar. He recognized Thin Buddha Hwang.

He asked, "Are you looking for someone?"

"Are you Lee Mo-bai?" Hwang asked.

"That's me." Lee Mo-bai wondered why Hwang came without being invited.

"Your fame is far-reaching. I'm Ku An-chi. I heard that Dae Wu, with your help, considers that he is number one in Beijing now. I also heard that you defeated Wu, Feng wu (five). You boasted that you'd duel with Saber King. Am I correct?"

"Yes, I said all of that and more, Mister Ku. I would also like to step on a well-known hypocrite and coward call 'Thin Buddha'." Lee Mo-bai despised that Hwang did not use his own name.

"Thin Buddha is kind and generous. You insult my friend. I'll punish you."

Lee Mo-bai knew that the cunning Hwang did not use his own name in case he would lose. "I don't care you are, a coward, a fake. Lee Mo-bai is at your service."

He deliberately let Hwang complete the whole sequence of a set of boxing moves but never let his fist even come close. Master Shih, the owner of a nearby eatery, walked in to watch the duel. Lee Mo-bai called out, "Watch out, I'll hit your left shoulder." Hwang was hit. He staggered back a few steps, and sweat from the pain. Master Shih called, "Bravo!"

Lee laughed, "You're Thin Buddha. Coward. You dared not use your own name."

"Master Lee, you are the number one in Beijing now, and you must have a very good martial arts teacher." the portly and short Shih said.

"I'm a beginner, Master Shih. Do you know martial arts?"

"Call me Fat Shih. I'm too fat to brandish a saber or a staff. I love to watch a duel. Master Lee, I would be very careful and watch my back all the time if I were you. Beware of *Thin Buddha* and his kind."

"Thanks. Tell me what you know about Thin Buddha Hwang and Huge Bo."

"They are rich and wicked. *Thin Buddha* helps the poor often to buy a good name. Huge Bo is a miser. He only uses the power of his wealth to do evil and to control many high positioned officials who owe him money. All the poor trollops, high or low, are afraid of Huge Bo. Ah! I don't know martial arts well; otherwise, I would beat up that wicked Huge Bo."

"I think you're just being modest," Lee Mo-bai said. Shih laughed and left.

Lee Mo-bai thought, *'Money is indeed power. I fight well and I write well, but I don't have silver and I can't find a satisfying job to support myself. And the two women I love are out of my reach. I cannot marry Yu Ceo-lian because there is a faceless man called Mon Zhi-an. I'm even willing to lower my standards and rebel against my uncle to marry Violet. Where can I find the silver to buy her out? Besides, she is used to luxury and she doesn't want to marry a poor man. Maybe I will be a guard for a while to earn some silver."*

He knew that 'indecision' was his worst enemy; there were too many 'maybes' and too many 'ifs. He couldn't make a clean cut. He practiced sword fighting until he was drenched in sweat. The bluish blade of his sword looked frosty cold and it mirrored his mood. He walked around the court restlessly.

It was hot and crowded at Shih's eatery. Many customers stared at Lee Mo-bai. They seemed to know that Lee Mo-bai had hit Thin Buddha. Master Shih set a table for Lee in the back yard.

"Master Lee, the owner of Fu-An fabric shop hanged himself," Fat Shih said.

"I was there and it looks prosperous. Why did the owner kill himself?"

"Huge Bo charged him exorbitant interest that compounded monthly. The good profit from his shop was not enough to pay the interest. That wicked Huge Bo pressed him to pay; he wanted to seize the business and his pretty daughter."

"Maybe I'll teach him a lesson he won't forget." Lee Mo-bai said.

He walked around town aimlessly to hold back his urge to visit Violet. In the end he gave in and went to her parlor. A servant stopped him and told him that Master Bo was visiting Violet. He heard a robust laughter mixed with Violet's pleasant voice. He was jealous and angry and his taut nerves snapped.

"Huge Bo, you murderer. You forced a man to hang himself. I'm here to punish you!"

"Who is here looking for trouble? I'll get you arrested." A fat man came out and shouted down from upstairs. Lee Mo-bai jumped up, threw Huge Bo down.

Violet shouted, "Lee Mo-bai, you beat my client. You'll ruin my business!"

"I'll marry you. I'll support and protect you and your mother," Lee Mo-bai declared.

"Can you support us? Yes, you can fight with your fist. But, tell me what you will use to support us? You only know how to make our lives more difficult." Violet cried. She went in and slammed the door shut.

The news of two of the wealthiest persons in Beijing being hit in one day spread fast and Lee Mo-bai became a celebrity. He decided that he would leave Beijing. When he went to say good-bye to Uncle Kao, the valet politely turned him down.

"My relative won't see me anymore; a prostitute won't see me anymore. I'm going to leave Beijing soon." Lee Mo-bai told Fat Shih.

"The sooner the better. It's dangerous for you to stay. Even if you decide to write the civil services examination, they will find a way to ban you. Where are you going?" Fat Shih said.

"Everywhere and nowhere. I need to find a missing person for a relative. You've been around. Have you ever heard of a young man called Mon Zhi-an? He had run away from the law. His father owns a security company at Da-ton, Shanxi Province."

"No, but I will ask around. Da-ton is part of the area called Inner Mongolia. He may have escaped to Mongolia or even Russia. You may find some information in Xian, or he might be hiding right here in Beijing. Have you heard the saying, '*Beijing is the place full of hidden dragons and crouching tigers*'? Look at you, before yesterday; were you not an obscure fighter veiled behind your scholarly look? Oh! You can't leave Beijing yet. I heard *Saber King* is on the way here to fight you. If you leave now, folks will think you're afraid and run away."

"That's right. I'll wait three days. Then I will meet him on my way home, I have to pass through Ba-tin."

"Saber King and Golden Spear Jao are famous. They are different like day and night: Feng sie (four) is righteous and Jao is wicked. If *Saber King* finds out that his brother was in the wrong, he would not fight you. Perhaps the animosity between you and him can be resolved. Master Lee, to have a friend is better than to have an enemy."

"It's up to Saber King. I'm not afraid of him. Now I'd like to go to bid Violet farewell. I mean to end it."

"I heard Violet is a nice lady. Why don't you buy her out? If she loves you, she won't mind a modest life-style. She is no longer young. To have an elegant husband like you is not a bad choice."

"Ah! I can support her and her mother only if I want to be a guard. I cannot make up my mind about her and my career."

Violet offered Lee Mo-bai a cup of tea nonchalantly.

"I'm leaving Beijing soon. I came to say goodbye."

"Master Lee. where are you going? When will you be back?" She was no longer cold and unresponsive.

"I'll go home first and then to Da-ton and Xian. I won't be back soon. Violet, I truly care for you and intend to save some money to buy you out and marry you even if I have to choose an unsatisfying job. But you've given me the cold shoulder. I should not beat up Huge Bo. I was so jealous."

"I care for you, too. But.." Violet said.

"I know you consider me a poor and bad tempered bully now. You don't know how long I have been in agony over you and Yu Ceo-lian, the other girl I told you about. I'm sorry that I lost control the other day. By now you probably know that I'm a highly trained martial arts fighter. If anyone wants to marry you by force, or your enemy wants to kill you, I will be back to fight them off. I'll protect you whether you want to marry me or not."

Violet threw herself into his arms and kept on sobbing. Finally she said, "Mo-bai you know I love you, but I know you are in a constant state of indecision. I'll wait for you to make up your mind. No matter how long I have to wait. Oh! It's my karma to be a prostitute and that you met her before you met me."

Not far from Violet's bungalow, Lee Mo-bai heard a noise and acted on it.

"*Ouch*! Let me go, Master Lee." Fat Shih tried to waggle out of Lee's grip.

"It's you. What are you doing here at this hour?"

"Your enemies are waiting for you at the temple. I came to warn you."

"Who are they? Saber King?"

"Yes. He and two others. Be careful. *Saber King* is a powerful man and his sabers are heavy and deadly. But, he won't play a dirty trick."

Not far from the gate of the temple, Lee Mo-bai heard "Mister, are you Master Lee Mo-bai?"

"I am. Who are you?" One of them held a lantern and another one held some weapons and the reins of three horses. The empty-handed one bowed politely and said, "Master Lee, I'm Feng sie (four) of Ba-tin Town. You said you want to fight me."

"You're the famous Saber King. Why do you await me in the dark?"

"You're right that I should have waited for the morning. But I'm angry and I want to meet you as soon as I came into town. See, I'm empty-handed. Please come to Universal Security tomorrow morning with your friend Dae Wu. We'll fight then."

"Dae Wu is out of town on business. I'll be there."

He could not sleep and thought, *"Violet is right. I simply cannot forget Yu Ceo-lian. Of course, Violet does not want to marry me knowing that I have another woman on my mind. That Saber King seems to be a good man. Whether I win or lose tomorrow, I can ask for his help to find Mon Zhi-an."*

Lee Mo-bai rode one of Fat Shih's horses across town. When he passed Grand Security, a guard stopped him and said, "Master Lieu would like to have a word with you."

"Mo-bai, I heard about the duel and I'd like to talk to you."

"Uncle Lieu, guide me. I never had a formal duel with anyone before."

"Is that right? You will definitely win. I'm asking you to be lenient when you fight *Saber King*. He is not your equal. He is proud, but he is a real honest man. Please indulge me an unreasonable request. I want you to spare him a humiliating defeat."

"You think too highly of me. He may defeat me. I'll not be aggressive if I have the upper hand. Is this what you want to advise me?"

"Yes. Mo-bai, we'll go there together."

All the guards and the martial arts fanatics in Beijing were gathered there. *Saber King* was rugged, compact and robust. Lee Mo-bai was thin, pale, a tired scholar. Even the seasoned Master Lieu started to worry that Lee Mo-bai would meet a shameful defeat.

"Welcome, Master Lee. There is no real animosity between us. You have challenged me to fight you, so let's have an honest boxing match without any dirty tricks or hidden steel darts. Agreed?" *Saber King* bowed low and politely.

"Master Feng, we'll fight fair and square. Weapons are sharp and we can have a match without them." Lee Mo-bai bowed equally low and polite.

"Bravo. Master Feng is a true hero." Said one onlooker.

"Lee Mo-bai bowed like a courtier or an opera actor.' another spectator.

"There's a saying that *'when two tigers fight, one will die.'* I'm on friendly terms with both of you. Please indulge an old man's suggestion that you two talk over your differences over a drink." Master Lieu stood between Lee and Feng and pleaded that they don't fight.

"Sorry, Uncle Lieu, I cannot obey you today. Lee Mo-bai boasted that he would defeat me. I rushed here in the heat to meet his challenge. If he apologizes now, we'll have a truce," Saber King said.

"Uncle Lieu, I can't obey you either." Lee Mo-bai said.

Someone shouted, "Master Feng, chop him up with your sabers. He is afraid of your sabers and that's why he agrees to have a boxing match." The powerful Saber King knew that the skinny Lee Mo-bai was definitely not an easy contender.

"We'll have a boxing match first." They bowed once to each other and started to fight. Saber King hurled at Lee with fast and powerful fists and kicks, each of his powerful movement came with whooshing sounds. Lee Mo-bai moved seemingly slow and gracefully. He knew he will win and he let Saber King's fist or foot hit him once in a while because he did not want to humiliate him with a quick and obvious defeat. All of the audience applauded loudly whenever *Saber King* hit Lee Mo-bai. Only Saber King himself knew that he had been spared. His powerful strokes seemed to lose power when they touched Lee's body and Lee's strokes at him were harmless, too. Sweat poured from Saber King and he hauled at Lee with all the strength he could muster. Lee waited until the last second and jumped three feet high, descended bird-like with one foot kick that sent Saber King rolling.

Saber King yelled, "Lee Mo-bai, dare to fight me with your sword?"

"Certainly." Each one got their weapons ready. Lee Mo-bai had a sword and Saber King had two heavy sabers.

Lee Mo-bai bowed and said, "Master Feng, you're the host. Please start."

Three sharp weapons moved too quickly for the lesser skilled guards to see which is which. Lee Mo-bai never let the heavy sabers clash with his lightweight sword. Saber King took it that Lee was afraid of his strength and the heavy sabers. He gained confidence and fought ferociously. Lee Mo-bai kept the same principle of not embarrassing *Saber King* and he delayed his sure victory. They fenced for a while and suddenly Lee Mo-bai shouted, "Stop!" and jumped aside. He bowed and said, "Thanks. It's a good fight."

"*Lee Mo-bai lost*," someone shouted.

"*Bravo, Saber King.*" Many voices shouted.

Feng wu (five) yelled at his brother, "Why didn't you chop him down. Don't be merciful."

"You fool. Master Lee spared my life. Thank you, Master Lee. You will have my unyielding gratitude and I wish to be your friend." *Saber King* raised his arm and showed everyone that a slight sword cut pierced his clothes which could very well have sliced his right shoulder off.

"Master Feng, it's a hard fight for me, too. You're a tough contender. If you can forgive my earlier offensive remarks, I'd be honored to be your friend," Lee Mo-bai said with sincerity. He had forgotten the rule of modesty when he openly challenged Saber King.

"Well said. I'm proud to have two worthy nephews," Master Lieu said.

Saber King laughed, "I had a torn sleeve and I get a friend. Fighting is a thirsty business. Let's drink and eat." He put his arm around Lee Mo-bai and led him to a well-laid banquet and sat him next to Master Lieu. Lee Mo-bai asked everyone present to help him to find Mon Zhi-an.

A shifty looking man, Ca leo (six), bowed to Lee Mo-bai. and said, "Master Lee, you have my immense gratitude. You saved and then buried Uncle Yu and escorted my sister Yu Ceo-lian to Da-ton. The carriage driver told us all about you kindness and bravery. Brother Su and I sincerely thank you." He told the details. Everyone praised Lee Mo-bai.

"I did what a decent man will do under the circumstances. I hope we can find Mon Zhi-an soon," Lee Mo-bai said. For the next few days, Lee Mo-bai fully enjoyed his earned friendship and popularity among the guards and warriors. He liked their candid manners and the openhanded comradeship. When Master Lieu asked him to escort the transportation of three months wages for military forces and administration fund to Xian, he accepted.

Thin Buddha Hwang paid Lee Mo-bai another visit and apologized for his ridiculous behaviors earlier. "Master Lee, it was foolish of me to use a faked name. I did it because I knew I would be defeated at your hand. Why should I feel ashamed of my defeat? Even Saber King had met defeat at your hand. Please accept my apology and be my friend."

Lee Mo-bai replied, "Thank you for overlooking my silly behavior." They parted as friends. He suspected that Hwang's unexpected change of attitude might be a scheme in disguise. He told Fat Shih about it. Shih was worried.

Two days later, Lee Mo-bai was arrested and jailed. The charge was that someone reported him as a highly skilled burglar. The arresting officers thanked Lee for his non-resistance, "Master Lee, we thank you for letting us do our job. You could kill all of us at will."

"Sergeant, I'm innocent. I do not hold any grudge against you." He wondered who the instigator was. They had extra strong manacles put on his feet and also a heavy chain on his neck. Huge Bo paid the captain well and asked him to have extra guards posted around Lee Mo-bai's cell.

In his favorite concubine's place, Huge Bo told the opium addicted Vice Minister Hsu of the arrest. "Now the troublemaker Lee Mo-bai is out of the way. Violet will be yours. Congratulation."

Violet understood why Lee Mo-bai was arrested. She put on her most charming smile and pleaded, "Lord Hsu, I'm so grateful of your patronage. That young upstart Lee Mo-bai is rude and crude. His boorish ways tired me." She rubbed Vice Minister Hsu's back and continued, "But, My Lord, I don't think Lee Mo-bai is a thief."

Huge Bo said, "Tell me then where did he get the silver? Come on! It does not come free for him to visit you so often. He does not have a job. He steals."

"Master Dae Wu gives him silver," Violet argued.

"Violet, I would be very careful. I heard that Lee Mo-bai jumped nearly three feet high when he kicked Saber King. No walls can stop him and he is a wanted thief, and soon he will be beheaded. Anyone associated with him will be treated as his accomplice. They will search your parlor and confiscate your belongings if they consider you his accomplice. Do you and your mother want to be arrested on his account? Only Lord Hsu can shelter you," Huge Bo threatened Violet.

Her mother knelt and begged, "My lord, please help us. I told Violet again and again that Lee Mo-bai is a bad lot."

"Madam, please get up. You'll soon be Lord Hsu's mother-in-law," Huge Bo pulled the old woman up gently.

"Brother Bo, I advise caution. Just give that insolent Lee Mo-bai a good clubbing. You can't keep him jailed too long. You know this kind of criminal has friends who can scale the wall and break into the jail. They can kill us during the night, too. You have to release him; give him silver and ask him to leave Beijing." Vice Minister Hsu said.

'My Lord. No need to worry. Dae Wu is away and only Saber King and a couple of guards are on friendly terms with Lee Mo-bai. Feng wu (five) and the others either hate him or are jealous of him. Master Hwang hates him, too. We should kill him as soon as possible."

Huge Bo coerced, threatened and bribed Violet into agreeing to be Hsu's concubine. Violet and her mother were to move in with another concubine of Hugo Bo's on an auspicious day. Violet wept all the way home.

A very fat, well-dressed short man awaited them. The visitor told Violet bluntly, "I'm Lee Mo-bai's friend and you know in your heart that Lee Mo-bai was framed. Huge Bo and Vice Minster Hsu schemed to get him jailed, and they wanted to kill him, too. We will get him out soon. Lee Mo-bai loves you and I am here to warn you not to let them buy you out with their filthy silver. Otherwise .." Fat Shih said.

"Otherwise what? No one can force me to marry or not to marry. Get out, get out my house," Violet said angrily.

"You should not have loved that Lee Mo-bai in the first place. Your father's soul would not forgive you if you marry a thief or anyone who knows martial arts. You forget how your father had been beaten to death. You had been beaten too. I always worry that the cruel Dart Mew will come and catch us. Only the rich and powerful Vice Minister Hsu can protect us. I want to live comfortable and well at my old age. You could have married Lord Hsu earlier if that rascal Lee Mo-bai had not won your heart," her mother scolded Violet.

Her father was pretty good at martial arts and he was also a very good artist. He wrote poems, too. He married a beautiful prostitute and they had only one child, Violet, whom he taught well. Violet's parents bought a little place to retire close to the historical city of Kaifeng. Kaifeng had been the capital of many dynasties and was famous for the rich collection of antiquities. Unfortunately a vicious bandit leader, Dart Mew, lived not far away from them.

Mew was a well-known former bandit. His throwing dart is deadly accurate. Many professional guards and martial arts masters were afraid of his darts. His nephew Jao nicknamed '*Golden Spear*' married a fierce female fighter nicknamed '*She Devil*'. Mew and the Jao terrorized the whole area around Kaifeng.

Mew had many young concubines. He got them either by force or silver. The pretty Violet became Dart Mew's victim. In the beginning, the sadistic Dart Mew treated Violet well, but he started to torture her same way he tortured the others after the novelty wore off. Her father plotted an escape but they were caught. Mew had Violet's father beaten to death. She and her mother were also beaten and then heavily guarded. Violet charmed Dart Mew and gradually the surveillance on her and her mother relaxed and they managed to escape to Beijing. Once her father told them that Beijing, being the Manchu's capital, would protect them from Dart Mew. He also suggested that Violet should marry a powerful rich man to shield them.

Violet cared for the scholarly Lee Mo-bai very much before his superior martial arts skills became known. He promised that he will fight off her enemies. She was certain that Lee Mo-bai could defeat Dart Mew, but now Lee was in jail. She and her mother might be compromised too. She also begrudged that Lee Mo-bai had sent the fat man here to threaten her. She decided to be Vice Minister Hsu's concubine.

5

Lee Mo-bai's arrest soon spread and conflicting rumors circulated. His enemies wanted him dead or jailed for life. His friends wanted to save him. Fat Shih brought him daily meals, rumors and news. Master Lieu and other guards came to visit him in jail. The soldiers dared not abuse him.

Saber King was half way to Ba-tin, he doubled back. He visited Lee Mo-bai and reassured Lee that he would help Lee Mo-bai without any reservation. Lee Mo-bai was touched. He told Lee, "I will have someone safe guard your personal belongings."

"That is great. Please take temporary custody of my books and my sword. It's my late father's sword."

Saber King's sworn brother Chin was a boxing instructor at Prince Te's. Saber King asked Chin to tell Prince Te that Lee Mo-bai was no thief and had been wrongly arrested.

Prince Te had just return from a half year administration duty in Manchuria. He and all the other sons of the Emperor were required to learn both literary arts and martial arts. Each prince would gather talented and capable men, Manchu and Han, around him to teach him, to be his counsel. Prince Te encouraged anyone to go to him with suggestions and opinions.

"Your Highness, Lee Mo-bai is a scholar and he is waiting to write the civil services examination. He is Master Dea-ti's friend, and he is also a highly trained martial arts master. When Saber King fought him, he could have sliced off Saber King's shoulder and arms but he controlled his sword so well that he only ripped the sleeve. He is no thief and he was framed." Chin requested an audience and told Prince Te.

"Master Chin, thanks for the information. I will look into it. I cannot believe Dae Wu would be a friend to a thief. I will not allow an innocent man be jailed."

Prince Ti always respected Dae Wu's broad-minded way of being friends with the Han. When Prince Te was told that Dae Wu and Lee Mo-bai were good friends, he was convinced that the righteous and sensible Dae Wu would never befriend a lowly thief. He also thought a man good at both the literary arts and martial arts would not need to be a thief. Prince Te ordered his staff to investigate the case.

Fat Shih brought Lee Mo-bai a meal and whispered, "There is a file at the bottom of the dish. Use it to break the chain. I will have a horse ready outside of East Gate for you. There is no moon tonight. Be ready." Lee Mo-bai also whispered, "I'm no criminal. If I escape, it would be my admission of the guilt. I'm grateful for your help. They cannot hold me long. Saber King told me that one of his friends told Prince Te of my innocence. Besides, If I want to escape, no chain could keep me."

Two days later, a uniformed Imperial guard came and got Lee Mo-bai out of the jail. Fat Shih congratulated Lee, "Great! Nobody dares to touch you in Beijing anymore. But you still have to be cautious." Fat Shih told Lee that Violet became a concubine, "Mo-bai, forget her. She is a prostitute."

Saber King invited Lee Mo-bai and his sworn brother Chin to have a drink. Lee Mo-bai thanked Chin for his help. "It's nothing. Master Lee, Master Gi saved my brother years ago. I'm glad to have a chance to do something for his student. I know of your father and Master Chiang, too." He then told Lee some anecdotes of the three of them. Chin also advised Lee Mo-bai to study hard to become an administrator. He said, "You're a scholar and now you have a powerful patron. You could become a high ranking administer or a general in time and you can really do something good for us the Hans. Mo-bai, don't waste your talent and time on fighting and senseless revenge. I'm older than you and I hope you don't mind my boring comments." Chin said. Lee Mo-bai bowed low and thanked Chin, "Thank you. Uncle Kao and Dae Wu advised me to do the same."

Two days later, Prince Te sent summoned Lee Mo-bai.

"Mo-bai, study hard, pass the examination and be an administrator, or follow your father's step to be a military attaché for a general. Emperor need talents." Prince Te advised him. They talked about the different sword fighting styles. Prince Te insisted that they should have a friendly duel. Lee Mo-bai hesitated and said, "It's not fitting for me to have a duel with Your Highness. The sword is sharp and.."

Prince Te laughed, "You wanted to say that you may wound me. Is that right? It's simple, we will wrap the swords with silk." They went to the training field and everyone crowded around to watch the duel. Prince Te put on a black suit. He ordered to have two swords wrapped with silk and coated with lime.

"The white spots on my black suit will tell me where you hit me. Mo-bai, I don't want you to have any reservation. Don't hold back. you hear?" Lee Mo-bai made the duel last a long time. When he saw that Prince Te showed signs of weary, he delivered the winning thrust. Someone called out, 'Watch out! The left shoulder." just before Lee Mo-bai's sword, flat, hit Prince Te's left shoulder. *'Ahe. He saw through my move, this person is an expert.'* Lee Mo-bai glanced at the direction where the voice came. He saw three young men there.

Prince Te said, "You're very good. There are only eleven white spots on my suit. *Ha. Ha.*" He then handed the sword he was using to Lee Mo-bai, "I'd like you to have it. It's a historically well-known piece."

"Your Highness, it's too valuable. I don't deserve it."

"If you don't deserve it, who else does? Keep it. Mo-bai."

They had supper together. Prince Te said, "I have spare rooms here. Why don't you have one?"

Lee Mo-bai said, "Thanks. I don't want to impose on you."

"You want freedom. *Ha Ha.*" Prince Te ordered his valet, "Get a carriage ready to take him home." On his way out, Lee Mo-bai asked the valet, "Do you know who called out the warning at the end of the duel?"

"It must be Yu Er (two). He works in the stable. He will be reprimanded for his insolence."

Lee Mo-bai walked around Violet's new home but he did not see her coming out of the house. Every day he drank heavily and ignored Fat Shih's advice of restraining. One night a noise woke the drunken Lee Mo-bai. He took his sword, staggered out of the room to check around and found no one. A man rushed out his room, holding the sword that Prince Te had given him. Lee Mo-bai shouted, "You came to steal the sword. I know who you are! Yu Er (two)." They fought and Lee Mo-bai met his first worthy opponent. Yu Er (two) was a more experienced fighter and he had a better sword. He also was more agile and in better shape since Lee Mo-bai did not sleep well for a long time. Yu Er (two) forced Lee Mo-bai back and jumped upon the roof and escaped. The bare-footed Lee Mo-bai chased after him but could not catch him.

Next day Lee Mo-bai went to Prince Te's and asked the guards at the gate about Yu Er (two). No one knew too much about him. One of them said, "A while ago, a Tibetan Monk brought him here and said he could tame horses. The manager let him work at the stable. Indeed he knows horses. Even the most difficult ones are docile at his hand." Lee Mo-bai could not go to the stable to seek Yu Er (two). He went to ask Master Lieu about him. Lieu said, "'Yu' is not a common surname like 'Lee' and 'Lieu'. I wonder whether he is related to the late Brother Yu." Lieu also told him the convoy to the west had been canceled. Lee Mo-bai could leave Beijing now but he was too proud to let Yu Er (two) walk away with stealing the sword right under his nose. '*He will come to fight me again. One of the days his hand will get itchy. I'll wait..*

It rained that night, Lee went to Violet's new home and wanted to know whether she is happy or not. '*If she is not happy, I'll take her with me and leave Beijing without that sword. Yu Er (two) can have it.*' He waited on the roof in the rain and heard Violet laughing and joking with another young woman. When he saw the other young woman come out of Violet's room, he slipped into it, and Violet said angrily, "Get out. How dare you have your friend threaten me! I'm happy and I feel safe here and I don't want to see you anymore."

"Who had threatened you? I know nothing."

"A fat man and he said he is your friend. Mo-bai, we've been good together. Let's keep the good memory of the time we were together. Please forget me," Violet sobbed. When Lee left, he saw the curtain of the other girl's room drew close. '*Ahe! The other girl saw me. I hope that I didn't cause Violet any trouble.*'

He went home sick. When he did not show up at Fat Shih's eatery, Fat Shih came and found Lee Mo-bai very sick. Shih said, "I'll be right back with some herbal medicine for your fever."

Lee Mo-bai dropped into another feverish sleep. He woke up suddenly and found Yu Er (two) standing beside the bed. He came to return the sword. Lee Mo-bai said weakly, "I know it's you. Brother Yu. You should keep it, you're a better swordsman."

"You're sick and you should not be alone. Your enemies may come to kill you. I'll stay with you." Lee nodded. Yu suddenly turned around when Fat Shih came. Lee said, "Brother Yu, he is a friend. Master Shih, this is the young accomplished warrior I told you about. He is Yu Er (two)." Fat Shih brought medicine and a kettle of hot tea, a pot of porridge.

"Brother Yu, thank god you're here. I cannot fight his enemies off if they come to harm him." Shih said. Yu Er (two) curled up in a corner on the *kon* (bed). During the night, Yu Er (two) helped Lee to drink some tea twice. Next morning Yu Er (two), Prince Te's valet and a doctor came. Lee Mo-bai had pneumonia. Yu Er (two) brought a charcoal burner, a pot to brew the herbs and also to cook rice porridge. Fat Shih brought them both meals every day and extra bedding and warm clothes for the cooler autumn. Some professional guards came to visit Lee Mo-bai often. When Lee asked where did Yu Er (two) learned martial arts so well, Yu Er (two) told him: a Tibetan monk had brought him to Master Hsu's place in Szechwan. Hawk Hsu's wife taught him. Chiang Nan-ho and his mute brother had stayed at Master Hsu's place for eight months before Master Hsu passed away. Both of them taught Yu Er (two) and the Mute particularly. The Mute liked Yu Er (two) very much. Lee Mo-bai said, "Ahe! That explains that some of our fighting styles are very similar. We're truly brothers. Chiang Nan-ho is my father's sworn brother. The last time I saw him I was eight years old. He took me to my uncle's after my parents died. I wished often that Uncle Chiang had adopted me and take me places." Lee wanted to ask about Yu Er (two)'s past but he did not want to probe. Yu Er (two) was reticent, he only told Lee Mo-bai that he had killed an evil man and he is in hiding.

A sergeant walked in, the same one who had arrested Lee Mo-bai earlier.

"Sergeant, I'm sick. Is this a follow-up check on me?"

"Master Lee, I came to see how you are. How long have you been sick?"

"Many days. I got sick shortly after I got out of the jail. I'm going nowhere."

"I can see that. Vice Minister Hsu and Master Bo were killed last night."

"Really? I'm glad." Lee Mo-bai said.

"It was not a burglary. We're holding both concubines for questioning. Master Bo's concubine implicated you."

"Did the woman say that I was the killer?"

"No. She said you were there one night but she said the killer is short and fat. Two women who worked there saw the killer and reported that the killer wrapped his fat legs and arms with strips of black cloth."

"Great, I'm tall and thin. Why do you come to me then, Sergeant?"

"I have to follow up the inquiries. I'm only doing my job."

"I know nothing. Huge Bo who got me jailed, but I would not murder him at night. It's not my style. I'm very sick."

"Master Lee, you are not a suspect."

"I'm glad to hear you say that. We all know that Hsu and Bo, with their filthy money and power, abused and ruined a lot of people. Their victims might have done it. Just between you and me, they deserved to be killed, sooner or later."

"I think I know who is the killer. I better leave Beijing as soon as I'm well. Brother Yu, will you like to go to Yin-kin, Shanxi with me? We may meet my friend Dae Wu there. Then we'll go to Da-ton." Lee Mo-bai said to Yu Er.

"Sorry, I cannot go to either city. Someone might recognize me there."

"We can ask Prince Te to clear your name. He will understand that you've killed an evil man."

"It would not be that easy. Brother Lee, I'd like to go down South to seek the Mute if he is still alive."

"Good idea, we'll go together. Uncle Chiang probably does not know that Teacher Gi had passed away. You know they were enemies first and then friends later. Master Chin told me that Uncle Chiang and Teacher Gi had fought over the same woman when they were young." Lee Mo-bai sighed and continued, "After Teacher Gi passed away, and I've been very lonely. My aunt cares for me very much but my uncle, a miser, only wants me to be an administrator to bring him wealth and status. I think of you as my true brother, Brother Yu."

"I'm honored. You did not judge me by my shabby appearance. You're the first true praiseworthy contender I have met. Here is your medicine." He handed Lee the medicine and continued, "Get well soon. I'd like to duel with you again, we can learn from each other."

"It is a deal." Lee Mo-bai laughed and coughed a little before he slept.

Close to midnight, Fat Shih came. There were strips of black cloth wrapped around his thick thighs. Lee Mo-bai laughed, "Master Shih, you finally show us your true identity."

"I never thought I could pull a fog over both of you. I came to say farewell."

"Did you know the sergeant came to question me this morning for the crime you've committed?"

"How can you say it is a crime? I consider it a heroic deed. Mo-bai, you're sick and you are under the future Emperor's protection. I know they cannot touch you." Fat Shih sat on the edge of the bed and continued, "I'm nicknamed *'Mountain Lizard'*. My enemies forced me to flee here to hide. Huge Bo and Master Hsu robbed you of a pretty woman, had you jailed and made you sick. On behalf of YOU and other countless victims suffering at their hands, I killed them. Violet is a widow now and you can marry her and live happily ever after. *Ha Ha*. Too bad we don't have wine to celebrate."

"Master Shih, I don't want to and I cannot afford to marry Violet. Thanks to you, she lost her powerful protector. I hope that the law treated her and her mother not too rough. She definitely will lose her income and somehow I have to help her." Lee Mo-bai complained.

"Fine. I knew you would not appreciate my effort. Here is some silver for Violet. I have to leave Beijing tonight. I want to warn you, Mo-bai, *Thin Buddha* Hwang pulled a lot of strings to have you jailed. He is evil. I heard he sent someone to fetch Dart Mew, *Golden Spear* Jao and others from Kaifeng here to fight you. Be prepared. Bye.' Fat Shih jumped upon the roof and left.

"I knew that you were jailed because of a pretty prostitute. Is Violet her name? Sorry, I shouldn't pry."

"I fell in love with Violet and I believe she loves me, too. But.. I don't want to marry her, because there is another woman who has haunted me ever since last spring. I went to Violet with the hope that I may forget the other woman. I hit Huge Bo. That's why I was jailed."

"May I ask you a very personal question?"

"I would not hide anything from you. You are a true brother."

"When you were delirious, you called out two names; Violet and Ceo-lian. You called out Ceo-lian more. Is she the woman of your dreams?"

Lee Mo-bai sighed, "She is. I can't have her and I can't forget her. For months I haven't had a good night's sleep and no food tastes good to me. I'm agonizing over her." Lee Mo-bai sobbed, "Let me tell you from the beginning._You're the second person I've poured my heart out to. Talking it out would give me some relief, too." Between sobbing and coughing, Lee told Yu Er (two) everything.

Yu Er (two) laughed hard at the ridiculous duel that Lee had wishfully thinking that he could win a wife with his sword. He laughed so hard that his tears came. He suddenly stood up and said, "I need to go to the market." In the semi-darkness, Lee Mo-bai did not see Yu Er (two)'s tears and sudden paleness.

Yu Er (two) stood at a corner, gulped air and tried to keep his emotions in check. *'Ahe! It's her. I wondered about it. Now I know it and I'm poor and I have to hide all my life. What should I do?'* He thought about telling Lee the truth about himself. Another thought came to him and he decided to keep quiet. Lee Mo-bai thought, *'Dart Mew will be here soon. It's said that Dart Mew uses poisonous darts. It's good that I have taught Ceo-lian how to avoid and to throw a dart. I hope she will keep up the exercise. I wonder how they are. Is the Mon family treating her mother and her well?'* His thoughts darted from Yu Ceo-lian to Violet, back and forth.

Yu Er (two) told Lee, "I'm grateful that you consider me your brother. I truly think you should marry Yu Ceo-lian whether the missing fiancé is found or not. You've done so much for her family. You're a scholar, Yu Ceo-lian could be a first-rank lady if you pass the examination and become an administrator. Your calligraphy is superb and I know you can pass the exam if you want to. that fugitive Mon Zhi-an is the son of a guard. He would not have your polished looks and he definitely could not make Yu Ceo-lian a lady and provide her a fine living even if he is not a wanted criminal."

"Thanks. Mon Zhi-an is a true hero; he had the courage to take justice in his own hands. He is her betrothal. I heard that he knows martial arts extremely well. He could be a famous guard if he changed his name. They are of the same background, Yu Ceo-lian will be happy with him. I have to find him for her. If you don't mind, I'd rather not talk about this anymore." Lee Mo-bai said. He closed his eyes and thought, *'I should not have been so open with him. He treats me with genuine concern, but he won't tell me anything about himself, not even his full name. 'Er' simply means he is a second son. I wonder what else he is hiding from me.'* He was worried about Violet and her mother, too. He asked Yu Er (two) to take some silver to them but Yu Er (two) could not find them. The only consolation that Lee Mo-bai had is that a pretty woman would soon find another rich man.

Yu Er (two) soon moved back to Prince Te's stable. It began getting colder each day. Lee Mo-bai put on his padded jackets and still felt the piercing cold wind when he visited Prince Te.

"Mo-bai, you have lost a lot of weight and you're still pale. You must have been pampered when you were at home. Let me find you a good wife to look after you," Prince Te said.

"Your Highness, thank you for everything and thank you for letting Yu Er (two) to take care of me. He is great."

"Oh! That's nothing. It was good of him to tell us that you were sick, I'll reward him." Prince Te's valet came in with a calling card. Lee Mo-bai tactfully ended his visit. He walked back to the stable and invited Yu Er (two) to have a drink. Lee Mo-bai shivered in the cold wind. Yu Er (two) showed no signs of being cold.

"Brother Yu, I miss your company. And I can't thank you enough for what you've done for me." Lee Mo-Bai said.

"You will do the same for me. I'll soon leave Beijing. Before I leave, I'd like to have a duel with you at daytime, not at night." Both of them laughed.

"I'd like that. Where are you going? Do you need help with traveling funds?"

"I can manage." Yu Er (two) did not tell Lee where he was going and why he wanted to leave.

"You're a true brother. I often think you're hiding your worry from me. Please open up to me like I did to you, maybe I can help."

"No. You can't." They drank in silence. "Brother Lee, one day you will know that I'm not a sly person. It's just I can't tell you everything now. I have my reasons. I truly value your friendship. Someday you'll know that I have your best interests in mind."

"Do you mind accepting some warm winter clothes?"

"Thank you, I need some warm clothes. I'd better get back to work. See you in the evening."

Lee Mo-bai went to see Master Lieu at Grand Security and thanked all the guards who were friendly to him. He asked them again whether they have heard a young warrior named Yu Er (two). Master Lieu said, "The only 'Yu' good at martial arts I know of was the late Master Yu. By the way, Mo-bai, your letter to Mrs. Yu was delivered. The carrier came back with the news that Mrs. Yu is very ill and there is no information of the missing Mon Zhi-an."

"Ahe! That's bad. I wish I was free to go to Da-ton to see Aunt Yu. But I have to wait for the imminent fight with Dart Mew and the others from Kaifeng."

"Mo-bai, take care of yourself. I hope you will be fully recovered when they come. We'll be on your side."

Lee Mo-bai went to the market and bought some warm clothes, fur hats and boots for Yu Er (two) and himself. He met Violet's mother. "Master Lee, Please come with me," the old woman begged in tears.

Violet and her mother lived with some other poor prostitutes in a shabby house. Vice Minister Hsu's wife confiscated all of their savings and kicked them out. The law officers were not kind to Violet either. She was sick.

"Master Lee, we have you to thank for all of our troubles," Violet said bitterly.

"I am truly sorry. I was sick for a long time and I did not kill Bo and Hsu."

"I know that you are sick. Can you say you're completely in the clear? Your fat friend killed them for you. If I had told the law that he's your friend. Master Lee, you would not be free of blame either."

"Fat Shih did not kill Bo and Hsu for you and me only. He killed them for all the other victims they had ruined."

"I said it before and I'll say it again. You men who know martial arts are all conceited and inconsiderate. You and your kind only understand fighting and killing. That fat friend of yours did not care whether I and my mother could survive without a powerful protector."

"Violet, I couldn't foretell and control what Fat Shih would do. He left me some silver for you," Lee Mo-bai put the silver which Fat Shih had left with him and three silver certificates worth fifty ounces each on a table and then continued, "Farewell, Violet. I'm in no shape for a quarrel. I'm leaving Beijing after I kill Jao and Dart Mew from Kaifeng. They killed Uncle Yu."

"Who? Did you say Dart Mew from Kaifeng would be here soon?" Her eyes were full of terror. Lee Mo-bai had a coughing spell so he did not notice it.

"Just as you said, all the ones who know martial arts like nothing better than fighting and revenge for something insignificant. They are coming from afar to challenge me and I have to kill them for revenge even they did not kill my uncle themselves. I wish you all the best. Farewell." Lee Mo bai coughed and then left with remorse. He wondered again about Violet's hidden daggers and why do they need powerful protectors. He wanted to ask her but he knew that she would not tell him. *'It's time to end the affair.'* He decided.

Yu Er (two) and Lee Mo-bai practiced and compared their fighting skills at dawn and dusk. Yu Er (two) had more real combat experience. His jumping skills were better and his swords thrusts were more powerful and deadly. Lee Mo-bai knew more advanced breathing exercises and *Tai Chi* boxing and swords fighting techniques, which the Mute could not make Yu Er (two) fully understand.

"The Mute showed me a two-volume martial arts manual full of illustrations and explanations in simple words. Chiang Nan-ho compiled them. He showed me some but I did not absorb it well. Someone who has a mind as sharp as yours could learn well from studying the manuals. I hope they will not fall into evil hands." Yu Er said.

"Manuals? I know nothing about it. We have to find it. The last time I saw Uncle Chiang, I was eight years old. You and I have to find Uncle Chiang and the Mute to learn more. Uncle Chiang is older than Teacher Gi. I don't know whether they are still around or not."

Their skills improved. Their friendship and the vigorous exercise cured Lee Mo-bai's insomnia and also stimulated his appetite. He got stronger.

One late afternoon, Dae Wu's servant came, "Master Lee, my master will be back soon. He sent someone ahead with this letter to you." It read, *'Mo-bai, we have been apart more than three months already. I still have some official business to do. I'll tell you in detail when we meet. I heard that you're out of jail but something else must keep you from coming to meet me. Master Yan-ti heard so much about you and he is coming to Beijing to meet you. He wants you to work for him if you want to be a guard. I have marvelous news. The lovely Yu Ceo-lian whom you cannot forget and for whom you have so many sleepless nights is here at Yin kin. Her mother passed away and she is here to ask Yan-ti about Mon Zhi-an. I told her that I'm your friend and she agrees to come to Beijing with us. So my dear Mo-bai, your dream and wish will be fulfilled soon. Be prepared. I'll have a grand wedding for you. Your humble brother Dae Wu.'*

He read the letter again and thought, *'Dae Wu is goodhearted but preposterous. Poor Ceo-lian, her mother passed away. From this letter, it seemed that Yu Ceo-lian might not object to marrying me. Am I dreaming again?'* He hit his thigh hard to see it whether it was a dream and continued his musing, *'but, it's absurd. What if Mon Zhi-an shows up one day? I can't marry her until we know for sure Mon Zhi-an is dead. But how long should I wait? How long should Yu Ceo-lian and I suffer the uncertainty and loneliness? And how about my relationship with Violet? I know Violet still wants me and I cannot forget her either.'*

He paced around, holding the wrinkled letter, laughed and sighed. The sweat covered his thin face.

"Brother Lee, what's the matter? Are you sick again?" Yu Er (two) came.

"I..I," Lee Mo-bai shook his head and handed Yu Er (two) the letter, "Yu Ceo-lian will be here soon. Dae Wu wants us to get married. How can I? Mon Zhi-an is her fiancé," Lee Mo-bai moaned. His eyes flashed and his face changed from pale to purple and back to a deathly white. Yu Er (two) took a long time to read the letter. He also paled and his hand shook when he put the letter on the table.

"It's great. Of course you should marry her. You deserve it. Compared to you, Mon Zhi-an did nothing for her family. He probably is poor and destitute and can't provide Yu Ceo-lian a decent living. Maybe he does not want to be found. You should marry Yu Ceo-lian." Yu Er (two) said very loud. He shouted.

Lee Mo bai stared at the usually sedate Yu Er (two) who was shouting now. He Suddenly noticed Yu Er (two)'s abrupt bloodless face and his trembling shoulders, he grabbed Yu Er (two)'s arm and shouted, "You.. You are Mon Zhi-an. I think I always knew…"

Yu Er (two) wrenched free and fled. Two streets later, the breathless Lee Mo-bai gave up the chase. He knew that even when he was at his best, he would have a hard time to catch Yu Er (two). *'In my mind, I think I always knew that he is Mon Zhi-an. When I told him about Yu Ceo-lian, didn't he laugh hysterically and pale suddenly. He found an excuse to leave the room and said that he had to go to the market. He must want to hide his emotional turmoil. He must love Yu Ceo-lian too since he uses her last name 'Yu' and 'Er' which means he is a second son. He guarded me and took care of me when I was sick and now I rob him of his betrothed. What kind of evil man am I? My indecision has caused Violet and her mother to be miserable and poor. Now, if Mon Zhi-an does not want to be found, it's also my fault a young couple separated. Mon Zhi-an obviously misunderstands me and thinks that there is an infatuation between Yu Ceo-lian and me. Where can I find him?'*

Lee Mo-bai rushed to Prince Te's palace in a wild hope that Mon Zhi-an would pick up his belongings. He asked the guards at the gate to allow him to go the stable directly, but Prince Te was just getting off a carriage and saw him. Prince Te said, "Mo-bai, Congratulations. Dae Wu wrote that you're going to be married soon. Oh! What's the matter? Are you ill again?"

"Your Highness, I'll explain later. I have to find Yu Er (two). I must see him before he leaves." Lee Mo-bai said with apparent urgency.

"What's wrong? I'll send Je to fetch him." Lee Mo-bai could not find Yu Er (two) in the stable and neither could Prince Te's valet. Lee Mo-bai gushed out everything from the beginning to Mon Zhi-an's disappearance.

"Je, pass my order, Close all the gates out of Beijing now, apprehend Yu Er and bring him to me" Prince T barked his order half way through the narrative.

"Mo-bai, I really feel for you. Now I can see why a conscientious young man could get mixed up with a prostitute. You were looking for a diversion then." Prince T. said after he had heard all.

"Your Highness, I am ashamed and I'm responsible for Violet's misfortune even though I did not kill Vice Minister Hsu myself. Now I'm responsible for breaking up a couple."

"Mo-bai, I'm ashamed, too. I did not recognize Yu Er (two) as a talented warrior while I paid a lot for mediocre ones. When he comes back, I'll clear his name and I'll offer him an instructor's post. He can marry Yu Ceo-lian then. I'm curious to know how good he is."

"He is better than me. Your Highness, I'm afraid that Mon Zhi-an won't be back. He insisted that I could provide Yu Ceo-lian a better life than he could."

"Mo-bai, there is some truth to it. If she marries you, Yu Ceo-lian could be a lady. If she marries Mon Zhi-an, she would be a wife of a guard and nothing more. Besides Mo-bai, you have done so much for her family and you're so good looking. I won't doubt that the girl admires you."

"Your Highness, I behave properly around her and I tried very hard to hide my feelings. I think Yu Ceo-lian only thinks of me as her older brother."

"Mo-bai, you tried to hide your feelings, and she probably did, too. I don't see why you cannot marry her. They have never met each other and now Mon Zhi-an obviously relinquishes his marital rights to let you marry her."

'*Someday you'll know that I have your best interests in mind.*' Mon Zhi-an, Yu Ear's words came back. Lee Mo-bai knew that Mon Zhi-an did not want to be found.

"You Highness, if I had never met Mon Zhi-an, or if Mon Zhi-an did not take care of me, I think I could marry Yu Ceo-lian after a certain length of time. Now, I can't and I won't marry her. I have to find Mon Zhi-an."

"Mo-bai, you can stay here tonight. I have ordered the guards at all the gates leading out of Beijing to watch for him. All the gates will be closed for the night. Tomorrow, I will get more men at each gate to catch him."

"Thanks, Your Highness, I think I better go back to my place. Maybe he is waiting for me there."

"Tell me immediately of any new development."

Back at his room at the temple, it was not Mon Zhi-an in person but a letter was waiting for Lee Mo-bai. It read, '*Brother Lee, please accept my blessings and marry Yu Ceo-lian. I have nothing to offer her whereas you have plenty to offer in addition to what great services you have already done for the family. I wish you two the best. Don't look for me. You can't find me. Farewell. PS. I took the sword Prince Te had given you again.*' Lee Mo-bai wept.

Prince Te often slept alone in his study. Sometime after midnight, sounds of soft footsteps woke up Prince Te. "Is that you, Je? Bring me a cup of tea!" No answer.

Prince Te unsheathed his sword. A young man walked in. It was Yu Er (two). "It's you! Lee Mo-bai waited for you all day. Now I know your real name and your problem. I can clear your name. Zhi-an." Price Te said warmly.

"Thank you, Your Highness. I must leave at once. I will borrow one of your horses."

"You can have a dozen horses. I want to talk to you, Zhi-an.'

"Sorry, I know what you want to tell me. I must leave. Farewell." Mon Zhi-an left as soundlessly as a breeze over the roofs.

"Je, wake up. Go to the stable and see which horse is missing. Be quiet about it," Prince Te ordered his valet.

"Your Highness, who would ride at this hour?" Je grumbled and left. He came back shortly and reported, "Your Highness. Yu Er (two) is not back yet. Your favorite black mare is missing and the stable gate was unlocked and left open. Should I order a thorough search?"

"Yu Er (two) left with the horse. No need to make a fuss. Bring me tea and go back to sleep." Prince Te thought, *'There are nine inner gates and fifteen outer gates in Beijing. No way to tell which gate he will take.'*

He sent for Lee Mo-bai at dawn and told him that Mon Zhi-an had taken the horse. Lee Mo-bai said, "Your Highness, we can't find him now. He took the sword you gave me last night again when I was here. Now he has a fast horse and a sharp sword. Who knows where he will go?"

"He came to me at midnight. I tried to talk some sense into him last night. He left without giving me a chance to say anything,"

"Your Highness, if I can't find him, how could I face Yu Ceo-lian?"

Prince Te thought a moment and then said, "Mo-bai, if you make up your mind that you can't and don't want to marry her, no one can force the issue. Just tell her the truth. You did not force him away. He left on his own. I have resources and manpower for you to draw on to help you find him."

"Thanks, Your Highness, I'm sorry I am not a pleasant company today."

"Mo-bai, you may leave. Prepare your mind and body for the impending fight with Dart Mew and his gang. Yu Er (two), Mon Zhi-an, is not here to help you. You're on your own."

6

Yu Ceo-lian and her mother suffered from indifference to downright abuse at their in-law's home. Mrs. Yu's stomach ulcer got worse. She constantly wept for her husband's death and her daughter's bleak future. Yu Ceo-lian had to work non-stop. She took care of her sick mother and she had to serve her demanding future mother-in-law. She also had to do the housework under her sister-in-law's critical eyes. Sometimes she was too busy to think about her misfortune and to cry.

Mrs. Mon was a demanding and bitter woman. It was her father's money and fame that established the Mon Security Company. She was a spoiled only daughter and she had never forgiven her husband for taking a concubine. She resented that her own son must share the family wealth with Mon Zhi-an, the son of the concubine. As expected, she did not like Yu Ceo-lian. When her own son's wife ordered Yu Ceo-lian around like a servant, she did not object. As a matter of fact, she would not let any chance gone by without insinuating that she had to mercifully take in the now destitute Mrs. Yu and Yu Ceo-lian.

Mon Zhi-chi, the elder son, was in charge of the family business. Yu Ceo-lian soon realized that the Mon Senior actually was afraid of his wife and his elder son. Old Master Mon was indifferent to Mrs. Yu's illness. Short Hsu and his wife were the only ones who were kind to Ceo-lian and her mother. Short Hsu found a doctor and also brought the medical herbs for Yu Ceo-lian to brew for her mother. When Short Hsu's wife realized that Ceo-lian sure had mixed feelings for Lee Mo-bai, she talked to Mrs. Yu and suggested that it will be all right for Ceo-lian to marry Lee Mo-bai if Mon Zhi-an could not be found soon. They encouraged Yu Ceo-lian to learn how to read and write. Short Hsu did not know his words well, but he taught Yu Ceo-lian whatever he knew.

254

Mrs. Mon and Yu Ceo-lian's sister-in-law verbally abused Ceo-lian and her mother often. Yu Ceo-lian's mother died. Master Mon ordered Short Hsu to make the funeral arrangements.

Mon Zhi-chi sought every opportunity to ogle the pretty Yu Ceo-lian. His wife was jealous and treated Yu Ceo-lian worse. Yu Ceo-lian decided to leave. She sought Short Hsu's advice. He sighed, "Sister, I know your difficulties very well and you want to leave. I need my job here and I can't go with you. Do you want to go back to Lu Town?"

His wife said, "How can she travel alone? She is so young."

"I know martial arts well. I can travel by myself. My sworn brother Lee Mo-bai is in Beijing. He wrote to us saying that he did not find Mon Zhi-an yet but he is still trying. I'm going there, he will help me. I know it's not very proper, but I have no one else."

Short Hsu said, "In this area, there are many young Mongolian and Manchu girls. They rode and wore their hairs in two braids. We'll get her a pair of boots and she could look like a Manchu girl traveling alone. Master Lee is indeed a very decent man, and he sure will help you. Before you go to Beijing, I suggest you go to visit the famous Master Yan-ti at Yin-kin Town. You have to pass there anyway. He knows the Mons, father and sons. He may give you some information."

"Do you know how to handle a horse? Ceo-lian"

"Yes I do. Brother Lee Mo-bai taught me everything: brushing the horse, riding and saddling a horse. I'm taller now. I can manage any horse," she said rather proudly and she thought about her father and the first time Lee Mo-bai helped her to mount her father's horse. Her tears came and she also blushed when she tried to recall the sensation of Lee Mo-bai's strong hands pushing her up the tall horse. That was the first time a man had touched her.

Short Hsu saddled a good horse for her. Yu Ceo-lian wore a dark blue cotton short set with a silver comb in her hair and wide strips of white cloth tied her braids. She also wore a white armband. She was in mourning. She carried two pairs of sabers, her own and her father's. A small package with some silver and silver certificates tied around her waist under her tunic. Short Hsu's wife helped her to sew a small pocket for the extra silver certificates, which could be stored between the linings of her undershirt. 'Aunt, you and Ceo-lian should have some silver.' Lee Mo-bai's words came clear to her. He had said after he sold her father's horse. 'Ahe! He is honest and he truly cares for us. He could *have kept my father's good horse for himself. I remembered that his horse is old and thin. He could have sold that old horse instead or not care to sell the horse at all. He wanted us to have some silver'* She remembered that Lee Mo-bai washed and brushed the horse before he sold it. *'We can get more silver for a clean horse."* He had explained.

Her clothes and other necessities were in the saddlebag. Wrapped tightly inside her spare clothes were a pair of gold hair combs and a sealed letter. The combs were the marriage keepsakes Master Mon gave her father six years ago when they arranged the marriage between her and Mon Zhi-an. When she finds *Mon Zhi-an, this pair of gold combs would identify her as his bride. Short Hsu handed her a sealed letter and said that she should hand it to Lee Mo-bai in* person. "Sister, give it to him, not his friend," Short Hsu told her. When she asked him what was in the letter. Short Hsu had said vaguely, "Probably something about your late father's unfinished business that he wanted Lee Mo-bai to handle for him."

She had diligently practiced the deep breathing technique Lee Mo-bai had taught her. She felt strong and her senses became sharper. When she found a quiet place along the road, she practiced the throwing darts technique, which Lee Mo-bai also taught her. *'Sister, try not to catch any dart your enemy throws at you. Just dodge it or push it away with your saber. The dart might be poisonous. If you really want to catch it, wear something that covers your hand.'* Everything she did brought Lee Mo-bai's words and image vividly to her mind. At night she slept with her clothes and shoes on and with her sabers beside her. She remembered that Lee Mo-bai had told her to be alert all the time.

When she stopped at the first inn, the clerk looked at her in awe as she carried two pairs of sabers under one arm and her saddlebag with one hand. The owner's wife came to her room carrying her meal and asked, "Miss, where are your folks? You cannot be traveling alone?" Ceo-lian replied, "Thank you for your concern. I can take care of myself." She ate her bowl of noodle soup mixed with her tears and thought, *'I have nobody'.* The owner found her a long bag for her sabers and helped her to tie the bag along the horse's flank. He said, "We don't want others to see your sabers."

She very disappointed when Yan-ti told her nothing about Mon Zhi-an's death or whereabouts.

"Master Yan-ti, I will go to Beijing. My sworn brother Lee Mo-bai is in Beijing. Here is the address of his relative. If you ever have any information, please send a letter to this address."

"I will. I have heard about Lee Mo-bai. He fights well," Yan-ti said.

Dae Wu was visiting Master Yan. He introduced himself, "Miss Yu, I overheard your conversation with Master Yan. I'm Lee Mo-bai's friend. He told me about you. My name is Dae Wu. Master Yan and I are going to Beijing soon. We can travel together." Yu Ceo-lian wanted to hear more about Lee Mo-bai and agreed to travel with them.

Yan-ti and Yu Ceo-lian rode alongside Dae Wu's carriage. They followed_the convoy of merchants and their goods that Yan-ti was escorting to Beijing. Dae Wu told Yu Ceo-lian that Lee Mo-bai made himself quite a name in Beijing. Lee Mo-bai knew many professional guards and made inquires about Mon Zhi-an's whereabouts. He did not mention that Lee was jailed because of a prostitute.

Two days later they entered the Gu-bai Pass. Yan-ti's assistant told them how Lee Mo-bai had chased away a group of bandits without drawing his sword. Dae Wu also mentioned how swiftly Lee Mo-bai defeated the bandit chieftain.

The chatted with each other and also became absorbed in their own thoughts.

Yan-ti thought, '*this young man, Lee Mo-bai, must be very good. How can I get him to work for me? Dae Wu said he is a scholar and he may not want to be a guard. It seems that Dae Wu wants Lee Mo-bai to marry Yu Ceo-lian. They both could work for me. I wonder whether Lee Mo-bai's family would allow him to marry a poor unlucky living widow with not properly bounded feet.*'

Dae Wu thought, '*Yu Ceo-lian is sure pretty. No wonder Lee Mo-bai lost his heart over her. If we can't find Mon Zhi-an, I'll help them get married.*'

Yu Ceo-lian thought, '*It's too bad that I was promised to marry the missing Mon Zhi-an. If no one can find him, I won't mind marrying Brother Lee if he still likes me.*' She blushed for her wishful ideas but she was sure that Lee Mo-bai loves her. '*The way he had looked at me! He could not hide his feelings. What if he has found a wife already?*' She felt a sudden chill.

Dae Wu stole a glance at Yu Ceo-lian's pinkish glow and thought, *'Mo-bai, no more sadness.'* He had sent two letters to Lee Mo-bai and Prince Te to tell them about Ceo-lian.

Dae Wu took Yu Ceo-lian home to meet his wife and his mother. They all liked her right away. They let Yu Ceo-lian have her own room and tried to make her feel at home. When Dae Wu whispered to his wife the hopeful marriage between Yu Ceo-lian and Lee Mo-bai, his wife got excited and said, "They are indeed a pair. Mo-bai is handsome and Yu Ceo-lian is very pretty. I'm going to congratulate her."

"Hold it. First, we have to be sure that Mon Zhi-an could not be found. Second, I have to get Lee Mo-bai's agreement."

"Why shouldn't he agree? Didn't you tell me that Yu Ceo-lian is the very girl of his dreams? I'm certain of the marriage like I know tomorrow will be coming after today."

"Let's be cautious. Lee Mo-bai is a bit stiff-necked. He rigidly upholds the codes of ethic and honor. We'll know soon enough."

Dae Wu went to Prince Ti's palace to report and found Lee Mo-bai there.

"Brother, I can't and I won't marry Yu Ceo-lian. She has a fiancé," Lee Mo-bai sighed and continued, "I know you're very kind and you do have my best interests in mind. But you don't know that I found Mon Zhi-an and I lost him again."

"What? Where did you find him and how did you lose him again?"

Prince Te said, "Dae Wu, it is awkward for Mo-bai now. Mon Zhi-an called himself Yu Er (two) and he is Mo-bai's best friend and took good care of him when he was sick. Unfortunately, Mo-bai told him his longing for Yu Ceo-lian. He did not know Mon Zhi-an gave himself an alias, Yu Er (two), and worked for me incognito. We have to find him and that's that."

"It's unbelievable. Mo-bai. Please tell me everything."

Lee Mo-bai explained in detail and Dae Wu was dumbfounded.

"Your Highness and Brother Dea, the worst is that I told Mon Zhi-an that the only way I could marry Yu Ceo-lian is if her missing fiancé is either missing forever or dead."

"Mo-bai, how could you be so gullible and stupid again?" Dae Wu was angry.

Prince Te said, "Dae Wu, don't blame him. Mo-bai is sick and lonely and he needs to have someone to talk to."

"I called out her name and .. 'Violet' when I was delirious. He was very reticent. He probably guessed it but he kept it to himself. He knew about and Violet. He asked me who Ceo-lian is, and...and I blurted out everything. I'm very grateful for his help and I did not want to hide anything when he asked me. And...and I need to talk about it." Lee Mo-bai moaned.

"Dae Wu, where is Yu Ceo-lian now? At your home?" Prince Te asked,

"Yes. My mother and my wife like her very much. She wants to see Mo-bai as soon as possible. What should I tell her, Mo-bai."

"Please don't tell her where I live. It's a temple and it's not fitting for her to visit me there. Tell her I will come to your home to meet her. But, what do I tell her if she asks me about Mon Zhi-an?"

"Tell her the truth. Mon Zhi-an is wanted by the law, he is on the run, and he used a faked name." Lee Mo-bai thought, *'How can I tell her the truth? that I called out her name when I was sick'* Dae Wu's carriage dropped him off at the corner close to the temple.

Fat Shih's assistant waited for Lee Mo-bai at the temple. He told Lee Mo-bai urgently, "Master Lee, my master is awaiting you at the South Gate. Come quickly, my master sent me here to tell you..."

Lee Mo-bai said, "Please inform Master Dae Wu that I have to leave town to find Master Mon in a hurry. DON'T tell him where I'm going."

"Brother Dea, when can I meet with Brother Lee? Will he come to visit you tomorrow?" Yu Ceo-lian asked him, she was with Mrs. Dae Du.

"I met Mo-bai at Prince Te's a short while ago. He said he would be here tomorrow. But, just now he sent someone to tell me that he has to leave Beijing in a hurry. He did not tell me where he is going and he probably will be back soon."

"Ceo-lian, you know all men are alike, they don't tell us a lot," Mrs. Dae Wu said.

Next morning, Mrs. Dae Wu circumspectly told Yu Ceo-lian that Lee Mo-bai had indeed found Mon Zhi-an and then Mon Zhi-an left town suddenly. Lee Mo-bai tried to find him again. Yu Ceo-lian wondered why and hoped that Lee will be back with Mon Zhi-an or at least bring back some definite information about the man she's supposed to marry.

Fat Shih had two horses ready and they wanted to rush to Kao-yon Town, south of Ba-tin Town but they could not rode fast on the busy highway out of Beijing. They talked.

"I met Yu Er (two) and he told me that you are his only true friend. He will die for you." Fat Shih said.

"His real name is Mon Zhi-an. He is the second son of Master Mon of Da-ton, Shanxi Province. He killed someone and he is on the run," Lee Mo-bai told Fat Shih.

"I see. I am wondering about what he wants to hide. He told me that he wanted to intercept your enemies and fight them off for you. He said modestly that he hopes to scare them away or at least curtail some of their arrogance. I admired his bravery and decided to accompany him."

"Mon Zhi-an fights better than me. I can't believe they could wound him"

"Mo-bai. He did fight very well. That evil Dart Mew's poisonous dart did him in. We met Golden Spear Jao and Dart Mew's gang just south of Kao-yon Town. Yu Er (two), Mon Zhi-an, stopped them first and wanted to reason with them. They ganged up on us. Mon Zhi-an's fast sword thrusts slightly pierced eight or nine of them in a flash…"

"Ahe! He is good. Wu-ton School of Martial Arts forbids us from killing unnecessarily," Lee Mo-bai praised.

"Dart Mew threw two darts at Mon Zhi-an. Mon caught one and threw one back at Mew. It scraped Mew's shoulder. Dart Mew pretended to be wounded badly and fell face down to feign a faint. Mon Zhi-an. was busy fighting Golden Spear Jao and more than seven gang members. Dart Mew threw a poisonous dart at Mon Zhi-an, Mon Zhi-an dodged and the dart just barely scraped his ear. It must have been a fast poison and Mon started to stagger. They ganged up on him and cut him up. The soldiers came and I dragged him to safety. A doctor purged him of the poison but the multiple wounds are fatal. Mon Zhi-an is holding his last breath to talk to you."

"If he dies, I can't live with my conscience. Literally, I'm his killer and poor Yu Ceo-lian….." Lee Mo-bai's chest tightened and he nearly fell off the horse.

"Mo-bai, take it easy. Who is Yu Ceo-lian? A pretty woman?" Lee Mo-bai told Fat Shih the entanglement among the three of them.

"Ahe! I wish that I could say something to ease your pain. I thought the root of your sadness is losing Violet. I did not know you have lost your heart to this Yu Ceo-lian before you met Violet. You're tight-mouthed."

"No, not tight enough. When Mon Zhi-an asked me about Violet, I told him that for me Violet is only a diversion. I told him the impossible love I had for Yu Ceo-lian. I had thought that Yu Er (two) might not be his real name. He lied and told me he had killed someone in Szechwan. I believed him and I never thought that he is Mon Zhi-an."

"Mo-bai, you were very sick then. You needed sympathy and you trusted him. Your guard was down." Fat Shih sighed.

Mon Zhi-an had a deep cut on his chest, two cuts on his left thigh and another wound on his right shoulder. He had lost a lot of blood. The doctor shook his head and said that he had done all he could. For two long days, Mon Zhi-an was not fully conscious. On the third day, Mon Zhi-an was momentarily clear and he told them, little by little, "My mother is a concubine. My brother is the wife's only son. They hated my mother and me because I'm entitled to half of the family estate. She abused my mother, my mother became deaf. When I was eight years old, I was kidnapped and now I believe that was a set up to get rid of me. The kidnappers took me to Szechwan. An old Tibetan monk saved me and started to teach me martial arts. Before his death he took me to Master Hsu's place. They took me in and they treated me well and taught me martial arts. Six years ago, I went back home for my mother, but she died soon afterwards. Brother Lee, you know the rest. I do sincerely think you will be a better husband for Yu Ceo-lian than I ever could be. I don't have many breaths left in me and I beg you to marry her. Please don't argue with a dying man and please pity her. If you don't marry her, she will be a living widow all her life. The superstitious folks will not have such an unlucky woman for a daughter-in-law. I'm certain that she loves you too. I beg you .. go to Szechwan.... Dirty trick, Dart Mew..You evil ..." Mon Zhi-an yelled and died. Lee Mo-bai understood the unfinished request was that he must go to Szechwan to check on Master Hsu's family and to kill Dart Mew.

They buried Mon Zhi-an and the sword at a nearby hillside. Lee Mo-bai wrote Mon Zhi-an's name and ordered a tombstone to be carved and erected later. His immensurable guilt and remorse tore him apart. Fat Shih had to drag him away from the tomb.

"Mo-bai, there's no time to lament. You better hurry back to Beijing to fight them and avenge Brother Mon's death. I hope we are not too late and I'm afraid this pack of jackals may have harassed Dae Wu already."

"Yes, I will ride Prince Te's black horse back to Beijing. I think Yu Ceo-lian and that famous Yan-ti will have no trouble to fend them off for a while." The black mare seemed to know that her beloved master was buried there and turned her head to look at the grave again and again.

In Beijing, Yu Ceo-lian killed Dart Mew with one of his own poisonous darts.

Sixty-five years old Dart Mew did not want to leave Kaifeng at first. He had a new young concubine. Ca leo (six), the man Thin Buddha Hwang sent to invite him, told him that his runaway concubine Chi Mi-neon is in Beijing and lives with Lee Mo-bai. "Master Mew, your runaway concubine calls herself 'Violet' now._She is a prostitute. Lee Mo-bai visits her often and they practically live together. She says that Lee Mo-bai will kill you for her." Dart Mew was furious. He, his nephew Golden Spear Jao, Jao's wife nicknamed '*She Devil*' and thirty some roughnecks left Kaifeng for Beijing. At Kao-yon Town, a young man fought them and Dart Mew's poisonous dart killed the young man.

Thin Buddha Hwang welcomed them warmly. Dart Mew told him, "That young man I might have killed was very good. Is he Lee Mo-bai?"

"How many days ago?"

"About a half-month ago."

"It cannot be Lee Mo-bai, my man spotted him and Dae Wu coming out of the palace about ten days ago." Thin Buddha had having his spies kept surveillance on Lee Mo-bai. When he heard the report that Lee Mo-bai was sick, he had sent someone to kill Lee. But he was told there was a young man staying with Lee. He thought that young man was Lee's classmate.

"Master Mew, did you say this young man fights well. He might be Lee Mo-bai's classmate or a friend. They are close. He might be still alive, I was told Lee Mo-bai left Beijing in a hurry."

"What does this Lee Mo-bai look like?"

"He is tall and thin with a pretty face. He is pretty like a woman. Dae Wu likes him very much *Ha Ha*."

"That young man was neither tall nor pretty. Master Hwang, find me some young girls, the younger the better. Does this Lee Mo-bai live with a prostitute called 'Violet?"

"Lee Mo-bai indeed visited Violet often and he was jailed for her. I heard she is sick and in destitute now. Master Mew, I will find you young girls."

"Master Hwang, send your man to find Violet, she was my concubine."

"Not too long ago, Lee Mo-bai killed her protector. She is around."

Violet was sacred after Lee Mo-bai had mentioned that Dart Mew would be in Beijing soon. Now someone told her that some famous martial arts experts from Kaifeng had come to Beijing to fight Lee Mo-bai and she knew that Dart Mew must be in Beijing. She asked her mother to find Lee Mo-bai. The old woman did not find Lee Mo-bai at the temple, and so she went to Dae Wu's house. Dae Wu was not in, a servant told Mrs. Dae Wu. Yu Ceo-lian came out. The old woman told her that Dart Mew wanted to kill her and her daughter.

"Is this Dart Mew from Kaifeng?" Ceo-lian asked.

"Yes, he forced my daughter to be his concubine, he killed my husband. We escaped and hide here in Beijing. Lee Mo-bai knows how to fight. Now She Devil and the Ho brothers are here to help Dart Mew to kill us. Master Lee loves my daughter; please tell him to help us. .. ..." She sobbed and told Ceo-lian everything.

Ahe, the Ho brothers are my father's murderers and now they are here in Beijing! I will kill them! Yu Ceo-lian was also curious and wanted to meet the woman Lee Mo-bai loves. She knew that she had no right to be jealous but she was.

"Aunty, I will help you. Lee Mo-bai is my sworn brother and the Ho brothers are my enemies, too." She helped the old woman get in the carriage._Violet's mother looked at Ceo-lian with doubt. *'She is a young girl. How can she help us?'*

Dart Mew and a few roughnecks had broken into the shabby house where Violet and her mother lived. Dart Mew slapped Violet hard and she slashed Dart Mew's face with the dagger hidden under the pillow. Dart Mew wanted to kill her right there but Ca leo (six) stopped him, "Master Mew. We are in Beijing, the capital. You cannot kill her." Mew told Violet that he would come to get them the next day. He told Ca leo (six) and three men, "Stay here. Don't let them escape."

Ca leo (six) recognized Yu Ceo-lian and ran. The other three men ganged up on Ceo-lian and shouted obscenities. Yu Ceo-lian seized a staff and chased them away. She wanted to go after Dart Mew right away at first and then she thought, *'I can't get Dae Wu involved. Besides, I need to have something to protect my hand because I may try to catch the darts automatically. Lee Mo-bai told me the darts might be poisonous'* She looked at Violet's swollen face and found she a beauty. She thought, *'Where is Lee Mo-bai? He should protect her!'*

She told Violet, "Lee Mo-bai is my sworn brother. Your neighbors called the soldiers and they are here now. I'm going back to talk with Master Dae Wu and see if we can find a way to keep you safe." Violet knew that Yu Ceo-lian was the young girl Lee Mo-bai had dreamed about. She noticed that Yu Ceo-lian still wore her hair in braids, the customary hairstyle for a maiden. Violet knew then that she had to let go her dream of marrying Lee Mo-bai. She wanted to show Ceo-lian the bloody dagger and tell her she also had courage to fight. Before Violet could do so, Ceo-lian left.

Yu Ceo-lian told Dae Wu what had happened, "Violet and her mother are in danger. Is there any way we can help them?"

"I'll ask my friend Captain Lu to have some soldiers there to guard their home for a short while. We will have to move them to somewhere safe until this Dart Mew and his like leave Beijing. We cannot have them here. She is a prostitute and I may lose my job." Dae Wu said.

Mrs. Dea wu suggested, "The soldiers could not be there all the time. We can send them to the Peace Convent. The abbess there came to see mother often and we always donate silver."

"That's a good idea. They will be safe in the convent. I was told that the abbess knows martial arts." Dae Wu sent his servants to move Violet and her mother to the convent.

Yu Ceo-lian and a maid sewed something like a glove for her right hand. Early next morning, she rode to the hotel where Dart Mew and his men were staying. She shouted a challenge and dashed out of the city gate. Ca leo (six) had told Dart Mew how beautiful and how tough Ceo-lian is. Dart Mew wanted to have her, he rode after her. Ceo-lian lured him a long way out of the city and then she slowed and deliberately let Dart Mew get closer. Dart Mew tried to capture her at first and he did not use a poisonous dart. But Ceo-lian dodged his dart quickly. Dart Mew then threw a poisonous one at her. Ceo-lian caught it and threw it back at him, aiming at his chest but she missed. The dart slid off the side of Dart Mew's head. Yu Ceo-lian was scared and she dashed for her life. When she found no horse behind, she carefully doubled back and saw Dart Mew lying on the ground, his face black and he died. The poisonous dart scratched where Violet's dagger had pierced Dart Mew's face and the poison worked fast. Yu Ceo-lian shook and vomited at the sight of his body.

Dae Wu was afraid that Golden Spear Jao would now come to kill Yu Ceo-lian and him. He sent a servant to ask Yan-ti to come over to help.

Meanwhile Golden Spear Jao challenged Viscount Chiu. The Ho brothers ganged up Viscount Chiu and wounded the count. Now a whole regiment of soldiers tried to catch Jao and his men. They hid at Hwang's place and left Beijing with Dart Mew's coffin.

Nothing happened for a couple of days. Yu Ceo-lian recalled Lee Mo-bai's word of the importance of being alert. *'Miss Yu, your enemies are bandits. We have to be alert at all hours.'* She thought that this unscrupulous group might come in at the dead of the night. She slept with her tight-fitting combat suit and shoes on.

She Devil and her two brothers came to kill her and Dae Wu one night. Yu Ceo-lian fought them off and chased after them. She came back and told Dea wu.

"Brother, they are not that good. I chased them a few streets down. Someone woke up and called the law. I don't want the soldiers spot me. they got away."

Dae Wu and his wife praised her for her readiness. Yu Ceo-lian said, "Brother Lee taught me a lot." Somehow Yu Ceo-lian blushed.

Dae Wu said, "Mo-bai told me that Mon Zhi-an is more experienced and fights better than him. Let's hope that Mo-bai will find him soon. Prince Te said he will pardon Mon Zhi-an and then he will be a free man. We will have a nice wedding."

When Yu Ceo-lian was alone with Mrs. Dae Wu, she asked, "I'm a country girl, and we don't hear much talk about prostitutes. Violet is very pretty, do you know anything about the prostitutes and ..her?"

"I presume that here are prostitutes in the country, too. In the big cities, they lived in a special area, called '*flower or red lantern*' district. Most of them are young and pretty. Whenever there is a flood or draught, the poor and the refugees would sell their girls to be trained as prostitutes. I'm lucky that my husband does not visit them, he only goes there to meet friends. You should hear the ridiculous tales he told me about them and their clients. He told me that Violet is a very special one. She is very artistic; she paints and she writes poems. Her clients enjoy her company and they can talk about poetry with her. She … but I remembered that Dae Wu said she is not young." Mrs. Dae Wu did not want to tell her that Lee Mo-bai visited Violet often and they read and wrote poems together. He was jailed because of her.

Yu Ceo-lian thought, *'My father is right, Lee Mo-bai is too sophisticated for me.'*

That night, Dae Wu told his wife, "Thin Buddha Hwang will be our foe forever. We better teach our sons martial arts."

"You can teach them yourself."

"No. I'm definitely not good enough. I wish Mo-bai would marry Yu Ceo-lian and both of them teach our sons. But, the waiting has gotten on my nerves."

"The other day, Yu Ceo-lian showed me the 'gold combs', the marriage token from the family of Mon. Ahe! Yu Ceo-lian is such a nice girl. It's not right these two young men…"

"Keep your voices down. Will you" Dae Wu whispered.

Yu Ceo-lian's now sharpened hearing could only catch a segment of the conversation. Now she was sure that Mon Zhi-an's sudden disappearance had something to do with Lee Mo-bai. If Mon Zhi-an did not want to be found and Lee Mo-bai would not talk to her about it, she should not stay here and wait. She cried herself to sleep and she decided to go back to Lu Town.

She told Mrs. Dae Wu the next morning, "If Brother Lee does not come back soon, and I'll go back home and make arrangements to move my parents' caskets back to the family lot in Lu Town."

"Ceo-lian, it could snow any day now. The ground will soon be frozen and you could not move the caskets. Please stay with us until next spring. If…if it's necessary, we'll find someone to accompany you home then." Mrs. Dae Wu said. Her unspoken word *'if Lee Mo-bai can't find your missing fiancé and Lee does not want to marry you either,'* hang heavily in the air.

"Thank you. I don't think I should celebrate the New Year with you. I'm in mourning."

"Why not? It must be one of your Han customs. We would like to have you, and your parents would like to see you have a good time. There will be a lot of festival activities here in Beijing. You don't want to miss it. You know that I really want you stay with us as long as you want to. I feel safe to have you around." Mrs. Dae Wu said.

Lee Mo-bai came back two days later at night.

"Mon Zhi-an is dead. I'm responsible for his death." There were tears streaked Lee Mo-bai's weary and dusty thin faces. He told Dae Wu briefly.

"Ahe! It's bad. Young Mon acted impulsively. You shouldn't blame yourself. How are we going to tell Yu Ceo-lian?"

"I'm damned. It's gods' way of punishing me for wanting another man's wife." Lee Mo-bai moaned.

"Take it easy. It's fate. You look awful, have you eaten?" Dae Wu asked with concern.

"I don't know. I.." Lee Mo-bai murmured something. A servant came in with a bowl of ginseng soup and then reported that a bath, a barber and a masseur were ready.

Lee Mo-bai asked the servant, "How is the black mare? I rode her hard."

"Master Lee, the groom rubbed her down and said she is a champion, one in ten thousand."

"Mo-bai, you rode Prince-Te's favorite mare back."

"Yes. Mon Zhi-an groomed her every day. The mare did not want to leave his grave."

Over drinks and a light snack, Lee filled in the details and said, "Tomorrow I'll kill Dart Mew. He killed Mon Zhi-an. That's the least I can do…"

Dae Wu said excitedly, "Yu Ceo-lian killed him with one of his own poisonous darts. The rest of the gang left Beijing with the casket. You see.." He explained.

"Ceo-lian must have improved her skills a great deal. Who said that Providence has no eyes? Ahe! she knows the dart is poisonous. Did she remember …"

"Yes. You taught her well. Yu Ceo-lian is very resourceful and she made some kind of hand cover herself. She did not want to involve me and lured him out of the city gate. Isn't she smart? She thinks the world of you. Mo-bai."

"Yes, Ceo-lian is smart. Ahe! Violet is a runaway concubine. I know she knows martial arts and that's why she had a dagger hidden. You're so kind to help her."

They talked about this and that for a while, avoiding the real issue. Finally Dae Wu said, "Mo-bai, what are we going to do? We have to tell Yu Ceo-lian the truth."

"I cannot face her now, please break the news to her."

"Mo-bai, of course I'll tell her the news. How about her future? The only sensible solution is that you marry her. Isn't this Mon Zhi-an's dying wish, too?" He continued after he stopped Lee's protest. "I don't mean now or the immediate future. You can marry her a year, or even two years later. At least give her something to hope for, poor girl."

"I can't. I made a bargain with the gods to keep Mon Zhi-an alive. I vowed that I won't covet his wife. Mon Zhi-an died for me. I can't marry Yu Ceo-lian. Don't you understand?"

"Mo-bai, you can't ignore his dying wish. He begged you to marry Yu Ceo-lian lest she would be a living widow forever."

"I understand, but I can't." Lee Mo-bai sobbed.

"Mo-bai, I know it's cruel but I have to say it. You escorted Yu Ceo-lian nearly for a half month on the road. I know you behaved most honorably but somehow her name was tarnished. Mon Zhi-an would naturally think there were infatuation between you two. I also think so. She blushed whenever your name was mentioned. Now, she cannot stay with the Mon family and she is alone. Of course she can stay with us forever if she wants to. We all like her a lot and she can protect us. But, a living widow at her tender age? Mo-bai, have mercy on her and on yourself."

"I can't. Please pardon me." Lee Mo-bai knelt.

Dae Wu told his wife everything. she said, "Poor Ceo-lian and poor Mo-bai. I feel for both of them. I'll break the bad news to her gently, but how can I tell her that Mo-bai does not want to talk to her. She is entitled to ask Lee Mo-bai the details."

"It's a dilemma. I know, you tell her that Lee is exhausted and he needs a couple of days to recuperate first. and.. tell her that Lee's uncle wants to see him immediately."

Lee Mo-bai slept in; he woke up shortly before Dae Wu came home at lunch hour. They reported to Prince Te together.

"Mo-bai, be strong and don't allow yourself to hide behind self-pity and self-loathing. Take the pain in stride and then face the future." Prince Te advised Lee.

"Thank you. Your Highness." Lee Mo-bai said.

"Your Highness," Dae Wu pleaded, "can you talk some common sense into his stubborn head and let him marry Yu Ceo-lian. Mo-bai looks up to you and he will listen to you."

Lee Mo-bai said in a hurry, "Your Highness, I can't and I won't marry her. Please don't order me to, I rather die." He knelt.

"Up! Mo-bai, I'm not going to force you," Turning to Dae Wu, Prince Te said, "I think I understand Mo-bai better. You are the lucky one to be happily married and never have to suffer from the torture of an impossible love."

"But, Your Highness. Mo-bai loves Yu Ceo-lian and how can he bear to see that Ceo-lian be a living widow?"

"Mo-bai can't marry Yu Ceo-lian at the present just because he loves and respects her deeply. In a way, it's his fault that Mo-Zhi-an chose to die. I hope time will heal everything and hopefully Mo-bai will change his mind later. To be honest, I doubt it will happen. I mean I can see no marriage between them. Besides, we have to consider Yu Ceo-lian's feelings. She might want to be a faithful living widow."

"Thank you, Your Highness. You truly understand me."

"I'd like to share a part of myself with both of you. Do you ever wonder why I, having a beautiful wife and two royal consorts, spend most of the time alone in my study? I fell in a desperate love with a maiden from a rival tribe but I can't marry her. My marriage is a political one. True love never dies and never changes. Woe for the pitiful ones who are under its spell. Mon Zhi-an died for Mo-bai. Mo-bai respects Yu Ceo-lian too much to covet her, his best friend's wife-to-be. But, Mo-bai, you have to be married to fulfill your duty to produce 'sons' like I did." Three of them sat in silence in a shared melancholy.

Prince Te sighed, "Mo-bai, My great grandfather Manchu Emperor Shoe Je fell in love with a woman he was forbidden to love. He, with his august position as an emperor, could not make her the empress, not even a formal royal consort. After her death, he died soon and left the throne to an eight years old boy, Emperor Kangxi."

Lee Mo-bai dared not to ask or to mention an emperor's name. Somehow, Prince Te sensed it and explained, "Emperor Shue Je died of a broken heart. The Han resistance forces spread rumors to discredit the Manchu and said he became a monk. You see, Mo-bai, you're not the first man, and not the last one either to suffer the torture of an impossible love. You have to be strong and look forward to the future."

Dae Wu said, "Mo-bai is a victim of a rigid custom. When Mo-bai first found out that Mon Zhi-an was missing, if he is not bound by the custom, he could have asked Yu Ceo-lian's hand in marriage. I think the Mon Senior would not say no."

Prince recited a well-known verse, *'after experiencing the mighty ocean, one can hardly settle with any smaller body of water'* and said, "Mo-bai, I don't think you will find another love easily."

"I'm always interested in *'Taoism'* and I want to be a Taoist priest."

Dae Wu said, "Mo-bai, you can't take the easy way out. You have your earthly duties. You should strive for a better future. Don't let us down now."

Prince Te said, "Mo-bai, you can keep the mare. She was an average looking horse. Mon Zhi-an was the one who recognized her rare quality form obscurity. It's too bad that I did not have the wisdom to recognized Mon Zhi-an's superiority."

7

"Mo-bai, your uncle and aunt are sick. You should go home right away."
Uncle Kao continued with a rather sarcastic tone, "Now you're the
number one martial arts master in Beijing and Prince Te's favorite. You
do not need, or more clearly, that no one dares to offer you, a minor
clerk position anymore. I don't think you ever need to find a job. By the
way, I should have you to thank for my promotion."

Aunt Kao said, "Look at you, you're so thin. You really should have
a wife to look after you and your uncle should let you have enough silver
to live comfortably. Ahe! It's not for us to say that your uncle should
relinquish his tight control on your inheritance long time ago. Now,
he is sick and he needs you home to collect the year-end rental income
from the tenants. I presume that he would have no choice but to let you
to manage your estate from now on."

Uncle Kao noticed Lee Mo-bai's puzzled look, he chuckled, and
"It fits. Your uncle did not tell you that you're a substantial landowner.
I've been wondering about why your uncle wants you to find a minor
position. You don't really need to work for silver. Your uncle likes to
live frugally and he does not let you spend your silver either. Mo-bai, I
presume that your uncle did not tell you that it was your father's reward
and salaries that bought all the choice farmland."

Lee Mo-bai told Dae Wu of his own uncle's fraud and sighed, "He
made me live like a pauper. I've always thought my uncle a grump but
nevertheless a generous man when he arranged a moderate funeral for
Teacher Gi. He was spending my inheritance."

Dae Wu counseled, "Bitterness does not suit you. Think of your
bright future. Now you have the means and time to travel and to do
what you want to do."

"Brother, you're right. My aunt really cares for me. I'll go home. I'd like to say goodbye to Prince Te and...Violet. And it gives me a reason for not seeing Ceo-lian now. I'll leave as soon as possible."

Lee Mo-bai did not want to call unwanted attention by riding a champion mare around and neither to have Dae Wu's personal carriage be seen at the Convent. He hired a carriage. He thought, *'Now I can afford to provide Violet and her mother a better life. But I don't think I should marry her. I cannot marry Ceo-lian now and I don't want to hurt her either.'*

The abbess told him that Violet wanted to be a nun and she did not want to see anyone. Lee Mo-bai felt sad and relieved at the same time. The abbess's posture and gait told him that she is a highly skilled martial arts master and she is modest. Lee Mo-bai now realized that his not being modest caused all his trouble. It started when he had provoked a fight with the bandit leader before he came to Beijing. After he defeated Feng wu (five), he should not have told him that he would fight his brother Saber King. The biggest mistake he had was to have a relationship with a prostitute, which cause him to beat Huge Bo and be jailed. He thought, *'if I'm not jailed, I would not meet Mon Zhi-an. Ahe! It's predestined.'*

Lee Mo-bai told Prince Te of his plans to go home and Violet's intention of becoming a nun.

"Mo-bai, I was going to suggest that you go home for a while. You have been through a lot. I'll miss your company until you come back next spring," He continued after a short silence. "It's a good solution for Violet to enter the convent. There she can fully develop her artistry. I understand she is getting old for her trade. Mo-bai, you know the Japanese have a more sensible way. Shogun Toranaga established a special class of 'Geisha', a different kind of prostitutes. The word 'Geisha' means artists or entertainers. A *Geisha* entertains the clients only with her arts, and then age is not a problem anymore."

"Yes, Your Highness. Violet indeed is very talented. She composed refined verses and her paintings of flowers are exquisite, too."

"She is beautiful and talented. The late Vice Minister Hsu was a renowned scholar. He would not fall for mere beauty. Mo-bai, how about your sister Ceo-lian, have you thought about a solution? I know you don't want to marry her yet."

"Your Highness, I thought a lot about it but I can't find any solution until now. Uncle Kao told me that I have some inheritance. I have means to help her now. Brother Su and Ceo-lian will have means to reestablish her father's security company," Lee Mo-bai chuckled mirthlessly, "And I will be a top-rank guard for her company then." He told in detail the conversation he had with Uncle Kao.

"Good. Mo-bai, I'm glad you're not poor anymore. To tell you the truth, I'm afraid that you would sell my black mare when you need silver. Now I feel better knowing you don't have to sell your horse like the famous General Chyn of the Tang Dynasty."

Lee Mo-bai laughed, "Your Highness, I actually did have to sell a horse when I first got here."

"Mo-bai, if Ceo-lian agrees, Dae Wu's mother can adopt her and she will have a nice home and she can protect them. Later, only if she agrees, a Manchu officer can marry her. I did not tell Dae Wu my idea yet. I want to discuss it with you first. You're her sworn brother. Of course, everything will be handled with sensitivity and subtlety" Lee Mo-bai agreed and thanked the Prince; he knelt and formerly bid his farewell.

It was early evening; Lee Mo-bai decided to leave Beijing immediately.

Dae Wu said, "It's getting dark and it looks like it will snow soon. Wait and leave tomorrow morning."

"No, I want to leave now. I need a fast run to clear my head."

"Mo-bai, I think that you're afraid of facing Ceo-lian. I'll see you off at South Gate." Lee Mo-bai rode, and Dae Wu followed in his carriage.

Fat Shih's assistant Chen stopped Dae Wu's carriage and informed him that Golden Spear Jao and his gang did not go back to Kaifeng. They stayed at Ba-tin and Thin Buddha Hwang kept communication with them. "Master Dae Wu, they might be plotting to harm you."

"Oh! I see. Here is some silver for your trouble. If you have any information, please come to see me." Dae Wu decided to be extra cautious.

"Brother Dae, when will Brother Lee come to tell me the details of my..Mon Zhi-an's death and where he was buried?" Ceo-lian asked him.

"Mo-bai had to rush home today. His uncle and aunt are sick. He told me that he probably would meet with Brother Su soon. Ceo-lian, please stay with us. Lee Mo-bai will be back in the spring."

Ceo-lian was disappointed. It snowed after supper. When she was alone in her room, she absentmindedly poked at the charcoal in the small burner. She reviewed in her mind in detail the events of the last eight months. She seemed to see again Lee Mo-bai's laughing eyes full of admiration when he picked her scarf off the first time they met. She also saw again his sad eyes full of concern the night before he left Da-ton for Beijing. It just did not make any sense. A caring Lee Mo-bai, patiently taught her martial arts skills, and anticipated her mother's and her needs when he escorted them to Da-ton. How could he turn suddenly so cold toward her? She thought, *'He just deliberately avoids me and he must know why and how Mon Zhi-an died. I don't care whether it's proper or not for me to talk to him alone. I must demand that he tells me the truth.'* Snow or blizzard, she decided to leave at early dawn to go after Lee Mo-bai.

Before dawn, Ceo-lian saddled her horse the way Lee Mo-bai had taught her.' *Why did he ignore me? Because I knew that he had visited a prostitute?'* Ceo-lian rode fast out of Beijing through a light snow. The snowflakes melted on her checks and tasted salty. She had been crying.

She was the lone rider on the road. On both sides of the road, graying fields with snow patches stretched ahead, touching the low overcast sky. The road was icy and slippery, Ceo-lian rode on carefully and she felt so alone. She sobbed aloud and murmured, *'Who cares whether I fall and die? Who cares whether I wail my head off? What if I catch up with Lee Mo-bai and he does not want to talk to me. I don't have any family and I'm going back to an empty house.'*

A rider came from behind passed her and shouted something like, "Let me pass! Lee Mo-bai, Brother Lee, wait for me." Ceo-lian thought, *'is he trying to go after Lee Mo-bai? Is he one of Lee's friends, or enemies? Is he going to report to the enemies to waylay Lee Mo-bai? Dae Wu mentioned that Lee Mo-bai is not well. I can help him to fight the enemies off.'*

She carried her two pairs of sabers and luggage with ease when she checked in a hotel. The innkeeper lit an oil lamp in a small room for her. The innkeeper told his servant to be polite and see to it that Ceo-lian is comfortable. "She carried four heavy sabers and luggage effortlessly. Nowadays, some women fight better than men."

Ceo-lian rested on the warm *'Kon* (bed) and thought; *'Mrs. Dae Wu must be worrying about me now. I know that they wanted very much for Lee Mo-bai and me get married. But, I'm not sure now that Lee Mo-bai wants to marry me.'* She forced back her tears and asked the clerk who brought her water and her supper.

"Do you think it will be clear tomorrow?"

"No, it's snowing heavy now. It may snow for a couple of days. Besides, the bandits are out. Stay with us and we'll make sure you're comfortable. When it's clear, you would be safe to travel with other travelers."

"Thanks, I'm not afraid of bandits." Ceo-lian replied somewhat proudly. The clerk looked puzzlingly at the sabers on the *kon* (bed) and her young face.

Early next morning, someone yelled in the courtyard, "Brother Lee, Lee Mo-bai."

"Please don't shout. A tall young man did not check in last night." the hotel clerk complained. Some travelers cursed.

"I checked the only other hotel in town and he is not there. He must have ridden through the night. Sorry. Everyone." Ceo-lian looked through a slit of the paper-paneled window and saw it was the same fat man who had passed her earlier.

She had a hasty breakfast and insisted on leaving. The innkeeper counted the silver Ceo-lian paid him and said, "Miss, the road is icy and slippery. At least wait until it warms up a bit."

It was treacherous to ride against the wind but Ceo-lian pushed on and thought that Lee Mo-bai might be not too far ahead. Another lone rider ahead of her, she pushed hard and saw it was Lee Mo-bai. She called, "Brother Lee, Lee Mo-bai. Wait! I'm Ceo-lian." The wind muffled her shouts and the preoccupied Lee Mo-bai did not hear her. Another rider coming from the opposite direction shouted, "Ahe, someone fell. Ahe! A woman!" Lee Mo-bai doubled back and saw her, "It's you. Miss Yu, are you all right?"

She had on a pair of fur boots that Mrs. Dae Wu said it was the smallest sized one. It was made for Manchu women's natural sized feet and it's too big for Ceo-lian's bound feet. She struggled and got up herself and evaded Lee Mo-bai's out reached hands, "Go Away, I hate you. You pretended that you did not hear me. I know you ignored my call deliberately."

Lee said, "Oh! I didn't know that you're behind me. Honestly, I did not hear you. Did you sprain your ankles?"

"Go away! I don't want your help now. You are a hypocrite." Ceo-lian cried.

A man led Ceo-lian's horse back to her and told Lee Mo-bai, "Friend, don't quarrel with your little wife now. It is too cold. I better leave you young couple to sort it out yourself." He chuckled.

"Don't go now. I did not hear you. I'm sorry. I want to talk to you. Give me a chance and I will explain everything." Lee Mo-bai chased after the now ashamed and infuriated Ceo-lian.

A few travelers looked at them. Lee Mo-bai did not want to call more attention and he also afraid that his chase might make the tensed Ceo-lian ride fast and fall again. He gave up the chase.

Ceo-lian sobbed and she was disappointed when she heard no more calls from Lee Mo-bai and no more sounds of hooves behind her. Now she blamed herself. '*I should have asked him the why and how of Mon Zhi-an's death. Isn't that why I came after him in the snow? Instead, I called him a hypocrite, he probably would be too proud to talk to me again. Ahe! He is very thin and looks ill. I wonder what had happened between him and Mon Zhi-an? It must be awful. It left one died, one sick and me, a widow. What I will do with the letter, the one my mother gave me and I was supposed to hand Lee Mo-bai in person?*' She could not wipe the frozen tears away and her feet hurt. '*It is no use to cry. I have to be strong and I only have myself to look after me. I'm going home to reopen my father's security company and I'll be a woman guard.*'

She checked into a hotel before noon. The innkeeper bought some hot medicine patch for her swollen ankles. She practiced the deep breathing technique and meditated the way Lee Mo-bai taught her to relieve the pain. Everything led her mind back to him. She opened the sealed letter to Lee Mo-bai that her mother wanted her to give to Lee Mo-bai in person.

There was a note and another smaller, sealed envelope. The note was from Short Hsu. It said that her mother had asked a letter writer wrote this enclosed letter to Lee Mo-bai. Ceo-lian tore the sealed envelope open. She could not fully understand the words but she thought that her mother thanked Lee Mo-bai first and then agreed that Lee Mo-bai could marry her if Mon Zhi-an could not be found or is dead. Ceo-lian cried again. She wanted to tear the letters in pieces at first but she decided to keep it. '*Oh! How can I tell anyone about it?*" she sighed.

It snowed on and off. She stayed two more days. Late afternoon on the third day, she had a visitor, the fat rider she had met before.

Fat Shih introduced himself and told Ceo-lian that he was Lee Mo-bai's friend. He did not tell her that he had met Lee Mo-bai the day before and upon Lee's request, to meet with Ceo-lian and then escort her home.

But, against Lee Mo-bai's specific instruction of not telling Ceo-lian the details of Mon Zhi-an's death, he told her everything. From the beginning of how the two men met, how Mon Zhi-an guarded and nursed the very sick Lee Mo-bai back to health and how the misunderstandings led to his death.

"Miss Yu, he did not want me to tell you this. But, I think you're entitled to know. Even acute grief is better than fogged suspicion and uncertainty."

"Thank you very much. Brother Shih, now I know why Master Dae Wu could not look at me straight in the eye when he told me about Mon Zhi-an's death. Thank you and now everything is clear to me. Please call me Ceo-lian," she said sincerely.

"Mon Zhi-an begged Lee Mo-bai to marry you with his last breath. I was there. That stiff-necked Lee Mo-bai said he couldn't marry you. I hope Dae Wu and Prince Te could talk some sense into his stubborn head, and so you and him can get married later. Ceo-lian, you can't be alone as a...."

"Living widow? Under these circumstances, I could not and I don't want to marry Brother Lee either. I'm not a widow of a man I had never met. Let's talk more tomorrow. I'd like to be alone now." Ceo-lian wept and wept for herself, for Lee Mo-bai and the dead Mon Zhi-an. She believed that the impossible three-sided involvement among them must be predestinated. After her mother's death, she hoped that she could find her fiancé, or she could marry Lee Mo-bai if no one can find Mon Zhi-an. Now she lost both. In her destitute state, she unsheathed a saber and wanted to kill herself. The cold, frosty, shining blade reminded her once more her duty to avenge her parents' murderers. During the long night, Ceo-lian gradually hardened her will as firm as the steel blade of her sabers. She had no more tears and she resolved to restore her father's honor and the fame of 'Iron Wings' with her sabers.

The next morning, Fat Shih found Ceo-lian a hard, determined woman.

"Thank you, Brother Shih, now I know everything. I'm going home first. Next spring when the earth is unfrozen, I will arrange to have my parents reburied at my family cemetery lots. Could you send word to Master Mon at Da-ton and tell him where Mon Zhi-an is buried so they can take him home." Regardless of her resolution, her voice chocked but no tears.

Fat Shih suggested, "Ceo-lian, we're not far from Brother Mon's grave at Kao-yon Town. Would you like to go there to say good bye?" Ceo-lian agreed.

Mon Zhi-an's tombstone was an expensive one with Lee Mo-bai's elegant calligraphy on it. Ceo-lian did not know the words enough but she recognized the name and the artistic quality of the writing. She bowed low and silently told Mon Zhi-an that there was no infatuation between Lee Mo-bai and her.

Ceo-lian touched the tombstone and asked, "Brother Shih, this is an expensive tombstone. Brother Lee is not rich, how could he pay for it?"

"It did not cost a thing. When we went to buy a tombstone, a member of another grieving family saw Lee's good writings and asked him to write their father's name and an epitaph on a tombstone. Lee wrote the name and composed a poem. They praised his work and paid for Mon Zhi-an's tombstone and the lot. Ceo-lian, Mo-bai is righteous, talented and considerate. He adores you so much and that's why he has called out your name when he was delirious. I hope you two will get married later. I hope that time will heal the pain."

Ceo-lian said nothing. Fat Shih said, "Ceo-lian, may I accompany you home?" He did not say that he thinks Ceo-lian should not be traveling alone at that moment.

"Thank you."

When they reached the town where her father was jailed after Lee Mo-bai helped them to repel She Devil and the others. Ceo-lian told Fat Shih about the situation in detail and said, "We knew our enemies were after us and we were forced to leave home last summer. We met Lee Mo-bai two days before the enemies ganged up on us. Now I regret that I did not want my father to ask for Lee Mo-bai's help when we met him. If Lee had been with us, my father would not have been jailed and died."

"It's fate. None of us can defy it." Shih sighed. Ceo-lian relived the past and said, "Lee Mo-bai met a kind and just Manchu officer and got my father released. After his release, my father refused Brother Lee's good intention to travel with us but he followed us any way. He saved my father from dying by the roadside. I owed him a lot."

"Ceo-lian, Mo-bai is conceited but a good man."

Two days short of reaching her home, Ceo-lian thanked Fat Shih again and said she will be all right to go home alone now.

Shih said, "It's not far from here to Nan-kon Village, I'll go to see Lee Mo-bai." Ceo-lian said, "If you hear anyone in Beijing dare harass Master Dae Wu, please come to fetch me, I'll defend him and his family."

"Ceo-lian, you're Dae Wu's worthy friend. Bye."

Ceo-lian cried as soon as Brother Han opened the gate for her. She told him that her mother had passed away, too. Han and his wife tried to make her comfortable first and then told her that Brother Su left for Da-ton to bring her mother and her home twenty days ago.

"Ceo-lian, Sam, the carriage driver, came back and told us everything; how Master Yu died and how the young Master Lee saved him, buried him and escorted you and your mother to Da-ton. He also told us that your fiancé is missing. We were all worried. We sold most of the weapons and vehicles to get enough silver for Brother Su to go to Da-ton. He wanted to take aunt and you back home in case you were not happy there. We did not know that Aunt Yu also passed away."

Ceo-lian sighed, "My mother had been sick ever since we left home. We paid a lot for the doctor and the medical herbs. You know that my father sold the small lot we rented out to a farmer. Now I only have enough silver to move my parents' caskets back and bury them at the family cemetery. We don't have any rental income and now we don't have weapons and vehicles to reopen the security company. What are we going to live on now? What am I going to do with the rest of my life? Why do all the gods abandon me?"

No one answered and she did not expect one either. Han hired himself out to do odd jobs. With his earnings to supplement the scant savings Ceo-lian had, they managed. Ceo-lian and Han's wife wanted to take home some sewing to make the ends meet. She did not have any close male relative to help her to claim her share of the Mons' estate. The cold winter was here and the New Year would be here soon.

Ten days later, a cart full of bags of wheat, rice, produce and a cage of live chickens came from Lee Mo-bai with a letter. Han and Ceo-lian could not fully understand the letter; they took the letter to the local letter writer.

"Miss Yu, we've been neighbors for a long time. I didn't know you have a brother." The letter writer said.

"Master Lee is my sworn brother."

The letter said, "Sister, greetings. Master Shih told me that you're home. I'm sending you some of the crops I collected from the tenants. I would like to come to see you soon to discuss some important matters with you. Your brother, Lee Mo-bai."

Ceo-lian paid the letter writer. On her way home, she wondered what the 'important matters' would be. She blushed when she thought, *'He changes his mind and wants to marry me, but why should he sign the letter as my own brother?'* Han and his wife secretly harbored the same hope. They were all grateful for the food.

Lee Mo-bai was very busy to manage the huge family holdings. For many years, his uncle completely depended on Ma, the overseer, to collect the year-end rent from the tenants who farmed the land rented from the Lees. Ma became greedy and give or withhold his favor from the tenants. He also pilfered the rental income. Short of using his fists, Lee Mo-bai put the bully Ma in his place. He applied justice; he curbed the rowdy ones and helped the ones in need. The year-end rental income nearly doubled. He was thinking of finding a trusted new overseer. At home, he helped his widowed sister-in-law care for his uncle and aunt. His uncle recovered but not his aunt. His widowed sister-in-law was only four years older than Ceo-lian. She was depressed. It painted Lee Mo-bai very much to see her being changed from a robust and stout young girl to a dispirited and thin young widow. Lee Mo-bai realized sharply what a miserable life Ceo-lian would face. *'It's all my fault.'* His guilt feelings doubled when he came to a sad realization that he actually loved Violet more when he leafed through the poems they composed together.

Lee Mo-bai blamed himself, *'I should not look down on Violet because she is a lowly prostitute. The fact that she is a prostitute influenced me not knowing my true feelings toward her. If I knew my true feelings that I loved her, she would willingly be mine. Didn't she often remind me that she is only a poor substitute of Ceo-lian, and she even said that she would be willing to be a concubine. If I married her after Fat Shih killed her protector, Mon Zhi-an would still be alive and he and Ceo-lian could be married. My indecision and ambiguity had caused the tragedy. I don't deserve to live.'*

So many 'ifs' and 'consequences' went through his mind over and over. Days and nights he lived through his insoluble misery. Finally he thought of ways of remedy. A remorse but resolute Lee Mo-bai went to see Ceo-lian. It was a painful and awkward moment for both of them.

"Sister, I came to ask for your forgiveness. It's my fault that Brother Mon died." Lee Mo-bai addressed Ceo-lian as a true brother should. He hoped to establish that he would think of her as a younger sister and nothing more.

Ceo-lian caught on immediately. She addressed him accordingly, "Brother, it's fate. Master Shih told me everything."

Lee Mo-bai managed a mirthless chuckle, "I bet he did not tell you that I'm no longer a poor man," he continued seriously, "My uncle finally relinquished his control and gave me back my right to my inheritance of more than ten lots of profitable farm lands. I only kept four lots and yield to him the rest providing my widowed sister-in-law would adopt a son. I'm giving you the two pieces closest to your hometown and I would appreciate if Brother Han would manage my two pieces for me."

"I'm grateful but I can't accept your generosity."

"Sister, you cannot refuse. I swore to look after you. I'm your brother and you're supposed to obey me. It's also for the deceased Brother Mon Zhi-an. You can say that it's my atonement. Next spring, I will go to Da-ton to demand your share of the estate. I'm not hesitating to use my sword if it's necessary." Ceo-lian thought, *'he does not want to marry me. We both know that the only way I can claim my share of the estate from the Mons is that I have to be a widow.'* She tried to force her tears back.

"Brother, thank you." Ceo-lian sobbed. Lee Mo-bai tried to cover the sob with a cough.

After a painful stretch of silence, Lee Mo-bai said with forced gaiety, "Sister, let's finish the transactions quickly. Don't you want me to teach you more martial arts skills before I leave? I'm an anxious teacher."

"I'm an eager student. I need to learn more. I must be good enough to kill my parents' murderers."

"We're in it together. Later, we'll get the security company in business again. You'll be a famous woman guard."

"We can't. The weapons and vehicles were sold." Ceo-lian sighed.

"We don't need weapons and vehicles. We have enough manpower. We can get your Short Brother back here to help us. We will specialize in escorting rich families and jewels," Lee Mo-bai assured Ceo-lian.

Before Lee Mo-bai left, he exchanged horses with Ceo-lian.

"This black beauty is Prince Te's champion horse. Brother Mon Zhi-an groomed her daily and cared for her very much. Sister, you should have her."

8

It was a mild winter, but Lee Mo-bai thought that it was the worst and coldest. His aunt was dying. He sat beside her bed and seriously considered whether he would become a Taoist priest.

His widowed sister-in-law adopted a baby boy of a poor distant cousin. She loved the baby. Her face now shone with joy and her gait became springy. Lee Mo-bai thought, '*Now, the continuation of the bloodline is secured and I'm free to do what I want to do. I'm now free to travel, to look for Uncle Chiang.*'

His aunt passed away shortly after the New Year. The customary mourning period called for seven sections of seven days, total of forty-nine days. Lee Mo-bai could not attend the final interment of Ceo-lian's parents. Fat Shih helped Ceo-lian with the transportation of the caskets and the final funeral. He came to visit Lee Mo-bai and kowtowed to the casket of Lee's aunt to show his respect.

He told Lee Mo-bai, "Ceo-lian is very grateful that you gave her two lots of farm land."

"That's the least I can do for her and Mon Zhi-an." Lee Mo-bai sighed.

"You know you can do better. You can carry out Mon Zhi-an's dying wish and marry Ceo-lian later." Lee Mo-bai only sighed.

"Mo-bai, if I fight better than you, I would beat the stubbornness out of you. You know Mon Zhi-an's dying wish overrules the customary rule against marrying another man's wife. Besides, they never met each other. It's no use to argue with you anymore. I'm going back to Beijing to see whether Dae Wu and Master Lieu of Grand Security could convince you. By the way, Dart Mew's nephew Golden Spear Jao and his gang did not return to Kaifeng. They stayed at Ba-tin, and they are cooking some evil plot to harm you and Dae Wu".

"When I passed Ba-tin last winter, they did not harass me."

"You left Beijing rather sudden. They dare not fight you in the open. They might have thought that you and Ceo-lian were traveling together. The rumor is that Ceo-lian is your woman."

"Please tell me if any harm comes to Dae Wu. I'll go to Beijing as soon as I can. I'm a free man with means now. Later we can go to Szechwan to check on the late Master Hsu's family. It's Mon Zhi-an's dying wish."

"It's a deal. On our way west, you can beat up some of my enemies."

The funeral and other family business came to a conclusion and Lee Mo-bai was ready to leave for Beijing. Fat Shih rushed in one late rainy night.

"Mo-bai, it's really bad. Dae Wu is in jail. Let me catch my breath."

Someone stole forty some big precious pearls and other art pieces from the Royal Palace before the New Year. Early this spring some of the missing goods were found in the stock of one of Master Yong's pawnshops. Master Yong is Dae Wu's friend, and Dae Wu tried to save him. *Thin Buddha* Hwang and a powerful eunuch implicated Dea Wu and other personages. Dae Wu was jailed and the soldiers searched Dae Wu's house twice. Some villains, obviously on *Thin Buddha's* payroll, harassed Dae Wu's family."

"Ahe! I remember meeting a fat man named Yong. I will go to Beijing immediately to help, at least to protect Dae Wu's family." Lee Mo-bai said.

"Great! We can leave at dawn."

"I'll leave right now. My indecisiveness and hesitation had caused enough misfortune already. Please go and get Ceo-lian. I want her in Beijing soon. She can protect the women."

Lee Mo-bai rushed. He checked into a hotel to rest every two days. He soon rode right up to the tightly closed gate of Dae Wu's mansion and knocked.

"My master is not home. We only open the gate to…"

"Fu, I'm Lee Mo-bai, your master's.."

The gate opened immediately, Fu, the coachman called excitedly, "Master Lee, my master is in jail. Please help us."

"I heard it so I rushed here. Please announce me to your mistress."

Mrs. Dae Wu received Lee Mo-bai in the inner court. She told him the details and the serious situation of the case.

"Mo-bai, the soldiers had thoroughly searched the whole house twice. We'll find some precious artifices and antiques missing after each search. We bribed the soldiers not to search Grandma's room. She thought that Dae Wu is on another business trip out of town. Some of the servants turned rowdy and I let them go. I only keep a few trusted ones. Some rough looking men had been here twice to collect some supposed loans. We never had to borrow any silver. Prince Te sent his valet here to see us a few days earlier, I told him the harassment. Prince Te sent some soldiers here for a couple days. But I don't think the soldiers will be here all the time. Mo-bai. I want you stay at the study."

"Thanks. I'll see to things and let no one come to bother you again. I've sent word to Ceo-lian, she probably will be here in a couple of days."

"Oh! Very good. I can sleep again without fear if she is here. Mo-bai, you look tired. Take a rest first."

"I'm fine. It's early, I'll go to see Brother Shih now."

Dae Wu was on friendly terms with Prince Te and Viscount Chiu. His cell was airy and clean and had a comfortable bed. He was not chained either.

"Brother Shih, Mo-bai is here."

"When did you get in?"

"This morning. Fat Shih told me everything and I rushed here. Ceo-lian is on the way here, too."

"Great! I'm grateful that I have good friends. Mo-bai, please be careful. THEY will try all means to provoke you to a fight, so they will have a reason to jail you. They already spread rumors that only you, since you have excellent night jumping skills, could steal the pearls."

"I see. I'll be careful. I'll go to visit Prince Te and see what else I can do to help."

"Mo-bai, don't come to see me every day. The jailers don't like it."

"Yes, I know." Le Mo-bai recalled that he had to bribe the jailer when the late Master Yu was jailed. His thoughts turned to Ceo-lian and he felt awful.

Prince Te and Viscount Chiu were discussing Dae Wu's case.

"Mo-bai, I want you to be extremely careful. *Thin Buddha* must have spent a fortune to get the eunuch Chang to implicate Dae Wu. Chang is the chief eunuch of Emperor's most royal favorite consort. My hands are tied. Don't give them an opportunity to jail you with some ridiculous cause."

"Your Highness, Viscount Chiu, I'll be careful. Yu Ceo-lian will be here soon and I'll warn her to be cautious."

"Oh! No! Mo-bai, don't let Ceo-lian ride through Beijing again. She and her horse will draw too much attention and we have enough trouble already," Prince Te said.

Lee Mo-bai could not help laughing, "She sure will draw attention. Your Highness, she has your favorite mare. I'll convince her that she should stay home."

"You gave her the horse," after a short silence, Prince Te continued, "I see your point. Mon Zhi-an loved that horse. She should have it."

Viscount Chiu asked, "Brother Lee, may I call you Mo-bai? Please" Drop the title when you address me."

"Thanks, Brother Chiu."

"Mo-bai, I'll tell you with confidence that Dae Wu will not be sentenced to beheading. The worst for him is a two-year exile. I was going to send my wife to tell Mrs. Dae Wu. Now you can tell her and ask her not to worry. The countess's visit her may call for unwanted attention. Also, my teacher Yan-ti will come soon."

"Mo-bai, you look tired and I won't keep you to have supper with us," Prince Te noticed Lee's white armband and continued, "I see you're in mourning. Please have my belated condolence."

"Thanks. Your Highness, my aunt passed away. She raised me since I was eight. My cousin died a few years ago. I wear white as her son."

"Another death! You've gone through a lot. Take care," Prince Te sighed with compassion.

On his way back, Lee Mo-bai did not close the curtain of the carriage. He wanted all the hooligans working for *Thin Buddha* Hwang to know that he is back. He then thought about the three deceased that he buried In less than a year. He buried Ceo-lian's father last summer. He buried Mon Zhi-an last autumn and he buried his aunt recently. He also thought about the deaths of Huge Bo and Vice Minister Hsu. Fat Shih killed them because they took Violet away from him. Lee Mo-bai did not do the real killing himself. Nevertheless he was responsible for their deaths and the incident that forced Violet to be a nun. He thought about the sufferings and the transience of life. He wanted to end it all or enter the priesthood.

"Master Lee, look! They are coming to demand loan payment again." Fu, the coachman called. Lee recognized the shifty-eyed Ca leo (six), Feng wu (five) and two clerks. He jumped out of the carriage when he heard Ca leo (six) say, "Today we'll chase them out of the house if they can't pay. Master Hwang will back us up."

Stop!" Everyone froze when they saw Lee Mo-bai.

"Show me the promissory note at once," Lee Mo-bai demanded. Ca leo (six) and Feng wu (five) ran away.

"Here it is. Master Lee, we are only doing our jobs." One of the clerks handed over a piece of folded paper. The note simply wrote that Dae Wu owed the Bo Loan Company twenty thousand ounces of silver. Witnessed and signed by Ca and Feng.

Lee Mo-bai said, "If they want silver, come to me to collect it. Tell them come with genuine notes, not these fakes." He let the two clerks go.

He told Mrs. Dae Wu that there would be no death penalty for Dae Wu. It might be a two-year exile. Mrs. Dae Wu was relieved.

A frightened Fu came to the study and told Lee that there was a tall, fierce looking man demanding to see him.

"Is he armed?"

"No. But he is very demanding." It was Brother Su, late Master Yu's student.

"Brother Lee, thank you for everything you have done for us," the tall husky Brother Su wanted to kneel. Lee Mo-bai stopped him.

"Brother Su, please call me Mo-bai."

"I came to Beijing ten days ago. Ca leo (six) is my sworn brother. He found me a guard position at Universal Security Company. He told me that you had harassed Master Hwang and he asked me to come here to beat you up. Of course I come as your friend. I could not beat you up even if I want to. You're super."

"Ca leo (six) is a bad lot."

"Yes, I have known it for quite a while, but I need a job. Master Hwang treated me royally and gave me silver twice already. Somehow I felt uneasy when they told me that Dae Wu and you persecuted them. They asked me to come here to fight you. I know better. Please tell me, why you and them are enemies?" Lee Mo bai told him.

"I'll beat Ca leo to pulp." The impatient Brother Su wanted to rush back to hit Ca leo (six). He tried and could not get away from Lee Mo-bai's restraining hand.

"Wait. Brother Su, I need your help. Please don't break up with Ca just now. Instead you should pretend that you're on their side and then you can forewarn me of their plot. Uncle Yu made me Ceo-lian's sworn brother, so you are my brother. I need your help. I'm alone and they are so many. Ceo-lian will be here soon. Dae Wu opened his home to her last year."

"Sure, Mo-bai, just tell me what to do." Brother Su was surprised at the pale and skinny Lee Mo-bai's strength.

"Please don't come here unless I sent for you. One of Master Shih's men, named Snake, will contact you."

"But, "Mo-bai, I told them that I admire you."

"Then tell them I'm conceited and I befriend rich Manchu. They will believe you."

Twice during the night, Lee Mo-bai scrutinized the mansion from the rooftops and found no danger. He chuckled when he recalled that Dae Wu had said that all the hooligans were afraid of him as mice to a cat.

He went to visit Uncle Lieu at Grand Security and told him the death of Mon Zhi-an and recommended Brother Su to Lieu. "Sure I'll hire him. *Iron Wing*'s student must be good. Mo-bai, we are all willing to help Master Dae Wu."

"Thank you, Uncle Lieu. If you hear anything, rumors.., talks... Anything concerning Dae Wu, please let me know."

"Sure, be careful Mo-bai. I heard that *Thin Buddha* Hwang practiced his martial arts skills and networked all his spies to prepare for pulling you down. Yesterday, he declared that you, not Dae Wu, are now his primary target. He was heard saying, '*Getting rid of that damned Lee Mo-bai and Dae Wu is nothing.*' Watch every step."

"I'll be cautious but I'm not afraid."

"Of course you're not afraid of any fight in the open. Please beware of their secret plots and false rumors to discredit you. Someone said you stole all the pearls."

"I also heard about it. I wonder who the thief is. He must be very good. Did you hear about any new highly skilled martial arts masters around?"

"No. If that person does not want to be known, no one can detect him. Mon Zhi-an is a good example. Up to today, I never knew about his existence. Beijing is worse than a jungle, who knows what's lurking around? The present Manchu emperor is kind and just. It's rumored that his father, the preceding Emperor, harbored a horde of highly skilled martial arts masters. With their help, he got the throne. It's said that a nun murdered him in his heavily guarded bed chamber." Lieu whispered.

"Ahe! A nun?" Lee Mo-bai thought, *'isn't the abbess of the convent where Violet stays a martial arts master, and a super one too.'*

"Yes, someone said she was the last Ming Emperor's daughter."

That night, Lee Mo-bai leafed through one of the anthologies and then thought about Violet. He wanted to visit her at the convent. *'Just a visit to see how she is'* he tried to convince himself but he continued his thought, *'to be honest, what if I find she did not want to shave her head and commit the last vow, I could not possibly ask her to marry me now. Mon Zhi-an died for me and I've caused Ceo-lian enough grief. My marrying Violet will push her further and deeper into her bottomless misery. I'm not blind to see that she wishes that I might eventually marry her. Could I marry Ceo-lian knowing Mon Zhi-an's death will be a perpetual shadow in my heart? I have dug my grave and I have to bear it as long as I live."* He tossed around all night long.

He went to the convent to look for Violet the next day. He was disappointed and at the same time had a sense of reprieve when he was told that Violet and her mother went to Japan. Her past caused a number of villains to keep pestering the convent, so the Abbess made the arrangements for her to teach the Japanese novices Chinese arts. Lee Mo-bai thought, *'Providence sure have dealt me a hard hand. When the exquisite Violet was for my asking, I dreamed about the untouchable Ceo-lian. Now Ceo-lian is available, and I could not get Violet out of my mind. What kind of man am I, evil or stupid? May be both.'*

Ceo-lian's arrival four days later relieved some of Lee Mo-bai's distress. He told her the situation and then warned Ceo-lian to be cautious. "Sister, Prince Te suggested that you stay in and protect the family."

"No need to worry. I have grown and I'm not childish anymore. I won't go out. I'll guard the inner court. It's inconvenient for you to do."

"Ceo-lian, Mo-bai, I 'm grateful to have you two good friends. Ceo-lian is here. I can sleep better," Mrs. Dae Wu said.

At midnight, Lee Mo-bai deliberately stepped a bit heavy on the roof. To his delight, Ceo-lian was out and on the roof immediately, fully clothed.

"It's me. Your hearing has improved. I hardly made any noise. And you're fast," Lee Mo-bai whispered happily.

"I have a good teacher," Ceo-lian whispered with her pleasant bell-like voice.

They sat companion-like on the roof. Lee Mo-bai told her the possibility that of a highly skilled, anonymous martial arts master stole the pearls. "I want you to be alert. Leave the fighting and chasing to me. Be assured that if anyone causes your suspicion that he's already under my surveillance. You have to protect the family. I heard some of the dark secrets of the ruling Manchu. Who knows if Dae Wu is a victim of a political scheme?"

"Oh! Do you know for sure?"

"No, I don't. I'll tell you the minute I know. Don't be scared."

"Do you remember that you said the same thing last year when we were traveling to Da-ton," Ceo-lian sobbed and continued, "I'm sad about the past but at least there are no barriers between us now, you're a true caring brother."

"We've been through a lot." He changed the subject and said, "I've thought about how to blend some of the quick sword thrusts into your saber fighting technique. Let's try it out sometime. Good night or good morning for now."

Another night when they met on the roof, Lee Mo-bai told Ceo-lian, "Thank you for helping Violet last year. You killed Dart Mew and set her free. She is a nun. Now, she and her mother are in a convent in Japan."

"I always wondered what had happened to them. Mrs. Dae Wu told me that she is not only beautiful, she also is very artistic and talented. I know she is also very brave; she threw a dagger at Dart Mew and slashed his face. The cut she inflicted on Mew's face had caused the poison on his own dart to kill him. Actually, I missed when I threw his dart back at him. I was so scared." She told Lee Mo-bai what happened that day when she killed Dart Mew.

"I know she had a dagger and she knows martial arts. She never talked about her past."

Many rumors discrediting Lee Mo-bai circulated in Beijing. Lee Mo-bai tried very hard to hold his temper in check. That's *Thin Buddha's* way to provoke him to fight and then they could arrest him for disturbing the peace. The pressure and the increasing hot weather weakened Lee Mo-bai and he kept on losing weight.

Ceo-lian jumped upon the roof every night, secretly wanting to meet and talk to Lee Mo-bai. But Lee Mo-bai usually read and wrote in the study. Ceo-lian saw his silhouette through the window and she knew that he must have heard her. She was sad.

Mrs. Dae Wu worried about Lee Mo-bai's health and also his seemingly warm but also distant attitude toward Ceo-lian. Behind the façade of brotherly affection, there could be deeper feelings that he tried to conceal and control. *'It's not quite like love, more like the feelings of remorse and deep sorrow'* Mrs. Dae Wu thought. Ceo-lian had told her that Violet had gone to Japan. That was good. No more third person. She harbored the hope that time will heal everything and eventually they will be married. Ceo-lian's feeling was transparent for everyone to see that she loved Lee, even though she tried her best to show that she thought of Lee as a true brother. Mrs. Dae Wu tried to bring them together and asked Lee to come in to dine with them often. Lee Mo-bai taught Ceo-lian martial arts. Mrs. Dae Wu taught Ceo-lian how to read and write.

Prince Te summoned Lee Mo-bai and told him that the sentencing would be very swift under the Manchu Law. Mrs. Dae Wu started to prepare extra clothes, common herbal preparations for Dae Wu's long trip and his two-year exile in the far west Xikang Province. It was about four thousand *Li* (mile) to the west of Beijing. Mrs. Dae Wu had to sell a parcel of land for silver.

Viscount Chiu invited all of Dae Wu's concerned friends to a dinner. Yan-ti, Viscount Chiu's teacher, offered to escort Dae Wu all the way to Xikang. He will not have any major escorting business during the summer. He would go with Dae Wu and be back in the fall. There were bandits everywhere and he wanted to make sure Dae Wu would get there safely.

Lee Mo-bai said, "I'd like to go, too. But my uncle is not well and he needs me at home." Actually, he wanted to stay behind and kill *Thin Buddha* Hwang.

Viscount Chiu said, "For the long trip, Teacher Yan is more experienced. My concern is that *Golden Spear* Jao and the late Dart Mew's gang might ambush Dae Wu at Ba-tin. I heard the bandit leader Wu, the one whom Mo-bai wounded last year is now in league with them. The two-faced *Thin Buddha* paid them to kill Dae Wu and Mo-bai."

Lee Mo-bai said, "That's easy. I'll follow the convoy to Ba-tin to fight them off. Brother Su (brother) could follow the convoy discreetly to Xikang. He has no family and he can stay there and escort Dae Wu back to Beijing two years later."

Viscount Chiu concluded, "And Miss Yu will stay and guard the family. My wife will visit them once in a while keep them informed."

The final sentencing came. Two men would be beheaded in the fall and Dae Wu and someone else were sentenced two years of exile. The Manchu law was swift. The prisoners and a company of soldiers would leave right after the sentence and only permit the prisoners to have a short farewell. Lee Mo-bai told Dae Wu the arrangements. Dae Wu could have two servants with him. One would be Ton, his valet, and the other one would be Yan-ti who carried silver and silver certificates. Brother Su would follow the convoy disguised as a merchant. The group of two carriages for the prisoners and a company of soldiers on horses left at noon.

Prince Te summoned Lee Mo-bai in the evening. He said, "Mo-bai, I know you have laboriously held back your anger at all the spiteful insults from *Thin Buddha* Hwang and his men for almost a month now, and you want to retaliate soon. That's why you did not escort Dae Wu yourself. I don't want you to do something drastic. It's not worth sacrificing your bright future for fighting the likes of them. You cannot fight them all unless you kill Thin Buddha. I won't allow it."

"Your Highness, I'll be cautious. But unless the evil Thin Buddha Hwang is eliminated, someone else in Beijing will suffer. And I bet he will find a way to harm Dae Wu two years later."

"So, you really want to kill him. A killer will be hanged and even I can't protect you. Mo-bai, leave it to me. I promise that I will find a subtle way to get rid of him and his influence. Don't do anything irrational. Mo-bai."

"Yes. Your Highness."

"Mo-bai, don't kill anyone who might waylay Dae Wu at Ba-tin. I permit you to wound them if you have to. *Thin Buddha* Hwang manipulated them and they are only puppets. I suggest you go home or travel to Szechwan, or to the South directly from Ba-tin. It's not good for you to come back to Beijing right away. You know the pearls are still missing. While the real thief is at large, you're the prime suspect. Have a safe trip and a good fight. Mo-bai."

Halfway home Fu yelled in pain, an arrow pierced his leg. A volley of arrows, aimed at the carriage, rained on them. Lee Mo-bai swiftly pulled out the seat pad and covered Fu with it. Ten or more men armed with long spears ganged up on Lee Mo-bai. He seized a spear, and with it he pierced three attackers quickly and the rest fled. Then shouts and soldiers with lanterns approached fast. This was a planned trap. Lee Mo-bai threw the spear away, got back on the carriage and ordered Fu to drive fast. He rearranged the seat pad and pulled the curtain of the carriage down.

"Hold!" The soldiers stopped them and accused Lee Mo-bai of piercing three men with a spear.

"Sergeant, I don't have the spear. There is no room in the carriage for a long spear. I also heard some commotion back there but I did not pay any attention."

"Lee Mo-bai, we know you. Who could have the skills to wound three and scared the rest away but you. Come with us for questioning."

"I just left Prince Te's palace. You know no one can bring any weapon to the palace. You should try to catch the hooligans. If I want to wound them, do you think anyone can get away alive?"

"Let's go," Lee Mo-bai ordered Fu.

His pounding heart told him that *Thin Buddha* Hwang had arranged the two-step ambush. First, Thin Buddha tried to kill him with arrows and gangs. If it failed, the soldiers would arrest him. Only his fighting skills and quick thinking of throwing the spear away saved him. *'How the soldiers can decide the wounds had been from no other weapons but a spear so quickly in the dark? They know.'* He renewed his oath to kill *Thin Buddha* Hwang regardless of Prince Te's admonition. He decided, *'Mon Zhi-an died for me. It's my fault that Ceo-lian is a living widow; I can't live in peace with the guilt. I'll kill Thin Buddha Hwang for all his victims in Beijing and let my best friend Dae Wu come back to live in peace. I'll be hanged. I wanted to die anyway and my death is worthwhile.'*

Lee Mo-bai sent a servant to ask Ceo-lian to come to the study.

"*Sister,* will you promise me something? I have a request, not for now, but for two years later. Dae Wu would be back then."

"Sure I will."

"Please go to Szechwan to look for Master Hsu's family. Help them if they need help. Mrs. Hsu gave Mon Zhi-an a home when he was a boy. It's one of his dying requests. I'd like you to carry it out if I can't. Please promise me."

"I promise. You will win the fight against Jao and the others at Ba-tin. Jao is not that good, but they all will gang up on you. I'll go with you."

"No, it's vital that you stay and protect the family. I better be on my way, the gate will soon be closed for the night. Bye."

Lee Mo-bai handed Ceo-lian Master Hsu's address in Szechwan, took a small bag and left.

"Ceo-lian, what did Lee Mo-bai tell you?" Mrs. Dae Wu sensed Ceo-lian's apprehension and asked.

"He asked me to go to Szechwan for him two years later. He should not have asked me so early. He was very strange and it almost sounded like a final goodbye. I'm worried."

Did he take his books? Ceo-lian"

"I don't think so. He took a small bag."

"Ceo-lian, he'll be back. He would definitely not leave his books and writings behind."

Fat Shih waited for Lee Mo-bai a short way out of the South Gate. "Mo-bai, I knew sooner or later you would pass through.

"I don't want them spotting me traveling with the convoy. If I'm recognized, they might change their plan and attack Dae Wu further on the road. I want to finish this business soon." Shih interrupted, "And then come back to kill *Thin Buddha* Hwang. Ha Ha! Mo-bai, I read you like an open book. Mo-bai, don't do it. I'll do it for you. You should not sacrifice your bright future for killing a viper. I know you'll get away with it but you will be a wanted man your entire life. Not worth it."

"Maybe I'll just scare him a bit." Lee Mo-bai did not want to say that he wanted to die anyway. After the killing, he will confess and hand himself in. The only way to completely assure a clear way for Dae Wu later got to be the killer be found and hanged. If Fat Shih could kill *Thin Buddha* Hwang and escape, Dae Wu and Lee Mo-bai would still be under suspicion for being the instigators. Also, Fat Shih might not be able to kill the highly skilled *Thin Buddha* Hwang. Then Dae Wu and him could never be clear of suspicion. He knew some of the authorities still suspected him being Huge Bo and Vice Minister Hsu's murderer even he was very sick when they were killed.

"Mo-bai, Saber King refused to join them. He denounced his two brothers,_Feng sam (three) and Feng wu (five). He also forbids his students to participate in the ambush.

"Saber King is righteous and a worthy friend to know. I will visit him sometime."

She Devil and a group of men circled the carriages first. Yan-ti and Brother Su fought on each side of the carriage. Lee Mo-bai moved in fast, he pierced Jao on the chest, and sliced off Wu's left shoulder and arm. The others tried to flee at first and then sank to their knees begging for mercy. The accompanying soldiers knelt and told Lee Mo-bai, "Please spare us. Thin Buddha Hwang paid us to stay out of the fight. We know we're in the wrong. We beg for mercy"

Dae Wu said," Mo-bai, they dare not disobey their boss. I'm sure they will treat me well now."

Lee Mo-bai said, "Have a good trip. Brother Dae, farewell." His tears came.

"Mo-bai, take care of yourself. Remember the saying; *'think twice before you take one step.'* I wish you a happy future. Come to visit me in Xikang. Ceo-lian will guard my family. You should not stay in Beijing. Bye."

9

Lee Mo-bai stood there and watched Dae Wu's carriage resume the long journey to the west. 'Farewell, my true friend and brother, we'll meet in the next life if there will be one. I'll buy you a peaceful future with my death.' Next day he led his horse to the stable to be fed. and to have new shoes. There was a big, strong white horse at the stable. A long, heavy sheathed sword was strapped at the horse's flank. He thought, *'Whoever could ride that horse and wield that sword would sure be a tough opponent. Is he the real thief? I hope whoever he is, is not one of my enemies.'* Ever since he noticed the abbess of the convent where Violet had stayed is a highly trained martial arts master, he realized that there must be other superior masters around.

Two days later at sunset, Lee Mo-bai was the lone rider on the last stretch to Beijing. A tall old man, on the tall white horse, the one he had seen two days before, came fast from behind. The old man laughed and whipped at LEE MO-BAI slightly at the shoulder when he rode past. Lee Mo-bai was annoyed, he pushed his mount ahead hard to pursue but the white horse and laughter faded fast. *'He is super. The old man looked familiar. He's no enemy and he only teased me. He seemed to know me and I wonder who he is. I wish I had time to find out who he is. It's close to Beijing now; I need to concentrate on how and where I could kill Thin Buddha.'*

He thought about the saying, *'hidden dragons and crouching tigers'* and he thought, *'Nothing is as it seems in Beijing. Violet, an exquisite artistic prostitute, knew martial arts and had the courage to wound a sadistic bandit leader. Fat Shih, the owner of an eatery, killed the rich loan shark for the poor. Mon Zhi-an, an obscure groom, turned out to be a highly skilled warrior. An aged abbess is a superb martial arts master. Thin Buddha Hwang, a known philanthropist, is a vicious snake in disguise while scheming for more power ruthlessly. That old man I just met is another highly skilled one; he or his student might be the real thief who stole the pearl. I wish I had time to find out. If I want to clear my name and Dae Wu's, I have to kill Thin Buddha Hwang. I had to use a different name and try to be inconspicuous, too. For a few days, I will be one of the crouching tigers.'*

Lee Mo-bai entered the city gate, boarded his horse at a stable with the instruction that the horse should be delivered to Master Lieu's security company four days later. *'I hope I can get it done in less than four days.'*

It took Lee Mo-bai two days to find *Thin Buddha* Hwang's hiding place and to corner him. *Thin Buddha* Hwang asked for mercy and offered him twenty thousand ounces of silver with a promise that he would do no more evil. Lee Mo-bai refused and killed him. He held the blood-dripping sword, and went to the nearby magistrate office and told the guard, "My name is Lee Mo-bai. I killed the evil *Thin Buddha* Hwang." They jailed him and he was heavily chained and handcuffed.

Beijing was in turmoil. Viscount Chiu sent his whole regiment of soldiers out to break out the crowds that formed everywhere. The venders ran back home and the stores also hastily closed. Dae Wu's coachman Fu rushed into the inner court to tell Ceo-lian. Ceo-lian told Fu to gather the servants. She told them to keep quiet and forbade any of them, except Fu, from leaving the house. Fu said, "Miss Yu, we'll be cautious, and we will keep it from the maids. Master Lee told us to obey your orders completely. A few of us have been working for the Dae-ti family for two or more generations. You can trust us."

No one dared to treat Lee Mo-bai as a common thief and put him in a clean, airy cell in the innermost court. The captain put a long heavy chains on Lee's ankles, and he was not handcuffed. They thanked Lee Mo-bai for his nonresistance. Viscount Chiu and Prince Te's servants brought Lee Mo-bai meals every day, and he told them to take the meals back. He said, "Please tell your masters that I had committed a horrible crime and I'm prepared to die for it." He refused to eat the jail food. He wanted to die soon, not wait for a lengthen trial and the death sentencing.

Prince Te told Viscount Chiu, "Lee Mo-bai wants to die and there is nothing we can do. His death will clear Dae Wu's name and ensure Dae Wu a peaceful life when he returns two years later. You know the

Emperor wants to complete a set of encyclopedias of Chinese literature, and he called for scholars to work on the project. I could recommend Lee Mo-bai for the project and I could get him a pardon. I sent Lee Mo-bai a letter telling him my plan to help him. He refused. It's bad. He is such a talented young man."

Without eating and drinking, Lee Mo-bai knew and felt he would die soon. He was dizzy and lethargic and his senses dulled. On the third night, he woke up and heard a whisper, "Mo-bai, we come to get you out of here." It was Fat Shih who was working to loosen the chains on Lee Mo-bai's feet.

"Brother Shih, you know for sure that if I want to escape, no chains can hold me. Let me die to end my troubled and guilt-ridden miserable life. Please leave."

"Mo-bai, Ceo-lian is here, too."

"Please come with us. We will carry you out," Ceo-lian begged.

"Ceo-Lian, this is not a place for you. Leave quickly. You have to guard Dae Wu's family for me. Knowing you're there to guard them, I can die in peace. Please leave quickly."

Ceo-lian sobbed, "I won't go. You know that I can't live without you. If you don't want to leave, I'll stay and let us die together. There was nothing for me to live for anymore." She embraced him.

"Mon Zhi-an died for me. I wanted to die the day we buried him. I am to blame for your misfortune. I can't live with my conscience. Obey me and leave. I ruined both your and Violet's chance to be happy. I want to die. Only death could redeem my guilt. Leave! Ceo-lian, I want you to get married someday, don't let the unreasonable custom bind you. You had never met Mon Zhi-an."

Ceo-lian sobbed even harder, she threw herself on Lee Mo-bai's shoulder.

The sound of the night patrol's footsteps got closer. Fat Shih pulled Ceo-lian off Lee Mo-bai and they left.

The authority found the locks and chain to Lee Mo-bay's cell had been tempered with. They increased surveillance. For the next two nights, Fat Shih and Ceo-lian could not get close to the cell.

On the night of the sixth day, Fat Shih sent his assistant to warn Ceo-lian, "Too dangerous, don't go tonight." Ceo-lian could not stop herself from going. She couldn't bear to think that her beloved Lee Mo-bai might have died or are dying in the cell. She wanted to go to see him one last time and to tell him that she would love him forever and she won't marry another man. She even thought about holding him and dying together. Her life would be meaningless without him, and there was nothing for her to live for anymore.

There were more soldiers on patrol. She could not even get close to the court where the cell is. She walked through the narrow lanes surrounding the prison, trying to find a way to slip in. Suddenly, someone patted her shoulder. She turned around with her dagger ready and asked the tall old man who stood behind her, "Hi, old man, who are you? How dare you...!" The old man with long white beard said urgently with a Southerner's accent, "Go home quickly! Go home!" and disappeared as suddenly as he had come.

'Ahe! A ghost! Was that my father's spirit coming to warn me? But my father was not that tall. I did not hear any sound of his coming and going. Anyway, ghost or man, he means me no harm. He could have killed me' the hair on her arms stood up. She did not want to give up and keep walking around. Finally she got to Lee Mo-bai's cell and found the door ajar. She went in and groped around the bed and the floor in the dark and found nothing. She went home scared. 'Did that old man kill Lee Mo-bai? But where is the body? If he killed Lee, why did he take the body out and to where? He must be really super given how he moved around soundlessly. Who is he?' Many questions came to her mind but no answers.

Early next morning, a maid told her that a man wanted to see her immediately. Ceo-lian dressed quickly and went to the front. It was Master Shih's assistant. He said urgently, "Master Lee Mo-bai escaped last night. Someone got him out. There are soldiers everywhere. Master Shih escaped. Could you give me some silver?"

"Sure, can you ride?"

"I better escape on foot." Ceo-lian gave him some silver and she asked a servant to get a package of food for him. She said, "Come back when it's safe."

Ceo-lian ordered Fu, "Keep everyone at home for a few days. You're the only one who can go out to do some marketing. I want you to go out shortly before noon and find out whatever you can for me. We don't want Mrs. Dae Wu and the maids to know anything."

She went back to her room and waited until the time she usually gets up. She chatted and joked with Mrs. Dae Wu, sat with grandma, and tried to act as if it was just another normal day. Her mind kept going back to Lee's escape and that strange old man she met. She thought, '*If he killed him why did he not leave his body in the cell? Besides, he would kill me, too. Is he Lee Mo-bai's Teacher? But Lee Mo-bai told me that his Teacher had passed away five years ago. He must have saved Lee Mo-bai and took him away. Lee Mo-bai is alive. Of course he is alive, the old man wouldn't carry a corpse out!*' Her hope soared.

She could not concentrate when Mrs. Dae Wu taught her reading and writing in the afternoon. She said she had a headache. Indeed her head was aching from speculations. A maid told her that Fu was back. She went to the study to meet him.

Fu said, "Miss Yu the authority said that a short, fat man helped Master Lee to escape last night. Some soldiers reported that they saw this short man and another one lingered about the areas surrounding the prison. They started their door-to door search."

"Will they come here and search us?" Ceo-lian asked.

"No, they are only searching the districts where the Han live. They won't search us." Fu continued, "There is all kind of rumors. Someone said the late Thin Buddha Hwang's men killed Master Lee and used some kind of powder to turn the body into water. Someone said Master Lee knew magic and turned into a big bird and flew away. Someone said a fat man helped him to escape. Most of the folks are happy that Master Lee escaped. They said killing the two-faced Thin Buddha Hwang is a heroic deed."

Ceo-lian sent Fu out every day to gather news for the next few days. There were no new developments. Everything started to be normal again.

On the hot night of the sixth day after Lee Mo-bai's dramatic escape, Ceo-lian had a troubled sleep and she dreamed of being with her parents and she also dreamed that Lee Mo-bai hugged her. She woke up and turned over trying to sleep again when her bare arm touched something long and cold like a snake. She was scared and started to yell, 'Ahe!' But she immediately stopped herself. She lit the oil lamp and she almost yelled again. There was an unsheathed sword on top of a piece of paper with words on it beside her pillow. She grabbed one of her sabers, went out and jumped upon the roof and saw no one and heard nothing. She trembled from fear and came back to check the window and found no sign of a breaking in. Now she felt hairs standing on her arm. Her hand shook when she picked up the paper to read. It wrote,

'*He is now with Chiang Nan-ho. His sword is for you to keep.*' Ceo-lian recognized Lee Mo-bai's sword immediately and she blushed. She had learned enough to understand the words. Chiang Nan-ho must be the name of that strange old man she met the night Lee Mo-bai escaped. The old man saved Lee Mo-bai. She wanted to shout, '*He is alive!*' She was so happy, she cried.

The sword was a plain and heavy one. Lee Mo-bai once told her that it was his father's sword. '*Ahe! The old man wants me to keep it as a marriage token. Where did he get the sword? They must have confiscated it when they jailed him. At least the note told me that Lee Mo-bai is alive. Oh! I don't know what to think any more.*' Ceo-lian carefully put the sword and note away. She could not and would not tell anyone about the whole bizarre affair.

Ceo-lian spent her days teaching Dae Wu's two sons martial arts, and also learning reading and writing. Every morning and every night she practiced martial arts. Whenever she practiced the skills that Lee Mo-bai had taught her, her mind wondered about the sword, the note, the strange old man and Lee Mo-bai. Once in a while when she was alone, Ceo-lian would take out the 'gold combs' and look at them. They were her marriage token to Mon Zhi-an, the husband-to-be whom she had never met. '*Fat Shih told me that Lee Mo-bai thought very highly of him. Lee Mo-bai is usually conceited but he had told Fat Shih and Dae Wu that Mon-Zhi-an was a better fighter than him. Mon-Zhi-an must be a hero and was very courageous when he killed the evil rich man. He also must be a very caring person when he guarded and took care of the very ill Lee Mo-bai. Oh! He must have loved me deeply in his heart when he called himself 'Yu Er (two)' He was using my surname. and ..and ..*' She started to understand the guilt Lee Mo-bai felt. She could have married Mon-Zhi an if Lee Mo-bai did not tell Mon Zhi-an his longing for her. She also kept speculating about the 'sword'. The old man Chiang Nan-ho wanted Lee Mo-bai and her to get married later.

Once Mrs. Dae Wu asked why Lee Mo-bai did not come to see them anymore. Ceo-lian told her that Lee Mo-bai probably went to Xikang to be with Dae Wu. Three months later, Yan-Ti came back from Xikang and said that Dae Wu was well. Her Brother Su would stay there for the next two years and then he would escort Dae Wu back home. Ceo-lian was content. There were maids to see to her needs and Mrs. Dae Wu was a good teacher and company. Mrs. Dae Wu would take her to visit Countess Chiu and the Countess would come to visit them. Both of them were refined and educated ladies. Ceo-lian was no longer the ignorant country girl. Ceo-lian was glad that Countess Chiu had never talked about Lee Mo-bai's escape. She presumed that Viscount Chiu had told his wife not to talk about it.

Time went fast as a throwing dart. Seasons changed from winter to summer and soon the third summer came. Dae Wu and Brother Su came home from Xikang. The two-year exile ended. Dae Wu was happy to be home again. Mrs. Dae Wu cried and laughed happily that her husband was home again. Both of them thanked Ceo-lian for keeping the family safe. Then Ceo-lian told them both everything; Lee Mo-bai killed *Thin Buddha* Hwang and he had disappeared from the jail. There was no news about Lee Mo-bai for two years. She showed them the sword, the note and told them about the strange old man whom she had met the night Lee Mo-bai escaped.

Dae Wu laughed happily and said, "No need to worry any more. Chiang Nan-ho is his father's sworn brother. He rescued Lee Mo-bai from the jail and took him away. Now my dear Brother Lee must have learned more advanced martial_arts. I'm home again, I think he will soon sneak back to Beijing and come to visit us. *Ha Ha.*" He handed back the sword and note to her, "Ceo-lian, keep them safe."

"Please tell me more about this Chiang Nan-ho," Ceo-lian asked.

"Chiang Nan-ho, Gi Kon-jii, and Lee Mo-bai's father Lee Feng-jii were about the same age. Gi was Lee Mo-bai's Teacher. When they were young, they fought with each other and later they became close friends. Chiang Nan-ho is Lee Feng-jii's sworn brother and that made him Mo-bai's uncle Mo-bai's parents died when Lee Mo-bai was eight years old. Chiang Nan-ho took him to Nan-ko Village to live with his uncle. Chiang Nan-ho must have arranged for Gi Kon-jii to teach Mo-bai martial arts. I always wondered about that. Gi Kon-jii's home was in Szechwan." He did not tell Ceo-lian that it was obvious that Chiang Nan-ho gave her the sword as a marriage token for his nephew. '*She knows.*' Dae Wu smiled at his wife and she smiled back. They were happy for Ceo-lian.

Dae Wu told Prince Te about the note and the sword. Prince Te said, "I knew that someone with super skills took Lee Mo-bai out of the jail. They said it was an owner of a restaurant who did it. I never believed it. To take a nearly dying Mo-bai out of a heavily guarded jail surely was not an easy task. It required strength and skills. I'm happy to know that Lee Mo-bai is alive somewhere. I miss him."

"So do I, Your Highness."

"Dae wu, "Chiang Nan-ho took the sword from my study. The sword was on that desk." Prince Te pointed to the desk in a corner. "After Mo-bai escaped, I asked for Mo-bai's sword as a memento, and I put it on that desk. One day it was gone. I did not want to make a big issue of it. How did he know it was Mo-bai's sword? And how did he know it was here?"

"Your Highness, Chiang Nan-ho knew the sword because Mo-bai was using his late father's sword. He must have watched you when you put the sword there."

"Thank all the gods that he is no assassin. It must be it. I remembered telling Je to find a sheath for it. I must have mentioned that it was Mo-bai's sword. Chiang Nan-ho must be a super expert, you know that I have the security increased after the night Mo-Zhi-an paid me a visit."

"Your Highness, you know Mo-bai had made quite a name for himself in Beijing. Chiang Nan-ho must have heard about it and came to meet his nephew. He came just in time to save Mo-bai. It is another divine intervention."

"He took the sword and gave it to Ceo-lian as a marriage token. I hope Mo-bai will obey him and marry Ceo-lian later. Dae Wu, you have to find a way to keep Ceo-lian here. She knows martial arts. If she gets restless and wanders all over China, even Chiang Nan-ho will not find her easily."

"Your Highness, I plan to buy a small house close to mine for her to live. My wife gets along with her very well and my mother also likes her. My wife is teaching her reading and writing. Her Brother Su came back with me and now he is a guard at Grand Security where Ceo-lian's father used to be a guard. I think she will stay; she does not have any other family."

"Poor girl, I feel for her. I'm glad that you give her a home. Dae Wu, I want you to be careful. The case of the stolen pearls is not closed yet. When Lee Mo-bai was jailed, two of the pearls showed up at a jewel store at Ba-tin Town. Someone still thinks Lee Mo-bai's the thief even he was in jail."

Dae Wu bought a small house not far from his house for Ceo-lian to live. Her Brother Su came to visit her often. Ceo-lian was content to stay. '*Lee Mo-bai definitely would come back to visit Dae Wu.*' Sometimes she would look at the two marriages tokens; the gold combs from Mon Zhi-an, the sword from Lee Mo-bai, she would shed a few tears.

She had never met Mon Zhi-an. Lee Mo-bai said, "Mon Zhi-an died for me. I am to be blamed for your being a widow." on that last night she went into his jail. Sometime Ceo-lian thought that she would be happy if Mon Zhi-an married her. Her parents had never met each other until their wedding night. So did a lot of others. Some parents even arranged their children's marriage before they were born. One father would tell another father, "My wife is with child. She told me that your wife is with child, too. My child will marry yours or they will be sworn brothers or sisters." Now Mon Zhi-an was dead, and she would be considered his widow even though they did not have a wedding. That is the tradition. Unless another man who is brave enough and not superstitious and has his parents' approval wants to marry her. Not many parents would approve their son to marry such an unlucky woman.

She loves Lee Mo-bai very much but she does not understand him. She learned to be quiet when she sensed Lee Mo-bai was deep in thoughts on their journey to Da-ton. She also knew Lee Mo-bai still has some feelings for her even though he tried to hide it. But reading books and writing would take him to a faraway place she could never reach or understand. She wanted to learn the words and be prepared. She hoped and she waited. Sometimes she wondered whether she would be happy if Lee Mo-bai would marry her. She would have a chance to be happy with Lee Mo-bai if he met any other prostitute but the artistic Violet. '*I want Ceo-lian to be happy. Marriage between a man and a woman of the same class with similar backgrounds somehow could make a good marriage. Lee Mo-bai is too well educated for my Ceo-lian*' She once overheard that her father said it when her mother suggested a marriage between Lee Mo-bai and her.

Once Mrs. Dae Wu and Countess Chiu were talking about how well written Lee Mo-bai's poems were. Countess Chiu mentioned that Prince Te had commented that Lee Mo-bai's talent in writing poems might be even better than his swordsmanship. Ceo-lian felt that she was somewhat inadequate then.

The moon should be perfectly round and extra bright on the fifteenth day of the eighth month of the lunar calendar. It's the Mid-Autumn Festival, the Moon Festival. It is an event to celebrate the union of the family and the good harvest. Dae Wu would have the first family gathering in three years. Dae Wu invited Brother Su, of course, Ceo-lian to the traditional family dinner and to eat the round shaped moon cakes. Mrs. Dae Wu sighed and voiced out for everyone, "I wish Mo-bai is here with us."

To lighten the mood, Dae Wu opened a moon cake and chuckled, "No slip of paper with the message to call for killing the Manchu. *Ha Ha*! Hans and Manchu are sitting together at my table. Let's drink to it." Everyone joined in.

His elder son asked, "Daddy, why do the Hans want to kill us?"

"I hope not. Our Emperor is just; he treats Han and Manchu equally. Many ministers and generals are capable Hans. I'm talking about something that happened more than three hundred years ago. Genghis Khan led the Mongols breached the Great Wall and conquered China and establish the Yuan (Mongol) Dynasty. The Hans resisted them. One year, the Han resistance distributed thousands of 'moon cakes' to the Hans only in Beijing and asked them to eat the cakes at a specific divine hour on the night of the moon festival. They put slips of paper in the 'cakes' with the words asking them to kill Mongols. One night the Han regained control of Beijing and then overthrew the Mongol Dynasty. The Mongols ruled China for about one hundred years."

Brother Su chuckled. "Don't worry. We are friends aren't we?"

Mrs. Dae Wu said, "Sure we are friends. The Emperor encourages the Manchu to learn everything from the superiorly cultured Han. The other day, Countess Chiu told me that the Emperor hired many Han scholars to work on editing the history books. If Lee Mo-bai was here, he would be pardoned and given a very good position for sure."

Brother Su said, "One day, Brother Lee will show up and surprise us."

It was an enjoyable evening. Ceo-lian felt so alone afterwards, she cried herself to sleep.

It's getting chilly. One morning Dae Wu's two sons came to her earlier than usual for their martial arts lessons. The older boy told her, "Aunt Yu, my father sent us here. He was upset and he did not want to teach us this morning."

Ceo-lian asked, "Why? Did something unpleasant happen?"

"I don't know. My father sighed and wrote Uncle Lee's name again and again. He paced around the study and sighed." Ceo-lian felt uneasy.

Half way through the workout, Brother Su walked in and said, "That wicked Ca leo (six) scattered rumors all over saying that Lee Mobai drowned in the Yangtze River. Steady! Ceo-lian. It's only a rumor." Ceo-lian turned white and faltered.

"Tell me more. Please"

"Feng wu's (five) friends came from the South. The younger Tan Brother said Lee Mo-bai is his Teacher. Lee Mo-bai stayed at his home for a few months two years ago. An old monk and six students fought a lone Lee Mo-bai on a boat because Lee Mo-bai stole a manual of *'Tien Hsueh'*. Lee Mo-bai fell off the boat into the mighty Yangtze River and drowned. That's all I have heard."

Ceo-lian told the boys, "Go and tell your father, we are coming to see him."

Dae Wu said, "Ceo-lian, I heard the rumor, too. But, I have doubts. Chiang Nan-ho knows *'Tien Hsueh'*. There is no need for Lee Mo-bai to steal and to fight the monks over the manual."

"What is *'Tien Hsueh'*? My father mentioned it once," Ceo-lian asked.

"I don't know too much about it either. It is one of the elite secret skills. From what I have heard, one who knows it can kill or cripple a man, or make him mute instantly with two fingers. Master Lieu of Grand Security may know something about it."

Dae Wu continued, "Mo-bai came to the North when he was eight years old. I don't know if he can swim or not. Let's hope he knows how to swim." Ceo-Lian thought, *'Could Lee Mo-bai swim so well that he can survive the huge Yangtze River?'*

A few days later, Mrs. Dae Wu and Ceo-lian came back late. A man and a sobbing girl waited for Ceo-lian at the gate at Dae Wu's house. A servant said, "Miss Yu, they came here to see you. You were not home so we let them wait here. We gave them some water to drink."

The girl knelt and cried, "Aunt Yu please help me. Uncle Lee Mo-bai told me to come to you if I need any help. They killed grandpa and kidnapped my sister..."

The man said, "I'm a neighbor. We live just outside of the South Gate. Before dawn, some men came to rob them. they killed her grandpa. Her elder sister was gone. I found her hiding under a bed. She told me that they kidnapped her sister and wanted me to take her here to ask you to help her. We walked all the way here and we got lost before someone told us how to get here. Poor girl. Please help her."

Ceo-lian's maid asked, "Have you had any supper yet?"

The man said, "No."

Ceo-lian put her arm around the girl and said, "You must be hungry and cold. You wash up a little bit and eat. Then you tell me everything." She turned to the man and said, "You're a good neighbor, eat something and stay here tonight. The city gate must have closed."

She sent someone to ask Dae Wu to come. Mrs. Dew Wu came also.

"My name is Yan Li-fon. My sister's name is Yan Li-in. My brother is Yan Bo (lcopard). We are orphans. Someone murdered our parents. My mother was a concubine. After she died, the chief wife abused us. The old man we call Grandpa has the same last name but we're not related. He saved us and raised us. Some bad men crippled Grandpa and Grandpa Chiang came. He saved us and helped us move up here. We grow flowers for a living. Grandpa and my brother sold the flowers in Beijing. Early this morning we were still sleeping when four bad men came. They killed Grandpa and took my sister away. I hid under the bed. I heard one of them say they will sell my sister." Between sobs, Yan Li-fon told them.

"Why did they kill your grandpa?"

"I don't know."

"Where is your brother?"

"Grandpa called him a thief and chased him away."

"A thief? When was that? Do you remember?"

"Two years ago, about the same time that Grandpa Chiang carried Uncle Lee Mo-bai on his back to our home."

"How long did Uncle Lee stay with you?"

"Almost two months. He was very sick for a long time. Grandpa knew medicine and Grandpa Chiang treated him with 'Tien Hsueh', too. They said that Uncle Lee's lung was not good."

Mrs. Dae Wu pulled the girl close to her, tenderly wiped her tears and said, "I've always wanted to have a daughter and I have one now. Ceo-lian, you have a niece." Yan Li-fon sobbed even harder; she clung to Mrs. Dae Wu. Ceo-lian shed a few tears too.

Ceo-lian's maid altered some of Ceo-lian's old clothes for Yan Li-fon.

Next day, Ceo-lian, Yan Li-fon and a servant went with the neighbor to the girl's home. They reported the break-in and murder to the authority and buried the crippled old grandpa. Ceo-lian asked the neighbor to look after the house and told the neighbor to send the girl's brother to Dae Wu's place if he comes home.

Mrs. Dew Wu ordered for new warmer cloths to be made for Yan Li-fon.

Dae Wu asked, "Li-fon, did Grandpa Chiang visit you often?"

"No. I only remembered that he came twice. When I was five, Grandpa Chiang came with a Mute. They stayed with us for a long time. They taught my brother martial arts. Two years ago, he came again. He was out often and one night he carried Uncle Lee Mo-bai back to our home. Uncle Lee told me that I could come to ask Aunt Yu for help anytime. He wrote down the address on a slip of paper."

Mrs. Dae Wu asked, "Li-fon, how old are you?"

"I'm thirteen, my sister is sixteen, and my brother is nineteen."

Dae Wu asked, "Tell me about the Mute, how old is he?"

"He is old but he is very nice. He gave us pieces of silver and he smiled a lot. Grandpa Chiang told us the mute is his classmate."

"Did you remember anything Grandpa Chiang and Uncle Lee were talking about two years ago?

"Uncle Lee knelt and told Grandpa Chiang someone died. Grandpa Chiang scolded Uncle Lee and said Uncle Lee was not modest, and he should not show off his martial arts skills. My sister and I felt sorry for Uncle Lee then."

"Did Uncle Lee leave your home with Grandpa Chiang?"

"No, Grandpa Chiang left earlier. Uncle Lee stayed with us until he was well. I'm the one who brought him food. Grandpa said that my sister is older and it is not fitting for her to take care of Uncle Lee."

"Why did your Grandpa make your brother leave? Is he really a thief?" Dae Wu asked.

"Grandpa did not want my brother to learn martial arts. Another friend of my parents took him to a Master Chen to learn martial arts somewhere near Kaifeng. He learned well and came back three years ago. He wanted to avenge my parent's murders. But we had no silver and Grandpa did not want him to go. My brother and grandpa sold flowers everywhere in Beijing. He knew where the rich people live. He must have stolen something. My grandpa called him a thief and chased him out. Uncle Lee was still sick in bed. When Uncle Lee left us, I begged him to find my brother and to look after him."

Brother Su came. Ceo-lian told him about the killing and the kidnapping. He said immediately, "Feng wu (five) and the Tan brothers did this. Yesterday, I went to them to ask about Lee Mo-bai's supposed drowning, I was told they left Beijing in a hurry with a carriage. The Tan brothers told someone that they came to seek revenge. Yan Bo killed their father."

Ceo-lian said, "Li-fon heard one of them said that they wanted to sell her sister to a rich man. Where would they go?"

Dae Wu said, "They might go to Ba-tin, Feng wu (five)'s hometown. You remember that the dead Dart Mew and his nephew Jao had friends there. Mo-bai might have that Jao when they waylaid me on my way to Xikang. I bet the remaining gang are still there."

"We have to find Li-fon's sister before they sell her." Ceo-lian and Brother Su would leave immediately.

Yan Li-fon begged Ceo-lian, "Aunt Yu, please find my brother, too. He is almost as tall as Uncle Su." She sobbed again. Mrs. Dae Wu held her. Ceo-lian put her arms around the girl and said, "Li-fon, I hope that we can bring your sister back and both of you will stay with me. I am your big sister."

10

Dae Wu told Ceo-lian, "Yan Bo might have something to do with the stolen pearls. If so, he might be in danger. Greedy people may want to rob him, and he won't be able to fight off everyone. Sooner or later he will be killed. If you find him, ask him to hand them to Prince Te. Prince Te could help him."

"He was only seventeen two years ago. He wouldn't have enough experience to steal the pearls from the heavily guarded royal palace inside the Forbidden City."

"He didn't. Prince Te told me that the pearls were stolen from a secret chamber for the storage of rare treasures. A eunuch or a minister stole the pearls and hid them in his home. Someone very good at night jumping skills stole them from his home. Mo-bai was a suspect until someone sold two pearls at Ba-tin at the time Mo-bai was dying in jail. They said a tall young man sold the pearls at Ba-tin." Dae Wu explained.

"Yan Bo fits the description and the timing is right. It won't be difficult to find him if so many want to rob him. We'll keep our eyes open."

Dae Wu suggested, "When you stop at an inn, let Brother Su sleep in the mass sleeping room for single travelers. He could hear things and save some silver, too."

It worked. Brother Su heard a lot.

--*'Yan Bo is indeed formidable. He had three classmates with him. They unscrupulously killed whoever wanted to rob them of the pearls. Now the officials are searching in every province for him and he is probably hiding somewhere near Kaifeng.'*

-- *'Lee Mo-bai changed his name to Yan Bo. Who else could be that good?'*

--'That's not true. Yan Bo is husky and very tall; Lee Mo-bai is pale and thin and looks like a scholar. Besides, Lee Mo-bai drowned. More than six monks fought him on a boat, he fell into the Yangtze River.'

--'Lee Mo-bai is not dead. I heard that the monks are still looking for him.'

--'I heard that the Tan brothers killed Yan Bo's grandfather and kidnapped his sister. Yan Bo killed their father.'

--'The elder Tan gathered more than thirty fighters to rob Yan Bo. Yan Bo and his three classmates killed half of Tan's men. The Tan brothers are cowards, they dare not fight Yan Bo and they killed the crippled old man instead.'

--'The Tan family owns a shipping fleet along the Yangtze River. They're rich and they don't need to rob.'

--'They are greedy. The Tan brothers don't have long to live. Yan Bo will kill them.'

--'Golden Spear Jao of Kaifeng gathered more friends. He declares that he will fight Yu Ceo-lian to the death to avenge his uncle 'Dart Mew's death.'

Brother Su told Ceo-lian, "That Yan Bo must be real good. But he is doomed. He won't be able to run forever from both the law and the greedy ones."

"You're right. It's odd that no one talked about where Feng wu (five) and the Tan brothers are. Maybe everyone is afraid of Saber King Feng sie (four). We'll go to see him, he should know where his brother is." Ceo-lian said.

"Feng sie (four) is a good man. Lee Mo-bai defeated him, but he held no grudge against Mo-bai. It was his friend told Prince Te about Mo-bai's innocence. Prince Te got Mo-bai out of jail."

Ceo-lian said, "I can see we'll have a lot of trouble. Everyone knows that Lee Mo-bai is not here to help us. But, I'm confident that I can beat them." She did not tell Brother Su that she had a bad feeling that a young man might be tailing them.

Brother Su said hesitantly, "Sister I almost beat someone when he called you names."

Ceo-lian sighed, "It cannot be helped. The enemies will discredit us any way they can. I'm glad that you held your temper. If Feng wu (five) hears we're after him, he may hide Yan Li-in or even kill her."

They were noticed. For the next two nights, whenever Brother Su checked into the communal room of an inn, most travelers only joked about inconsequential things. At Ba-tin, Ceo-lian whispered, "I understand that the Feng brothers are well-known and powerful here. We better find out more about them first."

Ceo-lian asked the hotel clerk about the Feng wu (five).

The clerk said with obvious contempt, "Feng wu (five) dares not come home. No one around here has seen him for three years now. Feng wu (five) is notoriously wicked; his brother 'Saber King' disowned him and forbad him to come home. Feng sie (four) is not home either; he and his wife are visiting their in-laws. But Feng ie (one), Feng sam (three) are home."

Brother Su told Ceo-lian, "Sister, we should check the Feng Villa out. Feng wu (five) knew that his brother's away, he may hide the young girl there."

Ceo-lian reluctantly agreed, "We may find out where Feng wu (five) might have taken the girl to. Brother Su, please remember that we could only apprehend Feng wu (five), not his brothers."

Feng ie (one), a retired guard, rudely exchanged words with the impatient Brother Su and called Ceo-lian 'a wanton woman'.

But Ceo-lian used the back of her saber to disable Feng ie (one).

Someone told Ceo-lian that Feng wu (five) probably escaped to Kaifeng to seek *Golden Spear* Jao's help. A beggar told Ceo-lian that he saw Feng wu (five). He said, "I saw Feng wu (five) ride to Master Lin's villa yesterday. Master Lin is rich and always pays well for a pretty girl. Give me some silver, I'll take you there."

Ceo-lian asked, "Did you see him come with a carriage?"

"No, he was alone."

Master Lin lived in a fortified villa with tall and thick surrounding walls. The moat was dry. One drawbridge led to a heavy iron-coated gate. Master Lin invited Ceo-lian and Brother Su to his study cordially but denied seeing Feng wu (five) lately.

The beggar yelled outside the window, "Feng wu (five) rides away. Feng wu (five) is escaping to the South and on a white horse."

Brother Su whipped Master Lin hard. Although Ceo-lian's champion horse was swift, Feng wu (five) had a good start so they did not catch him. When they came back to Master Lin's villa, the drawbridge was up and the gate was closed.

Ceo-lian told the angry Brother Su, "We'll be back tonight, although I don't think the girl is here."

"Sister, the thick stone wall is too high. We can't scale it, and I don't think you have the skills to jump so high."

"No, But we can...." Ceo-lian remembered a story that her father told her.

Ceo-lian asked Brother Su to buy a length of strong cord, and a heavy hook. In the dark, Brother Su threw the hook attached to the cord up a low section of the wall and hooked it on a post securely. He held the cord and climbed up the wall and then pulled Ceo-lian up. The night watch sounded the second night call and shouted 'beware of fire' and the whole village was dark, only a few rooms with lights on.

"The rich stays up late. *Sister*, let's go where the light is." Brother Su said.

"Wait! Let's plan our retreat route first.... Did you hear that? They sounded the alarm. Must be another intruder."

By now, the whole villa was up with torches and loud shouting. A few came upon the wall. Ceo-lian quickly whipped a guard hard and told Brother Su to throw him down from the wall. They found a lowest part of the wall and jumped down to the debris filled moat.

Their captive, who survived from the fall, told them that Feng wu (five) was here yesterday but he did not have a young woman with him. Tonight, a young man with a sword killed Master Lin in bed with a concubine. The concubine called for help."

"Ahe! The killer was a young man with a sword, Who was he?"

"Is Lee Mo-bai?" Brother Su asked.

"No, I don't think so. Brother Lee does not kill unnecessarily."

They sat in Ceo-lian's room and speculated without any conclusion. and someone outside her window sneered, "A single man and a single woman in one room! Shame on you!" the man sounded like a Southerner.

Ceo-lian scanned the rooftops and the surrounding areas. She did not see anyone. '*This man must have followed us to the Lin Villa, and then killed Master Lin. His jumping skills must be better than mine. As a matter of fact, he shadowed us from Beijing and he knew what we're doing.*' Ceo-lian felt uneasy. On their way to Kaifeng the next day, Ceo-lian was subdued. Feng sie (four), *Saber King*, caught up with them and challenged them.

"Miss Yu, I know my brother Feng wu (five) is bad and I will punish him. But you should not have wounded my elder brother."

Ceo-lian said, "Master Feng, your brother insulted me first...."

Brother Su and Feng sie (four) locked in a fierce fight. Two men were equally powerful and the three heavy sabers, Feng sie (four) had two and Brother Su had one, clashed and clanged loudly. When Ceo-lian noticed that her Brother Su could no longer keep up, she called, "Brother Su, let me fight him."

She was very skilled in avoiding Feng sie (four)'s powerful saber strikes and surprised the heavy-set man with the quick thrusts that Lee Mo-bai had taught her. But Ceo-lian was soon exhausted. Suddenly, a young man with a sword rushed in and started fighting Feng sie (four). "Three to one! I will fight all of you." Feng sie (four) yelled.

Ceo-lian jumped away and shouted, "Stop! All of you, let's straighten out who's fighting who."

"Miss Yu, I helped you last night and I come to help you again. I'm Chen from Nanjing. I want to marry you."

"Brother Feng, I don't know this man. You have to believe me. He might be one of the men who killed Brother Lee Mo-bai." Ceo-lian said and she started fighting the young man.

"Lee Mo-bai is my friend. Miss Yu, Brother Su, let's forget our differences and join hands to fight him."

Three of them fought the young man Chen. He fought them bravely and sneered, "The three of you fight me. You Northerners sure know how to win a fight."

Ceo-lian retorted, "You Southerners are no better. Seven monks fought a lone Lee Mo-bai and forced him to fall into the river."

"Lee Mo-bai is a thief. He stole something from my Teacher. I was not there to fight Lee Mo-bai then. If I were there, I would have killed him." *Saber King* yelled, "Braggart!"

Chen's arms numbed and hurt from the impact of the two powerful men's heavy sabers, and Ceo-lian's surprising quick thrusts were also hard to fend off. With agility and ferocity, Chen forced the three of them back momentarily and jumped on his horse and galloped away.

Ceo-lian's champion mare almost caught up with him but bolted when the cunning Chen threw back a piece of red cloth. Brother Su threw the hook with the long cord and hooked onto a leg of Chen's horse. Chen managed to jump free and ran away through the narrow lanes between the fields.

Feng sie (four) said, "We cannot tramp on the crops to chase him. Is it true that Brother Lee is dead?"

"Brother Feng, I know nothing more than the rumors." Ceo-lian told Feng sie (four) that his brother Feng wu (five) kidnapped a young woman from Beijing and she saw Feng wu (five) escape from Master Lin's villa yesterday.

"I will punish my brother if I catch him. He probably ran to Kaifeng to ask Jao to help him."

Brother Su led Chen's white horse to Ceo-lian and said, "The horse is all right."

Ceo-lian said, "Let's search his saddlebag, we may find out something about him and why he came to the North."

"What is this heavy whip for?" Brother Su found a heavy whip of twined steel and cords among some clothes, a bag of silver and a letter.

"I don't know. Let's see what the letter could tell us."

The letter was from Monk Pure to his student Chen. It said, "After you left the South, the rumor that the enemy is still alive and is on his way North was confirmed. If you meet him, don't fight him alone, but ask him to return our valuables. He had them for almost two years now and probably learned well how to use it. Be careful. Signed, Monk Pure."

Ceo-lian's hands shook. She whispered, "Brother Su, This letter said that Lee Mo-bai is alive and is on his way North too."

"Ah! That's great. Are you sure?"

"I can read, but I would like to find a scribe to read it again. It is only a three-day-ride to home. Let's go home first to visit my parents' graves. I also want to keep my mare at home lest it gets hurt when I have to fight someone." Twice she sensed that the Southerner Chen was tailing them. She was happy. '*He wants us to lead him to Lee Mo-bai. Lee Mo-bai must be alive.*'

Brother Han told them, "If you two came back yesterday, you could have met Brother Wei. He came to ask you to help him."

"What's wrong?" Brother Su asked.

"Poor Brother Wei is a cripple now. Someone wounded him and seized his security company. He lost two fingers on his left hand and a half of his right foot."

"Tell us more." Ceo-lian asked.

"Jade Town is not far from Kaifeng. *Golden Spear* Jao vowed to eliminate his archenemies, Lee Mo-bai and you. He considered Brother Wei an enemy and tried to ruin Wei's business. Brother Wei had to pay a huge indemnity last year when the bandits robbed the merchant who bought his protection. The bandits actually were Jao's men. Jao wounded him and seized his business, house, vehicles, furniture and weapons."

"I did not forget that it was this Golden Spear Jao who had forced my parents to flee and die. We'll go to Jade Town first and then Kaifeng." Ceo-lian said.

They visited her parents' graves and also found a scribe to read the letter they found in Chen's saddlebag. It confirmed that Lee Mo-bai is alive. She happily wrote Dae Wu the good news herself.

Ceo-lian and Brother Su stopped to lunch at a small town two day's ride to Jade Town. There were horses and carriages parked there. When Ceo-lian unhooked her pair of sabers from the saddle, she heard someone call out her name. She saw a man look at her, and wondered, '*that's odd, I don't know this man and how can he know my name? He does not look hostile.*'

"*Sister,* you're well known with your sabers. I wouldn't worry."

Brother Wei lost his own home and now he lived with his aging father-in-law. He told them, "Tiger Jao is related to Golden Spear Jao of Kaifeng. They wanted to monopolize the security business in Henan Province. My company is not the only one they seized by force. Tiger Jao wounded me. A friend of his named Pai came. This Pai is a top-notch fighter. They threatened that they will kill my family and me if I dare go to the authority. They boasted that they will give me back my business if I or my friends could defeat them."

"Let's go to fight them now." Brother Su shouted.

Ceo-lian agreed, "It's early. Let's finish this business soon. We have to find the kidnapped girl." Briefly, she told Brother Wei their mission on the way to Brother Wei's security station.

As to be expected, Brother Su challenged Tiger Jao first. After thirty rounds, he chopped Tiger Jao heavily on the thigh. Ceo-lian stopped him in time to hold back the killing strike. The wounded Tiger Jao yelled, "Brother Pai, help me. Are you not my friend?"

A tall, robust and very good-looking young man came out and locked in a fight with the equally tall Brother Su. Both of them fought with a single heavy saber. After two rounds, Brother Su could hardly defend himself, and Ceo-lian immediately relieved him. She and Pai fought more than ten rounds and no one could gain an inch.

Pai forced Ceo-lian back a few steps and called with genuine Beijing tongue, "*Miss*, we don't have enough room here in the yard to fight properly. Can we have a duel tomorrow afternoon at the Su ShiaeTomb out of town? I'm Pai. Please tell me your name."

Before Ceo-lian could answer, Brother Su shouted, "My sister is the famous Yu Ceo-lian. She killed Dart Mew three years ago in Beijing. You better surrender now and hand us back the property."

Pai ignored the remarks and said politely to Ceo-lian, "Miss Yu, your good name is far-reaching. I'm only a guest here, but I cannot let my friend be injured. Let's have the duel tomorrow to decide who will get the station."

Ceo-lian replied, "I agree."

Brother Su said, "This Pai fights better than Feng sie (four). I wonder why no one knows him in Beijing."

Ceo-lian said, "He fights even better than that conceited Chen from the South. But, I think he is in hiding. He won't tell us his first name. Brother Wei, do you know anything about him?"

"No, I only know he has been around a couple of months. He seldom leaves his room."

"Lee Mo-bai once mentioned that many Hans secretly resist the Manchu is constantly in hiding. But, this Pai is too young to know of the Manchu's atrocities when they invaded China." Ceo-lian said.

"Sister, it's no use to speculate, we'll know tomorrow."

After supper, Ceo-lian mentally reviewed the winning techniques Lee Mo-bai taught her. She seemed to hear him say, '*To confuse your opponent, use your right saber to defend and your left saber to attack. You're a woman so your strength is limited but you can move fast, I will teach you how to blend some of the swift sword thrusts into your accustomed saber techniques.*'

Pai bowed to Ceo-lian and said, "We don't have enormous animosity between us and we should not fight to the death. Since you're a woman, it won't be proper of us to have a fistfight. But, we will be careful with the sabers."

Brother Wei applaud, "It's very decent of you."

Ceo-lian said, "We will know defeat without drawing blood. Let's get on with it."

The duel began. Two persons moved closer or parted swiftly and their three sabers clashed and clanked continuously. They fought more than fifty rounds with no one winning but Ceo-lian started to show signs of weary, and she knew that Pai had been fighting in defense for a while.

When Brother Su was just about to join the fight, a rider came and shouted, "Stop! Stop! Brother Pai, I've an urgent message."

Pai jumped free. "Excuse me, we'll continue in a moment."

Ceo-lian took the chance to catch her breath. She noticed the newcomer was the same man who called her name two days earlier when she and Brother Su stopped to lunch.

Pai listened to the messenger's urgent tone intently. Then he stamped heavily and cried. He handed his saber to his friend and walked to Ceo-lian and Brother Wei empty-handed.

With tears in his eyes, he bowed low first and then said, "Miss Yu, your martial arts skills are superior to mine. Tiger Jao will return the property to Brother Wei in three days. Now, I have a family emergency and I have to leave immediately. If you insist on resuming the duel, I admit I'm beaten."

Ceo-lian asked, "Why? It's your suggestion that we duel today, and you know you're going to win."

"I was wrong to offend you. The property will be returned in three days."

"Original furniture and fittings must be left intact. Agreed?" Ceo-lian overrode Brother Su's loud interruptions.

"Sure, Miss Yu, you have my word. Bye." He and the newcomer galloped away.

Ceo-lian said, "Brother Wei, what's going on? He would have won for sure. I met the other one, the messenger, two days earlier."

"I think the authorities caught wind of his hiding and are on the way here to arrest him. His friend rushed here to warn him to escape."

"That might be it. We will wait three days before leaving for Kaifeng to seek Feng wu (five) and to find the missing Yan Li-in. Wait, this young man came from Beijing and he is almost as tall as Brother Su ... I wonder..." Ceo-lian said.

Ceo-lian's intuition proved to be true when the same man she met two days before visited them that evening. He requested that the front gate be closed and he whispered, "I'm Lu Na-an. Yan Li-fon called me brother. The young man you dueled today is Yan Bo, the two girls' brother. I told him about the tragedy of his family and that you are his benefactor. He is hurrying back to Beijing to take revenge. Now, I have more to tell Miss Yu in private."

"They are my Brothers. I don't keep anything from them." Ceo-lian said.

Lu looked out of the window first and then took out a cloth bundle. Opening it, he showed them four lustrous big pearls. He whispered, "Yan Bo's father was poisonous and his beautiful mother committed suicide lest the corrupt magistrate would make her his concubine. Their grandpa had the same surname but was not related to them. He saved the children, raised them but refused to let Yan Bo take revenge. My Teacher also knows the family and taught Yan Bo martial arts. Yan Bo learned well. Three years ago, we heard that the evil magistrate was in Nanjing. Yan Bo asked his grandpa to give him some traveling fund, but the old man refused. Yan Bo sold flowers in Beijing every day; he knew where a rich and wicked man lives. One night he stole a package and found forty-four precious pearls and some silver certificates. These pearls are the very ones that caused three officials' beheading, Dae Wu and another man's exile. Yan Bo dared not use the silver certificates or sell the pearls. Somehow his grandpa sensed that he had stolen and chased him out of the house when your boy friend Lee Mo-bai was hiding in their home..."

Ceo-lian protested, "Lee Mo-bai is my sworn brother."

"After Yan Bo left home, he sold four pearls at Ba-tin and found me and two brothers to help him. But, the news of his pearls spread and many wanted to rob him. He killed and wounded all of them. Yan Bo killed the Tan brother's father when he tried to rob him. The Tan brothers killed Grandpa Yan and kidnapped Yan Li-in for revenge. Monk Pure's best student, Lee, waylaid us and killed two of my companions and wounded me. Yan Bo fought him three times and finally wounded him. Two months ago, the authorities recovered four pearls and are all out to catch him. Now he wants me to give you, Miss Yu, these four pearls."

"How dare you try to get my Sister in trouble. Ceo-Lian, don't accept them." Brother Su said angrily.

Brother Wei also said, "The pearls are royal property, coveting them will bring us disaster. Because of the pearls, Yan Bo killed the father and the sons ruined his family. Who said Providence has no eyes."

Lu Na-an solicited, "Yan Bo keeps the rest with him and won't give even one to anyone else. He wants to thank you." To Brother Su and Brother Wei's dismay, Ceo-lian accepted the pearls.

She told Lu, "Brother Lu, please tell Yan Bo not to sell any one of the pearls. Tell him I want to see him and talk to him. Brother Su and I are trying to rescue his sister. We heard the kidnapper, Feng wu (five), might be in Kaifeng. We're going there soon. It's no use for Yan Bo to rush back to Beijing. Would you please go after him and bring him back here? He might not have gone far. Then we'll rescue his sister together. I repeat, it's vital that I talk to him soon. Tell Yan Bo that his sister is at my house, not far from Dae Wu's place." She told Lu her address in Beijing.

Brother Wei complained, "Ceo-lian, you should not take the pearls. If the news leaks, everyone will want to rob you and the authorities will want to apprehend you. You may get Dae Wu in trouble again. Please keep them well hidden."

"Sister, what do you want the pearls for? You don't even have a husband. When and where will you wear them? Brother Wei is right. If anyone knows that you have the pearls, we'll have a catastrophe. You can never be in Beijing again." Brother Su echoed.

"Because I want to...," Ceo-lian hesitated and continued, "When Lu Na-an brings Yan Bo back, I'll ask him to give me the rest of them. I want..."

Brother Su interrupted her with open contempt, "Sister, you go after the pearls and I will go to Kaifeng to rescue the girl. Good night."

"You will understand when we go back to Beijing...." Ceo-lian wanted to tell them that she wanted to have all of the pearls Yan Bo had stolen and then return them to the palace. She wanted to clear Dae Wu's name permanently. She counted in her mind. *'Yan Bo stole forty-four, he sold four at Ba-tin and now. He gave me four. Yan Bo should have thirty-six pearls. Dae Wu said there were forty-eight pearls stolen from the palace. He was jailed and exiled because someone, probably the original thief, sold four of them at the shop of Dae Wu's best friend. No ordinary thief could get into the heavily guarded Royal Palace. Dae Wu had said the first thief must be someone working in the palace. He might be a eunuch.'*

Brother Wei sighed, "After we get back the property, I want to quit the security business and open a hotel instead. I'm crippled now and you cannot be here every day to protect me."

Ceo-lian nodded, "It's not a bad idea. It's better than competing with other conceited fighters who think they can fight better than anyone else. I learned my lesson on this trip. I cannot win every fight. As a matter of fact, no one can win every fight."

On the third day Brother Su shouted angrily. "These turtle eggs stole everything. They only left empty walls."

Brother Wei asked, "What? What did you say?"

"I said 'Tiger Jao' and his gang stole every piece of furniture, every piece of hardware and gave you back an empty building."

The yard and rooms were empty. All the furniture, pictures on the wall, even the wooden frames of windows and doors, vehicles in the yard, and horses in the stable were gone. Worse, the thieves defecated everywhere in the yard.

On a section of the whitewashed wall, a crude message challenged Brother Su and Ceo-lian to go to Ta-hon Mountain. It read, '*Su the Bully, Yu Ceo-lian the Wanton Woman, dare you meet me at Ta-hon Mountain. Choose to be heroes and come, or to be chickens and stay home. Tiger Jao*'. Brother Su scrubbed the words off with his saber and said, "Sister, I'll leave immediately."

"Ah! The bandit leader, Nin, there gathered more than a hundred desperadoes." Wei said.

Brother Su galloped to the west toward the Ta-hon Mountain alone. He left the package of silver Dae Wu handed him when they left Beijing and also the silver they found in Chen's saddlebag. Ceo-lian gave Brother Wei one hundred and fifty ounces of silver. She said, "I should not have trusted Yan Bo's word completely. Hope this silver will help you fix the building and start a hotel business. I'll leave for Ta-hon Mountain tomorrow."

"*Sister*, I heard that 'Tiger Jao' left some of his henchmen behind to harm me. I hope you can stay a couple of days, but I'm worried about Brother Su, too."

"If they have planned anything, it will be for tonight." Ceo-lian said.

Ceo-lian carefully sewed the pearls inside the lining of her undershirt. Then, she cleaned the blades of her saber with a piece of silk. She felt uneasy and restless and Lee Mo-bai's voice flashed through her mind. '*We have to be on our guard at all hours*.' Her tears came and she thought, '*Where are you? Lee Mo-bai, I miss you. I'm not hoping that you may marry me anymore. I'll be happy with just knowing you care and are around*.'

Loud dog barks sounded from both the houses next to Wei's house. Four men came to burn down the house. Ceo-lian wounded two and said, "We won't kill you, Take the wounded ones with you. Tell Tiger

Jao that I'm the one who wounded you. He's no hero if he dares not challenge me directly. Get out."

CL was ready to go, Brother Wei said, "It's overcast and it looks like it will rain. But, you better leave soon. I'm worried about Brother Su."

"I may go directly to Kaifeng and then Beijing from there. Send word to Lu Town or to Dae Wu's in Beijing if you need anything."

A few pedestrians walked with their heads lowered against the cold wind and drizzle. Ceo-lian galloped ahead cheerfully with the knowledge that Lee Mo-bai was alive, Yan Bo was not evil and a hope of recovering all the missing pearls. Dae Wu's name would be cleared when she could return the pearls to the palace.

"Did you see a tall, dark complexioned and robust man of his thirties pass by the last few days?" CL asked a waiter.

"A lot of men who fit your description passed through."

Ceo-lian finished eating and left. She did not notice two men leaving immediately after her. The cold wind whistled with sand and dirt flying. Ta-ho Mountain Range lay ahead like a dirty yellow dragon. Turning a corner, she saw another lone rider ahead of her. She pushed her mount but soon she lost sight of the rider and she regretted that she was not riding her black champion mare.

The drizzle turned into heavy rain and the wind turned colder. Ceo-lian stopped at a dilapidated house and knocked on the shakily gate.

A man opened the gate and let Ceo-lian in. He said, "Come in, Miss, stay with us and share our poor food." He stared at her horse and weapons.

Ceo-lian cautioned herself that this man might be a thief. The house is very close to the mountain. On her second thought that she might find a clue readily.

It rained even harder, the man said, "Miss, stay here tonight and leave tomorrow when it's clear. Where are you going in this foul weather?"

Ceo-lian replied, "I come to find someone."

The wife said, "Miss, it's not safe to travel alone."

"I'm not afraid. I have sabers and I know how to kill." Ceo-lian said.

The husband said, "You must know martial arts. Last month a woman wearing a red outfit and riding a chestnut mare came in town. She carried a pair of swords. I heard she fights very well."

Ceo-lian never heard of a woman like this. She said, "With so many bandits around, no one is safe without carrying weapons. Someone told me that a tall, husky guard called Su passed through here had been robbed."

"Please don't listen to rumors. I saw the man you mentioned two days ago. He passed the mountain unharmed."

Ceo-lian slept fully clothed. Shortly before dawn, she woke to hushed voices. Poking a hole in the paper window panel with a moisten finger, she peeked outside and found five or six armed bandits, with her host among them, were getting ready to attack her.

She chopped two of them down with lightening speed.

"Dare you ambush me!" The other three who ganged upon her. Ceo-lian wounded two more bandits down and the last one escaped likes a scared hare.

One dead. Her host had a big gash on his thigh, moaned in pain.

Ceo-lian said, "I saw through you when I came and showed you my sabers deliberately. Don't you know who I am? I better kill you now lest you rob and murder other travelers."

"Your Highness, please spare me. You were spotted and followed after lunch yesterday. If I did not notify them, they would come any way. Please spare me."

"Tell me what happened to Master Su?"

"Tiger Jao escaped to here from Jade Town. Master Su chased him here. He wounded and killed more than fifteen of us before we managed to capture him."

"Did you kill him?"

"No, our chief wants to kill you and him together. He knows that you would surely come. But, someone rescued Su two nights ago."

"You're lying." Ceo-lian flashed her saber and demanded, "The truth!"

"It's the truth. Someone saved him at night. Filed through the heavy chains we put on Master Su and saved him. Su's wounds were not fatal."

Ceo-lian knocked him out with the back of her saber and rode toward the mountain.

11

Ceo-lian rode through the dissipating fog against the nippy wind of the early dawn to the mountain. After the rain, the curving narrow mountain path was dangerously slippery; her mount nearly lost its footing twice. The sun broke through the clouds; she climbed up a clearing on a peak. Looking down to the west, she spotted a cloister of mud huts half hidden in a ravine. Assuming that must be the den of the bandits, Ceo-lian carefully descended. Twenty some bandits swamped out of their cave-like shelters and charged at her. Only one third of them were on horses.

One of the bandits shouted insults, "You are a whore, and our leader is waiting to bed you."

Ceo-lian was angry. She rode downward quickly to meet them and fell into a trap. Her sabers, her legs and the horse nearly buried in the rubble. The wounded horse cried pitifully and the bandits threw stones and dirt or tried to aim their sharp hooks down the deep hole to hit her. Ceo-lian pushed the dirt off her. She could not find her sabers and luggage. She stood upon the back of the horse and jumped out of the hole, seized a staff and fought with the bandits. Her ankles and legs pained her, so she turned and ran up the steep rocky slope. The bandits chased her a while and gave up with an insulting taunt, "You are afraid to fight us, aren't you? Come down and fight us. We will give you two sabers. Don't be a coward."

Ceo-lian ignored them and came down to the mountain path she passed earlier. She nearly fell and her legs wobbled. She trudged painfully back to the house where she stayed last night thinking that she could find a weapon to use. The yard and the house were empty but a broken staff remained. Using it as a cane, Ceo-lian walked into the first inn in town. Her clothes were covered with dirt and she had no luggage. The hotel clerk saw her and said, "Miss, you've been robbed! I'll take you to a room."

Ceo-lian said breathlessly, "Thanks, no need to worry; my brother will come for me soon." She immediately sat on the raised warm *kon* (bed) and stretched out her legs.

The manager said, "Miss, You may stay with us as long as you need to rest up. Don't worry about silver. Buddha will bless us if we help our guests in need. We will bring you meals and hot water with soothing herbs to bath your legs. I have some ointment too."

"You're very kind. I'm a guard. Twenty bandits robbed me of my weapon, horse and luggage. I will ask your local security station to help me to seize back my belongings."

The hotel manager shook his head, went out to look around to make sure there was no one around. He then whispered, "Miss, rest well and leave town as soon as possible. We'll even help you with some silver. We have two security stations and all the guards are in league with the bandits. The bandit leader calls himself a 'Lord' and the villagers are all bandits. Even the authorities have their eyes closed."

The herbs and ointment helped her legs heal somewhat. Next morning, she went out. It was a market day. There were some axes, sickles for sale. She could use an ax or a sickle to fight the bandits but she had no silver besides the hidden pearls.

--"*She's coming, look, 'Red Hornet' is back.*"

--"*She shacks up with a guard called 'Yellow Tiger', a close friend of 'Tiger Joe' pretty soon, we will have a tiger ranch here. Ha! Ha!*"

--"*This woman is nothing but a whore. I heard she threw herself at Lee Mo-bai before. She lied to her brother Master Lieu that Lee intended to rape her. Lee wounded her brother and seized his super sharp sword; the one can cut through metals. The monks had to use heavy whips to fight Lee Mo-bai.....*"

--"*I also heard lately that she begged 'Sword Chen' to marry her and was turned down again. She has no shame, that woman! No decent woman will dress the way she does.*"

Buyers and sellers ridiculed a pretty young woman dressed in red on a chestnut mare. A pair of swords with red cord hung from the saddle.

Ceo-lian heard the babble and remembered that hateful 'Sword Chen' who had a heavy whip. Now, she lost the white horse she had seized from him. She smiled and thought, '*by luck the letter in his saddlebag confirmed that Lee Mo-bai is alive.'* She was angry that this woman in red marred Lee Mo-bai's reputation. She thought of a plan. *'her man probably is a bandit anyway. I'll take her swords and horse.'*

Ceo-lian followed the woman in red, until there were fewer pedestrians.

"Lee Mo-bai would not have looked at you twice." Ceo-lian taunted her.

"Who are you? You dare ridicule me!"

To Ceo-lian's delight, the woman in red jumped down from her horse, drew her swords and charged at Ceo-lian. Ceo-lian swiftly overpowered her, seized the swords and galloped away on the chestnut mare through the gathering crowd.

She reentered the mountain path. Three riders chased after her with threatening shouts. A group of bandits could not stop her and she rode right up to the brim of the trap where she fell. She looked down and saw only rubble. The bandits had her sabers and luggage.

The three riders gained on her and more bandits gathered. Ceo-lian fought them. The bandit leader holding a long, heavy steel rod stopped his men and shouted at Ceo-lian, "It's between you and me. Don't injure my men. They are not trained fighters."

The three riders also shouted, "We're guards and we won't gang up on you. Yu Ceo-lian. Give us back the swords and horse."

"Let's fight. Winner will get it all." Ceo-lian showed no fear.

She fought the bandit leader's heavy rod defiantly with the borrowed swords. The three guards joined the fight. Like a tigress, Ceo-lian brandished the two swords snakelike and pierced two of them.

"Stop! We admit defeat. Yu Ceo-lian, we will give you back your sabers and luggage. We will also give you a horse." the bandit leader shouted. He ordered one of his men to fetch her luggage and sabers.

"Where is Brother Su? Release him." Ceo-lian demanded.

"He killed ten of my men and then fell into the same trap four days earlier. His legs were injured, but he escaped."

Ceo-lian said, "How convincing. I don't believe you."

"It's the truth. Tiger Jao wanted to kill Su but I wanted to hold him hostage. An old friend of mine, Brother Shih, happened to visit us the next day. He volunteered to guard the prisoner for us. They escaped together. They stole two of my good horses and also some silver. I sent my lieutenants to go after them and they're not back yet. If my best lieutenants were here to help me, Yu Ceo-lian, you wouldn't win."

"Unbelievable lies. What's this Shih's name?" Ceo-lian asked and thought about Fat Shih and the failed attempt to free the jailed Lee Mo-bai in Beijing three years ago.

"Shih Nin, nicked named '*Mountain Lizard*'. He is short and fat."

"Miss Yu, we also admit defeat. Please give us back Sister Lieu's swords and horse. Her man is away and asked us to take care of her. You have wounded her. Her brother Master Lieu is a man of prominence," the three guards told Ceo-lian.

The bandit whom the leader had sent to get Ceo-lian's belongings came back with her luggage only and reported, "Chief, Tiger Jao ran away with her sabers."

"I must have them back. My father specially ordered that pair of sabers to be made for me. Where did Tiger Jao go?" No one answered her. Ceo-lian mounted the chestnut mare again and was ready to leave.

"Wait, Miss Yu, give us back Sister Lieu's horse and swords," the three guards yelled.

"I will return them when I get back my own. No sooner. You can get them back with force if you dare."

Back at the inn, her legs and ankles pained her so she decided to stay another night and bought more medicated salve for her legs.

"*Miss*, you better leave. They won't let you get away lightly. Two of their best guards are away and I heard they have sent for their friends to come here to help them fight you."

"I'm not afraid of them. I will leave tomorrow morning, but no one can scare me away," Ceo-lian replied.

Fat Shih came to visit her in the evening and told her that Brother Su was recuperating at one of his friends' home not far away. Ceo-lian thanked Fat Shih and asked him to tell Brother Su to go back to Beijing afterwards. She decided she could function better without the jittery Brother Su. They reminisced about the past and talked about Ceo-lian's present mission.

Fat Shih said, "I knew about Yan Bo and the stolen pearls but I don't know they kidnapped his sister and killed the old man. I heard that Feng wu (five) hid at Golden Spear Jao's security station at Kaifeng. Jao gathered all his cronies including the bandits here to help him to eliminate Lee Mo-bai and you."

Ceo-lian said, "Brother Shih, I'm here so why didn't they kill me?"

Fat Shih laughed, "They sure tried but you are better. Besides, two of their best fighters are away. Be careful, Ceo-lian, they will trail you."

"Thank you. I will be on guard and I'm not afraid. You're a true brother."

"Ceo-lian, I heard Lee Mo-bai is alive and Monk Pure sent his students north to find him."

Ceo-lian blushed and remembered that night Fat Shih and she tried to free Lee Mo-bai from the jail. Fat Shih definitely saw her naked feelings toward Lee Mo-bai. She told Fat Shih the letter she found in Chen's luggage confirming that Lee Mo-bai is not dead.

"I'm glad. Mo-bai's skills will be even more advanced. See you soon, Ceo-lian." Fat Shih vanished in the night. Ceo-lian's legs hurt even more the next morning when she rode toward Kaifeng. The drizzle and the biting cold wind intensified her discomfort and her feelings of self-pity after her meeting with Fat Shih. Tears rolled down her cheeks, she did not bother to wipe the tears and rode slowly on the nearly empty road. A carriage with blue cloth skirting came from the opposite direction and the passenger drew the curtain closed.

Ceo-lian had a glimpse of the passenger wearing the habit of a Taoist Priest and a pointed hat. She wondered why a Taoist Priest would be shy. Then she assumed that the priest must disapprove of her wearing a short, tight combat suit and riding alone, and she wished again that she were a pampered, protected wife.

On the flat ferry Ceo-lian stood beside her horse. She felt dizzy from watching the seemingly endless muddy colored Yellow River. She doubted that Lee Mo-bai could survive after falling in the even mightier Yangtze River. She checked into the first inn after the crossing.

"Miss, you probably are not used to riding, I'll bring medicated hot water for you to soothe your legs with." She sat on the warm *kon* (bed) and rubbed her sore legs.

"Thank you. How far is Kaifeng from here?" Ceo-lian asked.

"Not far, a day's ride if you ride fast. We have noodle soup and fresh fish."

"Bring me some. Tomorrow, I'd like to have a simple breakfast early."

Ceo-lian thought about the kidnapped Yan Li-in who has been with her captors for at least a month. If the girl has a strong character and resisted her fate, she probably was killed. If she were weak and submissive, she would certainly lose her virginity by now.

The hotel clerk coughed outside her window first and knocked.

"Come in," Ceo-lian said.

"Miss, are you Miss Lieu?"

"No, I'm..." Ceo-lian did not want to say her real name and for a moment she could not think of another name besides her dead fiancé's, "Mrs. Mon of Da-ton. Is this for the register?" Further away from Beijing, most inns did not follow the rule of having the guest to register.

"Guard Ton said he recognized the chestnut mare and thought you are its owner Miss Lieu. I'll tell him that he made a mistake."

Ceo-lian knew someone must recognize the horse. She waited for the impending fight but everything was peaceful. She slept fully clothed.

Suddenly something or someone heavy fell to the ground outside her window jerked Ceo-lian wide-awake. She heard more than one person moan in pain and another guest yelled, "Thief! Thieves!"

"Who goes there?" and "Who are you?"

More than twenty guests and servants stood around two men on the ground right beneath Ceo-lian's window with their sabers beside them. Ceo-lian was scared stiff and a cold sweat poured out of her. She was not afraid of the two men who came to kill her. She was afraid of the person who helped her and disabled her enemies. This person obviously trailed her without her knowing, and she wondered how long this person had her movements covered. She was also puzzled. The two men were obviously in pain but no visible wounds and blood showed.

--"You thieves dare come with sabers. You mean to kill, don't you?"

--"Tie them up and hand them to the authorities."

--"Which one of us do you want to rob? To kill?"

--"No blood but they cannot move. That's odd."

--"It's 'Tien Hsueh' you don't say that Respectful old Monk Pure caught them! I heard that the reverent old one is around here looking for his student, the famous 'Sword Chen'. We better....."

A hotel clerks was surprise, "Master Ton, what are you doing here at this hour?" He told the angry guests, "Honorable guests, they are not thieves. Master Ton is one of the most respected guards in town. Please don't kick them anymore." The 'kicks' seemed to loosen the men's stiffness somewhat. Ton sat up and shouted, "I'm no thief. I've property in town. Tonight I came here to apprehend a female thief."

Now, everyone stared at the only woman there. Ceo-lian shouted, "I'm the only woman here. How dare you accuse me of being a thief?" She kicked Ton.

Another guest said, "Miss, they fell off the roof and they are thieves."

Ton sneered, "Yu Ceo-lian, you stole a horse and two swords. You're a thief and you're a murderer. You killed six men and wounded fifteen men. Two of the wounded are professional guards and my friends. Your friend disabled us tonight. We admit defeat this time, but, sooner or later, we'll kill you."

Everyone stared at the famous woman fighter in awe. Ceo-lian replied, "Come after me anytime, I'm not afraid of you."

Ceo-lian was wondering who was her protector. She decided, '*It must be 'Sword Chen'. He hopes that I will lead him to Lee Mo-bai somehow. But, his skills are not much better than mine. How could I hear nothing? I must be deadly tired.*" Ceo-lian slept with a happy thought that if 'Sword Chen' wanted her to lead him to Lee Mo-bai, then Lee must be alive. She was afraid that her presence and the incident of the night would reach Kaifeng fast and scare Feng wu (five) away, so she left before dawn.

Ceo-lian ate at a food stall and saw a carriage with blue cloth skirting parked outside another inn. At first, she thought that it was odd that the same carriage she saw yesterday on the other side of the Yellow River had followed her here. Then she blamed her vivid imagination and thought, '*I'm sure paranoid now. Most carriages around here all look alike. They all have the blue cloth skirting.*"

She ignored the dull pain of her legs and pushed on and got to Kaifeng in the evening. Someone told her that Golden Spear Jao had two security stations in town. The one close to the East Gate was his residence and all the guards stayed at the bigger one near the North Gate just an arrow's away from the inn she is staying.

A huge white silk banner with black trimming and 'Victorious Golden Spear Jao Un-jing' embroidered in red hanged across the gate of the security station. Two clerk-typed persons met Ceo-lian and giggled, "Miss Lieu, how come you're not wearing red today. Don't tell me 'Yellow Tiger' wore you out. *Ha! Ha!*"

"You have made a mistake. I'm here to see Master Feng wu (five) from Beijing," Ceo-lian replied coldly, but the clerks kept on looking at the chestnut mare and the swords with the red cord.

"Sorry, we thought you're Miss Lieu. I'll go in and ask," one said.

A moment later, Ho chi (seven) came out and rushed back in again. Ceo-lian recognized him and called, "Wait. Brother Ho, I'm not here to fight you. I'm here to catch Feng wu (five)."

Ho chi (seven) came out again with his brother Ho sam (three). Ho sam (three) pleaded, "Miss Yu, please let go of our animosity. Your father killed my daddy but we did not kill your father. You already wounded my sister and killed Uncle Mew. Are you not satisfied? We know we're not your match, but we'll fight you anyway if we have to."

Ceo-lian sighed, "I agree that we better let the past sleep. I'm here to catch Feng wu (five). He killed a crippled old man and kidnapped a young woman in Beijing."

Ho sam (three) said with genuine sincerity, "Thank you for letting the past rest. We all know of Feng wu (five)'s criminal behavior. He came here to ask my brother-in-law to shield him from your pursuit. He and Jao left Kaifeng two days ago and they probably will be back soon. We'll help you to catch him. I promise."

"I'll stay and wait. But, if I know you two help him to escape, I will not let you get away without a scratch," Ceo-lian said.

"We won't help them. To tell you the truth, we, my brother and me, would like to see Golden Spear's downfall. He has concubines and he does not treat my sister well. He looks down upon us and belittles us often," Ho sam (three) said.

More travelers checked into the inn where Ceo-lian was staying next day. A long-robed Taoist priest stood talking with a clerk in front of a room. On seeing Ceo-lian, the Taoist priest turned around and entered the room quickly. She did not have a good look at the Taoist Priest but she wondered whether that's the same shy one she met before.

"Miss Yu, Feng wu (five) must have sold the girl," Ho sam (three) came and told her, "He came here with silver and my brother-in-law treated him royally and let him disparage us. He's indeed out of town, but he probably will be back tomorrow. Golden Spear Jao married my sister and used my family's wealth to run the security stations. He treats us shabbily. I tell you this because I want you to believe my sincerity. Beware of Golden Spear Jao! He plots to destroy you. He gathers many friends to help him kill you and Lee Mo-bai. He hates Lee Mo-bai the most, not only because Lee almost killed him three years ago. Jao slept with most of Dart Mew's concubines, but Violet despised him and later she loved Lee Mo-bai." The outspoken Ho sam (three) did not consider Ceo-lian's sensibility.

At midnight, Ceo-lian went out of her room holding one sword. The whole hotel was dark but the Taoist priest's room. Ceo-lian saw the silhouette of a man writing through the paper window panels. She shook off her feeling of De-ja vu and went on to scrutinize Jao's security station from the rooftop and saw nothing suspicious. She recalled that four years ago when Lee Mo-bai escorted her to Da-ton, she had sneaked by Lee Mo-bai's hotel room while he was writing. Her tears blurred her vision and she wondered when she would see Lee Mo-bai again. A sound on the roof of her room jerked Ceo-lian awake from her reverie. She was on the roof and thrust a sword forward, but stopped when she heard, "Hold it, Sister Ceo-lian, I'm Ho Su-an. My brother told me that you forgo the animosity between our families. I come here with good intentions."

"I am not your sister. Get lost," Ceo-lian said.

"Please help me kill Jao. I'll help you catch Feng wu (five)."

"What, you want your husband dead?" Ceo-lian shouted in surprise.

"Miss Yu, my husband has many women and treats me and my bothers like dirt. The other day he raped one of my maids in front of me. He, Feng wu (five) and others insult my brothers often. We need your help to get back my family's property. Our fathers were sworn brothers so we are practically sisters. Please help us."

"I don't want to have any part in it. You better leave."

"I will. Yu Ceo-lian, my husband hates you. I warn you that he plots to ruin you. When you fight my husband, my brothers and I will be on your side."

"I don't need your help. Leave now."

She thought about Lee Mo-bai as usual. Lee's image came to her more sharply that night. She also thought about the shy Taoist priest. His height and the way he stood looked familiar. She shook her head and told herself that it was impossible and she had imagined too much.

"I saw a Taoist priest in the other court yesterday. Why would a priest not stay at a temple? He must be rich." Ceo-lian asked the clerk casually next morning.

"Priest Cao has a horse and a tea plantation in the South. He left before dawn." The clerk smiled at Ceo-lian, he must have wondered why a young woman would show so much interest in a Taoist priest.

"You say his surname is Cao, not Yu. I thought he might be my distant cousin who entered priesthood. My aunt is worried about him," Ceo-lian said in a way of explanation. She felt somewhat disappointed that the priest had left.

"Do you know whether that famous guard Golden Spear is in town?" Ceo-lian asked again when the same clerk brought her breakfast.

"He and a couple of our guests went to the rich Master Tu's birthday party, a yearly event around here."

"Thank you." Ceo-lian decided to rest her sore legs for a day.

At nightfall, just when Ceo-lian prepared to scrutinize the security station again, She Devil came and told her nervously, "Sister Ceo-lian, they are back and hiding at another house of ours. They plan to attack you."

"Where is the other house?" Ceo-lian asked.

"I'm here to fetch you. They are drinking at their favorite prostitutes' place now. Take your weapons and come with me, and we'll wait and ambush them."

"Just tell me where the house is. I'll find my way there." Ceo-lian did not completely trust her.

"The house is outside of East Gate and it's quite a way from here. I've a carriage waiting. We better hurry. The East Gate will be closed soon," She Devil urged Ceo-lian.

A banquet with only two seats was set in a spacious room. She Devil invited Ceo-lian to have a drink, "They won't be back so soon. You know how men are with prostitutes. I'd like to celebrate our renewed friendship. I'm so glad that we're no longer enemies, Sister Ceo-lian."

"It's karma. We cannot change the past and bring the dead back to life," Ceo-lian sighed.

"Sister Ceo-lian, a toast to seal our friendship" She Devil raised her cup.

Ceo-lian raised the cup and pretended to sip the wine, "Pardon me, I hardly drink." She looked around and thought she saw another room behind an elaborate carved wood screen.

"Is there another room behind the screen?" she asked.

"Yes, it's cooler to sleep there in the summer," She Devil held the chopsticks a while before she answered.

They talked. Two huge candles burned nearly halfway and it was pitch dark outside. Ceo-lian said impatiently, "It's late and they probably won't be back tonight. I better leave."

"You're not afraid of the dark, are you? Who knows when we will meet again? Stay a bit longer. Both of us are lonely," She Devil said.

Suddenly the sounds of weapons clashing and wounded men's moaning came from the room behind the lattice. She Devil turned pale and yelled, "What's happening?"

"You tricked me here and set up an ambush, didn't you? Move forward!" Ceo-lian thrust the point of her sword against She Devil's back and ordered. She also took a candle.

Two men were on the floor amongst the toppled furniture and broken weapons. Cold night air blew in from the open window. One man died and Ceo-lian thought the fatally wounded one must be Golden Spear Jao. She immediately killed him and shouted, "You faked our friendship and set up a trap. Where can you run?" She pierced She Devil on her shoulder. Before Ceo-lian could deliver the final thrust, someone called her from outside the window, "Get out of here fast."

Ceo-lian jumped out of the open window and got a glimpse of a shadow upon the opposite roof.

"Who are you? Why are you helping me?" Ceo-lian found no one. She scanned around and was at a lost at what direction she should take when she heard the shouts of soldiers. "Thief, a woman thief."

"Hurry, don't let the soldiers catch you." The voice came from three houses away.

Ceo-lian dashed to that direction and asked, "Who are you? Wait. Please help me again. Are you...?"

"Tomorrow at dawn, you will find Feng wu (five) at White Temple, ten miles south of South Gate." The slightly Southern Chinese accented voice trailed away and led her to a lower section of the city wall. She jumped down and nearly fell. The shadowy figure ahead turned around. It seemed that he was concerned. Ceo-lian stood up and the man faded into the night again.

"Wait, Lee Mo-bai....Brother Lee....?" Ceo-lian shouted but no reply.

Her heart pounded loudly, Ceo-lian realized that she could be killed if she loses, or caught for murder and buggery if she wins. She trudged back to her hotel room with a happy thought and murmured to her imaginary listener, *'you don't want to face me. Are you afraid that seeing me may cause you to weaken your resolution to be a Taoist priest? You shadowed me and protected me. If this is the game you want to play,*

I'll gladly oblige you,' Ceo-lian was not quite sure of her assumption. She wished that she could know for sure.

Ceo-lian prayed to her deceased parents that she now successfully avenged their murderers. She killed Dart Mew three years ago and she killed Golden Spear Jao and wounded She Devil tonight.

She rushed to White Temple and saw nothing but tombs through the dense fog next morning. Then she heard, "Mercy! Help me!"

"Who are you?" Ceo-lian followed the voice and found a man lying by the roadside. The man kept quiet.

Ceo-lian caught on and asked, "You are Feng wu (five), aren't you? Tell me the truth!"

"You must be Yu Ceo-lian. Please spare me. I did not kill the old man in Beijing. The elder Tan brother did. Golden Spear Jao and his wife She Devil plotted to trap you last night. I warned them and tried to stop them. They wouldn't listen and I hid at a pimp's home. A man caught me, tied me up and threw me here."

"Do you know the man who captured you?" Ceo-lian asked.

"No, he only asked for my name once. He sounded a little like a Southerner. Is he Sword Chen? I heard he wants to marry you."

"Are you sure your captor is not Lee Mo-bai?" Holding her breath, Ceo-lian waited.

"I don't think so. My captor is huskier and definitely unlike the skinny and soft Lee Mo-bai. Tan brothers told me that Lee Mo-bai drowned."

"Is the Yan girl dead? The truth!"

"She's alive. I sold her to Master Kim, south of Ba-tin. You and Brother Su were hard on my tail. I had to sell her for less."

"Tell me exactly the location of her new home. NOW!"

"About forty *li* (miles) south of Ba-tin. It's a huge villa with tall trees around and besides a small creek. Please spare me."

"You have to be punished for your atrocity." Ceo-lian killed him

She decided to go back to make sure that Brother Wei's hotel business was fine and then visited the kidnapped Yan girl at her new master's home before returning to Beijing.

Ceo-lian could not push her mount forward. Her legs and ankles hurt her less than her own feelings of self-doubt, disappointment and destitution. The cruel realization that she could neither kill her father's murderer Jao nor find out where Feng wu (five) sold the Yan girl without assistance from her mysterious protector. Besides, if her protector was Lee Mo-bai, why did he not talk to her? Of course she understood that Lee Mo-bai was now a wanted criminal, but he had ample chances to communicate with her secretly. Thinking about the letter in which her dying mother requested for Lee Mo-bai to marry her, she regretted again that she could not let go of her shyness, jealousy and show it to Dae Wu. Lee Mo-bai would marry her out of honor even though he might not whole-heartedly in love_with her. Then he would not have killed Thin Buddha Hwang. He would not have to become a wanted criminal and he would not be forced down the boat and drowned.

Brother Wei's hotel business was prosperous. A chiropractor treated her injured legs and ankles. Ceo-lian decided to have a good rest before returning to Beijing. Also, she even could not explain to herself whether she was actually waiting for someone or something to happen soon. Two days later, a boisterous Fat Shih came with her ill-tempered Brother Su.

Brother Wei welcomed them and went out to order a banquet, but then he came back in a flash holding a pair of sabers, Ceo-lian's missing sabers.

"A Taoist priest stopped me and asked me to give them to you after he confirmed that I'm your Brother ...Wait, Ceo-lian, What's wrong?"

Ceo-lian rushed out but she soon came back flustered with disappointment.

"What's wrong, Ceo-lian? He could not be an enemy, couldn't he?"

"What does the Taoist priest look like? Is he young? Is he tall?" Ceo-lian asked quickly.

"He's taller than me but shorter than Brother Su. Ceo-lian, what's wrong? He looks like a scholar and he is very polite. He would not tell me his name and simply said that he wanted to return your missing sabers and then walked away swiftly. Ceo-lian, he knows you. Is he an official detective traveling incognito and has something to do with the pearls?"

"I.... don't think so. I.....never mind, I'm glad to have my sabers back," Ceo-lian said and sat in a stupor.

"Ceo-lian, how could you, a proper woman, befriend a Taoist priest?" Brother Su complained as usual.

Fat Shih and Brother Wei exchanged unsettled looks. Fat Shih left, a strange and purposeful look on his face. Fat Shih found two of his trusted men, and he also met by chance 'Little Snake', his long time trusted underling in Beijing who knows Lee Mo-bai by sight. They found out which hotel the Taoist priest is staying at and set a trap. Three of them made catcalls from the rooftop, lured the Taoist priest away from his room. Fat Shih sneaked into the priest's room and found a package on the bed with some silver and books, secular clothes and a Taoist priest's long robe.

Fat Shih chuckled, "I'm glad. Not a real priest. You can marry...."

A shadow came into the room, punched Fat Shih on the bed, grabbed the luggage and left. Fat Shih was satisfied. He did not tell anyone, even his trusted men, and his discovery.

Ceo-lian wanted to go back to Beijing alone, Brother Wei advised that she should wait for the nearly recovered Brother Su to accompany her. Ceo-lian indicated that she preferred traveling alone, Fat Shih smiled and said, "No need to worry. A guardian will see to it that Ceo-lian meets no danger."

Brother Wei complained, "Brother Shih, be serious. There are enemies awaiting Ceo-lian everywhere."

Fat Shih only laughed louder and Ceo-lian blushed.

12

Winter came early that year. Ceo-lian had on new warmer clothes and a hooded cape when she set out alone to the north. She'd like to go back to Beijing before the first snow, but somehow she felt lethargic and a deep melancholy seized her. She felt so alone. Lee Mo-bai's sword and the note that Chiang Nan-ho had put beside her pillow had sustained her with expectation for two long years. Chiang Nan-ho had given her the sword as a marriage token from his nephew Lee Mo-bai. She hoped and hoped that one day Lee Mo-bai would obey his uncle's wish and marry her. Then the news of Lee Mo-bai's drowning shocked her into despair. Now she was sure that Lee Mo-bai's alive. but why didn't he come forward to see her and talk to her? She thought, *'Am I that ugly and ignorant that he does not want to marry me? I am certain that he loved me very much when he escorted my mother and me on the long trip to Da-ton. Mrs. Dae Wu thought that the prostitute Violet was a replacement of me, too. When and why did he change his mind? Does he not love me enough to marry me? He's avoiding me and it hurts.'* The passing brownish empty fields and the leafless trees mirrored her desolation.

She crossed the Yellow River, passed Kaifeng and rode to Master Kim's villa south of Ba-tin. A well-mannered servant took her to an elegantly furnished study where she met Master Kim and his mother. Ceo-lian told them that Yan Li-in was kidnapped. The dignified old woman said, "We bought her last month and she is still intact. We would like to keep her. But since you told us that she was kidnapped, you can take her home with you."

Ceo-lian said, "You are very generous. why did you buy her?"

Madam Kim looked at her son and said, "My son's wife is dying. My son has been married for nine years and they don't have any children. They are a loving couple. Yan Li-in is a very pretty girl. We bought her to be my son's wife. My son will formerly marry her when …" She sighed and then continued, "My daughter-in-law likes the girl, too."

Master Kim looked like an older version of Lee Mo-bai. He has the same sad eyes and the same scholarly look. He told Ceo-lian, "The doctor told us that my wife will die soon. I honor my wife and I won't take a concubine. Later, I'll marry and cherish Yan Li-in. you have the right to take her back to her home."

Ceo-lian said, "Actually she has no home to go back to. Their parents were murdered. The kidnappers killed the old man who had raised them. Her brother left home. Her younger sister is staying with my friend in Beijing. I want to ask her whether she wants to stay with you or not. I do believe you'll treat her with decency if she wishes to stay. Can I have a moment alone with her?"

Madam Kim said, "Certainly. I have only one son and I would like to have a daughter. I hope she'd like to be my son's wife. Do you want me to call her here to meet you, or would you rather go to her room to see her?" Ceo-lian wanted to see the way Yan Li-in lives. She replied, "Please take me to her room"

A maid took Ceo-lian to a nicely decorated room. Ceo-lian was surprised to see that Yan Li-in was a good mannered, elegantly but not over fancily dressed beautiful girl. She noticed the resemblance among the siblings and thought, *'Ahe! The three of them are all very good-looking. Their mother must be a beauty'*. She said, "I'm Yu Ceo-lian, your sister Li-fon calls me Aunt Yu. Lee Mo-bai is my sworn brother. I want to take you home if you don't want to stay here with Master Kim." The girl blushed and told Ceo-lian that they have treated her very well and she would like to stay with them. She said, "Master Kim teaches me how to read and write. Madame Kim thinks and treats me as her own daughter. I'd like to stay," she sobbed and then continued, "Aunt Yu, they killed Grandpa, They tied me up, put me in a carriage, and sometime put me in a locked room... and I'm lucky Madam Kim bought me. How is my sister? Li-fon is so little."

"Li-fon came to me and asked me to find you. She is staying with my good friend Master Dae Wu in Beijing. I also met your brother but I did not have a chance to talk to him. Do you know where your brother stole .. the ..valuables from?"

"He told me that it was from a big house in Beijing where he often went to sell flowers to the maids. I don't know the location. Wait, he said that the maids there all have small feet."

"I'm glad that you have a good home. I'll bring Li-fon here to see you sometime. Take care. Li-in." The girls sobbed.

Ceo-lian thanked Madam Kim for giving Li-in a good home. Madam Kim told Ceo-lian, "I'm glad she likes to stay with us, we'll treat her well. If her sister wants to live with us, we'll welcome her and we'll see to it that she also will have a good marriage, too."

Before she left Beijing, Mrs. Dae Wu told her that she would like to have Li-fon for her elder son. Ceo-lian was happy that both of the Yan girls will have a good home. If she could find Yan Bo in time, they would have a brother. She sighed, '*I have no one and Lee Mo-bai is avoiding me.*'

It was not too much out of her way for her to go home first and then to Beijing. She missed the black mare. In her mind, the horse provided her with the only tangible connection to the two men in her life: Mon Zhi-an and Lee Mo-bai. Mon Zhi-an passed away, and Lee Mo-bai was ever elusive. She could not get either of them out of her mind. She was tired of traveling and fighting and she decided that she would stay home for a while to rest and to sort out her confused feelings. Three years ago, she killed Dart Mew and then repelled the Ho brothers when they sneaked into Dae Wu's home at night. She was rather proud and thought her fighting skills were superior to a lot of others. But now she realized that she would need to practice more and learn more. Since she left Beijing, she met Sword Chen who was better than her, and then she had a hard time fighting Feng sie (four) even with Brother Su (brother) on her side. Yan Bo would defeat her and her secret protector definitely possessed higher skills.

She and Mrs. Han sew new clothes and shoes for her during the day, and she practiced martial arts at night. She practiced 'dart throwing'. Lee Mo-bai had taught her how to throw a handful of pebbles and now she wanted to throw steel darts, which would supplement her lack of manly strength and increase her odds of winning. A blacksmith made some slender and sharp darts small enough for her to hold two of them in her palm. She also had a leather pouch. Which she could hide under her top. With her sabers belted on her back, she practiced throwing two darts in quick succession at the targets on foot and on horseback. In a few days, she became good at it. One night, she had a visitor. The wounded rider fell off his horse at the gate of her home. It was Sword Chen, the Southern sword master she disliked. Chen lost his left arm and part of his left shoulder.

Chen told Ceo-lian, "I will die soon. I came to warn you that my Teacher and others are on their way here to capture you to draw Lee Mo-bai out in the open."

Ceo-lian asked, "Brother Chen, who did this to you?"

"Monk Ta, my classmate. I found out that he is the one who convinced my Teacher and everyone that Lee Mo-bai stole the manual. He is my teacher's most favorite student, but behind my teacher's back he is wicked. My Teacher taught him and Monk Guo 'Tien Hsueh'. Teacher ordered Monk Guo to safeguard the manual. Monk Ta coveted the manual and he was killing Monk Guo with some slow-acting poison. Monk Guo knew it. Monk Guo met Lee Mo-bai and they became good friends and he gave Lee Mo-bai the manual. He did not want the wicked Monk Ta to learn it well and use the deadly skills to do evil. Monk Guo died ten days ago, he told me the truth before he died. I told my teacher but he did not want to believe it and he insisted that Lee Mo-bai stole the manual. Monk Ta 'Tien Hsueh' me and wounded me. My Teacher wants to capture you..." Chen died.

Ceo-lian told Brother Han, "They are after me. If I stay, you all will be in danger." She left for Beijing immediately. She was very afraid of the monks' 'Tien_Hsueh' techniques. She wanted to run to Ba-tin to ask Feng sie (four) to help her, or at least she could hide in Feng's big villa for a while. She hoped Lee Mo-bai would come to help her. She thought, 'Lee Mo-bai is not a thief. He had the manual for two years and now he must know how to 'Tien Hsueh'. Maybe he is afraid of the monks and that's why he did not want to talk to me.' Somehow she felt better knowing her hero Lee Mo-bai was not a thief.

Before she could reach Ba-tin Town, the first snow turned into a blizzard. She was lost and stopped at a house. The old man kindly let her stay for the night. It snowed even harder the next day and she was forced to stay longer. There were only two sleeping rooms, the old man and his son slept in one room, Ceo-lian, the old woman and her daughter-in-law crowded into the smaller room. They were very kind to her. When Ceo-lian told them her identity and the old man seemed not surprised. Ceo-lian felt uneasy.

The old man told her, "Miss Yu, I know of you and Lee Mo-bai. You're heroes. When I was young, I used to work at a security company at Ba-tin Town and now I still have some connection. I also know of your father, the famous 'Iron Wings'. I heard that the monks are looking for you at Ba-tin. They said that you killed one of Monk Pure's secular students, Sword Chen, and they want to kill you. You're safe here. Besides, no one can go out for a couple of days. My son has to stay home, too,"

The son added, "They are waiting to rob Yan Bo, too. Monk Ta is rapacious. He is Feng wu (five)'s friend. They said that you killed Feng wu (five). He told Feng sie (four), Saber King and tried to get him to fight you. Feng sie (four) refused."

Ceo-lian said, "Feng sie (four) is a righteous man. I did not kill Chen, Monk Ta did. I'm afraid of Monk Pure's 'Tien Hsueh', which he seems to use at liberty. But, I must find Yan Bo and save him." She then told them the tragedy of Yan Bo's family.

The old man said, "We know some of it. When it's clear, let my son go to Ba-tin first to get more information for you."

The snowstorm turned into icy rains. It was not safe to travel. Two days later, the son ventured into Ba-tin Town. He came back with the news that the old Monk Pure was sick and turned back to the South. Monk Ta and the other greedy roughnecks had waylaid Yan Bo. Yan Bo was severely wounded because Monk Ta had 'Tien Hsueh' him and the others knifed him. Two of Yan Bo's brothers died. A Taoist priest came, fought the gang off and carried the wounded Yan Bo away. The monks are looking for them."

Ceo-lian thought, 'It's Lee Mo-bai all right. Why did he have to hide his identity?' She asked the old man, "How old is this Monk Pure? He sounds like a superb martial arts master."

"Indeed he is. Monk Pure is about seventy years old. It's said that he and Chiang Nan-ho met when they were teenagers. They are friends. Monk Pure is famous of his unique 'Tien Hsueh' techniques. He taught many students. Two of the good ones are not monks. I heard that Yan Bo impaired Lee and the other one was Sword Chen. Old Monk Pure enjoys being flattered and cannot stand for anyone who is more famous than him." The old man added, "His favorite student Monk Ta gets his ear completely. Behind his teacher's back, Monk Ta is an incarnation of greed and evil."

The son said, "You and Lee Mo-bai are their arch enemies. They want to kill you. I dare not ask too many questions lest I lead them to you. Someone also said that old Monk Pure might feign sickness to trick you. The majority believes that the old monk was not here. They thought that the Taoist priest could not get away if the old Monk was here. I'll go back to Ba-tin and try to find more news."

Ceo-lian asked, "What does Monk Ta look like?"

"He is of average height but he looks square in the shoulders and thick around the middle. His weapon is a thin foot-long steel rod with a spiky point. He uses it to '*Tien Hsueh*' instead of pointing two fingers at the opponents."

"Did you hear anything about Lee Mo-bai?" Ceo-lian asked again.

"Not really. The same old news said Lee Mo-bai and Yan Bo are the same person." Ceo-lian thought, '*I'll just keep moving fast and I won't give my enemy a chance to be close to me. Of course I'll try to block Monk Ta's steel rod.*'

She asked her host, "Uncle, have you heard of any ways to avoid '*Tien Hsueh*'?"

"Someone said that if one were hit, or a near thing, one should roll away fast. The rolling movements can prevent or loosen the effect of the attack. The danger of it is that the person rolling on the ground is defenseless." He added, "A man could do it easily. It is not proper and convenient for a woman to do so." Ceo-lian decided that she would keep moving fast to avoid being hit.

Ceo-lian was anxious to find Yan Bo and to recover the missing pearls. She wanted to visit Feng sie (four) and tell him that Lee Mo-bai did not steal the manual. She thought that Feng sie (four) might have some news about Lee Mo-bai. Something inside her pushed her hard to find Lee Mo-bai. It was a treacherous ride. She stopped at Ba-tin Town to have lunch. Besides the usual stares she received for being a lone woman with weapons, no one harassed her.

At late afternoon, Ceo-lian arrived at the outskirts of Feng sie (four)'s huge villa. There the monks waylaid her. Five monks attacked her. Ceo-lian rode fast and threw the steel darts fast and hit two of them before her horse bolted. She jumped down from the horse and brandished her two sabers to block the attacks from all the directions. She spotted Monk Ta holding a steel rod and he tried to '*Tien Hsueh*' her. She moved swiftly and wounded two other monks. Monk Ta tried to attack her from behind but Ceo-lian twirled around and chopped at Monk Ta's steel rod. An old, short monk silently came from nowhere and applied '*Tien Hsueh*' her leg, she fell. Then her forehead was hit. Feng sie (four)'s tenants and fighters came, "Stop! We'll call the law."

The monks hurried away before they could carry the inert Ceo-lian away.

When Ceo-lian came to, Lee Mo-bai was massaging her forehead. Feng sie (four) was rotating her leg.

"Sister, don't talk. Close your eyes and try to relax. Breathe in slowly and hold it then released it gradually." Ceo-lian felt his strong fingers and she was so happy and her tears came. Lee Mo-bai continued, "You have been out three days. Monk Pure could have killed you. I don't know why he changed his mind and did not attack your 'death cavity'. I rescued Yan Bo took him to a deserted temple. Yesterday I carried Yan Bo here to seek Feng sie (four)'s help. Feng sie (four)'s men had saved you and caught your mare."

Feng sie (four) added, "Miss Yu, I heard about the monk's scheme of robbing Yan Bo of the precious pearls. When my greedy 3rd brother, Feng sam (three), came to me and tried to talk me into robbing Yan Bo, I refused. Then I heard that Brother Lee did not drown and the monks wanted to kidnap you to draw Brother Lee out. I told my men to be on alert. We saved you in time."

Ceo-lian managed to tell them that Yan Li-in will marry a very decent man, and Yan Li-fon will marry Dae Wu's son. Yan Bo could die any moment and he should know that both his sisters would be with good families.

"Sister, I'm going to put you into a deep sleep. Don't worry. You'll be all right." Lee Mo-bai said. Ceo-lian slept with a smile on her face.

Lee Mo-bai looked at her and thought, '*She is still in love with me. Somehow I just do not want to marry her after the death of Mon Zhi-an. I love Violet. I cannot get Violet out of my mind. I am afraid that the shadows of Mon Zhi-an and Violet will stay between us if I ever marry Ceo-lian. The saying 'time will cure everything' does not work for me here. I'm confused and I cannot get rid of my guilt, remorse and my love for Violet.. Oh! What can I do? How can I let her know that I care for her very much but I don't want to marry her?*

Feng sie (four) said, "Brother Lee, a man should be strong enough to forget and forgive. I'd like to see you forget the past and forgive yourself for Brother Mon's untimely death. You and Miss Yu will make a nice couple. I'm your friend and I'm outspoken."

"Brother Feng, you're a true friend. What you just said is right and true, but I'm sorry that I just cannot do it. I care for Yu Ceo-lian very much but I think her only as my sister now. You know about Violet. I still have strong feelings for Violet. Sometimes I'm confused, too. Please also forgive me for catching your brother Feng wu (five) and Ceo-lian killed him. I don't deserve to be forgiven but it is the truth and I'd like you to know."

Feng sie (four) sighed, "My brother is a bad lot. Our family is very rich; one of our ancestors was a very successful silk and fabric merchant. We don't really_need to work for a living. But my brothers are greedy and wicked. They had never helped me to manage the estate and they harassed and terrorized the neighbors with the family wealth. I chased them out. You and Yu Ceo-lian have the right to kill Feng wu (five) for his atrocity. I'm sad about his death but I'm your friend."

"Thank you very much." Lee Mo-bai bowed very low.

They went to the secret room in the servants' quarter to see the fatally wounded Yan Bo. Two doctors, who had treated Ceo-lian and were Feng sie (four)'s trusted friends, shook their heads. One of them said, "It's no use. The wounds are too many and too deep; he had lost too much blood. He is hanging on, he must have some unfinished, and important matters on his mind."

Lee Mo-bai bent down and said, "Yan Bo, Aunt Yu is here. She is sleeping off her serious injuries right now. She will come to see you soon. She said that your sister Yan Li-in is going to be a very nice man's wife, not a concubine. Li-fon will marry Dae Wu's on. Aunt Yu killed the kidnapper."

Yan Bo said weakly, "Great. I want to tell you," then he indicated that Lee Mo-bai should bend down closer to his mouth, and he whispered. "Li-fon has them. Hu (Tiger) a brother…" He died.

Ceo-lian slept a long time. When she was told of Yan Bo's death, she sighed, "Poor Yan Bo. You know they are orphans. Their parents' murderers are still at large. At least the two girls all have good homes." She sighed and continued, "Yan Bo is dead because he needed silver for revenge. It's too bad. He learned martial arts so well." They buried Yan Bo quietly at a corner of Feng sie (four)'s property.

Lee Mo-bai took Feng sie (four) into his confidence and told him and Ceo-lian where the missing pearls are.

Ceo-lian said, "Brother Dae Wu had been jailed and exiled for four pearls. The officials confiscated four of them from one of the pawnshop at Ba-tin. Yan_Bo's friend gave me four. There should be thirty-six pearls in Beijing at Dae Wu's home. Brother Lee, we better go back Beijing right away. I'm fine now. We must return the pearls to the palace to clear Brother Dae Wu's name."

Feng sie (four) said, "My men reported to me that the monks are still looking for both of you everywhere. They came to my house to ask about you. My men politely but firmly turned them away. I also think you two should go back to Beijing to finish the business of the pearls. I advise you to leave here soon. I know Brother Lee is not afraid of fighting them. But it will cause more delay. I'm honored that you have taken me into your confidence. I have so many servants and the news of Yan Bo's death will eventually get out. Then everyone would rush here to find the missing pearls. I'm not afraid of fighting them off but it sure causes more delay and trouble for you."

Lee Mo-bai said, "Brother Feng, you're absolutely right. I think I'll go to Beijing first. Miss Yu should not travel so soon."

Feng sie (four) said, "It will be conspicuous for a Taoist priest and a young woman with weapons travel together. Sister Yu is welcome to stay here as long as she needs to. My wife will keep her company."

Lee Mo-bai said, "I'd like to tell both of you that I did not steal the 'Tien Hsueh' manual from the monks."

Both Feng sie (four) and Ceo-lian said at the same time, "I know."

"How did you know?"

Ceo-lian said first, "The Southerner Sword Chen came to warn me that they are after me. He told me before he died...." She told them Chen came to her home at Lu Town with blood all over him and told her everything.

"Yes. Monk Guo did not want the wicked Monk Ta to have the manual. He knew that he had been poisoned to a slow death. He gave me the manual," Lee Mo-bai said.

Feng sie (four) said, "We know for a long time that Monk Ta is wicked. The rumor has it that he stole the manual and hid it and then he accused Brother Lee of stealing."

"Another thing I want you to know that I'm not afraid of Monk Pure now that I learned 'Tien Hsueh'. I have to disguise my true identity because I do not want to have a confrontation with the monks. Miss Yu, I did not talk to you because I'm afraid that they will hold you as a hostage to draw me out in the open. I have studied the manual thoroughly for two years now. I'm confident that Monk Pure cannot defeat me anymore." Lee Mo-bai knew that he had not been honest with her and with himself. He was avoiding Ceo-lian. He dreaded facing her after that night two and a half years ago when he was jailed and wanted to die. Ceo-lian told him that she loved him. She said something like this, *"If you die, I will die, too. Without you, I have no life and I cannot live without you."*

Feng asked, "Brother Lee, if you're not afraid of them, why did you not fight them to clear your name? I would."

Lee sighed, "Many times I wanted to do just that. But, I'm afraid of my Teacher Chiang Nan-ho."

"I thought you are Gi Kon-jii's student."

"He was my first Teacher. Now, Chiang Han-ho teaches me. It's a long story. I did not know any of this until Chiang Nan-ho saved me three years ago."

Ceo-lian asked, "Brother, tell us where you have been the last three years. Will you? I know about the Tan brothers, I know you stayed with Yan Bo's family for a while and then you also stayed with the Tan brother's family. I had met *'Red Hornet'* the woman others said that she wanted to marry you."

He answered, "Sister, after I got the manual, I went up to my Teacher's tea farm on Joe-hua Peak to study *'tien hseuh'* from the manual. That's about it. Sister, your internal wound may not be completely healed. I and Brother Feng would massage your vital points again after lunch, I'll tell you more."

He did not want to scare Ceo-lian and tell her that Monk Pure intended to cripple her or even kill her. She may need more than one session of massage. The massage would drain energy from the persons who would do it. He explained to Feng sie (four) clearly and Feng was willing to help her. Lee Mo-bai thought, *'I may not be able to leave soon. The monks might be still around and I have to rest well to fight all of them.'*

Lee Mo-bai sat on the bed and firmly but gently massaged Ceo-lian's forehead. Feng sie (four) sat on a chair next to the bed and moved her legs. Lee Mo-bai said, "Chiang Nan-ho is not only my Teacher, he is my uncle, too. He and my late father were sworn brothers. The three of them, my late father, Master Gi Kon-jii and him were friends and sometimes enemies when they were young. I did not know anything about the past until I met Brother Ma who worked at the tea farm. His father raised the orphaned Chiang Nan-ho for a couple of years and he knows a lot about the tragic love affairs, an eternal triangle, between Chiang Nan-ho, Gi Kon-jii and the granddaughter of the man who killed Chiang Nan-ho's father."

Feng said, "Ah! Now I remember that I heard some elders talk about the legend of the three Wu-ton superior warriors. Was your father Lee Feng-jii?"

"Yes. I lost my parents when I was eight years old. We used to live in Nanjing. I remember that Uncle Chiang taught me how to swim in Yangtze River."

Ceo-lian said, "So you're a good swimmer. That's why you did not drown. Dae Wu was wondering whether you are a good swimmer."

Lee continued, "Uncle Chiang took me to my real uncle at Nan-Kon Village. My uncle did not want me to learn martial arts and he was rude to Uncle Chiang. Later my uncle wanted my cousin and me to learn some martial arts for self-defense. One year Uncle Chiang met Master Gi Kon-jii, who was a scholar and knew both martial arts and literary arts well. So they arranged for Master Gi to set up a school close to my home and taught us. I passed the first level of civil examination when I was seventeen. You may have heard that my late father was a poet as well as a Wu-ton school sword master."

"Brother, your calligraphy is superb and Mrs. Dae Wu mentioned often that you wrote excellent poems. I wish that I can read well to understand them." Ceo-lian said.

A cloud of sadness washed over Lee Mo-bai when he recalled the time he had with Violet and the beautiful verses they had composed together. He sighed, "That's the trouble and I was conceited. Chiang Nan-ho saved me from the jail and scolded me for being mixed up with a prostitute, for being proud and showing off my martial arts skills, for. ...anyway he sent me to visit his good friend Tan first and then Monk Pure." Lee Mo-bai stopped. He asked Ceo-lian to lie on her stomach and showed Feng sie (four) how to massage the back of her calves. He started to massage the back of Ceo-lian's head.

Feng thought, *'Chiang Nan-ho is right to say that Lee Mo-bai is too proud. He defeated my brother and openly challenged me. He was indeed very proud at that time. But I think he has grown out of it now.'*

Lee Mo-bai continued, "Next to Tan's estate, lived a woman who wears red all the time. Everyone called her *'Red Hornet'*. Her brother Lieu Pa-ye wounded my host Tan's elder son. I pierced him and seized

'Green Destiny', a historical famous super sharp sword, which could cut through metal. I went to Nanjing to visit Monk Pure. Uncle Chiang told me to show Monk Pure the highest respect. He wanted me to compare my leanings with Monk Pure's students. I met Monk Guo and we became good friends. Monk Pure's father was very nice to uncle Chiang when he was a homeless orphan. Later, Monk Pure saved the only woman whom Uncle Chiang intended to marry. For that, Uncle Chiang is forever grateful. Now Monk Pure accused me of stealing his manual and tries to force me to give it back to him. I know that I'm innocent but Uncle Chiang does not know that I was framed. He may very well believe that I had stolen it." He did not want to tell them that Uncle Chiang did not want to teach him 'Tien Hsueh'. "Mo-bai, you're too proud, until you truly understand what it is to be modest, I would not teach you 'Tien Hsueh' and other unique skills of the Wu-ton school." He did not tell Uncle Chiang that he had the manual and he studied from it secretly. Also Chiang Nan-ho wanted him to marry Ceo-lian. Uncle Chiang had said, "You cannot revive the dead any way. You cannot let that poor young woman be a living widow. You should marry her." He did want to talk much about 'Red Hornet' either. She looks a lot like Violet with the same crescent-shaped eyebrows, the long dark eyelashes, and the delicate neck. The first time they met, Lee Mo-bai could not stop looking at her

Feng said, "Mo-bai, Chiang Nan-ho must care for you a lot. Maybe I can intercede for you and I could tell him that you did not steal the manual. You may want to consider telling Monk Pure the truth and then give him back the manual. I believe you have learned well enough."

Ceo-lian said, "I will tell your Uncle Chiang the truth, too. You can lead us to him."

Lee Mo-bai said, "Thank you both. The truth is that I don't know where Uncle Chiang is. He is coming and going all the time and he is looking for his own missing manuals all over the country," He continued, "For two years, Monk Pure presumed that I drowned. Now he calls me a thief and threatens my friend. I won't give him back his manual so easily."

Ceo-lian asked, "Were you following me? How did you know where I was?"

"Sister, I did not even know you had left Beijing. I was following Yan Bo and tried to help him. Yan Li-fon asked me to. Every year at this time, I come down from Joe-hua Peak to sell the tea and I heard all about Yan Bo's predicament. I spotted you by chance."

Lee Mo-bai told Ceo-lian to turn over and to lie on her back. He told her that he was going to *'Tien Hsueh'* her, to put her into a deep sleep. Both men left Ceo-lian's room in the women's court. They knew that it was very improper of them to give a woman, especially an unmarried young woman, massages. But the difficult circumstance called for a compromise. They were treating her together, not alone.

A letter came from Monk Pure. It read, *"Greetings, Master Feng. We honor your position and we do not want to search your villa for Lee Mo-bai and Yu Ceo-lian. Please inform them that I am holding a fat man. I would like to have a duel with Lee Mo-bai to settle the matter of the manual. I will wait for them at Peace Temple for three days. If Lee Mo-bai does not show up, I'll cripple the fat man. Signed, Monk Pure."*

Feng said, "How presumptuous! I'll gather all my friends in Ba-tin to fight them. They have to behave themselves around here."

Lee Mo-bai said, "It's my problem and I will face them alone. Fat Shih is a dear friend. Brother Feng, you have your family to consider. We want to keep it quiet. I'll go to Peace Temple to meet them alone tomorrow morning. We better leave Miss Yu out of it. She needs complete rest."

"Brother Lee, you're alone and they are so many. Monk Pure's *'Tien Hsueh'* skills must be very tough to deal with. I will go with you. I promise that I'll not bring anyone with me. They may still call you a thief even after you beat Monk Pure. I will be a witness."

Lee Mo-bai hesitantly agreed. "Only you and me then. I will talk to the old man first. He is Uncle Chiang's friend; I really should not fight him. But he is truly merciless, and he want to kill Yu Ceo-lian. For that I'll fight him with all my might. Even I know he is not an easy contender."

Next morning when Lee Mo-bai and Feng sie (four) got there, seventeen people, fifteen monks and two others, were waiting. They tied Fat Shih to a post. Two monks guarded him.

Lee Mo-bai jumped down from his horse, *'Tien Hsueh'* and disabled the two monks on guard, twisted off the cord that tied Fat Shih to the post, held the heavy Fat Shih under his left arm, brandished the sword with his right hand and chopped the attacking Monk Ta's short steel rod in half, and forced another two monks back. He did all of that in quick succession.

Monk Pure shouted at his students," Stop! I want to talk to him first." He thought, '*Ah! He is tough. Two years ago, we could not catch him and we could only force him to fall into the rushing Yangtze River. It seems to me that he has learned 'Tien Hsueh' from the manual well; I may not be able to defeat him. I better try to talk to him first.*'

Monk Pure said, "Lee Mo-bai, hand me the manual! I won't punish you. I'll leave your friends alone. I knew your late father, your late Teacher Gi and your Uncle Chiang. I'll go easy on you"

Lee Mo-bai sneered, "I should respectfully call you 'Uncle' but you don't deserve it. I have the manual and I'll return it if you punish Monk Ta for spreading rumors that I stole it," Monk Ta tried to attack Lee again, but the old monk stopped him, "Let him talk. He won't get away!"

Lee Mo-bai laughed, "How could you detain me? Your student Monk Guo knew that Monk Ta had poisoned him. He did not want to let the evil one to have it and he gave it to me for safekeeping. Monk Ta also killed your secular student Chen. Chen told Yu Ceo-lian everything before he died. You are blind to the truth. If you punish Monk Ta the way he deserves to be punished, I'll give you back the manual. That's my final word." Lee Mo-bai's words came out loud and clear while he handed the inert Fat Shih to Feng sie (four).

Monk Pure shouted, "Rubbish! Yu Ceo-lian killed my student Chen and I want revenge. You stole the manual and I will get it back. No more talk. Let's fight."

Everyone ganged upon Lee Mo-bai. Lee Mo-bai whirled around and swung his super sharp sword. All the monks except Monk Pure could not even come close to him.

Monk Pure shouted, "Stop! all of you, I'll handle him myself."

Lee Mo-bai took this time to run up to where Fat Shih was and slapped a few places on Fat Shih's back, forehead and leg. Fat Shih moaned, "Mo-bai, that wicked old monk made me mute. Make him pay!"

Monk Pure rushed at Lee Mo-bai with a heavy long whip. Lee Mo-bai jumped free and said, "Wait. If you win, I'll hand the manual back to you, and I will kowtow to you and ask for forgiveness. But, what will you do if I win? I want to know."

"If you win, you can keep the manual. I'll not harass you and your friends anymore.'

"Sure. To honor your age, please have the first move." Lee Mo-bai stood still and waited.

Monk Pure attacked Lee immediately. They fought. Lee Mo-bai would not let the monk's heavy whip touch his light but super sharp sword and meanwhile he pierced at the monk in quick succession. Monk Pure was in a defensive position now. He shouted, "Stop! You are using a super sharp sword. You obviously have the advantage of a better weapon." Lee Mo-bai replied, "Let's fight with fists then." Actually he was thinking, *'He is old and he cannot last long with the heavy whip. It's no honor if I win and I don't want to hurt him or to humiliate him. Uncle Chiang will sure punish me if I do'.* He handed Feng sie (four) his sword and whispered to Feng and Fat Shih, "Prepare to get away. I know I'll win and I don't want to humiliate him. Let him chase us, so he can say that I am the one who ran away." Fat Shih said, "You do not have a horse."

"I can run fast."

He bowed low to Monk Pure and said, "You go first." They fought with fists for a while. Suddenly, Lee Mo-bai started to run, Feng and Fat Shih galloped alongside him. The monks started to pursue and soon failed. Monk Pure caught his breath and sighed, "Let him go for now." Monk Pure knew that he was beaten and he took his students back to Nanjing.

Lee Mo-bai and Feng treated both Ceo-lian and Fat Shih. Shih's wound was not serious. He decided to accompany Lee Mo-bai back to Beijing.

The second night they were on the road, Lee Mo-bai woke up to the sound of someone on the roof. He presumed that one of the monks came to attack. His sword cut off the right arm of the attacker before he heard a woman's voice. It was *Red Hornet*. She told him before she died, "I came to warn you that my brother wants his powerful friend in Ba-tin and Beijing to jail you as a criminal. They will provoke you to fight so the officials can arrest you. I always loved you." She died. Fat Shih blamed him, "Mo-bai, you're too hasty. She came to warn you."

"What have I done? I' m guilty." Lee Mo-bai sighed, "I never thought that she would show up here. How can I explain to anyone that I killed her by mistake? What should I do now?"

"It's done. Let's bury her."

Lee Mo-bai could not sleep after that for a long time. Before dawn he must have slept. He dreamed that he was swimming in the Yangtze River and the water was ice cold. It was freezing. He woke up and found the cotton quilt was not on him. The buttons on his top were undone. The pouch holding the 'manual' that was tied around his waist was gone. Cold sweat washed over him. *'Whoever it was, he could have killed me.'* He knew it was no use but nevertheless he jumped up on the roof and looked. As expected, he saw no one. He went back to his room crestfallen. Fat Shih woke up and found Lee Mo-bai just sitting there, holding his head in his arms. He asked with concern, "Mo-bai, are you ill? I know it was bad, but life goes on. There is nothing you can do about it now."

"Brother Shih, I want you go back to get Ceo-lian. She should be better now. You and she will go to Beijing and she has to manage things herself, or wait for me there. I have urgent personal business to attend to. I may see you in Beijing soon." He talked and packed his simple bag, saddled his horse and left. He left Fat Shih there dumbfounded.

At Feng sie (four)'s place, they all worried about what happened to Lee Mo-bai. Fat Shih thought, *'A big part of Lee's trouble is that he is afraid of facing Ceo-lian. He sure knows that Ceo-lian wants to marry him. All of his close friends and probably his Uncle Chiang too want them to get married. He keeps on saying that he cannot marry her, because Ceo-lian's fiancé Mon Zhi-an died for him. I'm not sure about that. Ahe! Red Hornet resembled Violet a little, and I think Lee Mo-bai is still in love with Violet. Didn't he mention that he might go to Japan? He wants to find Violet again. Poor Ceo-lian. Mo-bai was infatuated with her since she was the first pretty young girl he met who knows martial arts well. His true love is the sophisticated Violet.'*

In Beijing, Ceo-lian went to Dae Wu's home alone. Fat Shih was a wanted killer, he could only move around at night. So did Lee Mo-bai. One night when Ceo-lian, Dae Wu, and Mrs. Dae Wu were sitting around and talking, Lee Mo-bai walked in.

Dae Wu welcomed him warmly, "Mo-bai, how I missed you? Get up! Let me have a good look at you. You look stronger and your skills must be improved, you move soundlessly. Did you find what you have lost?"

Lee Mo-bai got up from the kneeling position and choked on his tears, "My Brother, You look well. I have so much to tell you. I did not find the missing article." He turned around and bowed low to Mrs. Dae Wu, "Sister-in-law greetings." He then greeted Ceo-lian.

Mrs. Dae Wu suggested, "Mo-bai, you're welcome to stay in the study. When you two stayed with us three years ago, I felt so safe. Dae Wu was in jail and the town rascals harassed us until you came. That was a nightmare." She sighed.

"I'm a wanted criminal. I cannot stay with you. I even cannot come to visit during the day. I don't want to compromise you. Uncle Chiang told me that I could stay at a dilapidated Tao Temple close to the East Gate. The abbot is Uncle Chiang's friend. That's where he would stay. I hope I will meet him there."

He then asked Ceo-lian, "Sister, did you do anything about the pearls?"

Mrs. Dae Wu heard the way he addressed Ceo-lian and thought, *'Oh! He does not want to marry her. He calls her sister. Violet is out of the picture. Did he meet someone else? He looks well and fit and he is very good-looking indeed. Poor Ceo-lian.'*

Dae Wu answered, "We have the pearls, all of them. Yan Bo brought them to Li-fon and told her to tell us that he wants us to return the pearls for him. It's too bad that I did not have a chance to talk to him. I could have asked Prince Te to help him. He could change his identity."

"Did he come to your house? The inner court? We need to have better security around." Lee Mo-bai asked.

"Mo-bai, you do not know that Ceo-lian is living in a house just behind us. Li-fon is staying at Ceo-lian's place and Ceo-lian's cleaning woman is looking after her." Mrs. Dae Wu explained.

"I met Yan Bo's friend and told him where Li-fon is staying. Yan Bo knew where he could find his sister." Ceo-lian said.

Dae Wu said, "We talked about it and we did not come up with a proper way to return the pearls to the palace. The Emperor is getting old and the royal princes are all trying to be the heir apparent. It's crucial that we don't cause Prince Te any trouble. I did not tell Prince Te that we have the pearls."

"I see. Did Li-fon ever tell you where Yan Bo stole the pearls? Did Li-fon and Li-in mention that they have another brother? Before he died, Yan Bo said something about '*Hu*' and a brother. '*Bo*' means leopard, maybe they have another brother called '*Hu*' (tiger)?"

Ceo-lian replied, "Really? Another brother named *Hu* (tiger), Sure I will ask them. Li-in told me that Yan Bo stole the pearls from a wealthy family, not a royal palace. He and his grandpa went there to sell flowers to the maids."

Dae Wu said, "We thought the first thief might be someone who worked in the palace. Yan Bo did not steal them from the palace."

"Did Yan Bo tell his sister whether the wealthy family is Manchu or Han?" Lee Mo-bai asked.

"No. Wait! It's probably a rich Han family. Li-in mentioned that her brother told her the maids who bought flowers from him all have tiny feet. You know the maids here are Manchu women with big feet."

Mrs. Dae Wu laughed, "Indeed most of our maids are Manchu. My mother-in-law did not like to see the Han women working hard on their tiny feet. Ceo-lian, I'm amazed that you can fight and jump around on your small feet."

Ceo-lian said, "It's a way of life. Rich or poor, the Han women all have their feet bound and they could do anything. Do you remember that night the Ho sister and brothers came here to attack us because I killed their Uncle Dart Mew? The woman has very tiny feet," She thought, *'the beautiful Violet must have tiny feet. Why should I think of her all the times? She is in Japan.'*

Dae Wu said, "A powerful Han official or a eunuch? He stole them from the royal palace. I was framed and some others were, too. We have to handle this matter with extra caution."

They decided that they would write an anonymous letter stating the truth and indicating the location where the pearls would be. Next night when the night call sounded three times, Lee Mo-bai and Ceo-lian went to the tallest tower adjacent to the palace. Ceo-lian kept watch while Lee Mo-bai, moving like a bobcat, climbed up the central peak of the highest tower. He counted the tiles on the roof and placed the bag of pearls under the third tile down from the top. They put the letter at the middle of the highest step leading to the Emperor's study.

Dae Wu was waiting for them in his study. When Lee Mo-bai and Ceo-lian were just about to enter the study, Lee Mo-bai got a glimpse of a dark form moving swiftly on the opposite roof. Immediately, he was on the roof and gone. Ceo-lian was also on the roof, she saw no one. She remembered that Lee Mo-bai had mentioned that he was staying at a Taoist temple adjacent to the East Gate, Ceo-lian ran there. The whole complex of the temple was dark but one small shed at the corner was glowing faintly. She approached it very cautiously. She heard, "you should not have stolen it. You should not kill that woman...Miss Yu come in!" a man sounding like a Southerner ordered. Ceo-lian went in and saw Lee Mo-bai kneeling in front of a tall old man. A bundle of cloths with pictures and writings on it was on the ground besides Lee Mo-bai.

"I'm Chiang Nan-ho. I met your late father once," He then ordered, "Mo-bai, get up."

"Reverent Uncle, Brother Lee did not steal the manual. The Southerner Chen told me ..." Ceo-lian explained.

"I also heard that Monk Ta is a bad lot. Mo-bai, return it as soon as possible. Ceo-lian, I'd like to have you as my daughter-in-law..." Lee Mo-bai sank to his knees again, "Uncle Chiang, I can't. I can't obey you. I'm her sworn brother. .." He repeated again the tragic death of Ceo-lian's fiancé and his guilt over it. "It's not right that I marry her."

"Listen to me..."

Ceo-lian said in a hurry, "Reverend Uncle, my father made us sworn siblings when he died. I honor the marriage that my late father had arranged for me. I won't marry anyone." Ceo-lian also knelt.

"Up! Both of you. The unreasonable traditions and customs should be eradicated long time ago. I'm a victim of one of them, too." With a heavy sigh, he told them briefly that he could not marry the granddaughter of his father's murderer.

"Ceo-lian, you're my niece then. You have to learn the 'Tien Hsueh' technique and other higher martial arts skills. Monk Pure, and his Teacher, Steel Rod Monk, would not have anyone fight better and be more famous. The monks are your enemies now. Mo-bai, take Ceo-lian with you up Jeo-hua peak. I'll teach both of you. I'm getting old, I'd like to have students."

Ceo-lian kowtowed, Chiang Nan-ho accepted and then said affectionately, "Ceo-lian, bring warm clothes. It's cold on the peak, and we don't have the warm *kon* (bed) in the South. The first winter will be hard for you. Brother Ma's young daughter-in-law will keep you company." He thought, '*I will try to find her a good husband. It's too cruel to let a young woman be a living widow. Maybe Mo-bai will change his mind, they will be together for some time.*"

Ceo-lian thought, *'At least I will be with him for a long while. I hope that he will change his mind. Besides hope, what else do I have?'* She tried hard not to cry.

-End-

Epilogue

Dea Wu checked the historical records of famous swords and identified that Lee Mo-bai's super sharp sword indeed was 'Green Destiny'. It was the personal sword of a king of the Wu State in the Three Kingdoms Period (280 A.D. to 229 A.D.) On the night before he and Yu Ceo-lian left Beijing for the South, Lee Mo-bai left it on a desk in Prince Te's study. It was his gift to Prince Te.

Three years later, Lee Mo-bai helped Yu Ceo-lian to reopen her father's security company and it did very well when everyone knew that Lee Mo-bai would firmly stand by Yu Ceo-lian.

Someone stole the sword 'Green Destiny'. Prince Te summoned Lee Mo-bai and Yu Ceo-lian to Beijing to investigate the case.

They traced the theft to an aristocratic young girl who had learned martial arts well from the manual written by Chiang Nan-ho. Lee Mo-bai recovered both the sword and the manual.

The theft of the sword also led them to Yan Li-fon's missing brother who fell in love with the aristocratic young girl. Yan Xia-hu (tiger) and Yan Li-fon averaged their parents 'murderers.

Lee Mo-bai became a true Taoist priest but he did not wear the habit.

CPSIA information can be obtained
at www.ICGtesting.com
Printed in the USA
BVHW07s2107070818
523863BV00001B/29/P